THE ENCHANTED PRINCE

ELLEN TANNER MARSH

Bestselling Author Of *If This Be Magic*

BEAUTY AND THE BEAST

"Damn you, Connor MacEowan!" Gemma yelled.

"Put that thing down before you hurt someone!" he yelled back, dancing around her flailing, panting form.

"I mean to kill you, not hurt you! Damn it, hold still!" Her eyes spewed emerald fire. "I wish you'd go to bloody hell!"

"You'd like to arrange that personally, wouldn't you?"

"You bet I would!"

"Then would you mind dispatching me with something a little less ignoble than a chamber pot?"

Instead of obliging, she hurled the chamber pot at him with all her might.

"Missed me!" he taunted; then out shot his big hands to encircle her birdlike wrists, squeezing just hard enough to subdue her without hurting her. "I ought to kill you," he said, his whiskey breath pelting her face.

Her chin tipped bravely. "Go ahead, do it! It would be better for both of us! They wouldn't charge you with murder—nobody cares if an angry husband slaughters his shrew of a wife!" Her voice faltered. "And nobody would care at all if I were dead."

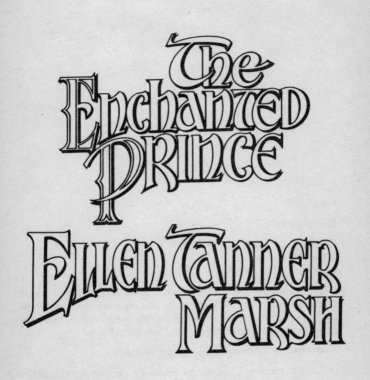

THE ENCHANTED PRINCE

ELLEN TANNER MARSH

LEISURE BOOKS **NEW YORK CITY**

A LEISURE BOOK®

June 1995

Published by

Dorchester Publishing Co., Inc.
276 Fifth Avenue
New York, NY 10001

Printed in the United States of America.

Prologue

Edinburgh, Scotland
October, 1853

Connor MacEowan lay in bed with the flu. His head pounded as he lolled beneath the rumpled sheets listening to the insistent drizzle beating against the window. Earlier, one of the servants had tiptoed in to stir the fire, but Connor hadn't opened his eyes or turned his head. Inquiring timidly if he needed anything, the servant had been rewarded with a string of savage curses.

Now, in the middle of his feverish musing concerning the diminishing likelihood of his recovery, came a loud knock on the bedroom door.

"Go away," he called irritably, but the hinges creaked nonetheless and several pairs of footsteps approached his ornately carved bed.

"So it *is* true! Jamie said you were languishing, but we refused to believe it."

"Hasta got the ague, Con, or just a wee too much whiskey at the pub last night?"

"Nay, if 'twere the pub he'd have a wench beside him, wouldn't he? Is that a woman betwixt the sheets or your own scurvy body, o mountainous one?"

Connor heard the male snickering and opened his eyes slowly. Turning his head on the pillow, he scowled at the three young men before him.

"It's the plague," he said darkly, "and now you've all caught it. Didn't Jamie warn you to keep out? I've not been given above a week to live."

Seeing their frightened faces, he knew they believed him. He was the oldest of the four and had been their leader since boyhood. They had never questioned anything he told them or dared accuse him of telling a lie. And he knew he certainly looked convincing enough with his feverish eyes and dark stubbled beard.

But then he laughed lustily and the three men looked at each other with sheepish relief.

"Actually, we're glad ye're ailin'," admitted Eachern MacEowan, who, like Connor, had inherited the MacEowan height but none of his dark coloring. "The fact that you're no in your looks could be a boon for us."

"Oh? In what way?" he asked, suspicious of his cousin's affable grin.

"We've worked out something new," explained Carter Sloane, the well-dressed dandy at Eachern's side. The youngest of the three and Eachern's close friend from university, he in many ways was the cleverest. Having twice lost a fortune at the gaming tables, Carter was not often eager to accept the wagers suggested by his friends, but never failed to dream up outrageous ones of his own.

Especially for Connor. In the dozen-odd years that the four of them had been attempting to outdo each other with one bold wager after another, none of them had as yet managed to best him. Surely his life had to be charmed, for he could agree to the most outrageous, damning, even dangerous bets, and always emerge, calm and unfazed, as the obvious winner.

"What is it you've got in mind?" he demanded. Sitting up, he let his probing gaze travel over the grinning countenances of his cousin and his friends. Eachern looked smug, Carter positively delighted, and the third, Reginald Spencer, whom everyone called "King," pityingly benign.

King, as Connor knew from long years of acquaintance, had something of a mean streak. Where most of their bets were basically harmless, King was not at all averse to throwing in a little added danger—or sometimes quite a lot, as had happened two years ago with that clergyman's daughter from High Dumferline. King had kidnapped her and plied her with brandy before slipping her, unconscious, into Connor's bed—because he had wagered that he could bring marriage-averse Connor to the altar.

Eachern and Carter had the good sense to be embarrassed, but Connor had been furious, for the girl's father had been a high official in the local church, and the ensuing scandal had been difficult to live down. But he had done so—admittedly in France, where he had managed to enjoy six months of undiluted pleasure in the company of countless beautiful and very willing Parisian ladies. He had even caught the eye of the Empress Eugénie herself and had been invited on occasion to court, where he had managed to pay King back in a fashion so splendid that Connor could still burst out laughing just remembering it.

But he was not laughing now as he crossed his arms across his chest and regarded his callers with a jaundiced eye. "You'll have to come back some other time. I'm in no mood for wagering right now, and certainly not on the scheme you've in mind for me. The three of you look like foxes digging their way into the proverbial henhouse. Go away."

"Excuse m-me, sir." The quavering voice was that of one of the downstairs maids.

Grinning, the three men surrounding Connor's bed moved aside. Taking one look at Connor's naked chest, the girl flushed scarlet beneath her mob cap while her mouth dropped open.

"What is it, Lucy?"

She raised her eyes from his chest to his face. "It's—it's half past three, s-sir. The gentlemen from the bank be here. Mr. Jamie's stepped out and . . . and they sent me up to l-let you know."

It was obvious that his staff had done so to scare the saucer-eyed creature half out of her wits. Feverish as he was, even Connor could see that the girl hadn't expected to find him abed in a state of near total undress, or suspected that his private chamber would be filled with a trio of finely clothed gentlemen.

"I'll be down shortly," he growled even though his head was aching. It was the last day of the month, and he had a long-standing appointment with his banker, Sir Duncan Campbell, and several of Sir Duncan's clerks, to go over the company books before the new month came in.

Lucy fled with unconcealed relief, her expression eliciting laughter from Eachern. "There! See? Not a woman on earth can resist ye, coz!"

Connor made no reply as he threw back the sheets, revealing his totally naked body, for he had torn off his nightshirt earlier in the throes of his fever. Now he crossed to the carved armoire in the corner of his dressing room and began rummaging through the shelves. He paid no attention to Eachern's remark; he had heard similar ones before.

"I wonder if he's angry with us," King mused. "Tomorrow's the first day of the new month, the deadline for our next wager. Were you hoping we'd be crying pax, Con?"

Connor straightened as he pulled on a white lawn shirt. Its long tail spilled down his back covering his flanks. "It crossed my mind," he admitted, busy with the buttons. "You've never taken this long to dream up something before."

"That's because your last wager was so impossible!" Carter complained, his boyish face wearing a look of annoyance.

Connor knew that Carter was referring to the expensive pair of coaching horses he had lost to Connor after Carter had failed to produce the scented white stockings of the Spanish Condesa de los Aquirales. Carter had sworn he could charm them off the lady when they both attended the christening of the newborn Prince Leopold at the Court of St. James last summer.

Carter's father had been furious over the loss of that blooded pair, a loss that galled Carter even more when

13

the icy Condesa's immediate interest had turned to Connor when he had shown up in London unannounced the following week.

"Come on, Carter!" Eachern said bracingly, slapping his friend on the shoulder. "Na need to look like that. We all agreed never to be bitter about losing, else there's na sense in making bets at all. Besides," he added with a wink, "he'll lose this ane for sure, will he no, King?"

"I daresay," he agreed mildly, looking Connor up and down as he drew a pair of well-tailored breeches over his thighs. "Don't you ever use a valet, man? Disgusting habit, dressing oneself."

"Like a peasant, don't ye think?" Eachern asked meaningfully.

"This must be a private joke," Connor said, turning to look at them as they dissolved into laughter. "Now what do the three of you find so amusing, I wonder?"

"You're too shrewd," Carter said, hiccuping and wiping his eyes.

Connor smiled dryly and shrugged into his coat. "All right, lads, you might as well tell me. But be quick about it. Campbell's downstairs and I don't care to keep him waiting. What's in store for me this time?"

Not that he was in the least bit worried. The three of them had been trying for years to get the better of him, plotting one outrageous wager after another in the hope of seeing him fall from what they liked to call his very high horse. Sometimes they surprised him and came up with tasks that forced him to use his wits—and his pistols, on occasion. But even if the bet was some minor sinecure he could wrap up in two weeks' time he always tackled it with relish. Anything to hold boredom at bay and give him an excuse to exercise his brains.

He bent over the washbasin and leisurely splashed his face. The icy water felt good against his hot skin. Straightening, he reached for a towel. "Well?"

"Go on, King," Carter prodded, grinning. "It was your idea. Tell him. We've seduction in mind."

Connor groaned. "Not again."

"Oh, no, my dear fellow," King drawled, "this time it's quite different. No more of watching you make the ladies swoon with just one glance into your ruggedly handsome face. It's your charm alone that's got to win some reluctant heart."

Carter and Eachern sniggered.

Adjusting the sleeves of his coat, Connor crossed to the window and peered down at the street. His elegant manor house stood in the most fashionable section of the old town, its cropped lawn sweeping right up to the Royal Mile. Holyrood Palace's towers and rooftops lay directly to the east, though they were obscured today by the low clouds and drizzle.

Nevertheless there was traffic below, for Edinburgh was a restless city just beginning to reap the spoils of the industrial revolution being fueled by young Queen Victoria's burgeoning empire. Connor himself was busier than ever these days, his ships departing regularly for London and the East carrying wool, china, and the tools and trade of the Empire, and returning with India's untold wealth.

Now, as his eyes turned away from the street his mind dwelt on his own growing wealth and the man who waited to meet with him downstairs. "So I'm to seduce someone," he repeated with a touch of impatience. "I thought you said this was something new."

"Oh, aye, it is," Eachern assured him.

"Well, get on with it, then."

"Actually we've agreed that you're not merely to seduce someone. You've got to make her fall in love with you as well."

Connor snorted. "Seduction, love, what's the difference?"

"Not infatuation, or sexual gratification, Con," King contradicted smugly. "*Love.* There's a world of difference."

"Is there?"

"Don't be sae damned cynical!" Eachern protested. "Oh, aye, 'tis true there's ladies what've sworn they're in love wi' ye, but it's yer wealth they be wantin'—"

"—or what's between your legs," Carter added, smirking.

"But this time you won't be allowed to use your wealth or your good looks to snare 'em," King explained.

"Oh?"

"You'll be incognito."

"Ugly," Eachern expounded enthusiastically.

"He means," King interjected, "that you've got to *disguise* yourself. Put on filthy clothes and grow out that beard. Cover that gorgeous cleft chin of yours and terrify women with your malodorous presence. No money, no looks, only your unalloyed charm will have to suffice to win the heart of some unsuspecting belle."

"There's the rub!" Carter crowed. "Your conquest is to be a total stranger!"

"Ah, but not just any stranger," King hastened to add. "Otherwise you'd latch onto some spotty-faced spinster only too grateful to spread her plump legs for a man. No, my dear lad, we've already saved you the trou-

16

ble of finding someone worthy of the challenge. I've selected a young lady, not known to me personally, but who is, I assure you, a singular beauty with a reputation for whistling every last manjack down the wind. I understand she's turned down every offer of marriage since her debut.''

"How old is she?" Connor asked, envisioning some aged harridan who had ''come out'' in the reign of George III.

"I'm not sure exactly, though certainly not yet twenty. My cousin's the one who found her. He hunts occasionally down in the Midlands where her uncle is said to own substantial property. You should have your work cut out for you trying to win her heart as an ugly pauper here in Derbyshire, where no one has ever heard of your fortune or your legendary exploits with women, and . . . Where the devil are you going?''

"Downstairs," he ground out. ''I've heard enough.''

"Methinks his fever has befuddled his brain," King said loudly as Connor walked toward the bedroom door. ''How else can we explain the fact that he's forgotten one of our most sacred rules? Refusing to accept a wager is tantamount to forfeiting.''

Connor halted, then turned slowly in the doorway. ''And what is it we're after this time?'' he inquired softly.

Both Carter and Eachern, younger and more easily daunted than the reckless King, refused suddenly to meet his narrowed eyes.

"Well?" Connor prompted.

"Glenarris," King said simply.

Glenarris. A vision rose in Connor's mind of the enormous fortress high on the moors above the Arris River.

17

He and all MacEowans before him had been born there. The first stone of the original keep had been laid by a MacEowan in the thirteenth century, and the MacEowan lairds had ruled all the land that could be seen from the castle's highest turret until the defeat of Bonnie Prince Charlie, the Stuart heir, in 1745. Even then, although their power and wealth had been cruelly diminished by England's vengeful king, the MacEowans had remained in possession of their castle, and although Connor, the present laird, preferred the bustle of Edinburgh to that isolated Northwest Highland fortress, he was not about to give up Glenarris while MacEowan blood ran in his veins.

Instead, suddenly he threw back his head and laughed. "You're mad, all of you," he said when he could speak.

Eachern cleared his throat. "I told them ye'd be furious."

"Furious?" He laughed again, his body quaking. God's blood, it was a challenge he'd relish! Forget his pounding head, his lethargy and the boring prospect of another gloomy winter in Auld Reekie. "Give me ten minutes with Campbell," he said over his shoulder, clattering down the stairs, "and I'll be back to discuss the details."

Chapter One

Gemma shivered and pulled the fur collar of her cloak more tightly about her throat. The wind whipped strands of her hair against her cheek and lashed her with icy rain. She wore no gloves, and her fingers were stiff as she guided Helios across the open road. The colt plodded along with lowered head, rain running in rivulets between his velvety ears.

It hadn't been raining when she had left her uncle's house. The autumn sun had been shining, and she had ridden halfway across the dale before the wind had shifted unexpectedly, driving in clouds from the north and, with them, this awful, icy rain. She and Helios had been caught unawares, and now they struggled against the elements as the threatening sky lowered and the daylight quickly waned.

With a feeling of relief she turned the colt onto a narrow cart track that left the open land behind and plunged into a dense stretch of forest. Here there was shelter from the rain, but it was very dark, and Helios snorted uneasily.

Gemma leaned forward to stroke his glossy golden neck. She had no fear of the forest and spoke soothingly to the skittish animal as he picked his way across the mossy floor.

Her head lowered, she rode with only one hand loose about the reins, the other into the folds of her cloak to warm her frozen fingers. Suddenly three men burst from the thickets, surrounding her with whoops and roars of laughter. Snorting, Helios reared and plunged, causing her to lose the reins and go flying from the saddle.

She landed on the hard ground with a blow that left her breathless. Before she could recover her wits, a big hand clamped itself about her waist and she was hauled up against a huge, hairy man who tossed her over the withers of his horse. Gemma could hear Helios squealing in fright and she gasped as she saw him fighting to free himself from the two other men who were dragging at his reins. The young colt had never known anything but her light touch, and the metal bit sawing cruelly into his sensitive mouth obviously was causing him pain. Snorting and bucking, he lashed out with his slender legs.

"Stop it!" she screamed. "You're hurting him!"

She struggled, but her captor clamped his hand over her mouth. She bit down as hard as she could through the stiff leather glove. The man yelped with astonished pain and swung down a cudgel, dealing her a cruel blow to her temple.

Pain exploded in her head. Reeling, she fought weakly against the blackness that overwhelmed her, and before losing consciousness she had the most astounding hallucination. She saw an animal, a big, hairy animal, come crashing out of the thickets on the other side of the clearing and launch itself at the two men who were fighting her colt. She heard a howl of pain and saw one of the men fall, writhing, while the loud report of a pistol exploded in the dark. Then her dimming vision blurred, and the entire fantastic scene ran together as everything faded.

Gemma groaned and slowly opened her eyes. The light stabbed them painfully and she quickly shut them again. There was movement above her, and then something cold and wet was pressed against the throbbing lump on the side of her head. Cautiously she pried open her lids and looked . . . and saw something infinitely horrible above her. Thick black fur and a pair of glowing black eyes hovered over her. She realized, without knowing how, that this was the animal that had sprung to her rescue. As for that cold, wet thing against her temple—surely it wasn't licking her with its tongue, was it?

She uttered a weak scream and tried to rise, only to be pushed back by a pair of very strong—and human—hands. Confused, she blinked, and the hairy face above her swam into focus. She saw now that it was a man, although the realization wasn't the least bit reassuring. He was heavily bearded, and his long, unkempt black hair fell into his unnervingly dark eyes. He was wrapped in a coat made of a dark brown pelt that gave off a horrible odor. She shrank instinctively from him, but the movement hurt her head again and she bit her lip against a moan of pain.

"Easy, now," the man said. His deep voice rumbled inside the hairy depths of his pelts. Taking away the cloth that was pressed against her brow, he wet it in a bucket and laid it once again to her wound. "That was a nasty blow. I imagine it hurts."

His deep voice had just the faintest inflection of a Scots burr, but that thought was completely usurped by the memory of what had happened to her, and to Helios. Pushing away the man's hands, she tried to sit up. Dizzily, she fell back with a groan.

"Lie still, you fool!"

"But my horse! I've got to find him!"

"In your condition?" the stranger asked scathingly.

Tears stung her eyes as she realized he was right. She couldn't even stand. Her head ached so that she was afraid she might faint. She caught at the thick fur of his sleeve. "Then you must go!"

"And get myself killed in the process? There are three of them, and only one of me."

"That didn't stop you before. I assume it *was* you I saw leaping out of the bushes?"

"Ah, but I had the element of surprise on my side then, *and* a shot left in my pistol."

She stared up at him. "I'll pay any price! Please!"

"Any price?" He sounded thoughtful.

She nodded, although the movement cost her dearly. She clutched her head and moaned.

"Well, then, I'll take a hot meal."

Her eyes shot open. "W-What?"

"A hot meal. It's been weeks since I've eaten decent food. If I get your horse back for you, will you take me home and feed me properly?"

It was the most absurd request Gemma had ever

22

heard. She stared at him, thinking he must be a halfwit, though there certainly wasn't anything vacuous in those heavily lashed eyes, which she saw now weren't black at all but a deep shade of blue, dark as the winter sky after the sun had gone down and the world hovered in that brief moment between darkness and light.

"Yes, yes," she said impatiently, "you'll have a meal fit for a king, on golden plate if you wish. Now *please*—"

"Your word on that?"

She stared at him, offended. "Of course."

"Very well, then. Come with me."

"I am not in the least bit capable—"

Her frigid words were lost amid the deep hairs of his smelly coat as he scooped her without warning against his chest. He was so huge that she was all but swallowed up in his arms. Before the rigid shock had even left her he was holding her up to a grimy windowpane. Gemma looked through it, and there, beneath the cover of a makeshift lean-to on the other side of a tree, stood Helios, apparently quite unharmed.

Her relief, however, was short-lived. Scarcely had the happy sigh escaped her lips before she turned on the man who held her. "You lied to me!" she spat. "He was here all this time! You're nothing but a bloody cheat!"

Two spots of color began to burn in his tanned cheeks above his heavy beard. Then Gemma was dropped with considerably less ceremony back upon the rough blankets. For a long moment they glared at each other, Gemma with her breasts heaving and the bearded man with his face filled with anger.

"You're a spoiled brat, you know that?"

"You tricked me!" she insisted.

"A decent meal," he jeered. "It's a small price to pay for your colt's safe return, wouldn't you think?"

Gemma had the good grace to feel embarrassed. It was certainly true. He could have demanded anything, anything at all, but he had simply asked for food. And Helios was safe. Wasn't that all that mattered?

She knew she ought to apologize, but instead she lifted her chin and glared at him. "Will you take me home now, please?"

"I can't."

Her eyes narrowed. "You can't, or you won't?"

"God above, what a sharp-tongued wretch you are! Do you think I mean to keep you here and ravage you, skinny lass that you are?"

He towered above her, dark-faced and hairy, exuding an almost animal aura that frightened her. For the first time she considered her predicament. He was nearly twice her size and looked capable of cracking her back in two with just a simple squeeze of his arms. And she was alone with him in this dingy room.

"We can't go anywhere at the moment," he continued harshly, interrupting her panic-stricken thoughts. "Haven't you noticed it's snowing outside?"

No, she hadn't. Now she tottered feebly to the window, and this time the hairy giant made no move to help her. Instead, he stood there with his huge arms folded over his chest watching as she pressed her nose to the glass in dismay.

Her concern for Helios had blotted her attention to the thick white flakes that swirled from the sky and drifted high over the roots of the trees. Several inches already covered the ground and it seemed likely that more would accumulate before the storm ended.

"It's daylight," she said, dazed. "How is that possible? Was I unconscious all night?"

"Aye. I was starting to wonder if you'd ever come around."

Her gaze followed his to the bucket near her bedside. She realized with unshakable certainty that he had stayed awake bathing the lump on her head throughout the long night. Once again she felt ashamed, and that annoyed her. Twice now he had made her feel that way, and she didn't like it at all!

Her lips compressed, she walked back to her makeshift bed and sank back amid the blankets spread on the packed earth floor. Not because she wanted to—they smelled as though they hadn't been washed in weeks— but simply because her wobbling knees wouldn't hold her upright any longer.

"I think it best we wait until morning before trying to leave," her towering rescuer said. "You don't seem up to it yet, and your colt strained a foreleg in yesterday's struggle. He's fine now," he added at her alarmed expression. "I packed it with snow and the swelling's gone down."

Her lips compressed even further. While she would not have thought twice about trying to get home no matter how weak she felt, she wasn't about to risk further injury to Helios. He was far too young and his legs still too delicate to expect him to flounder miles through the snow with a strained foreleg.

"I suppose you're right," she said irritably, and turned her head to survey her surroundings thoroughly for the first time. The mud-walled crude hut had a single, rough-cut window frame. A fire burned in the smoke-stained hearth although it provided little warmth in the drafty room.

She had never been here before but she did remember an abandoned shepherd's hut standing at the edge of a field across which she sometimes rode, and wondered if this might be the one. If so, her rescuer was probably right in suggesting they wait for the snow to end since the hut was some five miles or more from her uncle's house.

Uncle Archibald! Her breath caught. Surely he had sent someone to look for her when she failed to return home last night?

Even as the thought occurred to her her expectation of being found quickly waned. Her uncle's grooms would be searching in the direction of Penrose village, because that's where she had told them she was going. It wasn't until she had left her uncle's land behind that she had turned north instead. By the time anyone thought to check the old shepherd's hut off the Derby highway she'd already be home.

"I'm afraid I can't offer you anything to eat," the man said, propping a big shoulder against the wall as he looked down at her. "My pockets are empty."

"Did you have to mention food?" she asked irritably. Her stomach growled, for she had eaten nothing since noon the day before.

"Well, I did want to make your stay here a pleasant one."

Gemma gazed in annoyance into the stranger's laughing eyes. Was it possible that he was amused by her predicament? "While I realize that I owe you a great debt of gratitude for dispersing my attackers—" she began frostily.

''You're lucky I came along when I did,'' he agreed, interrupting her with a grin. His teeth were very white and even, and they flashed in his darkly bearded face. ''And that I had a shot left in my pistol. I think that's what convinced them more than anything that it would be prudent to retreat.''

That, and the terror that must have struck them down when this great, hairy man-beast had descended without warning into their midst!

She heaved a sigh of utter resignation. ''Since we seem to be trapped here,'' she began uncharitably, ''perhaps—''

''We ought to introduce ourselves,'' he finished, grinning in a manner that would have been entirely disarming but for his objectionable appearance. ''My thoughts exactly. Excuse me for being so remiss. My name is Connor MacEowan.''

She glared. That was not at all what she had meant to say! She would have preferred not telling him her name at all. God knows he'd only bandy it about publicly when he found out who she was, since she wasn't exactly unknown in these parts. Perhaps her uncle could buy him off? His looks suggested that he wouldn't be above accepting a few coppers in exchange for his silence.

''I'm Gemma Baird,'' she began, ''but what I wanted—''

''God's blood!'' he bellowed. ''You can't be serious!''

Her mouth snapped shut and she stared at him as if he'd lost his mind. ''I assure you that I am. What does it matter? Have you heard of me?''

Instead of answering he threw back his head and uttered a deep, throaty laugh that went on and on, filling the small room and echoing from the rafters.

She waited coldly until he was finished. "Would you mind telling me what's so amusing, Mr. . . . MacEowan, is it?"

"Why, nothing at all. I was just thinking to myself how capricious Fate can be."

"Exactly. And since she has forced the two of us to share close quarters until morning, I must insist that you take off your coat and place it outside."

"Eh?" His laughter stilled and he glared at her.

"Those furs or whatever they are," she explained as though speaking to a mentally impaired child. "They stink."

"It's a bearskin coat," he growled. "I shot it myself."

"Apparently nobody told you that you're supposed to scrape the animal parts out of it before you turn it into clothing."

For a moment he looked as though he would like to make a coat out of her. But then he obligingly undid the buckles and shrugged out of the sleeves. Opening the door, he tossed the coat into the snow, then slammed the door shut against the howling wind. He turned to her, his hands on his narrow hips. "Satisfied?"

No, she was not. He was wearing a stained, oily leather jacket beneath the coat, which also gave off whiffs of too many nights in the byre. She wrinkled her nose.

"What? This too?" he stormed.

She didn't answer and he tore the jacket from his body, muttering savagely beneath his breath. The jacket, too, followed the coat out into the snow, but his impulsive action did little to settle the matter as far as she could see. What remained of his clothing was a sweater of heather-colored Cheviot wool that must have been lovely once but was now stiffened with dirt and unraveling in numerous places. The collar of the white shirt that showed beneath it was badly yellowed and torn.

Across the length of the room his eyes met hers. Without another word he picked up the bucket and went outside. When he returned she saw that he had packed it with snow. Silently he hung it on a nail over the fire and stirred the embers with the toe of his boot.

She watched, wide-eyed, as he stripped off the sweater and tossed it onto the floor. It was quickly followed by his boots and stockings, which were equally as yellowed as the shirt. Unmindful of the chill, he began undoing the buttons of his shirt, and as he drew it off his broad shoulders, she gasped.

"What are you doing!"

He glared at her. "Exactly as you asked. Taking off my smelly clothes. All of them. I'm going to wash them in the bucket." Tugging off the shirt, he began to unfasten his worn calfskin breeches.

"Wait!" she squeaked.

He paused and looked at her questioningly.

"You—you aren't really going to undress c-completely, are you?"

"How else does one usually go about preparing for a bath?"

"A b-bath?"

"Yes, of course. To be perfectly honest, I smell as bad as my clothes. No sense in washing one without the other, is there? Though I daresay it'd be easier if I had a proper tub."

29

"B-but I didn't mean—"

He gave her a sly look. "No, I'm sure you didn't. But I certainly don't want to insult a fair lady's sensibilities, do I? You could always wait outside, although I wouldn't advise it. The temperature's dropped and your hands and feet will freeze. Don't worry, I won't be a minute."

"But won't you freeze in h-here as well without clothes on?" she asked desperately.

"My dear girl, I was born in the Highlands. The cold means nothing to me."

Gemma could only stare as he shrugged out of his breeches and kicked them aside and then, oh, horrors, he was standing there before her stark naked. He stretched his powerful arms to the rafters, revealing that he was every bit as hairy as the fur coat he had worn. The dark hair covered his muscular chest and his flat belly, tapering right down to—to—

She gasped and clapped her hands over her eyes. She heard his impudent laugh and then a splash of water. She peeked through her splayed fingers and saw him rinse himself off and then kneel on the floor. Humming a little beneath his breath, he began scrubbing his shirt, breeches, and underclothes.

"There," he told her, "I've spread them out in front of the fire. I think it's safe for you to look."

She lowered her hands and instantly wished she hadn't. While waiting for his clothes to dry he had wrapped himself in *her* cloak, the lovely green velvet one which had until recently been spread across the rough blankets on which she lay. Now it hugged his wide shoulders and spilled in emerald folds over his chest and down his narrow hips. But where its plush length had covered her down to her heels, it barely ended at mid-thigh on this mountainous barbarian.

Yes, barbarian, she thought furiously. After all, he was Scottish. Although Queen Victoria had begun making the much-hated Highlands respectable, even fashionable, of late with her purchase of Balmoral Castle, everyone knew that the Scots were still hopelessly uncivilized. Just like this one! How *could* he sit there looking at her with such an impudent grin on his bearded face when he was *stark naked* beneath her expensive velvet cloak?

I shall never wear it again! she thought furiously. I'll burn it and throw the ashes down the privy!

"I'm tired," she said coldly and, turning her back to him, closed her eyes and pretended to sleep.

Unperturbed, Connor laid another log on the fire and sat for a long time, watching the flames lick the sizzling wood. He was hungry and not a little tired himself, having stayed up all night bathing the wounded temple of the yon proud, golden-haired beauty.

A silent laugh shook his body. How Eachern and the others would howl when he told them the story of how Miss Gemma Baird had literally fallen into his lap! Lucky for him he'd been near enough to hear her screams when she was attacked, and lucky for her, too.

His smile dissolved into a frown. Tiny as she was, she would never have fended off those three scalawags, although she had certainly struggled valiantly. Why in the hell had she been riding alone through the forest? Hadn't anyone insisted that she ride out with a groom? As wealthy as King Spencer claimed she was, she should have been traveling with a veritable train of outriders. Though many of the more notorious highwaymen had been driven from Derbyshire long before Queen Victoria had ascended the throne, there were still unscrupulous vagabonds who sought the ample booty that traveled along the great coaching road between Derby, Sheffield, and Leeds.

Sighing, he drew up his knees and rested his arms on them. Outside the daylight had long since faded, but inside the fire lit the hut with a strangely intimate glow. From the deep, even breathing of the small bundle lying nearby, Connor assumed that the girl had fallen asleep. He wasn't surprised, considering that she had taken a blow to the head that could easily have killed her.

He turned quietly to look at her. Covered to the chin by rough blankets, there wasn't much to see but a glimpse of yellow hair, torched red by the firelight.

So this was Gemma Baird—small, slim, with sparkling green eyes. But insufferably haughty. And pretty enough, he supposed, even with those wan cheeks and that pain-wracked brow. Still, she was not at all what he'd expected.

As he watched, Gemma stirred in her sleep and rolled over, revealing her upturned nose, the slim line of her jaw and throat, and the lovely curve of her breasts illuminated by the firelight. Watching them rise and fall to the gentle rhythm of her breathing, he became aware of a familiar stirring in his loins. Scowling, he turned his head away. Now *that* was something he hadn't expected either: to feel an undeniable pull of desire for the skinny little witch.

Stretching out on the hard floor as far away from her as possible, he wrapped the warm folds of her cloak about him and forced himself to fall asleep as well. To his annoyance, it took a long time.

Chapter Two

Sir Archibald sat in the library of his Georgian manor gloomily thinking about Gemma, who had failed to return from a ride to Penrose two nights ago. Inquiries in the village had yielded him nothing, and though it was a sunny morning, yesterday's heavy snowfall had prevented his servants from resuming the search for his niece.

Nonetheless, he was not particularly worried about her. The seventeen-year-old impetuous firebrand cared little for convention and was certainly not the faint-hearted sort who would likely fall victim to foul play. Reports of highwaymen in the area hadn't concerned him either. Gemma was quite capable of looking after herself, and as for highwaymen—he was more likely to feel sorry for anyone trying to kidnap *her* than the other way around.

There was a knock on the library door and a servant

poked his head inside. "They're coming, sir! William's just spotted 'em on the upper road!"

"Who?"

"Why, Miss Gemma, sir. She's been found by some wild creature dressed in animal skins."

Despite the freezing temperature, most of his staff had assembled in the front drive by the time his niece appeared on the far side of the gate. He knew that no one was particularly surprised to see her, for his household tended to take the same long-suffering view toward her madcap escapades that he did. As he waited, he heard the murmurings by his staff about the wild creature accompanying Gemma.

Unfortunately, the wild creature turned out to be nothing more than a man, though a shaggy one, and from the look of her, Gemma wasn't particularly pleased that he was bringing her home. Her colt halted behind them when his niece stopped in front of him, her pert nose reddened from the cold and her trim boots caked with ice.

"Helios met with an accident," she told him, clear enough for every interested ear to hear, "and this . . . this . . . gentleman was kind enough to bring me home. I promised him a decent meal. William," she added, addressing the groom standing behind Sir Archibald, "will you show him to the barn, please?"

Gemma started toward the stable with the colt following on a loose rein behind her, but Sir Archibald held up his hand. "If the fellow was kind enough to help you out, lass, then he deserves better than the barn."

"Aye, she promised me a meal fit for a king. On golden plate, no less," the big stranger informed him loudly.

34

The look Gemma turned on him would have slain a lesser man.

"Is this true, Gemma?" he demanded.

She nodded, and Sir Archibald saw her face tighten with disapproval.

"Then keep your word, girl! After all, it's that of a Baird."

He watched Gemma's proud little head turn slowly toward the hairy man behind her.

"My uncle asks that I bid you welcome." Her soft voice, so cultured and refined, dripped venom. "If you'd be so kind as to follow Worsham inside? I'm sure he'd be delighted to draw you a bath and provide you with a change of clothes."

Upstairs in her own room Gemma could hardly wait to shrug out of her sodden habit and stockings. She waited, shivering, while the maids scurried to fill her bathtub, exhorting them to make sure the water was scalding while ignoring their wide-eyed looks and giggled whispers.

A sigh escaped her as she slid into the tub at last and felt her frozen limbs begin to thaw. Leaning back, she closed her eyes and gave herself over to the pleasure of soaking in the hot, scented water. She knew that she would have a lot of explaining to do and that a tedious meal awaited her downstairs in the company of that unpleasant Connor MacEowan, but at the moment she didn't care. She was warm at last, and Helios was safe in the care of the Baird stablemaster. Nothing else mattered.

Getting out of the tub and then dressing, she toyed with the idea of pleading ill and missing dinner entirely.

Wouldn't it be wonderful if she never had to lay eyes on that objectionable MacEowan fellow again? But her sense of fairness grudgingly exerted itself. No, she had given her word, and like it or not, Uncle Archibald seemed determined to see that she kept it.

"At least he'll have washed and changed his clothes," she said aloud, and was mollified by the thought.

Connor and Sir Archibald were seated in the withdrawing room, and through the open double doors Connor saw Gemma step into the hall. The laughter he had been sharing with the older man stilled. He had thought Gemma Baird pretty enough back there in the shepherd's hut, but he certainly hadn't expected such a breathtaking transformation from the bedraggled waif he'd rescued to this properly cleaned and clothed lady.

Aye, King had been right. She was certainly the sort to turn a man's head. Her wheat-colored mass of hair curled riotously about her small head despite the attempt to confine it in a snug chignon. There was color in her cheeks and a sleek, satisfied look about her as the wide skirts of her dove-gray woolen gown rustled softly around her. Cut modestly at the scalloped neckline, the garment nonetheless revealed the creamy smoothness of Gemma's throat and shoulders, while the tucks at the bodice emphasized her tiny waist. He couldn't take his eyes off her.

Gemma immediately noticed that Connor MacEowan was wearing the same offensive clothing that he had tried—uselessly—to wash in the hut and which was even now stiffened with more dirt and worn through in countless places. He seemed to have washed his hands and brushed some of the dust out of his beard and long hair, but that scarcely improved his appearance. Her heart sank. Did she *really* have to sit with him while he ate?

Apparently so, for Sir Archibald ushered them both into the dining room the moment she appeared. The long table had been set at one end for three, and her eyes widened when she saw the Royal Worcester china laid out with gleaming silverware on the fine linen cloth. God above, her uncle had even sent Worsham down to the cellar for a bottle of Bordeaux—as if the uncouth ogre would have the sense to appreciate it!

Nevertheless, her nose twitched hungrily at the tantalizing smells emanating from beneath the lids of the serving dishes. While footmen moved about lighting candles, carrying in food, and uncorking the wine, she allowed herself to be seated at her uncle's right side. Connor, deliberately ignored by the servants, pulled up a chair opposite her.

"MacEowan and I were having quite an interesting chin wag," Uncle Archibald said, beaming at her.

Judging from the laughter she'd heard on her way downstairs, Gemma didn't doubt it. Her lips thinned.

"Small world, I might add. MacEowan says he was on his way here to ask for work when you stumbled o'er his path."

"Oh? Then he told you what happened?"

Uncle Archibald's tubby face reddened with amusement. "Every word."

Across the table her eyes met Connor's. He gave a small, negative shake of his head. Vastly relieved, she tossed her own head and looked away.

Her uncle kept talking as the servants doled out gargantuan proportions of braised meat, plump fowl, fresh bread, and root-cellar vegetables which Gemma fell upon, half starved. Only when the worst of her hunger had been appeased did she steal a glance at the man opposite her. She stiffened, seeing that he was making no use of the silverware but was eating everything with his fingers. Why, he was fairly *growling* as he used his teeth to yank the skin off the fowl, and after every gulp of wine he had the gall to wipe his mouth with the back of his hand and belch loudly. Horrified, she looked away.

"—isn't that right, MacEowan?" Uncle Archibald finished, beaming at his guest.

Why, he actually likes the man! she thought in disbelief. And that after he had sent Worsham down to the cellar for two more bottles of wine! That was his best Bordeaux, which he hated to share with anyone!

Gemma sat tight-lipped throughout the remainder of the meal, not touching another thing, not even the wonderful desserts that were rolled in from the kitchen on a cart. Connor MacEowan, on the other hand, helped himself to everything, and swallowed it down with a haste she found thoroughly offensive. When the last of his plates had been cleared away by the poker-faced footmen, he pushed back his chair and stretched his long arms to the ceiling. Yawning hugely, he grinned and patted his stomach.

She took this as a cue that he was finished and shot to her feet.

"Just a minute, m' girl," her uncle said.

She eyed him distrustfully.

"MacEowan and I went ahead and discussed a few things before you came down. We've made some arrangements you'll be needing to hear."

"Oh, Uncle, you didn't offer him work!" she burst out in dismay.

Sir Archibald startled her by exploding into laughter. "Nay, girl, I've done better 'n that."

She sank back in her chair, eyeing him suspiciously. "What do you mean?"

"Why, only that he's offered to marry you, and I've agreed."

For a moment no one said anything. Gemma made no move at all. Only a wave of heat rushed into her face.

"That's not funny, Uncle Archibald," she said at last.

"Oh, I'm not teasing," he assured her, picking his teeth with a fork. "Listen here, gel, you spent two nights alone with the man. Your return in his company was witnessed by every last person in this house. MacEowan was generous enough to consider your reputation, which won't be worth—"

"How could you!" she shrieked, leaping to her feet. "Have you lost your mind?"

"Now, Gemma, girl—"

Lifting a pitcher of clotted cream, she smashed it onto the table and stormed from the room.

Connor heard her stomp up the stairs, then a thundering rumble that was followed by the far-off slamming of a door.

After a moment Connor said, "I think you were a wee bit hasty."

"Not at all." Sir Archibald dipped his finger into the cream and licked it with obvious enjoyment. "It's the only way to handle Gemma: quick and off the shoulder, so she won't have time to hit back." He laughed and waggled a pudgy hand. "Trust me, m' boy. Been that way since she first came here, barely six years old, when

39

my brother and his wife were drowned crossing the channel on their way to France. Shameless piece of baggage even then! It's the truth, and I've always wondered if the little heathen wasn't what drove my Druscilla to an early grave. Never had children of our own, thank God.''

Connor, who had been hard-pressed to hide his amusement while playing the savage for Gemma's benefit, now regarded the older man soberly. "So what happens now?''

"Why, we'll call in the preacher. Tie the knot afore m' servants have the chance to spread the tale far and wide. It's what we agreed, ain't it?''

"No, I mean the girl.''

"Gemma?'' Sir Archibald flapped his hand in dismissal. "Oh, she's had enough time by now to get over the shock and throw some of her duds into a valise. I expect she'll be sneaking down to the stable at this very moment.''

Connor straightened. "Then perhaps I should—''

"Sit down, sit down, m'boy! Yours is the last face she'd care to see just now. Can't say as I blame her,'' Sir Archibald added, grinning as he peered into Connor's bearded face. "I'd never have known you m'self if you hadn't said your name aloud. Egad, what a disguise!''

"Aye, it's quite a difference,'' Connor agreed impatiently. He had no recollection of having met Sir Archibald Baird at the British embassy in Paris six years ago, but apparently the bald-headed old man remembered the event quite clearly. In fact, they had discussed the coincidence more than enough before Gemma had joined them for dinner. "Now as for your niece—''

"There she is now," Sir Archibald declared as an outer door slammed and a woman's high, breathless voice shouting curses rang out. "Curt'll be takin' her upstairs. He's under standing orders to lock her in whenever she tries to run away."

Connor's brow rose. "Does she do so often?"

"Only when I try to arrange marriages for her."

The sounds of cursing and kicking continued until an upper door slammed. Then, abruptly, there was silence. A hulking fellow with arms like sides of beef appeared in the doorway, disheveled and out of breath.

"I locked 'er in as usual, zur."

"Thank you, Curt. That'll do."

"And now?" Connor asked, frowning.

Sir Archibald consulted the clock on the buffet. "Why, she'll start breaking things, I suppose. Fortunately there ain't much left." He winced as the sound of shattering porcelain exploded on the floor above. "Must've forgotten that one."

Settling himself back in his chair, he laced his fingers over the bulge where his waistcoat and stomach didn't quite meet. "Capital idea, this wager of yours. Even better than the one you were embroiled in when we met in Paris. Though I'm almost sorry I'm in on this one so soon. Would've enjoyed watching you tame her while posing as one of my farm hands, b'gad!"

"I assure you," Connor said arrogantly, "that had you given me work, I would still have managed—"

More breaking glass shattered the stillness above them. Several footmen entered the dining room to serve port and cigars. Crash! Crash! Crash! None of the footmen so much as blinked an eye.

Sir Archibald waited until they were gone before

41

speaking again. "Sure you still want to marry her? Won't be easy, y'know. Turned down more offers than we've got fingers and toes, and frightened half as many more clean away. Though I suppose you're not intending to lose this wager, eh?"

Connor's expression closed. "No."

"Well, b'gad," Sir Archibald went on, and it was clear that he was enjoying himself hugely, "better send for the preacher first thing."

"It's very quiet upstairs," Connor said.

"Eh? Oh, that'll be Gemma again. Knotting the bed linens together to make good her escape. I'll send Curt round back to catch her when she jumps."

"No need," Connor said, coming to his feet. "I can manage."

An icy wind lashed at him the moment Connor stepped outside. The house and the park lay in complete darkness. Only the snow-dusted lawn shone faintly in the starlight. Crunching over the ice, he wondered about the wild Gemma Baird. He had already gotten over the shock of having been recognized by her rascally uncle, and the ease with which every detail of the wager's end had fallen into place. The fat old scalawag had been only too happy to turn the girl over to him, suggesting marriage as a means to win the bet and spare them all the scandal that would erupt when it became known that Gemma had spent two nights alone in a shepherd's hut in the company of a man.

Aye, a tidy solution to everything, he thought, and only Gemma seemed determined to prevent the situation from ending smoothly. Too determined, he amended, turning the corner and seeing the open window on the floor above—and the slim, dark figure descending hand over hand down the face of the wall, her legs dangling, her hair blowing in the wind.

He stared, incredulous, for he hadn't really believed that Sir Archibald was telling the truth about the girl's determination to escape. Had she gone mad? One slip and she'd fall to her death on the stone walk below! How the devil could she manage such an impossible stunt?

Because she was wearing trousers, like a man. Heavy skirts would obviously have hindered her progress, and as Gemma let go of the rope and plunged the last few feet right into his waiting arms, he felt a flash of admiration for her. But that ended the instant she began writhing and twisting like a demon in his grasp.

"Let me go!" she screamed, pummeling him with her fists.

But he was not the slow-thinking, subservient Curt. Instead he held her a little away from him so that her blows rained harmlessly upon his shoulders and chest. Patiently he waited until she had exhausted herself and lay panting in his arms.

"I'm going to let you go now," he said coldly. "I'd advise you not to run away."

"You!" she gasped. "I—I thought it was Curt!"

Connor couldn't see Gemma's face in the darkness, but he could hear the hatred throbbing in her tone. It was the first time he had ever been so contemptuously addressed by a woman, and the experience was unpleasant. He set her down far more roughly than he would have a scant second earlier.

Gemma stood rubbing her arms and glaring up at him, her slim, trouser-clad form quivering with outrage.

Ellen Tanner Marsh

"Fortune hunter! Thief! I have no idea how you managed to convince my uncle to agree to this—this insanity, but I promise that you'll live to regret it! On my parents' grave I swear you'll not have me or my money! I'll see you dead first! I'll cut out your heart and feed it to the hogs! I'll—"

His hand covered her mouth, and with the other he caught her around the waist and pinned her tightly against his side so that she could neither struggle nor kick. He had already seen how painfully she could bite and was not about to make the same mistake of underestimating her as the highwayman had.

"I don't want your fortune, Gemma Baird," he said ominously. "You and I are going to be married and there's nothing you can do about it. The minister will be here first thing in the morning."

He loosened his hold on her head only long enough to look down into her face and make sure that she was listening. What he saw in her brimming eyes stabbed him for a moment with the realization that he was being an unspeakable cad. But the moment passed quickly, very quickly. There was Glenarris to be thought of.

Wordlessly he picked her up in his arms and carried her back into the house.

Chapter Three

Gemma stood at the tall bedroom window overlooking the park as the minister's carriage came bowling up the drive, the horses plodding through the slush. She had been up and dressed for hours, refusing breakfast and standing quietly, unnaturally so, while the maids dressed her and did up her hair.

There hadn't been time to procure a proper wedding gown. When marrying in indecent haste one had to make do with what one had, Gemma had thought numbly. In her case that meant a tea dress of ice-blue satin damask with yards of frilly white petticoats spilling over whalebone hoops. The spreading skirts were trimmed with blond lace, and, as was the current fashion, her shoulders were almost indecently bare and her neckline cut low in a daring décolletage.

Earlier, her hair had been curled with tongs and swept up on the crown of her head with pearl-studded combs.

When the time came for her to appear in the great hall, a veil would be lowered over her face, a veil the housekeeper had found in the attic last night among the long-deceased Lady Druscilla's belongings and which had been bleached and laundered in feverish haste.

Tiredly, she leaned against the window frame. She had scarcely slept a wink all night, which wasn't surprising considering that she had been locked in her room and actually tied to the bed. Ever since dawn she had, in her exhaustion, all but consigned herself to her fate.

Until now, when she saw the scrawny, black-clad form of Reverend Matlock descending from his carriage. He looked more like an undertaker than a man of God, and the sight of him stirred her into sudden action. She was too heavily guarded to run away or kill herself (a last resort which she wasn't above considering), but perhaps there was still time to make Connor MacEowan change his mind about wanting to marry her!

"I'm hungry," she said, whirling to address the sour-faced maid who had been charged with keeping an eye on her.

"Bain't no time for breakfast," the sullen creature insisted. "They'll be comin' for ye soon."

Gemma crossed to the door, the yards of shimmering damask foaming as she moved. "No matter. I'll find something in the kitchen."

Flattening her hoops to negotiate the narrow walkway, she took the back staircase with the disapproving maid scurrying behind. In the cavernous kitchen the cook and his staff were frantically preparing the wedding feast. Steam rose from the great cooking pots and the fire in the oven roared. Sauces sizzled and meat turned on the spit, and no one noticed as Gemma stole into the pantry.

The Enchanted Prince

A braid of garlic hung in the deep embrasure of the stone windowsill. Pulling a clove free, Gemma peeled away the flaky shell and popped it into her mouth. Shuddering, she forced herself to chew and swallow. Then she took an onion from the bin and peeled it as well. Her eyes watered and she gasped as she took a bite, but again she forced herself to chew slowly and swallow every bit.

Triumphantly she swept from the room and crossed into the main wing of the house. The wedding was to be held in the great hall, and she wisely avoided it, heading instead toward the reception rooms beyond, her sour-faced escort running to keep up with her.

"Miss Gemma, you slow down!"

She ignored the woman and pushed on. She had guessed that she would find her bridegroom in one of these rooms, and she was not mistaken. Poking her head through one door after another, she finally found Connor standing in front of the fire in a darkly furnished gentlemen's anteroom near the library.

To her amazement she saw that he had bathed and changed his clothing. His black hair, drawn back from his face and tied with velvet ribbon, gleamed in the firelight, and he was no longer wearing the stained and stinking attire. Nevertheless, the worn breeches and mended shirt that had obviously been borrowed from the brawniest of the Baird footmen did not make him look the least bit civilized. Not even one of her uncle's finest suits could have done that—even if the hairy giant had been able to shrug into it! No, not surprisingly, he still managed to look every inch a beggar, an unscrupulous, fortune-hunting beggar whom Gemma would dearly love strangling with her bare hands!

"Good morning," she said sweetly.

Connor, lost in thought, had not heard her come in. Now he whipped about and his face went blank as Gemma shut the door on her dour servant and crossed the room toward him. *Floated* was a more appropriate term, for she looked like an angel in her flowing skirts of ice blue, her golden hair, piled atop her small head, gleaming with pearl-studded combs, and her creamy shoulders prettily bared.

The modest wedding gown, however, did nothing to conceal Gemma's slim waist and her full breasts. In fact, there was something unintentionally seductive about this sensual mix of innocence and womanliness, and Connor could only stare. Small wonder that countless men before him had tried to win this golden temptress's hand! God's blood, the way she smiled with those green eyes of hers tilting at the corners and her soft, full mouth enchantingly curved made a man's pulses race! He had never seen her smile before.

Now she paused before him, all rustling, scented loveliness, and tipped back her pretty head in order to look him full in the face. "The minister is here. I wanted to make absolutely certain you hadn't changed your mind."

The garlic and onion on her breath hit him like an exploding cannonball. He stiffened as his stomach turned.

"Are you absolutely sure?" she breathed again, batting her thick lashes and looking utterly innocent.

"Oh, I'm sure," he said firmly, although he had retreated a step.

"I wouldn't want you to have second thoughts," she persisted, stalking him. " 'Twouldn't do for you to change your mind the moment Reverend Matlock says you're to *kiss the bride.*''

The last three words were expelled in a breathy rush that was overwhelmingly redolent of the cook house. He could feel his eyes water as he beat a hasty retreat. Scheming baggage! He had to grapple with the urge to take her over his knee. And fight the sudden, piercing desire that followed close on its heels to do exactly as she said and kiss those softly parted lips, onion breath and all. Now, wouldn't that serve to wipe the smug look off her lovely face, eh?

"Gemma! Where the devil are you, gel? It's time!" Sir Archibald bellowed from somewhere down the hall.

Gemma peered hopefully at Connor.

"Nice try," he told her, grinning, "but I still intend to marry you."

Her hopeful look changed to one of fury. "You'll be sorry."

"Oh, I don't doubt it," he agreed. Reaching for her arm, he started for the door only to have Gemma jerk out of his grasp. Whirling, he saw that she had planted her feet firmly on the thick rug and was glaring up at him, her jaw clenched, her fists on her hips, as though daring him to move her another step.

Connor grimaced, for he was learning very quickly what that mulish look of hers meant. "Now, Miss Baird—"

"I'm not going to marry you," she said ominously.

"Oh, yes, you are."

"You can't make me."

"Can't I?" He came toward her as he spoke, so close that she had to tilt back her head in order to look square into his face.

"I'll kill you if I have to."

"Go ahead."

"All right, I will."

"You haven't got a weapon."

She quickly searched the room with her eyes, and Connor laughed at the disappointed look that crept over her face as she realized he was right. He knew she couldn't reach the musket on the wall, the furniture was too cumbersome, and the urn near the fireplace too heavy for her to lift.

"What a bloodthirsty creature you are, Gemma Baird," he said, watching her with his arms crossed casually over his chest. "Last night I thought your uncle was being a little harsh in locking you up under guard. Now I'm beginning to realize I may have to do the same when you and I are married."

"And will you tie me to the bed the way he did?"

His eyes roved the lovely curve of her breasts. "I could be tempted, aye."

"You're a swine," she spat.

"I've been called worse. Now come on, your uncle's waiting." He reached out to grab her, but Gemma twisted out of reach.

"I won't marry you!" she shouted loud enough for the entire household to hear. "I'd rather die!"

"That can be arranged. *After* the wedding."

Gemma hurled herself at him, and taken completely by surprise, he was unable to prevent her from getting in one or two effective punches with her balled fists. He had never had much patience with difficult women, and Gemma Baird was worse than an army of them. Never mind that she was tiny and ridiculously unskilled at pugilism; her fists were relentless. Never mind that she

wore soft kid slippers beneath that foaming wedding
gown; the well-aimed kicks at his shins were painful.
God's blood, that last one had landed far too close to
his privates for comfort and Connor promptly lost his
temper.

Seizing Gemma's wrists in his hands, he twisted cruelly until she cried out and went slack against him. He
shook her, making her head snap back and forth like a
marionette.

"By God," he growled, "you really are an ill-
tempered witch! Try that again and I'll twist your head
right off your scrawny neck. Do you understand me?

"Well?" He shook her again, his fingers biting into
her flesh.

Gemma dropped her head and nodded.

"Gemma! Where the devil are you?" her uncle bellowed from down the hall.

Wordlessly Connor jerked her around and headed for
the door, uncaring that she stumbled. He didn't say anything as he pulled her into the corridor and whipped her
around to face her uncle.

"Here she is, Sir Archibald," he cheerfully announced, masking his anger. "Ready and eager to wed.
I'd keep a tight hold on her till you get her to the altar,
though. Shy young brides have been known to bolt."

Sir Archibald nodded vigorously. "Well, now, we
certainly don't want our wee Gemma to take fright on
such an important day, do we?" he said heartily and
gripped her wrist.

Gemma was silent as she allowed herself to be propelled to the front of the makeshift altar. Through the
thick film of her veil she watched Connor MacEowan

coming toward her at Reverend Matlock's side. How broad he was, and hairy and daunting! Her stomach churned.

Wait! she wanted to scream. *I can't do this! I don't know anything about this man except his name!* And the fact that he was coarse and ill kempt and unscrupulous enough to take advantage of a most unfortunate happenstance!

I hate you, Connor MacEowan, she thought, tears springing to her eyes so that her bridegroom's towering form blurred before her. I hate you and I'll run away from you the first chance I get. I'll go south, to London, where my mother's people came from. Neither you nor Uncle Archibald will ever find me there!

"Dearly beloved," the minister intoned, and at the sound of his high, nasal voice, a strange calm washed into her heart, erasing her anguish and the fear that Connor MacEowan had instilled within her in the anteroom.

Yes, she thought, she would go to London. Uncle Archibald had told her it was an enormous city, spreading for miles along the river Thames and beyond. She'd pawn her jewels and her gowns and have enough money on which to live until she could find work as a . . . a governess or a schoolteacher or something like that. Only Helios wouldn't be sold. She had assisted the stablemaster at the colt's birth and it was she alone who had raised and schooled him. He was all she had, the only thing she loved. She'd take him with her when she left.

Someone nudged her.

"What?" she asked irritably, then became aware that Reverend Matlock was looking down at her in unmistakable panic. "Oh!" she exclaimed as the minister cut his eyes repeatedly toward the big man at her side. "Yes," she said hastily, "yes, I do."

The reverend gave an audible sigh of relief. "Then I now pronounce you man and wife. You may kiss the bride."

She turned obediently to Connor. His big hands lifted away the veil. Beneath it she had crossed her eyes and had stuck out her tongue at him.

Instead of being shocked, Connor merely threw back his head and uttered a bark of lusty laughter. Then she felt his hands at her waist and the small of her back and he was drawing her body close, enfolding her in a huge embrace that all but swallowed her up. Then he lowered his head and his mouth closed over hers and for the first time in her life she was being kissed, really kissed, by a man.

It was nothing like the chaste pecks of her shy former suitors, or even the ardent caresses of some of the more emboldened ones. It was frightening and exhilarating all at the same time, with hardly any of the revulsion she had expected to feel. Even the scratching of his beard was somehow exciting, and the way his hot mouth covered hers made her lips part beneath his even though she didn't want them to.

Dear God, she was kissing him back, wasn't she? The instant the revelation hit, she tore free of his grasp. She would have loved to slap his face as hard as she could.

"Mrs. MacEowan?" Connor inquired, sounding a little breathless himself. "Shall we go?"

She stared at him stupidly for a moment, then looked down at the ring on her finger, the one Uncle Archibald had given his prospective nephew earlier that morning. Uncle Archibald liked flashy things, and he had purchased the trinket at one time to appease her Aunt Druscilla, who had never seemed to be pleased with anything when she was alive.

And now the delicate band of gold was hers although she had no memory of how it had gotten onto her hand. One thing was certain: its presence was cruel proof that she belonged to the bearded giant in front of her, an opportunistic savage whom she hated with all her heart but who had nonetheless managed to turn her knees to water with a simple kiss. What in God's name was she going to do about that?

"Mrs. MacEowan?" Connor repeated politely. "We're all waiting."

She looked up at him and he looked back at her calmly, patiently, so very sure of himself.

"Don't call me that!" she exploded. "Never call me that again!"

She heard Reverend Matlock gasp, and, her breasts heaving, she glared defiantly at her husband. Without another word Connor turned heel and left her standing at the altar, and Sir Archibald took her limp hand and led her away to the wedding feast.

She ate nothing of the sumptuous meal. The food stuck in her throat and she could no sooner swallow it than she could the great lump of tears lurking there as well. She sat like an alabaster statue while her uncle plied her husband and the Reverend Matlock with wine.

The talk was desultory, the atmosphere strained, but only her husband seemed unaware of it. He drank steadily and ate a veritable mountain of food while exhibiting the same execrable manners that had horrified her the night before. But now, his barbaric habits, and even his presence hardly mattered to her, and she did not look up when he scraped back his chair long before the meal was finished and rose.

"You've been more than generous, Sir Archibald," he said in a voice that was entirely steady despite the amount of alcohol he had consumed. "But now my wife and I will be off."

Her head jerked up. Off? Off where?

"I quite understand," her uncle was saying heartily. "You've a long journey ahead of you."

Journey? Where? Her eyes sought her uncle's, but he refused to look at her.

"Off so soon?" Reverend Matlock's voice quavered.

"I'm taking my wife to Scotland," Connor answered.

Reverend Matlock smiled thinly. "Oh? I take it you have a home there?"

"More or less," Connor ground out. "I'm obviously not a wealthy man."

"The lad's quite determined not to live off my largess," Sir Archibald said approvingly. "Plans to build a home for Gemma with his own hands. Told me so last night."

"I'd be just as happy in a cave," she said nastily.

"Don't be so quick to dismiss the possibility," Connor shot back.

She scowled and was ready to answer him when her uncle's voice stopped her.

"Go upstairs and pack your things, pet. I'm giving you one of my carriages as a wedding gift. If you hurry, you might make Yorkshire by nightfall."

But Gemma had no wish to accommodate her uncle's suggestion, for she stubbornly refused to leave home until every last one of her possessions had been packed. No, she would not leave behind even one of her dresses, or her bonnets, gloves, shoes, and shawls. As well, she intended bringing her brushes and combs, her music box and scent bottles, her drawing pads, pencils, music books, and novels. Mementos of her parents—and there were pitifully few—were packed away with great care into one of the trunks whose numbers were growing with alarming speed downstairs in the hall.

In the end Sir Archibald was forced to donate yet another carriage, this one packed to overflowing with her belongings. This meant, too, that another pair of coachmen had to be sent along to drive it.

One last obstacle remained: Gemma flatly refused to leave home without her colt. In this, her uncle was not inclined to be so generous, for he knew the value of her magnificent animal and was loath to see it leave his stable. But she was adamant. Her uncle could keep the mare that had given birth to the colt and had belonged to Gemma's mother, and the stallion that had sired Helios and had been given to Gemma on her thirteenth birthday from a nearby landowner with numerous unmarried sons. But his generosity had yielded him naught, for Gemma had turned down every last one of his boys in the interim years.

In the end, as usual, Gemma got her way.

Neither one spoke as the coach moved steadily toward their destination. Gemma sat stiffly, her face turned away from him, and Connor had no inkling of her thoughts. He could well imagine that they weren't kind. His own mood was, by contrast, much more charitable. After all, he was on his way back to Scotland, and in far more luxurious circumstances than when he'd left.

It was he who had suggested to Eachern and his

friends that he use public transportation to get to Derbyshire in the first place. In retrospect he had to admit that it had been an eye-opening experience, and while it was nothing he'd care to repeat, he couldn't for a moment claim to have been bored. And boredom had, for the whole of his adult life, been the bane of his existence.

The long miles of the journey south—many of them undertaken on foot—had certainly prepared him for his role. He'd slept on musty cots and in smelly barns and sometimes out in open fields. He'd earned money for his meals at odd jobs along the way, and once or twice had even begged a handout from some prosperous-looking gent just to see if he could get away with it. In the meantime he had let his hair and beard grow out, worn nothing but the clothes on his back day in and day out, and done his best to emulate the coarse manners of the unsavory characters he met.

All in all it had been an invigorating experience, and Connor could hardly wait to tell the others about it. Or wait to see their expressions when he paraded his very beautiful bride before their astounded eyes. Six months they'd given him to bring her back, the usual time for a wager as involved as this one, and here he was, a short week's journey from Edinburgh and at the end of a laughably simple task. As for yon proud beauty sulking on the seat opposite, well, she'd come around soon enough. And wouldn't it prove enjoyable to tame her in the meantime?

Yes indeed, he thought, crossing his arms behind his head and grinning at his bride's icy profile, once again Fate had been very, very kind to him.

Chapter Four

Gemma stirred from her sleep as she felt her shoulder being jostled. She opened her eyes, and for an instant did not recognize the bearded face that hovered over hers. Then she gasped and shrank back. Laughing, Connor motioned her out of the couch.

Light rain was falling and Gemma shivered as she stood in the torch-lit yard of a country inn. A woman approached her, introduced herself as the innkeeper's wife, and led Gemma inside and up a flight of creaking stairs. They entered a simply furnished but clean room where a fire was burning in the grate. Pulling off her gloves, Gemma gratefully warmed her hands.

"I'll be up in a moment with thy supper," the woman said and curtsied before hurrying out.

"I take it my uncle paid for this room?" Gemma asked nastily as Connor came in, his big frame blocking the doorway. "You'd not have been able to afford so much as a single bed, let alone supper, would you?''

"We only have a single bed,'' Connor pointed out calmly.

Her eyes followed his to the iron frame in the corner, which was covered with a plump feather tick and a pair of bolster pillows. She looked at him. "But where will you sleep?''

"Why, here, of course. You didn't think we had *two* rooms, did you?''

But that was exactly what she had thought, and now she stared at him in horror. Connor laughed at her expression and shrugged out of his coat. When he came to stand before the fire she moved quickly away to answer the knock at the door.

A slatternly serving girl carried in their supper, and Gemma watched the wench cast simpering looks at Connor. Inwardly she burned. It wasn't fair! *This* was the sort of woman Connor MacEowan deserved, a slovenly creature of no class or breeding who found his shaggy masculinity attractive and who would be delighted to share a pigsty with him!

"Where is it we're going?'' she inquired, itching for a fight after the girl had gone and the two of them sat down to their meal.

"To a small glen in the Northwest Highlands. I doubt you've ever heard of it.''

So did she. "Do you have a home there?''

"More or less.''

She scowled. Less, she imagined, envisioning the cave or the mud-floored cottage in which he had doubtless been born and raised. Go ahead and look as smug as you like! she thought furiously. You'll not be using a penny of my money to build yourself a fine manor house! The moment your back is turned I'm off to London, Connor MacEowan!

Connor studied Gemma as she ate, aware of her simmering anger. He suddenly realized that Gemma had never asked him one personal question. Now why was that? He also knew that she was not the sort of girl to retreat into herself the way she had ever since they'd exchanged their wedding vows earlier that morning. What evil was being plotted in that clever little brain of hers? An escape, perhaps?

Aye, that had to be it, because it would also explain her insistence on bringing along every last one of her countless belongings. Most of them would fetch a pretty penny in the secondhand shops of England's larger cities, probably enough to keep her comfortably in style until she could build a new future for herself. Which shouldn't prove too difficult for a girl of her intelligence and striking good looks.

His lips twitched at the thought. Scheming baggage! One had to admire her stubborn determination, and he had to admit that he was curious to see how she'd make good her escape. Of course he wasn't about to let her go just yet. Not until the wager was won and Glenarris was safe again.

Hungry as she was, Gemma found that she could eat very little. The hulking man's presence across from her put a definite damper on her appetite. Instead she sought sustenance from the wine carafe, drinking glass after glass of the grossly unpalatable stuff. Connor watched with heavy-lidded eyes, saying nothing, but when she moved to pour a fifth glass—or was it her sixth?—he stayed her with a hand around her wrist.

Her eyes swept up to meet his. "What are you doing?"

"Preventing you from getting drunk."

She tossed her head. "You're too late for that."

"I can see as much," he said, smiling, but still insisted on prying loose her fingers and setting the carafe on the floor beneath his chair.

She eyed him in mutinous silence. Her head was spinning, but she felt bold and unafraid. Without that big, hairy coat on, Connor looked almost human, and the manners he had exhibited so far tonight were immeasurably better than the horrendous ones she had observed during their wedding feast and when he had first brought her home.

"You know, you are a very mysterious man, Connor MacEowan."

He looked at her sharply. "Oh? In what way?"

"Lots of ways. For instance, why is it that your manners and the way you look befit the lowly beggar you are, but that you speak like an educated man? Even a gentleman, at times?"

"Do I?"

"You're not going to answer me, are you?"

In silence he studied her upturned face. The wine had brightened her leaf green eyes and brought a flush to her pale cheeks. Her lower lip protruded in a pout, and as his gaze fastened upon it he remembered how sweet her mouth had tasted when she had kissed him for that brief, disturbing moment during the wedding ceremony.

Gemma stared at him in alarm as he suddenly pushed back his chair and came to stand before her. Without a word he bent down and lifted her into his arms so that she was crushed tightly against his chest. He crossed the room and put her on the bed.

"Oh no!" she cried, and tried to scramble off.

Quickly he pinned her with the weight of his body, his arms propped on either side of her head. She stared at him, her breath coming quickly, her eyes no longer languid from the wine.

"Frightened, Mrs. MacEowan?" he taunted softly. "Why?"

"You know why!" she panted.

"I do," he agreed, savoring the feel of her slim body trapped beneath his own. "But do you?"

Gemma did not answer.

"Do you know what's going to happen, Gemma?" he persisted huskily. "You've never had a mother to tell you certain things. Do you know what happens between a man and a woman when they're together like this?"

Gemma closed her eyes. "Yes," she whispered.

The mattress sagged as he reached down and cupped his hand around the swell of her breast through the velvet of her traveling gown.

She gasped. "Stop that! Let me go!"

Rather than complying, he lowered his head until his mouth covered hers. His beard rasped against her jaw, and he felt her shiver. He deepened the kiss, grazing her stubbornly clamped lips with the tip of his tongue.

Gemma lashed out at him, and the well-aimed punch caught him square in the eye.

"Oww!" He reared back, glaring, his breath coming as fast as Gemma's. Disbelief and desire warred within him as he met her flashing eyes.

Desire won out, of course, despite the fact that he had never had such an unwilling woman lying beneath him.

He had planned to win her over with skillful love-making, knowing full well how to make a woman, especially such an innocent one, swoon with longing by touching her, kissing her. He was an old, experienced hand at love, but the resistance he saw in Gemma's eyes and could feel in her rigid body told him that she would not respond as expected to his expert touch.

Or would she?

Rising from the bed, he hastily shed his clothes, taking pleasure in the way her eyes went wide. She gasped as he pulled off his breeches.

"What's wrong?" he taunted. "It's nothing you haven't seen before."

Naked, he rejoined her on the bed, kneeling above her and trapping her between his thighs. Leaning down, he ripped the gown from her shoulders. The sight of the creamy skin beneath her embroidered corset excited him. His manhood throbbed as he unlaced her undergarments and sent her petticoats and stockings flying to the floor.

Gemma fought him, but his thighs pinned her naked body to the bed and he trapped her wrists in one hand above her head so that she could only writhe uselessly.

"I'll scream!" she hissed.

"No one will come. We are, after all, legally married."

Connor saw the green sparks that flashed in her eyes and, with a groan, fell upon her. It had been months since he had bedded a woman, which had to explain why this slim, unwilling girl was driving him to the breaking point. His mouth covered hers and he kissed her, parting her lips with his own and inserting his tongue in a compelling onslaught.

Panicked, Gemma writhed beneath Connor, but he

lowered his body across her, trapping her effectively without even lifting his mouth from hers. His hair-roughened skin melded with hers, burning her wherever it touched. She could feel his narrow hips pressing against hers and his throbbing manhood between her thighs. While her wrists were still imprisoned above her head, his free hand forced its way between their heated bodies, caressing her breasts with their sensitive nipples before traveling lower across her stomach to boldly insinuate itself between her legs.

"No!" she moaned against his mouth, but his hand continued to tease and caress, touching her in a place that had never been touched, making her writhe with an onslaught of sensations she had never known before. A strange ache began to seep into her limbs, making them feel heavy, languid, while odd currents of pleasure pulsed through her.

Dear God, it had to be the wine . . .

And still the delicious torment continued, driving her resistance and fear away and leaving a rising pleasure in its wake. Her breath caught as delicious sensations rippled through her. The heat began to build, wrapping her in mindless wonder, while Connor continued to worship her with his lips and his hands. She could feel her hatred for him seeping away into a storm of swirling pleasure. Oh, God, what was happening to her?

The fever built, tormenting her, and as though with a will of their own, her hips lifted hesitantly to meet his. Groaning, Connor forced her legs apart with his knee and thrust deep inside her.

Although she was warm and slickly wet from his expert manipulations, she was not prepared for the shattering pain and the savage tearing of her delicate membrane, which marked the end of her girlhood. A scream erupted in her throat, passing between her tightly clenched lips as a throbbing moan.

Connor caught her to him, his hands sliding beneath her firm buttocks so that he could lift her against him and stroke wildly in and out. Never had he known the stabbing pleasure of burying himself in such a soft creature whose moans were driving him half mad with excitement.

It was only a matter of moments before he climaxed, surging against her as he groaned and turned his face into the soft curve of her neck. Arching, he pounded into her, gasped, and lay still.

For a long moment neither of them moved. Utterly spent, Connor lay atop his young wife, savoring the feel of their bodies' intimate joining. Then he stirred and slowly eased himself away from her.

Instantly Gemma turned away, her face buried in the crook of her arm as great sobs wracked her tiny frame. Startled, he laid his hand on her shoulder.

"Stay away from me!" she shrieked loud enough for every last person in the inn to hear. "I'll kill you if you touch me again!"

He cringed in astonishment. This was the thanks he got for trying to make their wedding night a pleasurable one? By God, no woman had ever raged at him like a she-devil after making love! What on earth was wrong with her?

But of course he knew, and the knowledge shamed him unexpectedly. Lashed by remorse and a mounting sense of anger, he got out of bed and threw on his clothes. He was sorely tempted to stalk from the room but knew better than to leave his cunning wife to her own devices.

On the other hand, he was not about to skulk away with his tail between his legs, not on her account, by God! Nor was he going to give the girl the chance to run away and make him look the fool. Snatching up his bearskin coat, he made a bed for himself on the floor right in front of the door.

There he remained for what was left of the night, cold and supremely uncomfortable, and in an utterly villainous frame of mind because on the bed the muffled sobs continued unabated for hour after endless hour.

Chapter Five

Connor watched the serving girl who brought breakfast shiver as she set down the tray and crossed the room to stoke the fire.

"I'll do that," he snapped, rising from the chair in which he had been brooding since long before daylight. "Get out."

The girl looked at his face and fled. Massaging his aching muscles, he went to the grate and violently stirred the embers. Once the logs were blazing he sat down at the table and poured himself tea.

"Come and eat before it gets cold," he commanded, but there was no response from the bed.

He scowled. All night long he had lain awake listening to Gemma tossing and turning. Only after he'd given up on sleep himself and sat down in that cursed chair had she quieted at last. Doubtless she had finally dropped off to sleep from sheer exhaustion.

Let her sleep, he thought. At least it would spare him her tearful recriminations until she did get up!

The thought made his scowl deepen. He was immeasurably annoyed with himself for being unable to forget the tears she had shed last night, knowing full well that he had been the sole cause of them. God above, what had come over him anyway? He had taken his wife like some lusting animal! She was by no means the first virgin he had ever deflowered, and he knew perfectly well that a man had to be endlessly gentle and patient with young girls. Instead he had forgotten himself and turned on her like a rutting boar, hurting her cruelly and probably shattering any illusions she might have had that lovemaking could be pleasurable for the woman as well as the man.

Well, damn it, who could blame him? He'd gone for weeks without a woman, and Gemma Baird was certainly enough of a woman despite her inexperience to make any man lose his head! Why, even now his body stirred at the thought of what had happened between them last night. Aye, he wanted her again, but it didn't seem likely that he'd be having the pleasure anytime soon.

Throughout breakfast he brooded, waiting for Gemma to stir, but no movement came from the bed. After a while he began to suspect that she was awake but deliberately pretending to sleep in order to avoid him. The realization made him feel more like a cad than ever. He was sure that she was starving and that she urgently needed to use the chamberpot, not to mention that she was probably desperate to clean herself up after he'd left her bruised and bleeding the night before.

A low growl erupted from his throat. Pushing back his chair in one savage motion, he rose. "I'm leaving," he snarled, shrugging into his coat. "I'll not disturb you till it's time to go."

When the door slammed Gemma cautiously pushed the blanket aside and got out of bed. Then she ran to the basin and bent over it, certain that she was going to throw up. All morning she had been fighting back the nausea and pain of what he had done to her and the horror of knowing that she had actually responded to, even enjoyed, his brutish attack.

She groaned and bent further over the bowl, but nothing came up. After a moment she tottered to the chamberpot, then washed the blood from her thighs. Oh, God, how she hated him! She had to run away from him now, *now,* before they stopped for the night at some other inn and the same horrible thing happened again!

Collapsing in a chair at the table, she ate everything Connor had left for her despite the fact that the food was cold and she had no stomach for it. She knew that she must keep up her strength in order to elude him. If only Uncle Archibald had given her some money, or at least the keys to the casket that held all of her jewels! But no, he had made a point of handing everything over to Connor, and now she wondered if perhaps he hadn't done so deliberately. Did both of them suspect that she would try to run away?

If so, there was little chance that she would be able to outsmart a man like Connor MacEowan when his suspicions were aroused. He was as clever as he was dastardly and disgusting; so clever in fact that he had probably been keeping a hawk's eye on her all along without her even being aware of it.

"I'll have to think of something else," she whispered.

''There has to be some way of catching him off guard.''

But how? Tears pricked her eyes but she wiped them fiercely away. She'd done enough crying the night before. Hysterics would do her no good at all, not when she must remain entirely calm and clear-eyed in order to think of a way out of this horrible mess.

I could kill him, she thought hopefully, then instantly rejected the idea. She didn't relish the thought of cold-blooded murder and, besides, she didn't have a weapon.

Nevertheless, the bloodthirsty bent of her thoughts brought the first hint of a smile. She was actually feeling better thanks to the food in her belly and the amusing diversion of her vengeful daydreams. She had never been one to dwell in the depths of despair, and even Connor's unkindness and her uncle's duplicity couldn't defeat her overly long.

Well, Uncle Archibald might have washed his hands of her and Connor might consider the matter settled now that she wore a wedding band, but both of them were sorely mistaken in dismissing her so casually. If Connor Mac-Eowan thought for a moment that she'd willingly turn over her fortune—and her body!—to him, he was in for a rude awakening. True, he was clever, manipulative, and certainly far stronger than she was. But she was clever, too, and tough and resilient and certainly up to the challenge of taking on a lowborn pauper whose wits had been dulled by greed!

There was a knock on the door and Gemma sprang up from the chair, ready to leap into the fray. But it was only the innkeeper's wife with a fresh pot of tea and the smiling message that her husband was awaiting her downstairs. The carriages had been loaded and he was ready to go.

"I'll be down shortly," Gemma promised, setting her chin at a very determined angle.

The silence between them in the carriage that morning was as cold as the outside air. Not once since they had taken their respective seats had Gemma so much as glanced his way or uttered a single word to him.

Connor had never been so coldly and thoroughly snubbed, and his pride was sorely pricked. But two could play at this game, he decided, and so he, too, sat brooding and silent on the bench opposite her. Nevertheless, the irritating fact soon became apparent to him that he could not ignore Gemma as easily as she could him. Much as he tried, he could not deny that her mere presence in the narrow confines of the coach made him want her again.

Surreptitiously he studied the soft curve of her mouth as she sat with her face turned away from him, her chin tipped at an imperious angle. He remembered how deeply he had drunk of those sweet lips the night before, and how it had felt to trail his mouth down the silky length of her throat. Although she had pulled her traveling cloak tightly about her, he could still see the swell of her breasts where the ends of the fabric didn't quite come together.

His gut tightened. By God! Small as she was, she was made for love, and he ached to possess her.

I'll have you any time I wish, Gemma Baird, he thought arrogantly.

And next time she'd not be so unwilling.

The sun was just beginning to slide below the western horizon when their coaches rumbled into the crowded industrial city of Leeds. Catching sight of the smoking factory stacks and sooty houses beyond the coach window, Gemma gave a silent prayer of thanks. Connor had permitted them only the briefest of stops for dinner and tea, and her aching limbs were screaming with fatigue. The moment the vehicle halted in the cobbled yard of the first coaching inn they came to she leaped for the door.

In a flash Connor was there before her. A brief struggle ensued as she refused to give up the chance to be the first outside. Finally he lifted her by the waist and dropped her roughly onto the seat behind him. While she scrambled upright, he stepped quickly to the ground.

"I'll not have you running away from me," he warned, turning to look up at her, his bulk effectively blocking the steps.

"I just want to use the privy!" she snapped, glaring at him from the doorway. "Stand aside!"

"Forget it! You're not going anywhere without me!" Connor reached up as he spoke and grabbed her wrists to prevent her from bolting.

"You let me go!" she shouted, trying to tug free of his iron fingers.

"Hello! Is anything the matter here?"

Gemma and Connor turned to see two men in dark blue uniforms hurrying toward them from the street corner. Her eyes gleamed and her heart began to beat in joyous anticipation. Constables! Now wouldn't it be heavenly to watch Connor MacEowan land on his arse in jail?

As the lawmen approached the carriage, their expressions grew wary. They eyed Connor's beggarly attire and his hold on her wrists.

"Is this fellow giving you trouble, ma'am?" one constable asked, while the other slowly withdrew a nightstick from his belt.

She was quick to seize the opportunity. "Yes, yes he is!" she cried. "He was waiting for me the moment I opened the door, and when I refused to give him money, he tried to drag me from the coach! Help me, please!"

Her desperate plea was answered by a loud crack of the nightstick as one of the constables struck Connor a savage blow on the wrist. Bellowing, Connor released her and spun around to grab the man by the neck. Instantly the other officer leapt between them, and all at once the three of them were locked together, their fists flailing, their breathing coming harshly, the nightsticks crashing.

Ooh! This was too much! Leaping into the street, Gemma danced around the skirmishing trio, keeping well out of reach. Every time Connor's backside came into range she dealt him a series of enthusiastic kicks.

She could have laughed aloud at such glorious pleasure. Unfortunately, with a superhuman roar Connor broke free of the larger of the constables. The moment his arms were loose he spun on the balls of his feet, and several dizzying seconds later both of her would-be rescuers found themselves thrown into the gutter.

With a squeak of terror Gemma scrambled back into the coach, but Connor caught her on the steps. Seizing her arms, he shook her savagely. "Tell them the truth!" he grated. "Tell them before I wring your bloody neck!"

She tossed her head. "And miss the chance of throwing you in prison?"

"Do you want to come out of this alive or not?" he

asked through tightly clenched teeth.

Fortunately, his tone served to prick at her sense of self-preservation. Her enjoyment of the scene quickly faded. "Oh, very well," she said. "If you insist."

Connor shook her, and she could have sworn she heard her teeth rattle. "Then tell them!"

"This—this gentleman is my husband," she confessed reluctantly to the pair of officers still lying in the gutter. "We had a disagreement about where to stop for the night. I'm sorry if we gave you the wrong impression."

"Are you sure, ma'am?" asked one of the constables as the other picked himself up, groaning and dazed.

Connor's fingers bit into her flesh. "Yes," she said, attempting to sound contrite, but failing miserably. "Yes, I'm sure."

The constables looked at each other and then at her. Connor, breathing heavily, did not loosen his hold. His eyes blazed into hers. "I believe they still need convincing, my dear."

"Oh, very well," she said, annoyed, impatient, and by now extremely hungry. "If you must know, we were married this morning, and we've been having the most awful time traveling. Can you believe this man would be so boorish as to expect his bride to stop for her wedding night in Leeds? I wanted something romantic, and what did I get? Factories and smokestacks! Just look at this place, will you? It isn't at all what I expected of a—"

She broke off because the constables were beginning to look decidedly annoyed. *Poor fellow*, their looks plainly said, *married to such a poison-tongued virago!*

Dusting off their ruffled attire, they tipped their hats

and apologized—to Connor, not her, she noticed with wry amusement. Then they stole away with every evidence of enormous relief.

Not until they had disappeared around the corner did Connor release her, thrusting her away so unexpectedly that she staggered backward against the carriage seat. "Try that again and I'll kill you," he ground out.

She wisely held back her laughter. Oh, but he was sizzling! What was the matter? Did his buttocks hurt? By God, she certainly hoped so!

Acting suitably chastened, she stepped down from the coach and followed him past the Baird coachmen, who had been watching the entire fracas with slack-jawed astonishment from their seats high above. Into the inn Connor and Gemma marched, got the key to their room from the innkeeper, and went up the creaking stairs to their room.

Connor locked her in without so much as a word, and uncaring for once that she had been made a prisoner, Gemma stood before the fire with her cloak wrapped about her, savoring her victory as she warmed herself. After all, there was plenty to gloat about. She had succeeded in goading Connor into losing his temper, vented a satisfying amount of her own anger on his hapless backside, and come a hair's-breadth away from seeing him tossed into prison. Not bad, she thought smugly, for a mere evening's work.

Hearing the key grate in the lock, she whirled, smoothing down her skirts and squaring her shoulders. She tried to appear unruffled as Connor came inside, followed by the innkeeper bringing their supper.

No one spoke as Connor motioned for the tray to be set on the table. After uncorking the wine, the innkeeper backed out of the room, bowing and looking relieved to get away.

The silence left in the man's wake remained unbroken while Connor shrugged out of his coat and tossed it over the back of a chair. Then he turned to her. She had already tipped her chin in anticipation of dueling with him. But instead of uttering a word, she gasped as she caught sight of the bloody gash over his right eye.

"You're hurt!"

Connor glared. "I'm aware of it, thank you. One of your . . . rescuers got in a lucky blow with his stick." Pulling up his chair, he sat down at the table and uncovered a platter containing a nicely browned hen.

"You should clean that up first," she told him.

"Why bother?"

She stared at him as if he'd lost his mind. "Because it'll get infected!"

When Connor made no move to comply, she made a disgusted sound and crossed to the nightstand to fetch the ewer and washbowl. Then she hunted in the pocket of her cape for a handkerchief.

"What the devil are you up to?" Connor asked suspiciously.

"What does it look like?" she countered.

"As though you actually give a damn about me," he jeered.

She threw him a look that clearly revealed the insanity of such a suggestion. Dipping her handkerchief into the water, she touched it to the cut on his brow. Connor grunted in pain.

"Hold still."

"You could be more gentle," he growled.

But she had no intention of being gentle even though

76

she couldn't help feeling a small pang of guilt knowing that she had been responsible for his injuries. Aye, there were others: bruises that were beginning to darken his cheekbone and temple, and a welt that was rising on the collarbone beneath his opened shirt. She suspected that before long he would be black and blue all over.

Serves him right! she told herself fiercely. This was just a fraction of the punishment he deserved for having married her against her will in order to get his hands on her money!

"Oww!" he roared.

She pushed him back in his chair. "Stay where you are!"

"Then stop torturing me!"

"It's only a small measure of what I'd really like to do to you!" she shot back.

They glared at each other, their angry faces nearly touching. But perhaps Gemma was beginning to feel some remorse after all for the stunts she had pulled, for she was far more gentle when she resumed rinsing his wound. So gentle, in fact, that her ministrations quickly became exquisite torture for Connor, who had never known kindness from her before.

He sat very still as her fingers brushed lightly against his skin. She was standing closer to him than she had ever stood before, except for those few times when he had kissed and bedded her, unwilling times when her body had been rigid with revulsion. But there was nothing rigid or disgusted in her stance now, and as she leaned closer, the lovely curve of her breasts all but filled his field of vision. He found he had to swallow hard and physically will himself to sit still.

"Stop squirming!" Gemma commanded.

"I'm not!"

"Yes, you are!"

She leaned even closer, making matters worse, for although they had traveled a long, hard distance that day she somehow still managed to smell clean and sweet. And all at once he ached to draw her down on his lap, to take her small face in his hands and kiss those stubborn lips until they yielded beneath his own. The thought made him groan. Instantly Gemma stepped away from him. "Sorry. But I'm done now. Lucky for you it won't need sewing."

She spoke briskly as she rinsed out her handkerchief and hung it from a mantel nail to dry. Dumping the bowl of bloody water out the window, she refilled it from the ewer and then dried off the table. She was glad for the chance to keep busy as it gave her time to marshal her thoughts and bury the momentary twinge of . . . of . . . tenderness she had felt while bathing Connor's wound.

God above, this is crazy! she told herself fiercely. She didn't feel sorry for him! She hated him!

Then why had her fingers grown gentle despite herself as she leaned over him, and her heart started tripping oddly at his nearness? Bah! More than likely her pulses had been hammering only because she'd wanted so badly to bash his arrogantly swollen head in!

Nevertheless, it had been her own taunting and scheming that had driven the constables to inflict those wounds on Connor in the first place. In retrospect it had been an underhanded thing to do, and no matter how hard she tried reminding herself that he deserved it, she simply couldn't feel smug any longer.

Her eyes sought him out as he sat unmoving at the table, his head bowed and his hands dangling between his knees. He was obviously in pain, and again she felt that odd cinching of her heart. Suddenly she was driven by an overwhelming urge to go to him and lay her hands on his shoulders and tell him she was sorry . . .

Connor turned his head and their eyes met across the darkening room. His expression was guarded and cold.

Instantly the spell was broken. Jerking up her chin, she deliberately turned her back on him.

"I'm going out," Connor snapped, scraping back the chair so savagely that it spun over on its side. The door slammed behind him before she could frame a reply. This time no key turned in the lock; only the sound of his fading footsteps came from the landing.

Somehow it didn't matter that he hadn't remembered to lock her in. She was suddenly too drained even to think about escaping. She was exhausted from the long day's travel and belatedly shaken by the unpleasant scene that had erupted outside in the innyard. Nothing else weighed heavily on her conscience at the moment, she told herself fiercely. Nothing!

Leaving her supper untouched, she crawled into bed fully clothed. Never mind that her heavy skirts tangled around her legs and that the lace at her collar and wrists scratched uncomfortably. She wasn't about to leave a bit of skin exposed to inadvertently tempt her barbaric, rutting husband when he returned!

But he did not, and as the night wore on, the traffic gradually quieted outside. The doors to neighboring rooms were closed to the accompanying murmur of tired voices. Though she tried hard to fight her own weariness, Gemma couldn't seem to keep her eyes open any longer. When she drifted off to sleep at last, she was still alone on the narrow iron bed.

Chapter Six

"Gemma."

She burrowed deeper amid the blankets.

"Gemma, wake up."

"Go away."

"Come on, lass! It's time to leave."

"I said go away."

A hand touched her shoulder, shaking her. Groaning, she lifted her head and saw Connor leaning over her. Pushing the hair from her eyes, she stared at him balefully.

"It's time to leave," he repeated curtly. "I let you sleep longer than I should have."

Slowly her foggy brain cleared. She saw that the cut on his brow had started to heal, but that the bruise on his cheekbone had darkened overnight, giving him the dangerous look of a taproom brawler. The image was heightened by the width of his shoulders, which blocked out the light as he leaned over her, a feral giant with a mane of black hair whose very nearness seemed to make her pulse hammer in her throat.

"Then go away so I can dress," she snapped.

"You are dressed," he taunted. "What's the matter? Too scared of being ravished to take your clothes off last night? Well, you needn't worry anymore. I'm not going to waste my time on unwilling little girls like you."

What did that mean? Had he found someone else? Where had he been all night anyway?

She felt an absurd stab of anger shoot through her. Absurd because she ought to be glad, not angry, that Connor was turning his objectionable attentions to someone else! Good God, if she didn't know any better she'd think she was jealous! The thought was so outrageous that she simply turned her face into the pillow without uttering another word.

Connor gave her another angry shake. "Gemma!" he bellowed, annoyed.

"I said go away!" Scrambling upright, she gave him a push, then recoiled as her palms made contact with his hard-muscled chest. Ye gods, he was a brute of a man! And only yesterday he had threatened twice to wring her neck!

I have to get away from him, she thought frantically as the door slammed none too gently on Connor's broad, retreating back. But how on earth was she going to manage that? She had no clue as to where they were headed; no idea how to flee his ever watchful gaze. To complicate matters further, she was not about to leave without Helios, and certainly not without her belongings, which her uncle had handsomely paid the Baird coach-

men to keep out of her grasp. Traveling alone and penniless down the backroads of England, Gemma
suspected, was probably no more pleasant than traveling
with the likes of Connor MacEowan.

Be patient, she cautioned herself, although it was the
last thing she wanted to do. Her best chance of making
good an escape was to wait until Connor brought her to
whichever hovel it was he called home and convince
him that he could trust her. Then she would slip away
before he knew what she was about—unless she succeeded in driving him utterly mad first, and he tossed
her out long before that!

No matter what, one thing remained certain: she was
not about to let him touch her again, especially not in
the way he had the other night.

A host of shameful images rose unbidden to her mind.
She could clearly picture Connor's big hands roving her
naked body, his mouth covering hers, his hair-roughened
legs tangled with hers as he forced his way inside her
body, touching her more intimately than she had ever
dreamed possible.

"Damn him to blazes!" she breathed. If he ever tried
to do that again she'd yank that damned thing right off
his body! See what good he'd be without his highly
prized manhood, the great, bloody besom.

And as for calling her a skinny, unwilling girl—

"Gemma!"

The shout was accompanied by heavy pounding on
the door that made the walls and floorboards shake. "It's
cold outside, woman! What the devil's taking you so
long?"

Picking up the washbowl, she dashed it with all her
might against the closed door. Water splashed and wood

splintered as the bowl clanged explosively to the floor.

In the utter silence that followed, the door creaked open a fraction and Connor's rugged face appeared. "Missed me," he smirked and closed it again.

Two days later they crossed into Scotland and Connor explained their route to her. They traveled by way of the Otterburn road, which led them past the ancient Roman ruins of Hadrian's wall and into the equally ancient Scottish border country. Connor pointed out that the ballad-rich land was where battles had raged for centuries between the English and the proud Scots, and Gemma admitted to herself that the ruins of countless castles and abbeys lent the rugged landscape an overwhelming beauty.

She had never traveled beyond Derbyshire in her life, and could not feign disinterest in the scenery no matter how much she wanted to. Fiery autumn had painted the hills scarlet where they rose in sharp folds to the immense blue of the sky. Many of them were covered with churning waterfalls and fast-running streams. Secretive valleys with wind-stunted trees were scored by shallow rivers so clear that she could see every colorful pebble in the riverbed. Late-blooming autumn flowers blazed along the roadside, and on the sheltered hillsides the heather had exploded in gorgeous hues of purple and pink.

The villages they encountered were few and very remote, but the passing of their two elegant coaches and her high-stepping colt in tow never failed to bring curious spectators out of the isolated huts that were scattered hither and yon throughout the numerous glens. According to Connor, most of the inhabitants were sharecroppers or shepherds accompanied by their wives and children, and Gemma noticed that all of them were poorly dressed, and not very clean. Despite the cold of the late-autumn afternoon, most of them had bare legs under their kilts and wore leather brogues with holes in them or no shoes at all.

What a scruffy lot, she thought. They're just like Connor—beggars, every last one of them!

She supposed she shouldn't be surprised. Scotland was Connor's land, after all, and every one of those peasants would no doubt prove the same filthy opportunists as Connor was if given half the chance.

"Any particular reason for that scowl?" he asked her unexpectedly. It was the first thing he'd said to her in over an hour.

"As a matter of fact, yes," she snapped, and went on to describe her opinions in detail, so that he would have no illusions as to how she really felt. She found that she enjoyed giving him the lash of her tongue, especially because it soon became obvious that Connor would have preferred removing it from her mouth than listening to another word.

"Furthermore, what about supper?" she added for good measure. "I confess I'm starved! I'd also like to breathe a little fresh air, if you don't mind. Is it really necessary to push so hard day after day? What's your hurry? Where are we going, anyway?"

Connor threw her a look that told her clearly how much he'd prefer putting her out of her misery—and his!—right now. But instead he said coldly, "I imagine you'd like to know that, wouldn't you?"

"To tell you the truth," she countered frigidly, "I've been trying not to think about it too much."

"We'll spend another night on the road," he said bluntly, "and then we'll abandon the coaches and send the luggage ahead on carts."

"What for?" she asked in sudden alarm.

"Because we're getting ready to cross the Coomb."

"The what?"

"The Coomb," he said smugly. "One of the mountains dividing the border country from the southern uplands. It's doubtful the vehicles will make it across at this time of year. There could well be snow in the upper passes."

She glared. "Then how will we get across?"

"On horseback."

On horseback? Like soldiers, itinerants, penniless journeymen? Her mouth thinned. "Never."

Connor's eyes narrowed. "My dear girl, I don't think you have a choice."

"Oh, yes I have."

"What will you do?" he taunted.

"Kill you. Run away. Both."

He grinned. "How can you kill me? You haven't got a weapon."

She clenched her hands into fists. "I'll think of something."

"Aye, I'm sure you will."

His indifference was infuriating. His total lack of regard for her feelings, her position, her own shattered hopes of happiness, was surprisingly wounding. Although she had successfully inured herself during the course of a lonely lifetime to other people's hurtful treatment and accepted the fact that she mattered to no one, she could still feel the unexpected tears clogging her throat. And that enraged her. She wasn't about to let

Connor MacEowan, of all people, make her cry! He was vermin, beneath notice, should be hung from the very next tree for the way he had manipulated her into marrying him!

"I hate you," she said, not caring how childish it sounded.

"I quite imagine you do," he answered softly.

Gemma remained silent as they traveled but gradually realized that Connor had been right. As the land grew increasingly inhospitable, so did the road. They climbed steadily all afternoon, jolting into ruts and rumbling over boulders, and as the glens fell away below them the landscape became extremely harsh and uninviting. Ahead of them lay the upland mountains, dark and craggy in the waning daylight, the tallest of them jutting above the timberline.

They're just like Connor, she thought, dark and brooding and ugly.

Unable to help herself, she shivered. Stop it! She mustn't let him frighten her now, no matter how much he resembled this empty, alien land. He was still nothing more than a contemptuous beggar, far below her in station and scruples, and a man who richly deserved all the revenge that she planned to heap upon him.

Her angry thoughts were interrupted when Connor leaned out of the window to shout directions up at the head coachman. She couldn't hear the coachman's answer, but the tone of the man's voice was decidedly surly.

The realization filled her with smug satisfaction. Apparently Uncle Archibald's servants didn't think much of Connor either. She only wished they would show her a bit of sympathy so that she could enlist their help in escaping! But that, of course, was impossible. Uncle Archibald had paid the greedy oafs far too well to expect any kindness from them!

Now, following Connor's orders, the coaches left the main road and turned down a side trail so uneven and poorly marked that Connor soon had to join the drivers outside to help navigate through the gathering darkness.

Alone in the cab with the daylight waning, she entertained tantalizing thoughts of escape, of throwing herself out of the door and rolling down a ravine before anyone noticed that she was gone. But of course that would never do. Not without money, and certainly not without Helios, whom she'd never be able to untie without being seen.

Besides, she thought, I can't simply slip away without giving that long-legged blackguard the comeuppance he so richly deserves!

It was pitch dark when the Baird coaches halted at last before a tiny inn of whitewashed stone that had been built on the edge of nowhere. Rather than bringing his wife to Edinburgh along the far more civilized Jedburgh-Galashiels road, Connor had chosen the more difficult— and largely deserted—northwesterly route into Moffat and up through the Pentland Hills. His plan was to stop each night in out-of-the-way inns like this one where there was absolutely no chance of his being recognized.

Since they were now less than two days away from Edinburgh, he wasn't about to risk running into anyone he knew, especially not in his current attire and in the company of his shrewish wife who wouldn't hesitate to claw his eyes out right in front of his acquaintances.

So he had brought Gemma to Kinkillie, this remote village of less than twelve souls nestled in a narrow glen on the western side of Loch Uido. The rocky coves and heavily forested shores of the loch had long been a haven for smugglers, thieves, and escaped convicts—anyone who had reason to avoid the main road and the constables patrolling the towns in between. Kinkillie was a place where anyone who needed shelter could find it, regardless of the circumstances. Kinkillie inhabitants had always known how to keep their mouths shut.

"You expect me to stay *here*?" Gemma asked when Connor leaped down from the box to open her door.

"Either in there or under the stars."

For a moment she was tempted to do just that, but the wind had picked up as the sun went down, and now it whistled through her cloak, making her shiver and long for the warmth of a fire.

The yawning windows in the inn were dark, and no one came out to help with the horses or the luggage. Nor did anyone answer Connor's knock, and he was forced to push hard on the low wooden door before it swung open and they could step inside.

Gemma gasped as a roiling cloud of black smoke overwhelmed her on the threshold. "What on earth are they burning?"

"Peat. There's no firewood out here. You'd better get used to it."

Her eyes stung and she wiped them with her handkerchief in order to see. Instantly she found herself wishing that she couldn't. That way she would never have noticed that the floor was made of packed earth so filthy that she doubted it had ever been swept. Nor would she have seen the grease-stained walls and blackened ceiling, or the rafters hanging so low that Connor had to duck his head in order to pass beneath them. Nor would she have been forced to lay eyes on the ugly little man with the open sores on his face who came out of the back room to meet them, leering at her openly while the grease from his interrupted supper coagulated in his beard.

"Aye, what'll it be?" the fellow growled.

"A room," Connor answered curtly, pushing a coin across the table.

"Bain't enough," the man rasped scornfully. Gemma noticed that most of his teeth were missing.

"I think it is."

Connor and the innkeeper looked at each other for a long, hostile moment. In the silence she could hear someone whispering excitedly in the back room, but she didn't dare turn her head to look. For the first time ever she was grateful for Connor's presence and she moved a little closer to him, just to be on the safe side.

Apparently the little innkeeper was also coming to the decision that this big, bearded traveler was not a man to be trifled with. Pocketing the coin, he indicated with a jerk of his head that they were to follow him inside.

Squinting in the smoky light, Gemma picked her way carefully across the uneven floor. Their room lay at the end of a dank, windowless corridor. The narrow door had neither a lock nor a latch. The hinges shrieked as the innkeeper pushed them open.

"Grub?" he growled, addressing Connor but continuing to leer at her. She shuddered and pushed her way quickly past him into the room.

"As soon as possible." Producing another coin, Con-

nor negotiated meals and sleeping arrangements for the
Baird coachmen while she untied the hood of her cloak
and turned to survey her surroundings.

What she saw made the breath catch in her throat and
her stomach roll with nausea. Dried rushes, the sort that
had last been used in medieval times, were strewn on
the bare dirt floor. Evidence of other travelers, other
meals, other neglected cleanings, were scattered among
them. The bed was nothing more than a straw mattress
pushed into the corner. The washbasin hadn't been emptied since the last guest had used it, and she didn't dare
look inside the chamberpot. Slowly, unsteadily, she went
over to the little stool propped beneath the window and
sank down.

Connor sent the innkeeper on his way and slid home
the iron bar that bolted the door. Lighting the lantern on
the rusty nail above him, he adjusted the wick and turned
to survey the room.

"I know it isn't much," he said at last, "but we'll
only be here one night. You can have the bed. I'll put
my coat on the floor and—" He broke off, seeing that
Gemma wasn't listening. She sat in the corner with her
head bowed and her hands in her lap, and he realized
with a queer sense of shock that her lower lip was trembling because she was trying not to cry.

"Oh, Damn—"

He spun away, running his fingers angrily through his
hair. He could tolerate Gemma's outbursts, her caustic
tongue, her surprisingly strong little fists; aye, he would
actually have welcomed them gladly at the moment in
place of this silent despair. He had no idea how to deal
with it, or with her, and he wasn't used to feeling so
helpless or out of control.

You're too much trouble for me, Gemma Baird!

Thank God they'd be in Edinburgh the day after tomorrow. He'd waste no time then in showing her off to Eachern, King, and Carter, before sending her posthaste back to Derbyshire. His lawyers could handle the marriage annulment while his banker sent a handsome draft to Archibald Baird to compensate him for his troubles. Glenarris would be safe and Connor's peace of mind restored.

Unfortunately, there was nothing he could do at the moment to dry Gemma's tiresome tears. All of the devices he had used on distraught females in the past—kisses, caresses, the presentation of some pretty bauble, or assurances of his undying love—would never work with Gemma. He rather suspected that she would try to kill him if he dared resort to any of those flip solutions.

Which was why he now did the only thing a self-respecting man could do. He turned tail and fled. More specifically, he all but ripped the door off its hinges in his haste to get outside.

He was seething. Damn the girl! Damn her to hell and back! What right did she have to do this to him? Why couldn't she have lost her temper instead of crying, or punched him silly and tried to kick him in the groin, the way she usually did? By God, *anything* would have been better than the wrenching sight of her sitting there defeated and close to tears!

Not that he cared. Not that he cared at all! He just hated troublesome females, and God above, Gemma Baird was the worst of 'em!

Gemma *MacEowan*, you great braw dolt! he reminded himself furiously. You married her, remember? She bears your name now, and your ring, and she promised to love and obey you until the day she dies!

Oh, God, it was all too much!

I'll crack their heads, he fumed, thinking of his three friends who had arranged this insufferable hoax in the first place. How dare they push him into marriage with the comeliest lass in Derbyshire when in fact she was little more than a witch, a virago, the last woman on earth he'd care to share a seat with on the public stage, let alone marry and drag all the way to Edinburgh!

And I didn't make her cry! I'm not the least bit responsible for her tears! It's Eachern and King and Carter who should pay for that—and they will! I'll wring their bloody necks with my bare hands next time I see them!

Marching to the front table, he demanded whiskey, the strongest the innkeeper had, and settled down in the corner to drown his troubles in the depths of the uncorked bottle.

Chapter Seven

Gemma was gone when Connor returned to their room a half hour later. His mood was even fouler than it had been earlier, what with all that inferior whiskey torturing his insides. Drawing up short in the doorway, he scanned the flickering shadows painted by the smoking lamp. The room was empty.

What the devil—? He whirled to peer down the corridor, more puzzled than angry. How in hell had the blasted girl gotten past him? He'd not turned his back on their door for even a moment while he'd been drinking, and the single window there in the corner was far too small for even a wee chit like Gemma to crawl through.

Cursing beneath his breath, he stepped inside for a closer look. He barely had enough time to throw himself aside when Gemma, hiding behind the door, swung at him with the heavy enamel chamberpot.

"Good God!" he roared, although he was laughing, delighted that she was once again in rare fighting form.

"Damn you, Connor MacEowan!" she yelled.

"Put that thing down before you hurt someone!" he yelled back, dancing around her flailing, panting form.

"I mean to kill you, not hurt you! Damn it, hold still!"

"Ha! Ha! Ha!"

Her eyes spewed emerald fire. "I wish you'd go to bloody hell!"

"You'd like to arrange that personally, wouldn't you?"

"You bet I would!"

"Then would you mind dispatching me with something a little less ignoble than a chamberpot?"

Instead of obliging, she hurled the chamberpot at him with all her might. Lucky for him it had been emptied earlier, but it still came within a hair's-breadth of smashing his skull.

"Missed me!" he taunted, though he had to move quite nimbly to dodge the chunks of plaster that exploded from the wall behind him upon impact. Oh, how he loved her when she behaved like this!

On the other hand, he didn't like being attacked with a chamberpot after asking politely for a different weapon, and he was going to make damned sure she knew it. He preferred handling her when she acted like this far better than when she sat slumped like a pathetic rag doll on a rickety stool ready to burst into tears.

Out shot his hands to encircle her birdlike wrists, squeezing just hard enough to subdue her without hurting her. Around she spun as he jerked her to him, landing hard against him, her thighs pressed against his, her breasts brushing his chest, her mutinous green eyes burning a hole through him.

"I ought to kill you," he said, his whiskey breath pelting her face.

Her chin tipped bravely. "Go ahead, do it! It would be better for both of us! They wouldn't charge you with murder—nobody cares if an angry husband slaughters his shrew of a wife!" Her voice faltered. "And—and nobody would care at all if I were dead."

Was it the whiskey sloshing around in his stomach that snuffed out his amusement? He told himself that it had to be. Nevertheless, he released her, so abruptly that she staggered a little before retreating and standing her ground. There followed a long silence while both of them struggled to control their breathing.

"I won't tolerate being ambushed again," he warned at last.

"And I won't tolerate spending the night in this—this pigsty!" Gemma countered.

Scowling, he looked around. In the corner near the window a rat was snuffling amid the filthy rushes. Frigid air streamed through the broken glass above. The single mattress was no doubt crawling with fleas. Gemma was right. No decent human being should be forced to spend the night here, no matter how dire his circumstances, or how deserving!

Without a word, he grabbed her arm and jerked her through the door. Startled, she came along without protest.

"Supper for my wife," he snapped at the innkeeper, plunking Gemma down at the pockmarked table in front of the fire. "I'll be right back," he growled in her ear. "You know better than to set foot outside, aye?"

95

Oh, aye, Gemma did. She already knew that deadly calm tone far too well. Connor would hunt her down ruthlessly if she dared slip away. Not that she'd get far in the frigid darkness with no idea of where to go! And Helios could easily break a leg among the rocks, which she wasn't about to risk.

On the other hand, she had no intention of setting foot back inside that hovel of a room! Would Connor relent if she asked him nicely enough to let her sleep in the coach? She doubted it. And her aching limbs rebelled at the thought of curling up on that cramped leather seat.

She sat and waited for her meal, her eyes stinging from the peat smoke, and her spirits sinking lower with every passing minute. Uncharacteristically, she began to wonder if maybe she shouldn't just give in. Maybe she *would* be better off dead. Maybe she ought to just go ahead and kill herself instead of trying to goad Connor into doing her the favor.

On the other hand, then he'd end up getting her fortune and being rid of her to boot. She wasn't about to let him win quite so handily. No. She'd stay around long enough to make him suffer before she left, and leave him poorer and far more miserable than he'd been before he laid eyes on her.

Hmm. The thought was certainly tempting. But—uggghhh! What on earth was that awful smell?

She looked up as the innkeeper emerged from the back room and sent an earthenware bowl clattering onto the table in front of her. Peering into it, she found herself confronted by some sort of pasty gray stew that made her hair stand on end. What on earth were those suspicious lumps swirling in the middle? Meat? Bread? Impossible to tell.

A chipped tankard was set down next, and being extremely thirsty, she lifted it and took a long draught. In the next moment she leaped to her feet, choking and sputtering and clawing at her throat.

Whiskey! Oh, and how it burned going down, making her eyes water worse than the peat smoke did.

Frantically she swallowed a spoonful of stew to dispel the terrible burning. She expected it to taste awful, and it did, a thousand times worse than anything she'd imagined. Gagging, she washed it down with more of the whiskey, then collapsed on the bench, fanning herself and stifling a nauseated moan.

By the time Connor reappeared, she had managed to quell her awful hunger pangs by fishing out the lumps of meat in the stew and rinsing them off in the tankard. Her mood was foul, her well-being questionable, for the whiskey had made her feel ridiculously lightheaded and the meat lay like a lump in her belly.

"What?" Gemma asked, looking up sullenly at Connor's outstretched hand.

"Time for bed."

"No."

"Don't be a fool. You're exhausted."

"I don't care."

"Well, I do."

She glanced at him quickly, but Connor didn't notice her surprise. Instead he said darkly, "I'll not have you getting ill on me and proving even more trouble than you already are."

"I hate you," she said, staring fuzzily into her lap.

"I know. You've told me so often enough. But you're still going to do as I say. And I say it's time for you to go to bed."

"Not in there I'm not."

"Why not?" Connor asked in a reasonable tone that made her want to poke sticks up his nostrils. "I've cleaned it up for you."

He had? Her head came up. She saw that Connor was still holding out his hand to her, waiting, and grinning. What the devil was so amusing?

In the end her curiosity won out, and she hesitantly placed her hand into Connor's big palm. A wave of dizziness overwhelmed her as he pulled her up. Oh, dear. The whiskey had certainly gone to her head. She wavered badly as she followed him down the dark corridor, but for once Connor didn't utter an unkind word.

"Oh!" she breathed as he led her through the wide standing door and into their room. He really *had* been telling the truth! Her disbelieving eyes took in all the changes he had wrought. A tea towel was tacked neatly over the window to keep out the cold, and the floor was swept bare of its disgusting rushes and covered with a length of clean linen that had been stored among the bolts of cloth she had brought with her from home. Connor had taken other items from her household trunks as well: blankets for the bed, a comfortable footstool, Aunt Druscilla's china washbowl and pitcher, and a length of pretty yellow muslin—intended for undergarments once Gemma found a seamstress in Scotland—which Connor had used to cover the bare wall next to the bed so that she wouldn't have to sleep with her nose nearly touching the dirty, peeling plaster.

The simple touches had brought about an incredible change, and she couldn't believe that Connor was responsible. How could a man who had lived all his life in abject poverty know enough about comfort and style to have created such homey touches?

She turned to look at him wonderingly.

"Go to bed," Connor said gruffly. "It's late."

"But where will you sleep?"

"Out in the hall."

"On the floor?" Her eyes widened.

"Aye. Make sure you slide the bolt behind you."

What for? she wondered. To protect herself from him, or from the riffraff in the front room?

But for once she didn't care. By now she was bleary-eyed with exhaustion and thoroughly numbed by the whiskey. Slowly, she looked again at the cozy room, then up at the man responsible for it. This was the first act of kindness he had ever shown her, and it had to be the whiskey befuddling her senses, because she suddenly found herself overwhelmed by the need to thank him.

"Connor—"

He froze in the doorway and turned to look at her with one eyebrow raised. "Aye?"

She fidgeted, her foot rubbing the back of her calf beneath her skirts. "Will—will you be all right out there on the floor?"

Muttering, he slammed the door.

She was by now quite used to Connor slamming doors in her face. And she knew quite well how she ought to react. Only this time she had no desire to smash Aunt Druscilla's lovely pitcher against the wall. Not when it was filled with cold, clean water and she desperately needed to wash away the grime of the day's journey.

"I hope you pick up lice down there on the floor," she told the closed door anyway, but her words lacked their usual vehemence. Yawning hugely, she prepared

99

for bed and then quietly snuffed out the lantern overhead.

The sound of hoofbeats striking stone awoke Gemma
not long after dawn the following morning. Groggily she
pushed back the tea towel and peered through the tiny
window. It was Connor mounted on one of the Baird
carriage horses, riding bareback and on a loose rein into
the stableyard with a brimming basket slung over the
crupper. Cold sunlight shone on his black hair and highlighted his haggard features.

He had obviously spent a sleepless night, and that
didn't delight her. Not that she felt sorry for him. Connor
deserved everything he got, and more. On the other
hand, she didn't like seeing him look so tired and gaunt
and . . . and old just because she'd made him sleep outside on the floor.

"No, I did not!" she told herself vehemently. "It was
his idea, and he could just as easily have slept in here
if he'd wan—"

Oh, now didn't *that* thought bring her up cold! As if
she honestly would have welcomed Connor into her narrow bed without punching him silly or smashing him on
the head with her shoe. As if she felt the least bit sorry
for him; as if she would dare acknowledge even under
the most dire circumstances that Connor was her legally
wedded husband and had every right to share her bed if
he chose.

I'd sooner kill myself—and him! she thought furiously. And he wasn't being a gentleman or gallant in
refusing to assert his marital rights. She suspected that
Connor was merely starting to realize that perhaps his

young bride wasn't worth all the trouble she was causing him.

That thought filled her with a good deal of satisfaction and restored a lot of her shaky self-esteem. The good Lord knew it had been crushed low enough by her uncle when he had callously given her away in marriage to a lout like Connor MacEowan merely to keep his own name free of scandal.

Maybe there was a way out of this yet, she thought triumphantly. Rubbing her hands together, she left the room in search of her poor, unsuspecting husband.

In the front room she found him unpacking the basket with the help of a slatternly woman who wore a stained tartan plaid and had the frowziest red hair Gemma had ever seen. Connor had brought a loaf of bread and fresh eggs from somewhere down the glen, as well as a ham and a big wedge of cheese. From the tone of his voice as he warned the woman to cook everything carefully and not pocket anything for herself, Gemma gathered that his mood was foul. Wisely, she thought better about provoking him, and instead went out into the chilly air to see about Helios.

The colt had spent the night in a shed behind the inn, a crumbling stone building without a roof or running water. But he seemed content enough to stand quietly munching the oats that Connor had brought back from the village.

Slipping into the stall beside him, she lovingly stroked his golden neck. He was in need of a good grooming, she noticed, but otherwise seemed fit enough.

His ears flicked in response as she spoke to him softly, and once or twice he paused in his eating to nuzzle her. The gesture warmed her heart, as it always did. Here, at least, was someone who had always loved her, who needed her and whom she could love in return.

If not for the golden colt's companionship, her life would have been empty indeed. Aunt Druscilla had despised her, Uncle Archibald had despaired of her, and the Baird servants had thought her an unholy little terror. But not Helios. Helios had never cared if she was rude or late or disheveled, that she talked back and had a temper, that she was an orphan living entirely on the largess of her long-suffering relations who, as they had so often reminded her, had never wanted her in the first place.

Helios had always accepted her, had never minded when she shed her unhappy tears into his glossy neck or whispered her secret yearnings to him in the darkness whenever she crept out of her bed to sleep beside him in the straw. In those days she had been terribly afraid of the dark, but Helios had never made a fuss about it the way Aunt Druscilla always did.

"I'm not afraid of the dark anymore," she told Helios now, leaning her cheek against his silky side.

But that was because there were so many other things to be scared of. Like her uncertain future with Connor MacEowan, and her growing concern for Helios, for she worried constantly that he was too young and delicate for this harsh, unyielding land. She had seen the squat, hardy little pit ponies that the border Scots rode and knew that her finely bred colt would have trouble thriving here. And where would she shelter him when winter came? She doubted that Connor had a stall, let alone a house in which to live.

"Don't worry," she whispered, standing on tiptoe to caress the colt's ears, which she knew he loved. "I'll get you out of here. I promise.''

''Gemma.''

She whirled. How long had Connor been standing there? How much had he heard? ''Y-yes?'' she squeaked.

''Come get your breakfast. Your uncle's men have already started and there won't be much left.''

So! Feeding the servants first and leaving her to scrounge for leftovers, was he? Tossing her head, she marched past him as though he didn't exist. Not once did she look back, not even when he started laughing.

Half an hour later they left Kinkillie behind them. Gemma had never been so happy to bid a place farewell. On the other hand, she kept having the nasty feeling that maybe Connor's house was going to be just as horrible as that pigsty of an inn. What was it he'd said last night when the peat smoke had overwhelmed her?

Better get used to it.

No, she wouldn't! Well, maybe just long enough to drive the disgusting clod who'd married her into an early grave!

''Glad to see you've still got some starch in your backbone.''

She lifted her head to find Connor watching her from the opposite seat. Did he always do that? she wondered. Stare at her with those heavy-lidded eyes that seemed to notice her every thought and feeling?

Be careful around him, she cautioned herself. He was craftier than he looked, and as dangerous as a wildcat. And just as smelly too. Despite herself, her nose wrinkled.

Connor uttered an uncaring laugh. ''I'll take a bath as soon as we stop for the night, I promise. Sleeping on dirt floors doesn't do a body good.''

But she wasn't at all appeased to hear this. It reminded her of that first bath Connor had taken in the shepherd's hut in Derbyshire. She remembered how appalled she had been when he had shed his clothes so casually in front of her and afterward had had the gall to laugh about it. And the second time she'd seen him naked . . .

Oooh, no! She wasn't going to think about that either, or about what his naked male body had done to hers afterward! Big, ugly lummox! She'd douse him in a horse trough before she let him take off a stitch of clothing in front of her again!

''I think—'' she began stiffly, but never had the chance to tell him what it was she thought as a shout came from the coachman sitting outside on the boot.

Instantly Connor was on his feet, moving with surprising speed for a man his size. ''What is it?'' he demanded through the window.

''Someone ahead!'' the coachman called back.

Her heart leaped. Quickly she peered from the opposite window. Disappointment washed over her when she saw a lone rider coming down the narrow trail toward them. The chance of rescue seemed unlikely considering that it would take at least half a dozen of those skinny, kilted fellows to overpower a man like Connor.

''Pull up!'' Connor commanded. ''Gemma, you wait here,'' he added, pointing his forefinger at her nose. Springing to the ground, he hailed the approaching rider with a shout and a wave.

Watching from the window, she was astonished to see the rider smile in relief and draw rein at Connor's side. What on earth was going on? Had this meeting been planned? Her breath caught as she saw the man take off his cap to Connor and touch his forelock in an unmistakable gesture of respect.

"Stop that!" she wanted to rail at him. "He's naught but a lowly beggar. You'd do just as well to spit at him as treat him like a lord."

But of course she said no such thing. She merely sat gawking as the kilted fellow reached into his vest and withdrew a folded parchment that he extended politely to Connor. Her nerves jangled with curiosity as she watched Connor break the seal and read it. Until that moment she hadn't even realized that he knew how to read. More importantly, who was that letter for? Certainly not for him! How could anyone know he was here, and what on earth would anyone wish to tell him?

After a moment, Connor rolled up the parchment and returned it to the kilted rider. She strained to overhear the brief conversation that followed, but the wind was gusting noisily and they were too far away for her to understand a single word. Disappointed, she watched the man pocket the letter before wheeling his mount and riding away. So much for trying to steal it from Connor!

Connor stomped back to the waiting carriage, his mouth set in a hard line above his bristling beard. There was no mistaking his anger, and Gemma's curiosity grew. What in blazes had that letter said?

Signaling the coachman forward, Connor swung inside and settled himself on the seat next to her. With a crack of the whip the coach lurched forward, the violence of the motion throwing her hard against him.

"Sit over there!" Connor barked.

She slid, meekly for once, into the opposite seat.

"You're more trouble than you're worth, do you

know that?'' he added before deliberately turning his back on her.

The admission should have brought a rush of elation to her hate-filled heart. But it didn't. Instead it made her hunch against the window, her face turned away from him, furtively wiping her eyes whenever the angry tears welled up, and hoping desperately that he wouldn't notice. She couldn't even begin to explain why she was crying. She could only suppose that Connor MacEowan was slowly and surely driving her mad. She had to get away from him. But how? *How?*

I've got to get away from her, Connor thought savagely. Not because she was sniffling there in the corner like a child whose fingers had been slapped. As a matter of fact, it had nothing at all to do with her. It was simply because of the message he'd just received, and the bad food and the lack of sleep he'd endured since leaving Edinburgh so many weeks ago. He'd had more than enough of playing the beggarman, thank you.

Unfortunately, a speedy return to his old familiar and extremely comfortable way of life had, thanks to that bloody letter, been delayed. He knew that he owed the girl on the seat opposite him the decency of an apology for snapping at her, but his disappointment was simply too keen. He was dead tired of eating offal unfit for dogs and drinking rotgut spirits like the whiskey that had left him tossing and turning on the floor of the Kinkillie inn last night. He was tired of wearing these stinking clothes and sporting this itching, annoying beard. He was tired of traveling in this claustrophobic coach and tired of watching Gemma cry.

Two more days were all he'd thought to have left of

this tiresome journey. How dare King Spencer and Carter Sloane go off and leave Edinburgh when they knew damned well he might show up at any time? Grouse hunting, no less—and without him! Bloody berks! They'd pay for this when he caught up with 'em!

And, aye, Gemma was as much to blame as anyone else, so let her go ahead and cry till her eyes were red. It was the least she deserved—which is why he settled into his own corner and turned his face away from her, so that for all intents and purposes he might have been alone.

Chapter Eight

"Gemma, wake up."

Instantly Gemma's eyes snapped open and she straightened quickly. "Oh! Did I fall asleep?"

"Aye."

"Where are we?"

"Alnadrochit."

"Why," Gemma asked irritably, sitting up and brushing the hair from her eyes, "do Scottish towns have to have such ridiculous names? Oh—!" she added in the next breath, gazing in dismay past Connor's broad shoulder.

Connor ordered the coaches to halt on a windswept moor near the crossroads of the tiny village. To the right lay several forlorn stone houses and a tiny whitewashed church, empty and deserted in the bleak afternoon light. To the left loomed the mountains, their summits cast adrift in swirling mist.

Good Lord, Connor thought, seeing the fear on Gemma's face, if she finds these mountains unnerving wait till we get to the Highlands!

But the thought of the Highlands merely served to reawaken his anger. Despite what he'd been telling her all along, he had never had any intention of taking her to the Highlands, not at the onset of winter, and certainly not when it meant enduring more lengthy travel while playing this disgusting role of a beggar. Edinburgh was closer, less than two days away from Alnadrochit, and he wanted nothing more than to be back in his comfortable townhouse on Edinburgh's fashionable Archdale Street sitting at a gaming table with decent liquor at his elbow and a comely wench in his lap.

He had sent a missive from Derbyshire on the morning of his marriage, in which he had requested sturdy horses for himself and his bride and given the approximate date that they would be arriving in Kinkillie. Rather than finding himself conveniently obliged with transportation, Connor had been presented instead with King's letter, telling him of his friends' hunting trip and that Connor shouldn't expect them home until All Saints Day—provided Connor himself returned to Edinburgh before then, which King had cheekily remarked he very much doubted.

Connor had been furious, but his anger had faded during the course of the long afternoon while Gemma slept fitfully on the carriage seat opposite him. He supposed he shouldn't really blame his friends for deserting Edinburgh until November. After all, who would have dreamed that he would be returning from England so soon?

Nevertheless, he now had to take Gemma to Glenarris

rather than Edinburgh. It would be far better to hide his wild little bride in that remote Highland glen than await his friends' return in a crowded city like Edinburgh, where everybody knew him and his servants would announce his marriage to the world.

Though I certainly could have used those horses, Connor thought now. Alnadrochit was as far as the Baird coaches could go, for not a half mile beyond the village the road ended and the steep mountain trail leading north began. The going would be rough, as he well knew, for he had hunted and camped along those same ridges often since boyhood. He had to admit that he had never imagined he would one day be doing the same with a tart-tongued wife for company, or that she would be dragging half her household behind her!

His patience with Gemma had worn decidedly thin by the time he paused in the doorway of the carriage to glare at her. ''We're turning north from Alnadrochit into those mountains,'' he informed her coldly. ''Time for the coaches to go back to your uncle's and for you to change into something suitable for riding.''

A wail of protest rose in her throat although Gemma knew better than to utter it. So the bloody blackguard really expected her to ride, did he? Well, ride she would, and without a whimper of complaint! She'd show that dirt-poor Highland squatter that there was more backbone to England's landed gentry than he realized!

While Connor took two of the Baird coachmen down to the village, Gemma rummaged through her trunks in search of something ''suitable.'' What in bloody hell did that mean? Suitable for endless days on some rocky, nonexistent trail, or perhaps for falling to one's death off a crumbling mountainside? Or maybe suitable for being mauled by starving wolves, because she had always heard that Scotland was full of them. What did wolves like to eat, anyway? Brushed velvet or a jacquard weave?

By the time Connor and the coachmen returned with two enormous draft horses and a shaggy pony pulling a cart, she had managed to wrestle out of her woolen traveling gown in the cramped confines of the coach. The riding habit she had donned was of sweeping black velvet, fashionably cut, the trim jacket piped with satin and brass buttons, the full skirt reaching all the way down to her booted ankles.

As she descended to the ground she saw Connor's brows twitch together. Instantly her chin snapped up and she regarded him balefully.

He strode toward her. "For God's sake, girl, we aren't riding to hounds! We're heading into the mountains! That getup will never do!"

"This 'getup' is all I have," she shot back frigidly. "If you find it inappropriate for your hair-raising journey then perhaps you should permit me to return to Derbyshire with the coaches."

Behind her the coachmen exchanged looks of alarm at the prospect. Gemma didn't see them, but Connor did. All at once an odd feeling of protectiveness welled up inside him for this proud little creature whom no one seemed to want, not her uncle, not her servants, least of all himself. Poor wee Gemma, the unsuspecting pawn in such an unkind game! What would happen to her when he finally sent her packing?

But that was something he didn't want to think about. That was something which served to stir his rarely acknowledged conscience, something which must never be permitted. So once again he reacted as he always did whenever Gemma touched him in a way he didn't want to be: with angry mockery.

"Very well," he sneered, crossing his arms over his chest. "If playing the fashionable huntress is what you wish to do, then by all means suit yourself. But don't come weeping to me when your wee buttocks get bruised and sore!" His gaze nailed the coachmen gathered around the other coach. "And as for you—"

Instantly their smiles were wiped from their faces and all of them snapped to respectful attention.

"I want my wife's belongings loaded onto the cart!" he ordered. "Step to it, if you please! Mr. Grieg?"

"Sir?" the head coachman answered.

"Your pistols, please." Connor held out his hand. "Both of them. And the powder."

Gemma, watching the servants scurrying to obey, couldn't help feeling uneasy. For the first time, the magnitude of her uncle's abandonment swept over her in its entirety. When the coaches left, she and Connor would be alone. She would be completely dependent upon him, a man she despised, and thrust with him into a terrain so harsh and dangerous that he saw the need to arm himself against it.

Her eyes suddenly fell on Helios, still tethered to the back of the second coach. In the harsh daylight he looked more delicate than ever. Another wave of alarm washed over her, but it was for the colt this time. She had the sinking feeling that it wasn't going to be as easy as she'd envisioned to sneak away with Helios once Connor let his guard down. Not in this empty, hostile land.

So at the moment there was nothing she could do save

allow Coachman Grieg to boost her onto the back of one of the horses. Thank God she had insisted on bringing her sidesaddle from home, because there was no way her legs would have fit around the big animal's belly while riding astride. She wondered if the drafter had ever been used for anything but plowing, for he seemed extremely reluctant to be ridden. She had to kick him hard before he would take so much as a single, grudging step.

Wheeling him, sawing on the reins because he was so damned heavy-mouthed, she watched as Connor oversaw the loading of the pony cart. The Baird servants were working fast, obviously eager to be away. Tears welled in her eyes when they rumbled off at last, for they represented her last link with England and the only home she had ever known.

Perhaps, she thought, the head coachman was also gripped with a sudden sense of disquiet, for he turned around to look at her a number of times before the vehicles disappeared from view behind a dip in the road.

But no one came back for her as Gemma wished, and after a moment it became obvious that they were gone for good and the silence of the mountains closed in around them. Behind her, Connor mounted the second horse with disgusting agility. Fuming, she noticed that he didn't seem to have the least bit of trouble handling the ill-tempered beast. He rode like a gentleman, with a proper seat and light hands, and this also helped to fan her bottomless resentment toward him. What was it about this man that made it so difficult to understand him?

"Who's going to handle the cart?" she demanded, gesturing to the heavy load of trunks and boxes, and to Helios tethered at the rear.

Connor didn't even bother looking at her. "I've hired a lad from the village. He'll be here as soon as he packs together a few . . . Ah, as a matter of fact, here he comes."

From one of the tiny houses at the bottom of the hill emerged a hulking fellow with a leather satchel slung over his broad back. He was dressed in simple homespun and wore a battered tam o'shanter scrunched over his red curls. He grinned cheerfully as he approached, seeming delighted with the prospect of embarking on an adventure.

"I gae t' coppers tae me mum, sir," he called out, speaking in a thick Lowland dialect that Gemma could barely understand. "We're sair grateful, sir."

"I suppose you paid him with my money," she whispered heatedly to Connor.

"But of course," he replied with an arrogance that made her want to smack him. "Dirk, this is Mrs. MacEowan. You're to look after her colt and her belongings as agreed."

Dirk's head bobbed enthusiastically. "Och, aye, sir." Blushing furiously, he tipped his cap at her. " 'Tis a pleasure, ma'am."

"Very well, Dirk," Connor added. "We'll see you in Bathgate. Come along, Gemma."

But she held back, incredulous. "MacEowan!" she whispered frantically to his retreating back.

With a loud sigh, Connor wheeled his horse and returned to her side. His knee brushed her skirts as he leaned down from the saddle to peer into her eyes while the grinning Dirk looked on. "What is it this time, lass?"

"Y-you're not going to simply leave him here with

my horse and all my things, are you?''

"Why not? We'll cover the distance twice as fast if we don't wait on him.''

"But—but—he's a simpleton!'' she hissed beneath her breath. "How do you know he won't run off with my trunks? How do you know he won't be waylaid traveling alone? And how can you trust him to see that Helios—''

Wordlessly Connor reached down and laid a finger across her lips. The intimate gesture surprised her so much that she fell silent. "Because I know the lad,'' he told her easily.

"Know him?''

"Aye. He's an old friend.''

"I don't understand, MacEowan. How can you possibly know him? You said we're still miles from your home.''

"It's a small country, lass.''

Scowling, she turned to look at the sturdy Scotsman. He was still standing next to the cart where they had left him, grinning up at them with mild brown eyes. She forced herself to smile back, although her scowl returned as she whipped back to confront Connor.

"All right, so perhaps you do know him. Even so, I don't like leaving him with Helios. Look at him! He doesn't seem at all capable of—''

"Gemma,'' Connor interrupted, and now his hard fingers were holding her wrist in a tight grip. "Never judge a man by his appearance, do you hear me? Never.''

There was an urgency in his tone that she had never heard before. Her gaze faltered beneath the intensity of his. Looking down, her eyes fell onto his long, dark fingers as they rested against the whiteness of her skin.

She swallowed hard, wishing he would let her go, wishing he wasn't bending quite so near.

Then another thought came to her. If Connor claimed to know this fellow, then obviously the fellow knew Connor, too. If she could only ask him a few questions about this awful man who'd married her, maybe learn where they were headed so that she could plan her escape. . . .

"Gemma, let's go," Connor repeated.

"But—"

"No buts. We're leaving."

Leaning down, Connor jerked her horse's reins. She had no choice but to allow herself to be led away.

Chapter Nine

For the first hour or more Gemma could think of nothing save Helios. She turned constantly in the saddle to look back at him, even long after the trail wound sharply uphill and the slow-moving cart was lost from sight. But after a while other worries began to claim her attention, chief among them being the rolling gait of the huge animal she rode, a gait that made her back and rump quite sore, just as Connor had predicted. But she would be damned if she let him catch wind of it!

Furthermore, she didn't like the way the trail kept leading ever higher into the mountains. She had always heard that the southern half of Scotland was beautiful; that it was the north, the Highlands, that were so utterly desolate and cold. But the good Lord knew these Lowland passes were bad enough!

She lifted her gaze to Connor's broad back as he rode ahead of her, his black hair spilling down to his shoulders. Unmindful of the chilly wind, he had removed his coat, and she could see the muscles bunching beneath his shirt with every swaying step of his mount.

I'd like to see a knife between those shoulder blades, she thought mutinously.

Connor must have sensed the smoldering intensity of her stare, because he turned to look at her. She saw the white flash of his grin against his bearded face and the lusty vitality glowing in his dark blue eyes before he saluted her and turned away.

Why, he's enjoying himself! she thought furiously, more determined than ever to kill him in a thoroughly bloodthirsty manner.

The daylight was nearly gone when Connor halted at last in a sheltered clearing. He did so without warning, and she quickly drew her mount alongside.

"What is it?" she demanded, half expecting to find a landslide blocking their path, or a hungry wolfpack gathered on the trail ahead.

"Nothing," he said. "We're stopping for the night."

"Here?"

"Where else?" he asked, tossing her a grin. "There's shelter from the wind, running water, and plenty of moss to make a good bed."

"You mean we're going to sleep on the ground? In the open?"

"Aye. What else did you—"

Gemma had had enough. This time he had finally gone too far! She waited only long enough for Connor to dismount before spurring her horse forward, nearly running him down in her haste to get by.

"Gemma!" Connor bellowed.

Cursing, he vaulted into the saddle and cantered off

in pursuit. Gemma refused to slow down, and he was forced to draw alongside her, a harrowing stunt on the narrow trail, before he could reach down and drag wildly on the reins.

Once they were halted, the horses stood side by side struggling to catch their breaths, while he and Gemma did the same. He could tell that she was furious. Even through the fast-settling darkness he could see the tight clench of her jaw and the green fire spewing from her eyes. Leaning from his saddle he caught her wrist and wordlessly rode back to the clearing without releasing it, the horses bumping each other.

Her head snapped up the moment they halted. "I won't stay here!"

He was no longer in the mood for jokes. "Aye, you will."

"You can't make me!"

"Can't I?"

"I hate you!"

"Aye, I know."

Without warning, Gemma lashed out at him, using her free hand as he still held the other one. Her balled fist caught him square in the eye. He bellowed like a wounded bull, which panicked Gemma's skittish horse. Snorting wildly, it reared and plunged down the trail, and since he still had a tight hold of her wrist, she was dragged loose from the saddle. Down she crashed onto the rocky trail while her horse took off at a bucking run, and Connor had all he could do to keep his own mount from bolting after it and trampling her.

Subduing his horse at last, he leaped to the ground and dragged her upright by the collar of her habit. "Now see what you've done!" he thundered.

"Me?" she shouted rebelliously, her feet swinging a full inch off the ground.

"You bloody pigheaded piece of baggage!" He shook her. "Now we'll have a devil of a time catching him, if he doesn't break his leg first. Come on, up with you. And I'll have no more trouble out of you, understand?"

He shook Gemma once more for good measure, then tossed her onto the saddle. He vaulted up behind her and his arms encircled her waist, one of them trapping her against him. He took up the reins and urged the horse forward at a dead run in the gathering darkness.

Gemma sat rigid with shock. She couldn't believe the way she'd been manhandled! Worse, she hadn't been forced this close to Connor since that awful night following their wedding, and, oh, she'd forgotten just how horribly big and objectionable he was! Sitting there with her rump nestled between his outspread thighs, she could feel every ridged muscle through the thin fabric of his breeches. Against her back she could feel the thrumming of his heart, while his strong arms were clamped far too intimately around her hips.

He was urging his horse along at a canter, an unsafe speed because the animal stumbled often on the uneven trail, throwing her backward so that her head constantly bumped against his big shoulder. Despicable! He smelled of leather and sweat and horses, a manly smell that she found far too overwhelming for her liking. Worse was the way her buttocks kept riding up toward his inner thighs, because she knew perfectly well what horrible *thing* lay directly between them. More than anything she dreaded coming into contact with it.

"Sit still!" Connor roared as she tried in vain to wiggle away.

She refused to obey. Uttering an oath, he clamped his arm around her and wedged her tightly against his chest.

"If you don't sit still," he warned in her ear, "you'll throw the horse off stride and break both our necks!"

She quieted, if only because she had no choice. Connor had her pinned like an ornament to his wide chest. And since she didn't relish the thought of dying, she forced herself to relax even further. Her stiffened spine went limp, which made her head fall back into the warm curve of his shoulder.

Oh, dear Lord! Never in a million years would she have guessed that a chest as hard and unyielding as Connor's could prove so comfortable to lay one's weary head against! She must have been far more tired than she'd thought, because all at once a strange lassitude seemed to seep into her limbs, replacing her earlier fury and fear. She fought to keep her eyelids from drooping, but it was a losing battle.

Connor felt the weight of her head growing heavier against him. With a gentle shifting of one arm he was able to nestle her down into the curve beneath his collarbone. Gemma murmured something that sounded like an insult, but then her cheek fell against him and she was still.

Poor wee bairn, he thought, overcome by an unexpected feeling of tenderness. He knew that he had been pushing her much too hard for the last few days and that she had endured more physical deprivation than even some men could tolerate. Small wonder she had reached the point of utter exhaustion.

Let her sleep, he thought, slowing his mount to a walk. At least that would spare him her caustic tongue for a while. But he couldn't oblige her by stopping just yet. Not when her horse was still out in the darkness somewhere. He would have to push on, even if it meant playing pillow to this slip of a girl, whose delectable rump kept pressing against his thighs, playing havoc with his self-control.

"You're a curse, Gemma MacEowan," he muttered aloud, but for once the statement lacked its usual vehemence. He soothed himself with the reminder that in just a few days' time Gemma would be a Baird again and he would be rid of her for good. That ought to make her happy.

And him too, by God!

Wouldn't it?

Gemma awoke feeling warm and surprisingly well rested. Morning had come, for she could feel the brightness of the sun on her face even before she opened her eyes. Sitting up, she pushed the hair from her brow and was surprised to find herself wrapped in thick fur. Alarmed, she threw it aside, then realized that she had been sleeping underneath Connor's bearskin coat. How in the world—?

"Awake at last, I see."

She turned quickly and saw Connor squatting in front of a crackling fire. He had fashioned a hook from a stout stick and was using it to hold a pot of water over the flames. The water was boiling, and as she watched he took a handful of loose tea and tossed it inside. The water sizzled, and she watched the flames lick along the bottom of the pot, blackening the silver and . . . Wait a minute! Silver?

"Hey!" She scrambled upright and stormed over to

him, sputtering with indignation. "Th—that's my silver bowl you're using!"

It was, in fact, a trophy Gemma had won while riding Helios's mother at a county fair many years ago, before Helios had even been born. She had always treasured that trophy highly because she had worked so hard to win it. She had schooled the difficult mare herself and had ridden secretly at a neighbor's farm whenever her aunt and uncle weren't home because they disapproved of such things and had strictly forbidden her to attend any horse shows.

She had been found out, of course, and punished for her transgressions, but the trophy had remained hidden in her trunk for years to avoid confiscation. And there it hung over the fire, the bottom blackened with soot while her loathsome husband brewed tea in it!

"Where did you get that?" she raged.

Connor didn't seem at all perturbed by her anger. "I took some things from your trunks before we left Al-nadrochit, things I knew we'd need along the way."

She glared at him. He seemed ridiculously mellow lounging there in the grass with his wrists dangling over his updrawn knees. He looked well rested and disgustingly fit, a rough man who seemed perfectly content to be back again in this very rough land.

But it was beautiful land, she had to admit, turning away from him with a snort of disgust and taking stock of her surroundings. They must have left the mountains last night, for they were camped now on the edge of a long, lifting moor that looked like a sea of darkly tufted grass. Heather bloomed on the treeless hillsides, and in the distance a lake glimmered silver in the early morning sun. It was a desolate scene, yet breathtaking in its grandeur.

"Where are we?" she asked almost reverently, the trophy forgotten.

"Local folk call it the Great Moor. Travel east for half a day"—he pointed with a long finger—"and you'll reach Edinburgh. West, Glasgow and the North Channel. The Grampians lie ahead."

She could not tear herself away from the view. "The what?"

"The Grampians. The mountains that divide the Scottish Lowlands from the Highlands. We should reach the foothills tomorrow night, if we're lucky."

"Connor—" she seated herself across the fire from him, folding the long skirts of her habit out of the way.

He looked at her sharply.

"Where are you taking me?"

Connor didn't answer her. Instead he took the tea from the fire and rummaged through the leather satchel beside him. From a clean linen napkin he unfolded two small loaves of bread and offered one to her. They shared the tea, drinking from the bowl itself although the metal was so hot that she had to be careful not to burn her lips.

"Glenarris," Connor said at last, leaning back in the grass and crossing his arms beneath his head.

Over the tea bowl her eyes met his. "Glenarris? What is it?"

"Home of the MacEowan clan."

"You mean there are more of you?" she asked, upset.

Laughter rumbled in his chest. "Not too many, you'll be glad to hear."

"But you have parents," she said, not wanting to

sound as if she were prying although she was desperately anxious to know. She knew nothing about this man who had married her for her money, and it was important to learn all that she could. Knowledge was strength, and she needed whatever strength she could muster to escape him. "And brothers and sisters, I suppose?"

"No. No parents either. Both are dead. And I'm an only child because they decided to stop having children after I came along."

"I can't imagine why," she muttered caustically.

A lazy grin crossed his bearded face. "I do have a younger cousin named Eachern. You'll meet him when we get there."

And hate him the way I do you, she thought fiercely. And where was "there"? "There" had a name now: Glenarris. But what in the world was it? A town? A valley? A moor as desolate as this one? She didn't have the courage to ask, nor did she really need to. She could well imagine what sort of place it would turn out to be.

They were silent after that, busy with their thoughts and with the task of eating their surprisingly pleasant breakfast.

"This is good," she remarked, waving aloft what was left of her oat-sprinkled cake.

"They're called bannocks. Dirk's mother sent them along."

"Bannocks. I've never had them before."

"They're Scottish, of course. Regional fare, like the tripe stew we had in Kinkillie."

Connor grinned at her grimace. "I daresay the bannocks taste a good deal better, hmm?"

"That awful stuff! What did you call it?"

"Tripe stew."

"Ugh! Do you mind telling me what tripe is?"

"Why, boiled sheep stomachs."

She stopped chewing and her eyes widened. "Sh—sheep stomachs?"

Connor, chewing with gusto, nodded.

She felt her stomach begin to churn. She could still remember the revolting taste and awful gray color of the stuff. Thank God she hadn't eaten much of it! But just knowing she'd had so much as a mouthful made her clutch her belly and moan.

"Gemma?"

She raised her eyes and saw Connor regarding her with undisguised amusement. Oh, how she hated it when he laughed at her! "What?" she demanded, her jaw clenched, her head thrust forward, daring him to say another word.

Wisely he held up his hands as though acknowledging surrender. "Here, you can have the rest of this, if you like."

She flapped her hand at the bannock he was holding out to her. "No thanks. I've lost my appetite."

"It could've been worse," he teased.

She arched an eyebrow at him. "I find that hard to believe."

"Do you? Next time you might try rumbledy thumps, or haggis, which—"

"Never mind, MacEowan. I can't begin to imagine what they are, and I don't want to know! It's a queer language you Scots speak, I'll grant you that."

For the first time Connor saw that Gemma was laughing as she passed judgment on his country. Apparently the meal and the good night's sleep had served to mellow her. Leaning back on his elbows, he watched as she

126

drank the rest of the tea and then carefully cleaned the soot from the bottom of her trophy bowl. He doubted that her slim white hands had ever performed such menial labor. In a way it was a shame that they'd been forced into it at all.

He continued to watch her as she rinsed her hands in the icy stream that murmured below their campsite, enjoying the slim lines of her body and the disheveled loveliness of her hair, which the rising sun had torched like molten gold. Such a tiny thing she was, but with the courage and the vocal cords of a man three times her size. She'd made him angry, miserable, repentant and wild with passion in turn during their madcap rush through the Borders, but he wasn't sure now if he'd trade a single moment of it for some well-deserved peace of mind. Life was certainly going to be dull once Gemma was gone.

For some inexplicable reason, that thought annoyed him. Frowning, he came to his feet. "If we push hard today we'll make Bathgate by nightfall," he said harshly. "You'll have an honest bed to sleep in then."

"An honest bed?" Gemma jeered. "And whose money is going to pay for it, eh?"

Angered, he spun away to fetch the horses. Bringing her horse, he extended his hand to help her mount, but she ignored it, hauling herself onto the broad, shaggy back. Lots of grunting, cursing, and indiscreet flashing of her petticoats and her trimly booted ankles accompanied the task, which served at least to soften Connor's anger.

His lips twitching, he doused the fire and packed their belongings, then swung up into his own saddle. Across the short distance separating them, his eyes met Gemma's. She deliberately looked away.

"Point that chin of yours any higher and you're liable to dislocate your neck," he warned her.

Her shoulders stiffened, but her chin didn't come down. Chuckling, he set his horse trotting off down the hillside, and Gemma's mount quickly followed.

They had ridden hard all day, covering miles of moorland and gorse-covered hills, pausing only to rest and water their horses beside peat-colored brooks that Connor called burns. Feeling curiously lightheaded all day, Gemma had attributed it to exhaustion. But the stomach cramps she had felt a little before high noon and which now had returned as the sun set had nothing to do with her being fatigued. As another cramp seized her, she gasped and dropped the reins. She straightened quickly the moment the spasm was over, and dabbing the sweat from her upper lip, she squared her shoulders and hurried to catch up with Connor.

But another cramp soon followed, one that was far worse. She doubled over and clutched at her belly until it passed. More of them followed as the minutes dragged by, accompanied now by acute nausea and heart-thumping chills. She could no longer control her mount, but fortunately the ill-bred creature had no desire to do anything but follow the lead horse. As her horse plodded along, she felt dizzy and slowly slid from her saddle.

Connor heard something hit the ground and his head whipped around.

He was beside Gemma in an instant, lifting her against him, his heart clubbing in his chest. Her face was a ghastly color in the fading daylight and beads of sweat dotted her brow.

"Gemma!"

She opened her eyes. "What is it?" she asked anxiously. Then she closed her eyes and turned her face into his chest, shuddering and moaning.

"Gemma, what's wrong?"

"L-leave me alone," she breathed. "I think I'm going to be s-sick."

And Gemma was, miserably so. He stroked her brow and tried to soothe her with gentle words as she retched and shuddered and retched again. Afterward he held water to her lips and bathed her face. Seeing that she could not stand, he carried her off the road and laid her in the soft grass beneath a spreading larch tree.

"How long?" he demanded fiercely.

"I—I don't know. Hours."

"Good God, lass, why didn't you tell me?"

Closing her eyes, she turned her head away and moaned again. "Leave me alone."

"Gemma—"

"Go away, please!" Her voice was feeble, pitiful, but he obeyed, taking the opportunity to go back for the horses and the bearskin coat. When he returned, Gemma was barely conscious and flushed with fever.

Taking a clean shirt from his saddle pack, he ripped it into strips, cursing his clumsiness as his big hands fumbled with the cloth. Wetting the strips in the nearby stream, he laid them one at a time across Gemma's brow, alternating them as the heat from her body warmed them.

As he did so, he mentally assessed the situation. Gemma was far too ill to spend the night out here on the moor. But how to remove her to Bathgate, which lay at least another hour's hard ride to the north? It was one thing to cradle a sleeping girl in his arms while he rode, the way he had last night. It was another to attempt transporting a thrashing, feverish Gemma.

For the first time he cursed himself for leaving Dirk and the pony cart behind. What he wouldn't give now to lay her inside it! And to be only an hour away from Edinburgh, where he knew of a number of medical specialists, while it was highly unlikely that Bathgate would have so much as a single doctor.

Gemma moved fretfully. Instantly he bent close. "Aye, lass?"

"Thirsty," she whispered.

He held her while she drank, but she wasn't able to keep the tiny sip down. This time he had to change her soiled clothes, and as he stripped off her jacket she began to shiver in the damp air.

"Goddamn it!" Breathing heavily, he laid her back as gently as he could and wrapped her up in his coat. Still she shivered and moaned.

"Easy, lass, easy," he whispered.

Driven by a sense of helplessness he'd never known before, he lifted his head and looked desperately around. Now that the daylight had faded and the heavens were filling with the first dusting of stars, a light winked far off across the moors. Squinting, he watched, but it never moved, indicating that there had to be a croft or a farmhouse near.

Leaning down he put a hand on her brow. So hot. Frighteningly hot. "Gemma?"

"Hmm?" Her eyes were closed and her breathing shallow.

"There's a house up the road a ways. I'm going to fetch a cart. You'll be safe here until I get back."

"You won't be coming back." She spoke so faintly that he had to put his ear to her lips to hear her.

"What's that, lass?"

"I said you won't be coming back. 'Tis just an excuse to . . . to leave me by the roadside." She spoke in a halting whisper. "G-good for you. You'll be . . . be rid of me now."

Her words twisted his heart in agony, and a moment later he was riding hell for leather toward the distant light.

Every nerve in his body protested the wisdom of abandoning her, although he knew that he must. She was weakened from exhaustion thanks to having been pushed so hard, and far thinner than he remembered. He had never realized until he had eased off her little jacket just how frail she had become. How could she possibly muster the strength to fight this violent sickness? God alone knew if she'd even be alive when he returned!

The thought was enough to send him galloping desperately onward.

Chapter Ten

There was a faint but steady roaring in Gemma's ears, dragging her unwillingly from the black depths of slumber. She thought there might be a river nearby, and wondered how that was possible. Had Connor made camp last night after she'd fallen asleep? She couldn't for the life of her remember stopping, or even dismounting. What an uncomfortable life, sleeping beneath the stars. It left one feeling so desperately tired.

Slowly, feebly, she opened her eyes. When her blurred vision cleared, she was mildly surprised to find herself looking not at the stars but at a freshly painted ceiling. On the wall opposite her head was a window. The curtains had been left open, and she saw that it was raining. Rivers of water seemed to gush down the panes and a steady downpour drummed on the roof.

Where was she? Not a cave or a hovel, surely, but a pleasant, whitewashed room with a table and chairs and a vase of late autumn flowers on the mantel. Her bed had real springs, too, and a coverlet of soft eiderdown. Bewildered, she fingered the silky material, but even this small movement exhausted her. Drained, she closed her eyes, and the darkness washed over her again.

She felt much better the next time she awoke. The rain had stopped, but the sky beyond the windowpanes remained overcast and bleak. She could make out a glimpse of a steeply pitched rooftop, but that was all. Where in heaven's name was she?

A door in the far wall opened and a kindly-looking woman tiptoed in. The tray she carried was covered with a muslin cloth, but from underneath it emanated the most delicious smells. Gemma slowly pushed herself upright, her nose twitching, and was rewarded with a happy smile.

"There! I kenned ye'd be wakin' when the hunger came on. Ye've na eaten for days, dearie. 'Tis high time."

"How long?" she croaked, her voice raw from disuse.

"Och, near a week! Coom, sit a wee bit higher, and I'll set the tray on yer lap. There. 'Twill do nicely, won't it?"

"Where—where is this place?"

The woman smiled again. She was small and neat and endlessly reassuring. "Stirling, dear. His Lordship brought ye in't cart, and the doctor's been lookin' in on ye daily. Won't 'e be pleased yer oop at last!"

Stirling? Where was Stirling? And who was "His Lordship?"

"Why, I mean yer husband, dearie," came the smiling response to Gemma's bewildered look. "Gone north tae Inverness, he has, but I daresay he'll be back the

133

noo. Here, try the oat cakes. And the tea. 'Tis nourishment ye're needin' after bein' sae ill.''

She went out, closing the door behind her without giving Gemma the chance to utter another word. For a moment she sat there with the tray unheeded on her lap, her head whirling, before she suddenly remembered.

That's right, she'd been ill! Somewhere near Bathgate she'd gotten sick, had agonizing stomach cramps, and thrown up repeatedly while Connor . . . But she couldn't remember anything he had said or done, save a jumbled impression of kindness and concern. She must have been delirious by then. He had never been kind to her, nor concerned, and why in bloody hell did that sweet little woman insist on calling him His Lordship? Strange folk, these Scots!

The simple task of thinking belligerent thoughts about Connor exhausted her. Pushing him from her mind, she forced herself to eat, although her throat hurt and she was simply too tired to lift the food to her mouth. But after a few feeble mouthfuls, she began to realize the full extent of her hunger, and then it was easier for her to eat.

By the time the woman returned for the tray, Gemma had managed a few bites of porridge, two bannocks, and half the small pot of tea. She felt infinitely better. So much so that she was able to smile at her hostess and thank her, though the words were promptly waved away.

"No need, dearie. We were all of us fair worried, and glad I am to see ye're better." She moved quietly to the window and drew the curtains together. "Sleep now."

"But—"

"Whist! 'Tis rest yer needin'. We'll talk later."

Which suited Gemma after all, for her eyelids were

already growing heavy. She was asleep before the door closed on the kindly woman.

When next she awoke it was early evening. Loud voices drifted up to her from the darkened street, but the house itself was quiet. She lay still for some time staring up at the whitewashed ceiling illuminated by the glow from the outside lanterns. When the familiar creaking of the room door came she turned quickly.

"Ach! Awake again, I see," exclaimed her kindly nurse. "Wonderful! Here, lassie, I brought supper, and thought ye'd like tae bathe thereafter."

"Oh, yes," Gemma said, brightening. "I'd like that very much."

While she ate, two strapping maids carried in a big brass tub. In no time at all they had filled it with steaming water from belowstairs and helped Gemma strip off her nightgown after she'd eaten her fill. Unaccustomed to the intimacy of having other females in her life, she felt deeply embarrassed to stand naked before them. But they were kindly, boisterous creatures whose laughter and good-natured teasing soon made her relax.

"Here, yer naught but skin and bones," the larger girl exclaimed, soaping Gemma's back. "Mrs. Kennerly said ye'd been ill, and well she meant it!"

"I'll wash yer hair for 'ee," the second one offered.

"Oh, no, that's all right," Gemma assured her quickly. "I can manage." As she spoke she put her hands to her head, then gasped and went rigid. An awful dread rose within her. "M-my hair! What's happened to my hair?"

The girls exchanged puzzled looks.

"Fetch me a mirror!" Gemma implored.

She nearly burst into tears when she looked into the

tiny glass and saw the pale, shorn creature reflected there. Gone was the wealth of golden curls that had always adorned her head and in its place was a . . . a mop! An uneven, bristling scrub brush of hair that made her look like a boy of ten!

"They cut it off," explained one of the girls as tears began to roll down Gemma's cheeks and plop into the bathwater.

"W-who did?"

"The doctor or Mrs. Kennerly, I'm thinkin'. Tae bring doon the fever. 'Is Lordship were fearin' 'twould nevair break."

His Lordship! His Lordship! Gemma wanted to scream at the pair that he wasn't a lord any more than they were ladies-in-waiting to the Queen of England. Furthermore it was Connor's fault, his fault alone, that her hair had been cut off and she looked worse than a Billingsgate guttersnipe!

In stoic silence she allowed herself to be lathered and shampooed. Taking her silence for interest, the girls discussed her welfare as they worked, recalling how Gemma's husband had brought her to Mrs. Kennerly's rooming house in the back of a cart, having traveled throughout the night and into the day from the tiny village of Bathgate to reach the town of Stirling, where a reliable doctor could be found.

Gemma had barely withstood the journey, and apparently neither the doctor nor Mrs. Kennerly had expected her to last through that first night. And so, after conferring with "His Lordship" they had cut off her hair and rubbed her body down with alcohol every hour in order to break the fever that consumed her.

"Who did?" Gemma asked, roused from her lethargy long enough to inquire after those responsible for such shocking impropriety.

"Why, Mrs. Kennerly, ma'am," the larger girl responded matter-of-factly. "And 'Is Lordship afore he rode off tae Inverness last night."

Heat flushed her cheeks. Oh, so Connor had tended her too, had he? The thought that he had dared touch her naked body while she was unconscious enraged her. Never mind that the doctor and Mrs. Kennerly had done the same. It was Connor she resented, Connor whom she blamed for everything.

"I'm tired," she said suddenly. "May I lie down again, please?"

The girls were instantly solicitous, fetching a fresh nightgown and drawing it over her head after they'd rubbed her dry with towels warmed in front of the fire. A vigorous toweling left her newly washed hair curling riotously around her face.

Exhausted, she crawled into bed and pulled the eiderdown to her chin. She pretended to sleep while the girls emptied the tub and carried it downstairs, although inwardly she could think of nothing save how best to kill Connor when she saw him again.

Ten minutes later she was startled from her drowsy musings by the sound of Connor's deep voice on the landing below, answered by Mrs. Kennerly's softer one. Then his familiar footsteps came pounding up the stairs, followed by an unexpectedly gentle knock on the door.

"Gemma? Are you awake?"

Oh, aye, she was awake! And ready to claw his eyes out the moment his dark, hairy face came round that door!

"Come in," she said sweetly.

But all thoughts of revenge fled like the wind the moment Connor stepped across the threshold and turned to face her. Her mouth fell open. This wasn't Connor! Not this tall, clean-shaven giant in form-fitting breeches and a white lawn shirt. A buckskin jacket was thrown casually across his shoulders, and the collar of his shirt was opened carelessly at the throat. His cheeks were reddened and his dark hair windblown as though he'd ridden in haste through the cold autumn night.

But what shocked her more than anything else was that he had shaved off his beard. She didn't recognize him; she would never have dreamed that his jaw was so lean and his chin so deeply clefted and that beneath all that hair he was as handsome as the devil himself! She was shaken, rendered speechless, and could even understand a little why Mrs. Kennerly and her maids had mistaken him for some highborn lord.

But just as quickly cold reason reasserted itself. It didn't matter that this darkly handsome, aristocratic-looking fellow was as different as night from day from the hairy, unwashed savage she had married. He was still Connor MacEowan. He proved as much when their eyes clashed, and then his gaze focused on her bristling haircut, and he threw back his head and burst into laughter.

She waited, tight-lipped, until his laughter had faded into chuckles and finally into amused silence. Then, as his bold eyes met hers again, she drew herself upright. "Are you quite finished?"

"Aye, lad . . . er . . . lassie."

But she would tolerate no teasing, especially from him. After all, it was his fault that she had fallen ill. He was the one who had dragged her to this godforsaken, unhealthy backwater of a country in the first place.

And how dare he shave off his beard and dress in decent clothes so that he no longer looked like the barbarian she still hated with all her being but at least had come to know and feel a tiny bit comfortable with! How on earth was she supposed to deal with him now? She'd never get used to that lean, shaven face. Never! Unnervingly handsome, unnervingly aristocratic, it was certainly not the face of the Connor MacEowan she knew.

On the other hand, Gemma had never in her life been daunted by good-looking men. Heaven knows, enough of them had danced attendance upon her, most of them begging for her hand, while others, less ambitious but no less eager, had tried to steal a kiss or a peek under her skirts. She had known quite well how to deal with them all, and while she'd not known how to handle the doltish beast she'd married, she did know how to foil the likes of someone as devilishly handsome as this windblown young god before her.

"Laugh at me again and I'll cut out your heart and eat it for breakfast," she told him in a voice that could have frozen water.

"I see you've recovered your temper as well as the use of your tongue. Obviously that means you're going to live," he said, strolling toward the bed.

"More's the pity for you, eh? Had I died, my fortune would still be yours, but you'd be free of me."

"A pity," Connor agreed.

They looked at one another, their eyes clashing.

Deep down, she couldn't help feeling a tiny bit relieved to see him. After all, good or bad, Connor was all she had to cling to in this strange, savage land. But she'd sooner die than admit as much, especially to him.

In the doorway Mrs. Kennerly appeared with another muslin-draped supper tray. "I've brought enou' for the two o' ye," she announced, beaming at Connor. "Yer wife'll be wantin' tae dine with 'ee, I'm sure."

"I very much doubt it," Connor said harshly. And without another glance at her, he stalked out.

Gemma kept her eyes downcast while Mrs. Kennerly began fussing with the tray.

"Dinna judge him badly, dear," the older woman soothed. "I dinna think he's slept a wink since bringing ye here, and then that hard ride tae Inverness and back. Tsk, tsk. 'Tis exhausted he'll be."

"What was he doing in Inverness?" Gemma demanded, hardening her heart against any twinge of pity she might feel toward Connor for his supposed sacrifices on her behalf.

"I dinna ken, dear. He didna say. Ye'll have to ask him."

But that was the last thing she wished to do. Still, she thought about it while she ate her supper, wondering what sort of business a penniless pauper like Connor could possibly have in the prosperous town of Inverness. Was that where this Glenarris place was located? And was that where he'd done the unthinkable: shaved off his beard, trimmed his hair, and found those simple but well-tailored clothes?

Whoever had said that clothing makes the man had certainly been talking about Connor MacEowan. She still couldn't get over the change in him. Why, he had looked downright . . . respectable in those buff breeches and that fine lawn shirt. Not exactly like a wealthy young lordling, whose class these days was wont to opt for dark serge suits with fashionable tails, silk top hats, and incredibly expensive tie pins and walking sticks, like her Uncle Archibald. But after spending all this time in Connor's company with him looking like a beggar and worse, even this small change was startling.

I'll never get used to it, she thought, bemused.

I'll never get used to it, Connor thought, striding angrily down the stairs, picturing Gemma's scrub-brushed hair and the way it had made her look like an owl-eyed lad of ten. He'd never realized before how much he'd enjoyed watching the sunlight glint off her silky tresses, especially those few, intimate times when she'd unpinned the golden mass and let it fall down her shoulders and back. Seductive, a woman's unbound hair, and he had always had a weakness for the honeyed hue of Gemma's.

I'll be accused of cradle robbing the minute anyone lays eyes on her now, he thought ruefully.

If things worked out the way he expected, that might well be soon. He had ridden hard to Inverness, where his cousin Eachern shared a sprawling townhouse with his spinster sister Janet just across the River Ness from the old market square. Before showing up at the house, he had purchased a set of secondhand clothes and spent a few hours at an inn little frequented by the gentry bathing and cutting off his beard and shaggy hair.

He'd found Janet home alone, and she had made no effort to hide her curiosity as to why he was in Inverness when Eachern and his other cronies weren't. His less than grand attire had also aroused considerable interest, but because Janet had always been somewhat intimidated by him, she hadn't dared ask questions.

No, she had informed Connor obligingly enough,

Eachern wasn't in. He was somewhere out beyond Ben Tor with Carter Sloane and Reginald Spencer. They had taken their guns and their servants and were supposedly off after grouse. Surely he knew that, she had added.

Ignoring her remark, he had demanded to know when they were expected to return. Janet had answered tomorrow or the day after. He then had penned a quick note explaining in vague terms (for Janet's benefit, who'd doubtless read it the moment he left) that the bet was won and that he was awaiting their immediate arrival in Stirling as his companion was ill and couldn't possibly be removed to Inverness. He had stressed once again that he expected them to join him posthaste and trusted they'd not disappoint him.

Now Connor sat in the taproom of Maida Kennerly's pleasant little rooming house drinking a tolerably good barley ale and trying to keep his thoughts from Gemma. Mercifully, the task wasn't difficult, for the public room was crowded with interesting locals to watch, and the comely wench who served them was making no attempt to conceal her interest in him. He knew by the gleam in her eye whenever their glances locked that he'd need only crook his finger to have her in his bed.

Odd how a little grooming went a long way in tempting a lass who'd probably have turned up her nose at him yesterday, he thought wryly. Though he certainly couldn't say the same for Gemma.

He sighed deeply and put his head in his hands. Wee, stubborn Gemma. Would she ever stop tormenting him? Whether she was with him or not, she somehow managed to annoy him, taunt him, get under his skin in a way he didn't like or understand. Worse was the way she kept tugging at his conscience now that she'd been reduced by illness to the pale little gamin he'd found upstairs in bed.

I should never have come back here, he thought angrily. I should have waited in Inverness for Eachern and the others to return, and sent them on to Stirling by themselves to take a look at her.

In the meantime he could have ridden on to Edinburgh and started making arrangements for Gemma's return to Derbyshire. There had been no real reason for him to come back here, none at all. Then why in God's name had he?

Maybe it's because I didn't get enough of her harping and cursing before I left, he thought, but his attempt at humor fell miserably flat. Draining the last of the ale, he rose to his feet and tossed a coin onto the table. Ignoring the disappointment that shone clearly in the serving girl's eyes, he strode swiftly into the darkness.

Chapter Eleven

"Connnnorrr," a woman's singsong voice whispered in the darkness.

"Hmmm," he murmured in his sleep.

"Connnorrr! Where are yoooouuu?"

He stirred, but the thick fog of whiskey-induced sleep refused to release him. Squinting, he tried to lift his spinning head. "Gemma?"

The floorboards creaked. In the utter blackness a shape materialized beside his bed. The covers fell from his body, eased back by an unseen hand. The cold night air caressed his naked skin.

"Hmmm," he said again, but not sleepily this time, because now the unseen hand was trailing lightly across his chest and down his tapered belly. "Gemma," he whispered softly as the hand went lower, sensuously lower . . . until suddenly he felt himself being grabbed by the testicles and squeezed, squeezed hard!

With a roar he shot to his feet, wondering if he was in the grip of a nightmare. All around him the room was deathly silent. The inn itself was silent. Nothing stirred on the street below. All was so still that he began to think that he had been dreaming. But then a woman's soft giggle came out of the darkness and his heart began to knock against his ribs.

"Gemma?"

"Aye?"

His heart thudded harder. What in God's name was she doing here? Why had she gotten out of bed and come to him when the rest of the household lay fast asleep? He didn't dare begin to believe—

"Connor?" Her voice sounded strange, but that was probably because she'd been so ill.

"Aye?" he whispered back.

"Darling, where are you?"

"I'm over—" he began, then stopped. Something was wrong. Gemma had never called him "darling" before. Fat-head, barbarian, bloody sot was more like it.

Without warning his arm shot out, his fingers curling around the woman's neck as he made contact with her body. Desperate choking sounds erupted as he began to squeeze. Hands clawed at him, trying to tear his fingers away, and with a start he realized that they were not the small, shapely hands of a woman.

"Judas!" he burst out, releasing his prey.

Whirling, he quickly struck a light. The flame sputtered and then brightened to a glow, illuminating his tiny room—and the figure half crouched in the shadows, still coughing and clutching its throat. Then it straightened, but instead of looking frightened or sorry it began to laugh.

"Connor, darling," Carter breathed in the same girlish voice he had used earlier. "Are you always so rough on the lassies who try sneaking into your bed?"

Connor collapsed on the mattress, burying his face in his hands. Desperately he fought to quell his murderous rage. What a fool! What an ass!

Disappointment and despair lashed at him, but after a long moment, when he looked up again, he, too, had decided it was best to laugh. "You deserved that, Carter," he said as jovially as he could. "God's blood, I've never had a lass treat me so rudely."

"Oh, come, Con. I'm sure plenty of women out there have tried more than once to pull your balls off."

Both of them laughed again, but this time Connor's eyes studied Carter intently, and his friend pulled the collar of his coat up over the red marks Connor had left around his throat.

"We came the moment we got back to Inverness and Janet handed us your missive."

Connor glanced toward the door. "We?"

"Aye. Eachern and King are here, too. They're waiting out in the hall."

"For God's sake, bring them in before they're seen!"

A moment later the three disheveled, laughing men were crowded into his small room. He said nothing as he watched them, his arms crossed over his naked chest, while they expended their glee over the the success of Carter's joke.

"Where's the chit?" King inquired at last, peering eagerly at Connor's bed, then frowning. He looked Connor up and down. "And what about you, dear boy? You don't look much like a barbarian. What's happened to your disguise?"

"What were you expecting, King?" Eachern mocked.

"A beard, tattered rags? Unwashed hair?"

"Why, of course."

Connor's mouth twitched. If only they had seen him two days ago!

"All right, then, Con, give over," King demanded. "Where's the chit?"

"My *wife*," he said distinctly, "has been extremely ill. She's resting in a room of her own on the floor above us."

"Are ye really married?" Eachern inquired, pop-eyed.

The look Connor shot him was answer enough. The three of them exchanged glances, and Connor was pleased to see them looking so disappointed. They obviously couldn't stand the thought that he'd completed his task so handily. If only they had an inkling of the hell they'd put him through!

"If it's all the same to you," he added smoothly, "I'd like to leave for Edinburgh first thing in the morning. Since this . . . joke was your idea, King, I'll leave you to mop up the mess."

"Oh?"

"Aye. Arrange to have the girl taken back to Archibald Baird's when she's well enough. She's got a fine colt out in the stable and a mountain of belongings locked away in the cellar that Dirk of Alnadrochit delivered for me. They'll have to be sent back as well. The bet's finished, as you can see, though I'll admit it had its moments. But next time, leave Glenarris out of it, hmm? Now go away. I'm tired, and I want to leave before first light."

"Ye'll not even stay to bid her farewell?" Eachern

demanded as Connor flopped back in the bed and drew the covers over him.

He snorted. "Whatever for? She'd only make a tiresome scene."

"Tears and hand-wringing, ye mean."

"Violence, more like. Impale me with a pike, run me through with a dirk. Cave in my head with a chamberpot." Despite himself he smiled. "She's tried it before."

Above the bed, King, Eachern, and Carter exchanged astonished glances.

"So," King said, tapping a finger against his lips. "Do we take this to mean that the chit hasn't been a dutiful wife?"

Connor snorted again. "Hardly."

"But my dear lad, then the bet is by no means won."

Connor's eyes narrowed. "What do you mean?" he demanded slowly. "She married me, didn't she?"

"Oh, aye, we're certain that she did, and we're fair dying to hear the details. But the conditions of the wager called for something other than marriage."

"Oh? Such as?" he demanded, his enjoyment in besting them now gone.

"Love. Remember that? You were specifically charged with making her fall in love with you. You as the penniless beggar, of course, not the dashing laird of the MacEowan clan."

"There's a world of difference between marriage and love," Carter added helpfully.

"But that's insane!" Connor exploded, sitting up.

"It's what we agreed on," King said silkily. "Remember?"

Good Lord, of course he did—now. But who would have guessed that the three of them would be so adamant about this bloody love part? Marriage was one thing, but he was well aware that he couldn't possibly make Gemma fall in love with him, not when she'd much prefer wiping her boots on his carcass.

"Forget it," he snapped.

Carter gaped. "Just like that?"

"Aye!"

"Call the bet off, and you've lost Glenarris," Eachern pointed out in a shaky voice.

"Once made, a bet can't be rescinded," King reminded him glibly. " 'Tis a rule you've made us uphold ourselves on many an occasion, Con."

"Aye," Carter agreed emphatically.

They stared at him expectantly.

So there it was, he thought. Trapped by the same rules he had never permitted the others to break. Bound by his own word, the word of a MacEowan, to make that spiteful little viper in the room above fall in love with him or risk losing Glenarris to King Spencer. The thought was appalling.

Folding his arms across his updrawn knees, he laid his head upon them. He did not speak, but the stillness surrounding him shouted volumes.

"You'll have to keep up the charade, of course," King remarked after a while. "Grow back the beard they told me you arrived with. And that moth-eaten bearskin coat. Pure genius. I'd very much like to see you in it."

I won't let him goad me, he thought, though he felt the blackness of murderous anger swirling before his eyes. He and King had clashed over a number of things during the course of their stormy youths—women, horses, cards—but this was no time to be wasting energy on choking the life out of the man. He had to concentrate on Gemma. Surely it wouldn't take much to win her over. He'd have to change his strategy, that was all; woo her with kindness, affection, and respect, instead of clashing with her at every turn. Why, it might even turn out to be enjoyable.

Abruptly his head came up and his eyes nailed each of his friends in turn. At least Eachern and Carter had the good grace to shuffle their feet and look self-conscious.

"So where shall I take her after she recovers? I can't bring her to Glenarris or Edinburgh without revealing who I am, and that's one of the most important conditions of the bet."

"Hmm," King said.

"That's a bit of a problem, ain't it?" Carter agreed.

"What about the old Dodson croft?" Eachern said suddenly. "It's been empty since the old fellow's death. 'Tis remote enough that ye'll no be recognized, provided ye keep awa' from the village."

"I can't take Gemma there!" he protested, envisioning the ramshackle hut that Eachern meant. Why, it was miles from the nearest neighbor, and at least several hours' ride from the village of Arris.

"Where else then?" Eachern argued. "Beggar that you are, what else can ye afford?"

"No. Not with winter coming on." He shook his head.

"I daresay it won't be that bad," King said bracingly. " 'Tis the time of year when the Highlands historically enjoy a spell of fine weather before the snow sets in, right, lads? And Connor here won't need but half that time to seduce his bonnie bride. I gather you've not had much luck with her yet, eh, Con?"

Connor had finally been pushed too far. He rose from the bed and scowled his expression to show them that the time for prudent retreat had arrived. Wisely they withdrew, making no effort to be quiet on the landing despite the lateness of the hour.

He listened to them go, his mouth a hard, grim line. So. They had him by the balls after all, and well they knew it. All right, then, he'd play along, but he'd kick them out in the morning without permitting King or Carter to lay eyes on Gemma. Eachern could be trusted to keep his mouth shut, but Connor would just as soon kill the other two as allow them to see the bristle-headed moppet he was still compelled to acknowledge was his wife!

Gemma was eating breakfast when Connor knocked on the door the next morning. Frantic, she smoothed her cropped curls, but of course it did no good. All she could do was bite her lips in the hopes of giving them a little color and draw the coverlet to her chin.

"Come in."

He had brought someone with him, a younger man who lacked his height and darkness, but whose angular jaw and cleft chin were the same as Connor's. Friendly blue eyes regarded her with avid interest while she stared back, flushing with embarrassment.

"Since we're family now, I saw no reason not to present my cousin Eachern MacEowan," Connor told her blandly.

"No," she agreed tartly, "but you might have given me some warning."

She saw the startled smile that lit Eachern's face at that, and strangely enough felt none of the animosity toward him that she always felt toward Connor. Eachern MacEowan was handsome and well groomed, and his tailored coat and custom boots suggested that his financial circumstances were far less dire than his cousin's.

Oh, why couldn't it have been *this* MacEowan who'd rescued her from the highwaymen on the Derby road? she thought mournfully.

"Won't you sit down, Mr. MacEowan?" she asked graciously, as if she were ushering him into the withdrawing room at her uncle's estate.

"I'd be delighted, and please, will ye call me Eachern?"

Her attitude softened. Here, at least, was a man with nicely polished manners. Again she couldn't help wishing that if she'd had to marry a MacEowan it could have been this pleasant fellow.

"Eachern has come down from Inverness at my request," Connor said, looking from one smiling young face to the other. Never had he seen Gemma so open and good-natured with a stranger before, and Eachern was obviously enjoying himself hugely. "I've asked him to look after Helios for the winter."

"What?" Gemma shouted.

Even Eachern looked startled. Good, Connor thought, as he pulled up a chair, flipped it around, and sat on it with his arms crossed casually in front of him. He was pleased that he'd managed to wipe that smug expression from his cousin's face.

Gemma, meanwhile, had begun bristling like a fighting cockerel. She sat up, unaware that her clinging nightgown was exposed as the blanket slipped from her shoulders. "What do you mean, he's taking Helios for the winter?"

"Aye, Connor," Eachern chimed in, "what d'ye mean?"

"We won't have anywhere to shelter him where we're going," he explained, his eyes on Gemma. "He could well die of exposure. Eachern has a stable, and a competent stableman to look after it. Helios will be well cared for, I promise."

"And I'm to take your word for it? Just like that?"

"I don't think you have a choice."

Gemma's eyes brimmed with tears, and she bowed her head. Above her, Eachern glanced helplessly at Connor.

Coming quickly to his feet, he all but shoved his cousin to the door. "I'm afraid it's time to go, laddie."

"Charmed, Miss B—" Eachern began but got no further before he was manhandled into the corridor.

"Don't say a word," Connor warned, stepping outside behind him. "Not one bloody word."

"But I never—Who is this Helios? And what in blazes happened tae her hair?"

"I cut it off," he said curtly. "And it's *Mrs. Mac-Eowan*, I'll charge you to remember. Now do me a favor and go."

"Where?"

"Back to Edinburgh, with Helios. I want that colt cared for in my own stable. Tell John Scoures he'd better do a proper job or I'll have his carcass for breakfast."

Eachern bristled. "I willna curse the man, Connor! You ken there's no ane better wi' horseflesh."

"Just tell him."

"All right, all right, I will! Ye dinna have to be so bloody bad-tempered about it." Wounded, Eachern made a great show of smoothing down his coat sleeves, which had been badly wrinkled when Connor hauled him outside.

"Here. I want you to take this, too."

From around his neck he withdrew a pouch tied with a leather thong. "They're Gemma's jewels," he explained, turning over Eachern's hand and placing the bulging pouch in his palm. "I lifted a few of them so she'd think I used them to pay for our lodgings here. Keep them safe, will you?"

"And just how do ye plan to pay your room bill now you've given 'em to me?"

He grinned. "Why, laddie, I thought you'd take care of that on your way out. I ken damned well you never travel without full pockets."

"Bugger you, Con."

"Make sure you tell Mrs. Kennerly that we'll be staying at least three more days. I want Gemma well rested before we head north."

Eachern pocketed the jewels and shook his head. "Poor lass. Barely out of the schoolroom, frae the look of her. She's no found an easy life with ye, I'll wager. But ye ken what, Con?"

"No," he said, scowling. "What?"

"I liked her." Eachern was grinning now. "I liked her just fine, owl-eyed, bushy-headed an' a'."

"Good for you," he retorted. Taking his cousin by the shoulders, he propelled him toward the stairs. "You're more than welcome to her after I'm through."

"That's na fair!" Eachern protested. "That's na fair, Con!" he repeated.

"Life never is," he replied coldly and, turning back toward Gemma's room, slammed the door behind him.

Chapter Twelve

Gemma sat huddled amid numerous boxes and trunks in the back of the pony cart. Burying her face in the fur of Connor's bearskin coat—the same coat she had once despised—she shivered and wondered despairingly if she would ever be warm again. On the seat in front of her, Connor's broad back swayed as the cart jolted along the rocky trail.

He, too, wore a coat, though it was of unlined leather and probably not as warm as hers. His dark hair, though trimmed, still curled at his collar, and she knew without his having to turn around that a new growth of stubble blackened his jaw. She wouldn't be at all surprised if he grew back the same bristling beard he'd had before they reached their final destination—wherever in bloody hell that was!

Yesterday, they had crossed the last of the Grampian mountains. The weather had been abominable, and the pony had slipped constantly on the icy footing while the howling wind drove snow into their faces. Gemma had burrowed between the trunks to protect herself from the wind, but it had lashed at Connor so that his fingers had been stiff and useless when they'd stopped at last for the night.

At least they'd been able to stop at an inn, though it had been equally as primitive as that awful one in Kinkillie. Uncaring, exhausted, she had fallen asleep the moment she was laid down on the straw pallet to which Connor had carried her.

The crossing of the Grampians had been a hardship the likes of which she had never endured in her pampered young life. Still weakened from illness, she had suffered through the grueling days in stoic silence, while in her heart she had deliberately kept alive the burning resentment she felt toward Connor, who was solely to blame for the extent of her misery.

They had exchanged fewer than a dozen words since leaving Stirling four insufferably weary days ago. Even when the cart had broken a wheel on two separate occasions by jolting into a rocky fissure and they'd had to climb out to make repairs. On neither occasion had Connor permitted her to help, so she had stood shivering on the shoulder of the nonexistent trail as he bucked and strained and lifted the cart by sheer force of will—something she doubted that twice as many men his size would have been able to accomplish.

He, too, had been silent and withdrawn both times. Not once during the course of those difficult days had he complained of the cold or his hunger. There weren't many places to stop along the way for food or drink, and they had long since run out of rations. Nor had he complained about the hard bed he made for himself beneath the cart on those nights when inns or crofts had been lacking altogether.

A croft, Connor had explained to her early on, was the Scottish equivalent of an English tenant farm whose inhabitants paid fealty and rents to the local laird. She was familiar with tenant farms back home in Derbyshire, but she had been horrified to discover that crofters here in Scotland were no better than peasants and that the land they worked was in truth just a skimpy patch of earth too poor to yield a harvest. As well, most of the crofts they had passed since leaving the mountains behind had been deserted, the stone chimneys crumbling, the fields overgrown with gorse.

"Highland clearances," Connor had explained when she asked, and there was a grimness in his voice that she had never heard before.

"I don't understand," she had replied.

"Most of our Highlanders were rounded up and driven out in the great clearances years ago," Connor had said harshly. "Robbed of their homes, their livelihoods, packed off like cattle in order to make way for the landed aristocrats' more profitable sheep."

She had been horrified. "But—but where did they go?"

"South to the Lowlands, some of them, but most went across the sea to Canada, America, New Zealand. A number of them ended up in prison, I warrant, or dead."

It was the first time she had heard Connor speak with so much passion on any subject. Had his own people been among those expelled from the country? He had once told her that both his parents were dead. Could they have been victims of such inhumane treatment? That would certainly explain Connor's own terrible poverty, which had always been incomprehensible to her, considering that he was a strong and able-bodied man, and clearly well educated.

But if that were indeed the case, why was he bringing her back here? Did he have in mind to use her fortune to reclaim the land he had lost?

You're a mystery, Connor MacEowan, she thought, certainly not for the first time. Once again she wished that she could have asked his cousin a number of questions about him. But Connor had made certain that Eachern left Stirling long before she was even strong enough to get out of bed.

At least in one thing Connor had been right: in his decision to send Helios away. Although Gemma missed the colt bitterly, she realized now that he would not have endured the mountainous crossing without injury. Even the shaggy pony pulling their cart looked decidedly scrawny and no longer trotted out smartly beneath the sting of Connor's whip.

She had never asked Connor what had become of dull-witted Dirk, and he had never said. He never said much about anything, she thought now. Lonely and miserable, she cowered amid the trunks and willed herself to sleep. The only way to escape the cold and the boredom was by dreaming of other things. And in not thinking of the future.

"Gemma?"

She thought she must have dozed off for just a few minutes, but when she lifted her head she was astonished to discover that evening had fallen. A magnificent sunset was painting the western sky, and she blinked as she sat up to find the cart standing at the edge of a wide moor.

In the distance, mountains ranked to the fiery sky, but here there was nothing save seemingly endless miles of peaty earth, scored by brooks that fled downhill to empty themselves into a shimmering lake.

There was no sign of human habitation anywhere. The landscape was as desolate as it must have been on some distant planet. She looked up at Connor, not understanding why he had awakened her.

"We're here," he explained, meeting her eyes.

Here? she thought, mystified. Where was *here?*

"Is this Glenarris?"

"What makes you think that?" He was clearly startled.

"You told me that's where we were going."

"Oh, no, this isn't Glenarris!" He laughed as if she had said something hilarious. "Our croft is just beyond the rise, there," he explained, grinning and pointing.

Her eyes followed his finger to the shore of the distant lake. She couldn't see anything but water and rocks and a few stunted pines. A nameless dread began to seep into her heart. This couldn't be Connor's home! He had to be joking!

"You can't see the cottage from here," he added." 'Twill come into view soon enough."

"Let's go, then," she snapped. "I'd like to get there before dark."

But there was no road across the moor, and the cart got bogged down frequently in the mossy earth. Twice Connor had to get down and push, while muttering something grossly unprintable concerning the weight of her trunks. She ignored him, knowing that the contents of those same trunks were the assurance of her freedom. The sale of her belongings would provide the funds she needed to get away from here, and from Connor.

Nevertheless, she found it difficult to keep up her spirits when they finally reached the rocky shores of the lake, or loch as Connor called it, and she saw their croft for the very first time. The night was dark, for the sun had long since slipped behind the mountains. There was no moon, but in the dim light of countless stars she could make out the stone walls of a tiny house with two windows peering out like sightless eyes. As they got nearer, she saw that little was left of the chimney and the thatched roof. Crumbling plaster lay everywhere. A low wall of lichen-covered stone led away from the hut to a small, enclosed field strewn with rubble.

Halting in the littered yard, Connor unhitched the weary pony from its traces. She made no move to climb down from the back of the cart. Hugging herself with her arms, she sat watching as Connor turned the pony loose and secured the sagging gate. Without looking at her, he crossed to the tiny cottage. He had to put his shoulder to the splintered wood a number of times before the door burst open, then duck his head as he stepped inside. Seconds later his shadow emerged into the starlight.

''Bring a light.''

She had no desire to help him out, but she was cold and tired, and so she rummaged through his leather satchel until she found the flint and tapers. He, of course, was much too poor to afford real matches.

She stood shivering in the doorway as Connor lit the candles and placed them in the shelter of the deep windowsills. Shadows leaped against the low ceiling as the flames brightened, and she gasped.

''Y-you expect us to live *here*?''

160

"It'll look better come morning."

She knew that wasn't true. How could this filthy pigsty possibly improve in the daylight? She could already see enough of it in the dark to know that it was a total disaster. Charred beams ran along the crumbling ceiling. Mounds of dirt, moldering furniture, and decaying garbage lay ankle-deep on the earthen floor. The place had the smell of a mildewed trunk that had never been aired.

"Come," Connor said, "there's a bed in the other room."

The "other room" turned out to be little more than a loft tucked away in one corner, accessible by a paltry little ladder. The bottom rung caved in the moment Connor put his weight on it.

"Never mind," she snapped. "I'm not sleeping up there." Even in the smoky candlelight she could see that the loft was nothing more than a ledge of uneven boards lashed haphazardly together. No telling how safe it was, or what had been nesting up there!

"Then where—" he began impatiently.

She interrupted him with a fit of coughing which had developed alarmingly during the last few days of travel. But she had managed to hide it from Connor by burying her face in the thick fur of his coat whenever a spasm overcame her. Tonight was different. The dampness of the air here by the loch had seriously aggravated her lungs, and she couldn't stop the paroxysm. Her head spun and her lungs burned as she struggled to breathe.

Through her agony she could feel Connor's arms around her. Scooping her up as though she weighed nothing at all, he carried her toward the ladder. She wasn't entirely sure how he was going to make it up to the loft. She wasn't entirely sure about anything anymore. She couldn't stop coughing long enough to catch her breath. She felt disoriented, dizzy, and discovered that it was strangely comforting to lay her head against his wide chest.

"Easy," he whispered into her hair. "Breathe slowly. You'll be all right."

Reassured, she closed her eyes and nestled her cheek into the curve of his shoulder.

Once in the loft, Connor went down on his knees and kept her propped in his lap. He tried to dust off the old mattress lying there and eased the bearskin coat from her shoulders.

Gemma protested weakly as he laid her down, but by the time he had carefully covered her she was fast asleep. Quietly he returned below.

Outside in the darkness the brook gurgled in its endless race toward the loch. The pony blew through its nostrils and the wind sighed over the moor. Inside, too, there was nothing to be heard save gentle nighttime sounds: the sputtering of the candles, the rustling of a mouse in the corner, Gemma's even breathing from the loft above.

But there was no rest for him as he stood in the doorway, troubled and awake. Aching with cold and exhaustion, he lowered himself at last onto a stool that had been left propped near the hearth. Like Gemma, he could scarcely conceal his dismay as he looked around him. Camping out in the open for sport and relaxation was one thing. Living like a caveman was another. How could Fergus Dodson, the croft's last inhabitant, have tolerated such grinding poverty?

Just like anyone else who was reduced to eking out a harsh living in the Highlands, he thought grimly. Unlike many of his fellow landowners, he had always been fair to his own crofters, listening to their complaints, sending them food when the harvest was bad, or fuel when the winter was bitter, and an extra annuity whenever anyone in the family became ill or disabled. The crofters respected him in turn, trusted him with their grievances, and were quick to invite him inside for a dram of precious whiskey or tea whenever he rode down from his great castle to look in on them.

But occasional visits and a sympathetic ear did not prepare a man for becoming one of them. Yet here he sat on Fergus Dodson's rickety stool, surrounded by the detritus of the crofter's pitiable life, condemned to battle out the winter with a shrew of a wife who was still too weak to endure such hardship. The thought was not at all to his liking.

Nor was Gemma's health.

A scowl knitted his brow. Somehow her illness had served to alter their relationship, at least from his point of view. Somehow, perhaps because he'd battled so hard in Stirling to save her, Gemma's life had become important to him. After all, he was the one who had spent numbing hours bathing her feverish body and holding her close when convulsions wracked her. He was the one who had patiently spoon-fed her endless bowls of steaming broth because she had been too ill to take nourishment for herself, or even to notice who it was that fed her.

She had been so weak when he had gotten her to Stirling that neither the doctor nor Mrs. Kennerly had expected her to last through the night. Admittedly he hadn't either, but he realized now that he had taken it as a personal accomplishment that he *had* coaxed her through it, and on through the next night and the next until it was clear to everyone that she was out of danger. Only then had he dared ride to Inverness to fetch Eachern and the others.

And had found himself totally unprepared for his reaction when he'd returned to Stirling and walked through Gemma's door to see the shorn moppet with the huge green eyes looking at him so solemnly from her bed. She had grown so thin that it hurt just to look at her.

But her painful thinness wasn't simply the result of her illness, he guiltily admitted now. It was the way he had been pushing her on the long journey north, scarcely giving her time to rest, and presenting her with the most unpalatable food imaginable, especially for a girl who had never known anything save her uncle's exquisite cuisine.

Tripe and bannocks, watery whiskey and poorly fermented ale. What sort of nourishment was that for a slip of a lass, especially when she'd been too frightened and miserable to have much of an appetite anyway?

Wearily he put his head in his hands. How was he supposed to help her get her strength back now? What on earth was he going to feed her? This disgusting lair was no place for a gently bred girl! Worse, how was he ever going to make her fall in love with him when he was the one responsible for bringing her to this manure pit in the first place?

I've got to call off the bet, he thought despairingly. Tomorrow, first thing, I'm taking Gemma to Glenarris.

Where King, Carter, and Eachern would fall all over themselves with glee watching him grovel for amnesty!

It was an intolerable thought. Red rage swam before his eyes.

Go to sleep, Connor. You're not thinking clearly, he told himself.

But where should he sleep? On the stool? On the filthy floor? Outside in the cart? He shuddered with distaste at such dismal choices.

Why not up in the loft?

His whirling thoughts skittered to a halt, then back-tracked. Images of his plush bearskin coat and Gemma's warm body wrapped inside it rose temptingly through the exhaustion fogging his brain.

In no time at all he had ascended the ladder. The space was narrow, but Gemma never stirred as he eased himself under the covers beside her. She lay on one side with her back to him, and he curled himself around her so that her rump nestled against his belly and his hips. It was a liberty he would never have dared to take had she been awake, and one which probably would see him stabbed the moment her eyes came open in the morning.

But at the moment he didn't care what the morrow would bring. It was enough to feel the softness of the bearskin beneath him, and the warmth of her body pressed intimately against his aching limbs. Closing his eyes, he allowed himself to drift off into a deep sleep that, for the first time in days, was entirely devoid of dreams.

Chapter Thirteen

The loud report of a gun awoke Gemma with a start. Scrambling out from under the bearskin, she raced down the ladder and threw open the door. The wide moor was empty, but the pony was standing with pricked ears at the far end of the enclosure. Shading her eyes, she peered in the same direction. She thought she caught a flash of movement amid the scattering of pine and gorse on the distant hillside.

Connor. What on earth was he doing?

Another shot rang out, sending a pair of rooks on the rooftop flapping away in alarm. From out on the moor came the raucous calling of a wild bird, then another, and another, and again the sharp crack of a gun.

So. He was hunting.

Hugging herself with her arms, she went back inside. The interior of the house was just as chilly as outside. Her nose wrinkled as she inspected the debris in the hearth. No sense in trying to light a fire until the fireplace was clean. No sense in doing anything until the entire place was clean.

She turned slowly to take stock of her new home, and her heart sank. It was a thousand times worse in the daylight. Four very bare stone walls, a packed-earth floor, a jumble of broken furniture and pottery shards. Mouse droppings everywhere. No rugs, no curtains, not even glass in the windows. A ceiling blackened from the smoke of countless peat fires. Looking up at it, she realized that she wouldn't have been able to light a fire even if the hearth was clean and the chimney repaired. She had no peat, and she had no idea where to go looking for it.

At least I can sweep, she thought glumly.

But the simple task exhausted her, and the dust she raised exacerbated her cough. When the fit ended, she collapsed on a stool. Sweet Jesu, how long would it take to get her strength back? No doubt weeks in surroundings like these, where even the simplest conveniences were sorely lacking.

Face it, she told herself grimly. You'll have to stay until you're well.

By which time it would be the dead of winter and impossible to cross the mountains.

I'm trapped here, she thought. Trapped for the entire winter in this ... this den of horrors with Connor MacEowan. It might be months before the mountain roads were passable again, and maybe just as long before they saw so much as another human being, let alone one to whom she could pawn her belongings for enough money to get to London!

If she didn't feel so utterly weary, she would have

gone outside and drowned herself in the loch. Or taken a rope and hanged herself from the rafters. Or stolen the pony and headed into the mountains somewhere, anywhere, where the cold and the snow would soon make an end of her.

But she had never been one to succumb to self-pity for long, and she was not about to let Connor win this battle for her freedom or her fortune.

Her desire for revenge now stiffened her backbone and brought a measure of courage to her faltering heart. She would not let that filthy, opportunistic husband of hers condemn her to a lifetime of poverty, farming this dismal little croft. She deserved better—and he deserved to pay!

I suppose a single winter is preferable to the rest of my life, she decided, resigning herself to the likelihood that she would have to remain here until the snows ended. She ought to have her health back come spring, and hopefully would have earned enough of Connor's trust by then to plan for her departure without rousing his suspicions. But she'd have to be careful, too, not to arouse them now. She must strike just the right balance of rebellion and acquiescence. She mustn't seem too eager to embrace her new life, nor too anxious to get away from it. Both extremes would only make Connor watch her more closely. Devious and clever as he was, she knew there was little sense in trying to get away from him unless his guard was down.

A shadow fell across the threshold. Her head came up. Connor stood blocking the doorway, holding aloft four partridges.

''Breakfast,'' he announced gaily.

Resentment surged through her. How dare he stand

there grinning at her as though he hadn't a care in the world, as though this was just a game for him and not a deadly struggle for survival?

"No need to scowl so," he chided, stepping inside. "I'll clean them this time, though you'll have to learn to do it sooner or later. Here, clear off the table, will you?"

She grudgingly did as he asked and watched as he laid down the birds and pulled the pistols her uncle's coachman had given him from the waistband beneath his jacket. Her eyes widened. "You didn't go hunting with those, did you?"

"I didn't catch our breakfast with my bare hands, now did I?"

Gingerly she lifted one of the birds with her thumb and forefinger, then inspected the others in a similar manner. All four of them had been shot cleanly through the head. Her eyes swept up to Connor's.

He shrugged. "The moors are teeming with game."

But pistols? Where had he come by such skill with those difficult firearms?

"I'll take them outside to gut them," Connor added. "Start a fire in the meantime, will you? And see if you can fashion something to use for a spit."

She promptly forgot her curiosity. Who in blasted hell did he think he was? How dare he issue her orders, and such menial ones at that?

But she forced herself to remember the importance of at least seeming as if she were trying to meet him halfway. And, hang it all, she was hungry!

Since the hearth had already been swept, she stacked the splintered remains of the cottage's furniture on the blackened stones. By the time Connor returned, she had built quite a cheerful fire out of chair legs and a broken washstand.

Bending to feed another piece of wood to the flames, she heard an approaching "Hmmm" behind her.

Her head whipped around.

"Nice and warm," Connor said hastily.

She indicated the collection of firewood she had piled nearby. "This won't last long."

"No, and some of the furniture is too good to burn. I can definitely repair that chair, and those boards will make fine shelving. I suppose that means I'll have to start digging peat as soon as possible."

"Digging peat?"

"Well, of course. Where did you think it came from?"

She had no idea. She could not even begin to imagine how people kept themselves warm in this godforsaken land with not a tree to be seen save that copse of spindly pines on the far side of the loch.

Connor, meanwhile, was using his penknife to whittle a spit for the neatly trussed birds. She watched him, scowling ferociously. No one had to tell her that Connor had obviously been shooting and preparing game since boyhood. Was there anything the arrogant besom couldn't do?

Absorbed in his task, Connor pretended to be unaware of Gemma's smoldering resentment. But of course he sensed it, even though she didn't utter a word. He knew that rigid jaw and those flashing eyes of hers far too well by now to mistake her feelings toward him as charitable ones. He half suspected that if she wasn't still so weak from her illness she would have broken a chair leg over his head by now.

Let her try, he thought gaily, feeling well rested and in a deuced good mood. As a matter of fact, he would actually relish a return to the old, feisty Gemma—not only because it would signify that she was indeed getting her strength and spirit back, but because he'd missed them.

Whistling beneath his breath, he took his time skewering the partridges and suspending them over the fire. Where yesterday he had felt defeated and unwilling to continue this pointless charade, he now felt a keen sense of anticipation for the coming day, and for the days and weeks to follow. That, he recalled, was why he had always accepted King Spencer's bets in the first place, no matter how outrageous they might be. They added a bit of interest, of challenge, to his life. And life in this primitive hovel was going to be exhilarating, to say the least, what with the rebellious Gemma hovering over him just itching to do battle.

Connor stole a glance at her from his place beside the fire. She was standing in the open doorway, her trim back to him, her arms folded beneath her sweet young breasts. At that moment he had to admit that a lot of his renewed enthusiasm for the fight came from arousal; the arousal he'd felt when he had awakened this morning to find Gemma nestled close to his side, her legs tangled intimately with his. Too much time had passed since he had first made love to her, and his body protested such lengthy abstinence.

Now that their journey was ended, he decided that it was time to begin wooing Gemma with all the considerable experience at his command. He would bide his time and seduce her properly, with flattery and a gentle hand, the way women liked to be seduced. Gemma didn't know it, but she was passionate and sensual, a woman made for loving.

Oh, he was well aware that he wasn't the first man to sense as much about her, but he swelled with pride to know that he had been her first lover and that he would teach her the pleasures of lovemaking. He had no doubt that Gemma would respond eagerly once she got past her initial loathing of him, and prove an apt and deeply satisfying pupil. He had sensed as much on that disastrous night following their wedding, when for a brief moment she had responded passionately, despite herself, to his ardent ministrations. And love? That would follow on its own. It always did.

Gemma could hear Connor humming as he squatted near the hearth roasting his birds. She had to grind her teeth to keep from turning around and pushing him into the flames. God, how it galled her that he was so thoroughly content! She hated knowing that this was all it took to make him happy, this . . . this contemptible way of life to which he had obviously been born.

Well, maybe you're happy living like this, Connor MacEowan, she thought furiously, but I'll never become a pauper like you! Never, do you hear?

"Gemma?"

"Yes?" She looked at him.

"We'll need someplace to put these birds when they come off the fire. See what you can find."

Connor's ignorance as to the croft's contents and its neglect confirmed Gemma's suspicions that he had never lived here, that he had come from elsewhere when he'd headed south to England in search of work. She pondered this mystery as she rummaged through the trunks he had left in the cart overnight. She knew less than ever about him now. Not only was she mystified about his origins, but why on earth had he brought her here to this place? Who did it belong to? And where was this Glenarris he had spoken of? Could it be the nearest town? Was there even a town within a hundred miles of here?

There was so much she needed to know if she intended to arm herself against him. But how to ask questions when she knew Connor was too closed-mouthed and suspicious to answer them? Time, Gemma thought. Give him time, and win his trust.

But it proved enormously difficult for her to focus on her strategy of kindness and trust toward Connor while sorting through the trunks containing all that remained of her old life, which he had so effectively destroyed. She forgot what she was looking for as she fingered the lovely table linens she had brought with her from Derbyshire. Her spirits sagged as she pictured them spread on the homemade table inside and trailing onto the dirt floor of the cottage. What about these silver candlesticks? How would they look, all tarnished from the cold air, in the glassless embrasure of the windowsill? And what of her sampler which she had stitched as a child under the punitive tutelage of her Aunt Druscilla? Where could she hang it now? And these bolts of fine cloth she'd brought along in the hopes of finding a seamstress to sew new dresses and undergarments for the winter . . .

"Oh, God," she said with a laugh that broke into a sob. "I'll go mad before the winter ends, I know it!" And just as fretfully she thought what on earth would she do with these things? They'd never fit inside that hovel, never!

"Gemma!"

Connor's shout was furious, the tone of a man not

used to having his orders disobeyed.

Grabbing a pair of lovely Worcester dishes (yes, she had stupidly brought along enough place settings to feed twelve), she stalked inside. "What is it?" she yelled back.

"What the devil's been keeping you? This meat is about to burn!"

She slapped the dishes onto the table with a force that almost shattered them. "There! You can take the birds off the spit now, but I'll thank you to ask more politely in the future. I am *not* your housekeeper!"

His expression was as black as their rapidly over-cooking breakfast. "Oh, but I'm afraid you are, my dear, and I suggest you get used to it."

"Never!"

"Aye!"

They stood glaring at each other, breathing harshly, like a pair of wild horses. Then, suddenly, she stamped her foot in a gesture as childish as their entire argument. Whirling, she ran outside.

"Come back here!" he yelled, but she was running now, her dark skirts trailing like a sail behind her.

Not until she reached the rough footing on the lake-shore did Connor catch up with her. Seizing her wrist, he spun her around so that she slammed hard against him.

"Let me go!"

"Stop kicking me and I will!"

Her breasts heaving, she glared at him. Connor hov-ered over her, hawklike. Then, all at once, his sensual mouth softened, the annoyance smoothed from his hand-some face, and he smiled. The change was sudden, dev-astating.

"Gemma, I'm sorry."

She stiffened, sensing danger. He sounded so sincere, so . . . gentle. Did that mean he was apologizing? Like a gentleman? And to her, of all people? She didn't know what to make of it. His instant turnabout had defused the full broadside of her anger so that it crumbled like ashes in her mouth. And in her heart something strange was stirring to life, something that could not help but respond to his endearingly boyish smile.

"Apology accepted," she told him huffily, and brushed past him, her head high.

Connor followed, grinning, for he had seen the color that pinked Gemma's cheeks even though she'd marched past him like a bandy Napoleon. So, in the end she was just like the rest of her sex, wasn't she? A fool for a man's melting smile.

Extremely pleased with himself, he stepped through the cottage door behind her. "Gemma, I think we'd better—"

A splash of water dashed him full in the face, shocking him with its iciness, and he yelped.

Dropping the bucket, Gemma came around the side of the door where she'd been lying in wait for him. "That's to remind you once and for all that I am not your housekeeper, Connor MacEowan! In the future you'll not address me thusly. Is that understood?"

Oh ho! Never in all his pampered life had he heard a more outrageous command, for no one he knew had ever dared speak to him so baldly. Did she wish him to treat her as an equal? This snippet of a girl he could crush with his bare hands? This ill-bred termagant he should have left to those highwaymen in Derbyshire in the first place? Woo her he would, of course, for he had no choice if he wanted to keep Glenarris, but first he would have to squelch that objectionable arrogance of hers once and for all.

Standing there with the water dripping from his hair, his chin, his shirt and breeches, he was sorely tempted to beat the haughtiness out of her. But he had never in his life raised his hand to a woman. Then again, this was no woman. This was a she-devil with the face of an angel, a spoiled brat who deserved to be turned over his knee.

He pulled her swiftly off the floor, turned her over, and placed her across his lap. With one hand he imprisoned her wrists and with the other he pulled up her skirts and began to paddle her behind with the palm of his hand. Hard!

"MacEowan! Stop!"

"Will you behave?"

"No!"

Whack! Whack! Whack!

The blows weren't really all that hard; he didn't have the heart for that. But the humiliation would certainly hurt a girl of Gemma's boundless pride, and that, he thought, would do her a world of good.

"MacEowan!"

Gemma was squirming to escape his hand, and he discovered that he had to oblige her very fast, because it was difficult to let her wiggle around on his lap without letting her know that she was having a dangerously arousing effect on him.

Gripping her upper arms, he flipped her over and eased her off him, then got up quickly to hide the very suspicious bulge in his breeches.

"There," he said somewhat breathlessly. "You've

had that coming for quite some time. Perhaps if your uncle had beaten you more often you'd not have turned into the monster you are.''

To his astonishment, Gemma recoiled as though he had struck her full in the face. Her reaction stunned him. What was this? Had he touched some raw nerve without realizing it? Surely Archibald Baird hadn't dared lift his hand against her!

Had he?

But why then would Gemma react like this, cowering as though he had brought alive some very real, very painful memories?

He wasn't used to feeling like a cad. It was a rare moment in his life when he found himself regretting his actions, and yet he was certainly regretting them now. From the moment of their first meeting he had seen Gemma in countless unexpected ways: in tears, in towering rages, defiant, defeated, and once—too temptingly brief—in smiling sweetness, but he had never known her to cringe from him like some wounded animal.

Oh, God. How on earth could he let her know how deeply he regretted opening old wounds? He was not a man who tended to apologize. Why, even the kindly words he had said to her on the loch shore had merely been intended to confuse her, to catch her off guard so that he might begin seducing her. But this was different. The look on Gemma's face made him want to kill someone, namely Archibald Baird.

But even as he hesitated, the chance was lost. Silently Gemma turned to the fire and plucked the forgotten meat from the spit. Taking the charred remains outside, she paused in the doorway. Without looking at him she said, ''You'll have to find us something else to eat.''

And so he returned to the moors, relieved to get away from the silent cottage and Gemma's painful withdrawal. Even so, the image of her white face haunted him as he strode for hours through the heather, unable to keep his mind on the quest for game. He knew that he would have to make it up to her, but for the first time in his life he didn't know where to start. The realization was a bitter one.

Chapter Fourteen

Connor returned to the cottage at noon with a plump goose slung over his shoulder. He had stayed by the loch to pluck and dress the bird, wanting to spare Gemma the bloody sight. At least that was what he had kept telling himself. In truth he was not particularly anxious to see her just yet. For some odd reason he was more ashamed than ever of what he'd said to her, what he'd done to her, and even the long hours out on the moor hadn't diminished the unwelcome feeling of being responsible for her pain.

Damn the lass! What was it about her that brought out the worst in him? Why did she get under his skin, rub him the wrong way, when he'd always been able to shrug off such irritations before?

Perhaps it had something to do with the odd fact that he couldn't simply walk away from her as he had from all the other women he'd become entangled with during

179

the course of his dissolute youth. He was married to this one, after all, and more important, the fate of Glenarris hung in the balance. And so it was with a good deal of uncertainty—a feeling unfamiliar to him—that he reached the doorway of the forlorn little cottage and peered cautiously inside. Was she still here, or had she run away during his absence?

That nasty possibility hadn't occurred to him before. Propelled by a fear he couldn't begin to explain, he burst through the door. What he saw made him forget everything else. His mouth fell open. Unslinging the goose, he let it drop to the floor and stepped slowly into the room.

Without his help, Gemma had managed to drag the heavy trunks from the cart and bring them inside to unpack. But not before she had swept the cottage clean, stacking great piles of debris into the hearth where they continued even now to spark and smolder.

The walls and rafters of the cottage had been cleaned of cobwebs, and the floor neatly swept. On top of the packed earth she had unrolled two of the rugs she had brought with her from England. He recognized one of them as an Aubusson, the other as an Oriental kilim. Surely Archibald Baird would never have let them leave his possession if he had had an inkling as to how they would be used!

And there was more, mind-boggling more to look at, for the walls themselves were hung with—God's blood, could it be? Slowly he crossed the room to finger the gorgeous tapestry hung from numerous rusty nails, his gaze roving the lovely scenes depicting the Three Fates woven in lush burgundy, emerald, and gold. Flemish, his experienced eyes told him, two hundred years old and more, and extremely valuable considering today's market for Belgian tapestries, Royal Gobelins, and the like.

Several oil paintings had been hung up as well, all of them pleasing landscapes rendered by unknown but inarguably talented artists. To the right of the hearth Gemma had fashioned a makeshift kitchen where she had stored away her china and silverware and assorted pitchers and utensils. On the other side she had grouped the rickety stool and another chair around the small table, which was covered now with an embroidered cloth of fine damask and a vase of cut crystal—either German or Belgian, he guessed.

Up in the loft she had stored away her personal belongings: tortoiseshell combs, mirror and brush, a trinket box and perfume bottles, and an alphabet sampler covering a spot on the wall where some of the stones had crumbled away.

His bearskin coat had been replaced by real bedding and a plump eiderdown tick. Somewhat to his surprise he saw that she had brushed out the coat and hung it neatly on a peg behind the door. On the other side of the door, in the far corner beneath the loft ladder, she had laid out towels and a porcelain washbowl and pitcher. The bucket she had upended over his head stood brimming with clear spring water on the floor nearby.

Connor stood staring with his hands on his hips, not knowing what on earth to make of such opulence. For the first time in his life he was bereft of words. The changes Gemma had wrought were nothing short of miraculous. The work she must have put into it in the few hours he'd been gone told him volumes about her sheer force of will. He had the sudden, intense urge to laugh and weep at the same time; to laugh because the place looked like a pirates' den crammed to bursting with stolen booty, and to weep because there was something so pitiful in seeing all this splendor reduced to gracing a tumbledown croft.

But of course he wasn't about to shed tears. He'd never cried over anything, not even when his mother had died shortly before his eighth birthday, leaving him in the indifferent care of his coldly autocratic father. The lonely years that followed had hardened him as nothing else could have done. His childhood had ended with his mother's death, replaced by rigorous years of training as Donal MacEowan groomed his only son to take over the MacEowan shipping lines, assuming the responsibilities of running Glenarris, and carrying out the duties of the MacEowan laird.

Difficult as those years had been, Connor had ultimately prospered, driven by the same ambitions that had driven his hard, demanding father. Never mind that after his mother's death all softness and warmth had vanished from his life. Neither he nor his father had seen the need for tenderness, and over the years no woman had ever managed to gain enough of a foothold in his masculine world to remind him that such things even existed.

Until now.

A shadow fell across the threshold and he turned slowly to see his wife framed in the doorway. She looked charmingly disheveled from having worked so hard, but also extremely drawn, and he was unpleasantly reminded of her recent illness.

"You shouldn't have done all this," he said more harshly than he intended, alarmed by the dark circles beneath her eyes.

"Who else would have done it?" she snapped. "You? I warrant you're more at home here when it looks like a privy, aren't you? Well, I'm not about to live like a savage even though you don't seem to care."

She tried to push past him, but he wouldn't let her. "It was too much for you, Gemma. You're too weak yet."

She thrust aside his outstretched hand and brushed past him to the corner that looked like a kitchen. "I'd better get used to hard work, though, hadn't I? I expect I'll have plenty now that I'm a *crofter's wife.*"

The last two words dripped so much venom that the effect was like a slap in the face. In that instant it was clear to him just how much Gemma reviled him. His mouth settled into a harsh line. Without another word he stalked across the room to retrieve the goose.

For the next half hour they studiously ignored each other. It was a difficult task, given that they had to share such a cramped and crowded room, and yet they managed brilliantly.

But soon the delicious smell of braising meat filled the cottage, reminding them of the far more elemental pull of hunger. Gemma and Connor sat down to dine upon the beautifully browned goose, using no cutlery. It was easier to tear the meat from the bones with their fingers, and faster, too.

The goose was washed down with icy water from the burn, and at the last he pulled a package from his jacket pocket and pushed it across the table toward her.

Gemma's shining eyes swept up to his when she opened it. "Chocolates! Where on earth did you—"

"Mrs. Kennerly sent them along when we left Stirling. I've been saving them for a special treat." He had to turn his head to hide his grin. He'd presented many a bauble—bloody expensive ones at that—to other women, but Gemma's childlike delight was by far the most satisfying thanks he had ever received. One would think she'd been handed the Kohinoor diamond instead of a tin of sweets.

Gemma divided them carefully, her brow furrowed in concentration while he watched, feeling an odd tugging at his heart. They shared their booty in companionable silence, their eyes meeting across the table in a candid look of enjoyment. A truce of sorts had been established.

"Where will you sleep?" Gemma inquired as darkness fell and she announced wearily that she would withdraw to the loft.

He had been sitting at the table cleaning his pistols. Now he turned to look at her. "Same place I slept last night."

Gemma looked around the room, confused. "Where was that?"

"In the loft."

"But—but that's where I—" Her voice trailed away. "You didn't—Are you saying—"

"Exactly."

He watched with a good deal of enjoyment as the bewilderment on her face gave way to disbelief, then comprehension, and finally, anger. How delightfully transparent she was!

"Gemma—"

"No!" she cried. "This time you've gone too far, MacEowan. You have no right to share that loft with me. None at all!"

The laughter died inside him. "Oh, haven't I?"

The Enchanted Prince

Hot color swept from Gemma's throat to the roots of her hair. "Our marriage is a sham and you know it."

"Not in the eyes of your household, or the church, or even God, I daresay."

"Is that so? I was coerced, and you damned well know it!"

He shrugged. "Few women take their marriage vows without some form of duress nowadays. It's an unfortunate circumstance for the fairer sex in this supposedly enlightened century. Perhaps some day that will change, but for the time being the laws of church and state insist that you and I are legally man and wife, and one of the perquisites of those laws is the right to share your bed."

Gemma glanced longingly at the pistols he'd left on the table. Following her gaze, he threw back his head and roared with laughter.

"Shoot me if you must, but not until morning, please! A man deserves a good night's sleep before his execution."

He saw Gemma's mouth soften and twitch despite her valiant efforts not to smile. Their gazes clashed and then slid away, only to return once again, as though neither of them could help themselves.

He pushed back his chair and rose slowly to his feet.

"N-no," Gemma said, backing away although he hadn't made the slightest move toward her.

"Gemma—"

"D-don't say my name like that!"

"Like what?"

He saw her eyes dilate and heard her breath hitch. He sensed her fear like a physical thing even from this distance. Before she could bolt, he came around the table and caught her by the wrists. Through the silky skin he could feel the blood thrumming in her veins.

Pulling her closer, he held her just a few inches away from him for a long, still moment. Then he lifted one of those narrow little wrists and pressed a kiss against the throbbing skin.

"MacEowan, don't—"

Her eyes were wide, and as dark and green as the loch beyond the door. They were eyes in which a man could easily lose himself.

"Aye, Gemma," he said softly. "It's time you learned about certain things."

"I already know m-more than enough!"

Gemma tried to twist away, but she halted and hung her head as the fight went out of her. Connor heard her swallow hard.

Aching remorse washed over him. Oh, no, Gemma, there's naught to fear, he longed to tell her. I give you my word it won't be like the last time.

Instead of speaking, for surely words would have been futile, he took her face in his hands and turned it up to his. Tears glittered in her eyes but he ignored them, knowing they would be his undoing. Instead he dropped his gaze to her mouth, that soft, sweet mouth that had tantalized him from the very first. Lowering his head, he kissed her, taking her lips between his own, aching to feel them open in welcome.

But of course they did not. Gemma stood rigid against him, her eyes shut tightly.

He ignored her lack of response as his mouth tasted and teased, compelled and commanded. And when she would have backed away from him he dropped his hands from her face and slid one of them around her waist and the other to her nape, his fingers threading through her closely cropped hair.

"No, please—" Gemma begged against his mouth, but his arm merely tightened and she was swept up against him. He was huge, muscular, overwhelming, and she steeled herself against the pain and humiliation she knew was to come.

But it did not. The touch of his mouth on hers was neither frightening nor unkind. He had kissed her before, but not like this. She had never dreamed he could be so gentle.

"Kiss me back, Gemma," he breathed against her lips. It was the first humble thing he had ever asked of her, and that, too, served to crumble her resistance into nothing. No one had ever touched the loneliness within her this way, making her feel that she mattered, that it was she whom this man wanted, even needed.

Disarmed, dazzled by the way her heart was stirring into unexpected life, she could no longer fight the emotions swamping her as Connor revered her with his mouth and hands. Up went her arms over his broad shoulders to link themselves around his neck. She had to stand on tiptoe to open herself completely to his kiss, and Connor groaned as she leaned into him and her lips parted at last beneath his own.

His arm tightened around her tiny waist and he bent her slightly backward so that her breasts, belly, and thighs were welded against the full length of his hard male body. His legs were tangled in her skirts, and still he managed to mold her even closer while his tongue found its way into her mouth. She gasped, for she had never dreamed that a man could do such a thing to a woman, or that his tongue grazing hers could feel so electrifying.

But there was more, so much more, as his hands

cupped her breasts through her gown and his lips moved down to the hollow of her throat, tracing a trail of fire along her skin. She gasped again and felt her knees give way. Connor lifted her to keep her from falling before he eased her gently onto the carpet that she had unrolled just that morning.

Cold air brushed her skin as he hitched her gown back from her shoulders. His hand moved down the curve of her rib cage to her hip while his dark head bent to her breasts. His breath was hot against her icy skin as he took her erect nipple into his mouth. Her own breathing became ragged, and the blood coursed through her weakening limbs. A fierce ache blossomed inside her, in that secret place between her legs where Connor had so shamelessly invaded her before.

But where his touch had inspired fear the last time, it aroused a desperate longing now. She could feel herself softening, reaching her dew point as Connor's tongue found her other breast, caressing her skin and teasing the nipple to aching tautness. When he lifted his head at last, it was all she could do not to thread her fingers through his hair and pull him back.

Rising on one knee, he extinguished the single candle that still glowed on the table. In the utter dark of the moonless night he bent over her, and the last of her petticoats and undergarments whispered to the floor. She heard him shifting beside her and knew that he was also undressing, and she kept her face buried in the crook of her arm, shaking with mingled shame and the urgency of her arousal.

His voice held an unmistakable note of tenderness as he found her hand in the darkness and lifted it from her face. "Don't be frightened, love. It won't hurt this time,

I promise. And you'll enjoy it so much more. I promise that, too."

His hands slid underneath her body, and as he lay down again on the soft rug he rolled her over with him so that she was fused to him. There was nothing soft about the ridged muscles and angular planes of his body. Nor could there be any denying his desire for her as his manhood throbbed between them.

Nevertheless, she felt a momentary stab of fear as the huge bulge came to rest against the soft curve of her belly. But to her surprise Connor did not thrust inside her right away. Instead he continued to hold her close while his hand stroked her hip and then slowly, softly, invaded the space between them.

"Connor—!" She gasped as he found the swelling bud of her womanhood. But already his fingers were working their magic. She gasped again, but not in fear, and her head lolled against his chest.

Dazed and aroused, she allowed him to kiss her, feeling his tongue tantalize and tease even as his hand brought her toward the peak of heated pleasure. Unashamed now, she arched against him.

"Connor," she choked, throbbing with need.

He responded to her plea by turning her gently onto her back. Reaching between them, he placed his manhood where seconds earlier his hand had been. As he slid hot and turgid into her, filling her, she felt as if her very bones were melting away. Connor moved inside her, stroking in and out in a timeless rhythm that ignited their passion.

Gemma felt the first shuddering delight of ecstasy ripple through her. "Ohh," she gasped in sublime pleasure, feeling the explosion growing, sizzling along her nerve endings into every fiber of her being. She writhed and clung to him, gasping his name, and Connor responded with a ragged oath. Turning his face into her shoulder, he arched against her, then, spent, lay quietly in her arms.

Long, long moments passed while the universe skittered and tilted out of control for Gemma. But inevitably the whirling darkness grew calm, and her frantic heartbeat slowed. She finally realized that she lay beneath Connor, joined to him in that most intimate of human touches, but she felt neither shame nor regret, only an aching sweetness that seeped through every limb.

Above her Connor held his breath while he waited for her to make the first move. He had felt the lash of her tongue and the pain of her blows far too often to dare do more than hold himself utterly still. Inwardly he ached to bury his face in the softness of her curls, and to touch his lips to hers in one final kiss.

When Gemma moved at last beneath him he jumped nervously. But she merely linked her arms around his neck and drew him back into her warmth.

"I never knew," she whispered haltingly. "I never dreamed—"

Her innocence disarmed him. Tenderly, almost reverently, his fingers entwined in the silky curls he had been forced to cut in a desperate attempt to bring down her raging fever. "If I'd only known sooner that it would be so easy to tame you with lovemaking—"

"Would you have tried harder?" Gemma teased as his words trailed away into wonder at the thought of what he had missed.

He couldn't see her face in the darkness, but he could hear the sweet laughter in her voice. His heart warmed so that he was unable to keep from smiling too. "Aye, ages ago. 'Twas all I could think of before you took ill."

"And after?"

"Aye, and after," he said. His hand trailed from her curls to her soft cheek. As he stroked her lip with his thumb, she opened her mouth and bit him. Hard.

"Show me again."

"Show you what?" he demanded, rearing back on his heels to nurse his throbbing thumb, although the sensuous attack had served to arouse him again.

"How you're going to tame this fearsome shrew you married."

Connor laughed as he caught her to him. And easily, triumphantly, he obliged her.

Chapter Fifteen

Gemma was stiff and sore when she opened her eyes the next morning. Every muscle in her body seemed to ache, and her lips felt swollen from Connor's kisses. But for once she was uncaring of her pain. After all, how could she have escaped with less after a night of love-making with such a passionate man?

She smiled, and lay in the loft savoring the languor that weighted her limbs while trying to remember when she had ever felt so deeply alive, and so aware of her own body. Last night Connor had shown her what it meant to be a woman, and she felt the heat rise on her face as she remembered how eagerly she had welcomed his tutoring.

Closing her eyes, she relived every exquisite moment. To her disappointment, she found that some of it was little more than a shimmering blur. How, for example, had she ended up here in the loft? Had Connor carried her or had she climbed the ladder herself? Had he laid her down amid the blankets or had she pulled him down beside her? She couldn't remember. She knew only what had come after, the way he had loved her, again and yet again.

She lay quiet beneath the heavy eiderdown, wrapped in a warmth that went beyond anything physical. But slowly, inevitably, she became aware of things beyond her dreamy musings. She felt the chill of the early morning air and smelled the smoky remnants of last night's fire and the goose they had eaten. And now she could hear a steady chop, chop, chop from somewhere beyond the walls of the house.

Yesterday, while cleaning the loft, she had discovered a chink in the crumbling stones near her bed. Taking down the framed sampler with which she had covered it, she put her eye to the hole and peered outside. She saw that the dawn had come in a wash of silvery light. The moor sparkled with frost, and she could just make out Connor digging in the earth below her. Despite the cold, he had taken off his shirt and was working in nothing more than his breeches. Sweat gleamed on his back, and she could see the muscles bulging as he worked the rocky ground.

She watched his dark head bend to his task and felt a possessive ache deep in her heart. She had never had anyone to call her own before, but now she had Connor, and suddenly, for the first time ever, it no longered mattered what sort of man he was.

Was she in love with him? She didn't know. She had never known what it felt like to love anyone. But the feeling in her heart warmed her through and through, making her laugh aloud and feel outrageously silly and gay. She raced to wash herself and dress so that she could be outside, with him.

But by the time she descended the ladder he had already come back indoors. They met in the middle of the cluttered room, and for a long moment they looked at each other without speaking. Her heart filled with anticipation while Connor's darkly handsome face appeared calm.

Say something, her heart urged, only she didn't know what. She swallowed hard while an edgy silence fell between them.

"You've been working," Gemma said, finally breaking the awkward moment.

"Aye. Cutting peat." Connor was relieved. He couldn't for the life of him remember a more uncomfortable morning after. God knows, there'd been enough of those during his lively bachelorhood, but somehow it was terribly important to say the right thing, to keep from destroying the bond that he and Gemma had tentatively forged last night. It was not a situation to which he was accustomed. For the first time in his life, he felt clumsy and out of his depth.

Peat was a safe enough topic, and he seized it like a drowning man might a spar in heavy seas. " 'Twill take a few days to dry," he explained, bending over the washbasin to rinse his hands. Maybe more, but how on earth would he know? He'd never had to keep himself warm in such a primitive fashion.

"In the meantime we can burn what's left of the furniture. I'm going to try to put by enough for the winter, but it will take time." He thought about how long it had taken him to dig the trench behind the cottage in a neat square from which he had cut slabs of earth and stacked them near the stone stall that housed their pony.

"But the soil here is rich in rotting matter," he added, turning to see her cross to the door and peer outside. "And when it's dried and compacted it burns for hours. One of my crof—eh—a neighbor of mine showed me how it's done."

Thankfully, Gemma didn't catch his slip of the tongue.

"Connor—" She whirled unexpectedly to face him.

Come to me, Gemma. Touch me, he thought, although he didn't dare ask as much aloud. He burned with indecision. Gemma had loathed him for so long, and he had treated her so badly that he couldn't possibly hope for so simple a reconciliation. Last night had been different; she'd been exhausted and therefore vulnerable. That towering pride of hers, that impressive force of will, couldn't have been breached so easily in the harsh light of day.

Uncertain, he gazed into her wide green eyes. "Are you hungry?" he asked, feeling as stupid and awkward as an untried schoolboy for posing such an obviously contrived question.

"A little."

"I've some fish on the fire. Caught fresh before the sun came up."

Gemma hadn't even noticed, but the thought of food was a good one to cling to since it gave her something else to dwell on other than Connor, who towered over her like a half-naked god, his black hair tousled, his blue eyes burning into hers in a way that made her shiver. She busied herself setting the table while he finished washing up.

He took the fish from the fire while she went outside to fetch drinking water from the spring. By the time she returned, he had pulled on his wool sweater and was

195

dividing the filets between them. She was secretly relieved that he had dressed, for she felt rattled and terribly out of her depth trying to talk to him, and to behave as though nothing were amiss, while his bronzed chest paraded temptingly before her eyes.

The familiar ritual of eating also helped soothe her battered nerves. She forgot her doubts and wants and yearnings and discovered that her appetite was more keen than it had ever been. Was it the delicious fish, or the sharp mountain air, or the contentment of a woman who had been shamelessly well loved the night before?

The thought brought a warmth to her cheeks. For the first time she dared steal a glance at Connor. She found him watching her across the small table, and something stirred in her heart as her eyes met his. She searched frantically for something to say that would distance them from the compelling pull of intimacy.

"I've been meaning to ask you about my jewels."

His head came up. "Oh?"

"I couldn't find them when I unpacked yesterday. Have you seen them? They were in a casket about so big"—she made a shape with her hands—"that had a padlock and a key. I hope they weren't left behind."

"I'm afraid they're gone, Gemma."

She smiled at him, not understanding. "They're what?"

"I used them to pay Mrs. Kennerly for our stay in Stirling, and the doctor for your care. And I used a lot more of them to purchase this croft from its former owner. The transaction was handled when I rode to Inverness while you were ill. We had nowhere else to stay the winter, you see. My cousin Eachern promised to keep the rest in safekeeping until—"

She jumped up, knocking her stool over backwards.

"Damn you to hell, MacEowan! You had no right!"

"Gemma—"

"You had no right to take them!" she shrieked, enraged. "You could have used anything else I owned, anything! Why not the silver or the taspestries or the oils? Those jewels were worth thousands more than you paid for this stinking fox's lair! Obviously you let yourself be taken because you didn't have a clue as to their worth, did you? And do you know why? Because you're ignorant! Ignorant and lowborn and dumb! I—I hate you, you bloody pauper!"

Throbbing with anger, she quickly went up to the loft and threw herself onto the bed, bursting into tears.

Below her the cottage door slammed.

It was amazing how much work a man could accomplish when fury whipped him on. Throughout the long morning and into the afternoon Connor cut peat. Sweat poured from him and his back and shoulders ached, yet still he wielded the shovel and the pick, which he had rescued earlier from the debris Gemma had piled outside the cottage door. Twice he had to stop and repair the handles, not knowing—or caring—whether it was the rotten wood or the rage with which he wielded the tools that splintered them in two.

After the peat had been stacked in a wall as high and long as the one surrounding the croft, he set to work on the roof and chimney. Stones were dragged from the loch shore, thatch cut from the gorse in the neglected field, and a rough-and-ready cement was made with river sand and clay. By now the bleak sun was high overhead and he was weakened with hunger. But still he hammered and sawed and spackled. Fury drove him like a madman, a fury unabated as the hours dragged by and still the image of Gemma's wounded eyes continued to haunt him. God, how he hated her!

She was proud and selfish and insufferably spoiled. He should have known she was rotten to the core the moment he saw the wealth and privilege that surrounded her in Derbyshire. Oh, the signs of corruption had been evident: a defiant hoyden riding out without a groom, disobeying orders, showing her elders and ostensibly her numerous suitors no respect, keeping her long-suffering uncle and his household dancing to her every whim.

Oh, aye, he knew her kind well enough! Sir Archibald had assured him that her fortune—which was still drawing interest in a Derbyshire bank—could buy ten times more jewelry than the tawdry necklaces, rings, and bracelets he had found in that casket! So why make such an ungodly fuss because those few fripperies were gone? Why not go out and simply buy some more?

Lowborn, uneducated pauper, was he? Well, she was a spoiled, ill-tempered bitch! Just see if he'd ever set foot in that silly dress-up house of hers again!

But in the end, hunger and thirst proved greater than his despairing anger. And a good measure of his sour mood faded as he stepped back to admire the repairs he had made on the chimney, the roof and walls of the house, and the gate and fence in the pony's yard. While he worked long hours in his shipping offices off Queensferry Road and put in equally endless days setting matters to rights as laird of Glenarris, he doubted he had ever worked so hard with his hands on any given day in his life. Strange, how satisfying the sense of accomplishment one got from knowing that the sweat of one's brow alone was responsible for such dramatic changes.

But the glow of pleasure faded the moment he returned to the cottage to find Gemma still huddled on her bed up in the loft. She neither moved nor made a sound, although he was certain she could hear him prowling around. At least her crying had stopped! He had never been able to tolerate a woman's noisy tears.

Several pieces of fish remained in the pan in the hearth. Heating them quickly, he washed them down with water, then grimaced as he wiped his mouth on his sleeve. Faugh! There was nothing worse than old fish for dinner. In fact, he was heartily sick of meat and water as his only food.

"Gemma!" he bellowed, hauling on his bearskin coat. "I'm riding into town for provisions! I'll be back tomorrow!"

"I'm coming with you!" she bellowed back, peering down at him.

His lips thinned as he caught sight of her tear-swollen face. The last thing he wanted was to drag the whining chit to Glenarris, where everyone in the village knew him on sight, and where the ancestral home of the MacEowan lairds brooded high above the river just waiting to be pointed out to her. "No, you're not."

"Why not?"

"Because you can't."

"Why can't I?"

"Because I said so." My, how mature and reasonable *that* sounded! He tried another tack. "You're not strong enough yet."

"Hah! That didn't matter when you dragged me here from Stirling, did it?" she countered furiously.

"I've things to do there, damn it!" he yelled, annoyed. "I can't spend all my time looking after you!"

She smiled down at him archly. "Afraid I'll run away, are you?"

"I may be uneducated," he coldly echoed her previous insult, "but I'm not a fool."

He busied himself with packing his leather satchel. "There's a pole and a gaff down by the loch," he said, not looking up at her. "The water's teeming with fish. You shouldn't have any trouble catching dinner. And breakfast, too."

It's the least she deserves, he thought, feeling her furious gaze burning through him hotly enough to fuse his very bones. Maybe a taste of primitive homesteading will show her there's more in life worth weeping over than a few lost diamonds.

"I'm leaving my pistols here," he told her coldly. "They're both primed. Don't use them unless you absolutely must."

Gemma would have liked to use them on Connor, but the thought of being left alone in this desolate place unnerved her too much even to think about killing him. She saw now that he hadn't been joking when he said he was going off without her. He had put on his coat and slung his bag over his shoulder, and now he was looking up at her with an expression on his darkly handsome face that she couldn't understand.

"Gemma, come down here."

She obeyed, not because he'd asked her in a surprisingly gentle tone, but because she hoped to make him change his mind by appearing amenable herself. But that hope was dashed when she paused before him. There was a grim shade around his mouth as he tipped up her chin with his knuckles.

"I may be gone a few days. You must promise me,

Gemma, on your word as a Baird, not to run away.''

As a Baird? Oh, ho, he was digging deep, wasn't he! Bloody clever of him, to appeal to her sense of honor, well aware that she'd spit in his face if he dared call her a MacEowan! She stared mutinously at him and wrenched her head away.

''For God's sake!'' Connor exploded. ''Don't be a fool! There'll be snow in the upper passes by now, and you won't survive a day on foot.'' His hands came up to take her roughly by the shoulders. ''Gemma, this has nothing to do with my losing your fortune if you go, I swear it. Promise me, for your own sake, that you'll not try to leave.''

He was gripping her shoulders tightly, and his voice was more urgent than she had ever heard it. For an aching moment she allowed herself to pretend that she mattered to him, that he would be sorry if anything happened to her.

Then cold reality asserted itself. Her head snapped up and she wrenched free of his grasp. ''Don't worry about me, MacEowan, I'm not going anywhere! I've only one aim left in life: to make sure that yours is utterly miserable!''

''Fine,'' he ground out. Whirling on his heels, he left, slamming the door behind him.

Through the heavy stone walls she could hear him speaking to the pony and then the cart rumbling off with a crack of the whip. Running to the window, she stood on tiptoe and was aghast to see that he was actually leaving her, just as he'd said he would.

She watched until the slow-moving cart had vanished across the moor, his broad-shouldered form sitting stiffly on the driver's seat.

Not once did he turn his head to look back.

Chapter Sixteen

No sooner had the cart vanished beyond the hills than a sense of desolation swept over Gemma. The little croft that had seemed so cozy the night before was empty now, and much too quiet.

Pulling on her cloak, she fled to the loch. Beneath the cold blue sky the water shimmered, the dark depths made uneasy by the freshening wind. Connor had left a crudely fashioned pole and an evil-looking metal rod with a hooked end—the gaff—tucked in the shelter of a weathered tree. Despite her hunger, she didn't care to use them.

The smooth stones rattled underfoot as she walked along the shore. A recent storm had flung kelp and mussels and driftwood up above the waterline, and she wondered if this sort of flotsam meant that the ocean was near.

Lifting her head, she looked to the west, or where she

imagined the west to be now that the sun was beginning to set. It was unnerving, not knowing where she was, or if there was anyone else to be found for miles. Connor's leaving had left her with a profound sense of her own isolation, and it frightened her a little.

Oh, very well, it frightened her a lot. She didn't like the vast emptiness of the mountains that brooded in the fading half-light all around her. She didn't care for the thought that night was coming on and that she had no one to help keep the darkness at bay. But she wasn't scared of the dark anymore. She wasn't!

Still, she only just managed to keep from breaking into a run on her way back to the cottage. Once inside, she stirred the ashes in the hearth with a stick and was surprised and pleased when they sprang easily to life. Yet her pleasure quickly dissipated as her thoughts returned to Connor. She still felt murderously uncharitable toward him for everything—her pawned jewels, her abandonment, the entire, miserable marriage he had forced upon her.

All of the budding love she had felt toward him last night seemed to be gone, crushed beneath his uncaring heel.

If only she had Helios!

Tears brimmed in her eyes. What she wouldn't give right now to bury her nose in his soft neck and whisper her heartache into his ear! Her beloved colt would have listened calmly, and nuzzled her to show his sympathy. Helios's love for her had never faltered.

As the daylight waned, the cottage grew darker, and she lit one candle after another. There was no bolt on the door, so she slid one of her trunks in front of it and then heaped as many others as she could on top. She knew that she was being silly, and kept reminding herself that she had nothing to fear. There were no wolves in this part of the Highlands (surely Connor would have warned her if there were?), and at the moment she would gladly welcome an entire company of thieves intent on robbing her because then she'd have someone to talk to!

"They'd make better company than Connor," she said out loud. But the sound of her voice echoed strangely in the empty room, and she wondered how so small a cottage could seem so big and unfriendly without him there.

She withdrew to the loft early, before the candles had burned low, and even tried to pull the ladder up behind her, which was utterly ridiculous. There wasn't any room for it, and who on earth was she protecting herself from?

Nevertheless, she slept with both pistols near at hand, and started uneasily as strange birds called throughout the night and the wind soughed mournfully in the eaves.

By morning she was bleary-eyed and understandably crabby. She didn't catch a single fish for breakfast, despite what Connor had said about it being easy to do, and had to content herself with digging for mussels in the icy water and frying them without fat in the pan. As expected, they tasted disgusting, and she wondered fleetingly if Connor hadn't been hoping she'd starve to death while he was gone.

She wouldn't, she vowed. She was too bloody mad at him to die.

And then, that afternoon, her flux began. It was the proverbial last straw. If Connor had been there at that moment, she would have unloaded both pistols into his heart without a second's remorse.

The Enchanted Prince

At least at home in England she had always been able to rest on a daybed when afflicted by the curse, and had worn the demure protection adopted in recent years by ladies of gentle breeding. But here there was only a hard stool to sit on when her cramps began, and itchy rags to stuff between her legs to stanch the bright red flow.

I hate you, Connor MacEowan. I hate you, hate you, hate you! she raged inwardly.

At least she could soothe herself with the knowledge that he hadn't got her with child!

But despite her anger, her hunger, and her misery, she watched for him as the endless day crawled at long last toward darkness. She wasn't looking forward to another night alone, and even Connor's company would have been welcome at this point. But every time she peeped hopefully from the window, she found the dark moor as empty as before.

Damn his blasted hide, she missed him! Try as she might, she couldn't rekindle her earlier anger toward him at all. Not that she didn't try by deliberately recalling to mind every awful, unpardonable thing he had ever done to her. Especially selling off her jewels. She would never be able to forgive him for that. Never! He could have taken anything else she owned to buy this horrid place, anything!

Not that her jewels had been of exceptional quality, even though she had been correct in claiming they were worth far more than the ramshackle croft Connor had purchased. Their value to her lay solely in that they had once belonged to her mother.

She had few memories of her parents and understandably treasured every one of them, even though they were often little better than vague impressions of warmth and kindness. Sometimes, when the veils of time lifted momentarily, she could recall clearly the last time she'd seen them, on the morning of their departure for France. She could not remember the reason for their going, for her aunt and uncle had never troubled to answer her questions while she was growing up, but she could remember clearly waiting to bid them farewell in her nursery in the enormous house her father had owned somewhere in the lush green countryside of Kent.

She could easily recall the massive ceilings and the lovely scrolled paneling of her playroom, and the beautiful little bed with the satin coverlet and hand-stitched netting in the bedchamber beyond. Her nanny had been loving and kind, although nowadays Gemma could conjure up neither the woman's face nor her name.

But she had not been as kind as Gemma's mama. No one else in her lonely life before or since had ever come close.

Regrettably, a catalog of features was all that the years had preserved of the woman who had been Annabelle Baird; a pale, tired, but very sweet face with eyes as green as her own. A musical voice and soft, caressing hands, hands that had been shaking a little on the morning of her departure as Annabelle pulled Gemma onto her lap and presented her with a pretty casket. Gemma, gasping, had opened it revealing a shimmering treasure. The scene of that long-ago morning came vividly to her mind.

"You're not old enough to wear them yet," Annabelle had said, while Gemma reverently touched the emeralds, diamonds, and pearls on the blue velvet lining. "But when I return you shall be."

"I'm almost six," she remembered insisting.

"And soon you shall be seven, quite a young lady. And ready to wear all your mama's pretty things without losing them, won't you?"

"Promise," Gemma had said solemnly, for even at so tender an age she was self-assured.

Annabelle had smiled, though the smile hadn't seemed like a happy one to Gemma. She had wanted to ask her mother why she seemed so sad, but a blond gentleman had appeared in the nursery door.

"Oh, George," Mama had said a little breathlessly, "can't we take her with us?"

"Now, Annabelle," Gemma's father had chided in that gruffly tender way he always used when speaking to her mother. "You'll never regain your health if you don't rest, and there's no rest with that child underfoot."

But he, too, had looked lovingly at Gemma as he spoke, and she had preened beneath his gaze. Gemma had never doubted that her father adored her, even when he had started seeming so sad. She had never really understood the cause of his sadness, but she had suspected that it had something to do with her mother's illness, which had begun after Gemma's infant brother arrived and then disappeared, under mysterious circumstances, before Gemma had even been permitted to see him.

"Take care of your jewels, my own dear jewel, my darling little gem," Mama had whispered, her voice breaking, and Gemma had thrown herself into those thin, loving arms with her usual boundless enthusiasm.

"There, you see?" her father had said as her mother rocked a little beneath the onslaught of Gemma's clinging body. "Time to go, love, or we'll miss the packet."

But they hadn't missed it, which was why they had drowned, and why Gemma had been whisked away by her whey-faced Aunt Druscilla to the emptiness of the Derbyshire countryside and the colorless lives led by the dull, humorless Bairds.

But she had kept her promise to her mother by holding tightly to her jewels, safeguarding the casket with stubborn determination for many months before a maid discovered the jewels in their hiding place beneath the windowseat. She had whisked them away while Gemma had clung, screaming and struggling, to her skirts.

From that day forward the casket had remained under Aunt Druscilla's stern care, and Gemma had not succeeded in persuading her to give the jewels back. In fact, she had not seen them for more than a decade after they were confiscated—not until Uncle Archibald had turned the casket over to Connor, who in turn had sold the treasured contents for a patch of useless land.

But somehow the appalling thought no longer angered her as she brooded alone in front of the window of the ill-gotten croft. She felt only a deep sense of loss, and a sudden, intense longing for the love and safety that had surrounded her when her parents had been alive. And which, though she wouldn't dare bring herself to admit as much aloud, she had recaptured in some measure in Connor's arms the other night.

The thought of him stirred her from her lethargy as the loss of her parents and her jewels had failed to do. Cursed longshanks! Where was he? He had said he'd be gone two days, and now—

Sudden anxiety stabbed at her. Suppose something had happened to him? Suppose he'd met with some sort of accident on the road home? Her frightened imagination immediately presented her with a number of nasty possibilities: a fall from the cart, a tumble down the mountainside, an encounter with thieves or wolves or bears . . . Were there bears in Scotland?

"I've got to go out and look for him!" she cried, as though speaking to someone in the room with her.

But the thought filled her with terror. She had no desire to brave the desolate mountains with nothing more than a torch to dispel the darkness. On the other hand, if something had happened to Connor—

"Oh, bloody hell!" Scrambling into her boots and cloak, she crossed to the door and threw it open. She was brought up short by the impenetrable darkness outside. Sweet Jesu! Why did it have to be so cursed black?

Looking around, she realized that she didn't have anything to use as a torch. A piece of wood would burn too quickly, and the uncured peat not at all. She had a sudden, absurd image of stumbling across the moor carrying a big, smoking lump of peat that did nothing to disperse the darkness.

She laughed, but the sound was strained, and in the end she took only Connor's pistols. They were much heavier than she had imagined, and she had to tuck one of them into the folds of her cloak and the other into her left bootleg because they made her wrists ache when she tried carrying them.

Regrettably, they gave her only a small sense of comfort, for it was the darkness she feared and not what might be lurking abroad at night. For a long moment she lingered just beyond the door, breathing deeply and calmly before setting off.

But she had taken no more than half a dozen steps when the faint creaking of leather came to her on the wind. Freezing in mid-stride, she caught her breath on a crazy mix of hope and fear.

Her eyes strained through the darkness for a glimpse of what she most longed to see.

Connor saw her, silhouetted against the squares of light falling from the windows of the cottage. He had managed to approach stealthily to the outer wall of the tiny property, owing to the spongy moor grass that muffled the pony's hooves, and the fact that he had repaired and oiled the cart wheels before loading up and leaving Glenarris. Now he drew hard on the reins and halted the pony nearly on top of her.

"What the devil are you doing out here?" he cracked. His voice was sharp because he had just noticed the pistols tucked into her cloak and the top of her boot.

He vaulted to the ground and strode toward her.

"I thought I heard a noise," she informed him, sounding cool. "I was coming out to investigate."

He halted before her, his face in the shadows. "Bristling with weapons?"

She said quellingly, "I had no idea what I might find. You never told me if there were wolves or bears on the moors."

"There aren't," he said, and was glad that Gemma couldn't see his face, because he was having a devil of a time keeping a grin off it. Liar! She'd not been worried about wolves or bears.

But he knew better than to pry an explanation from her, so he let the matter drop. Nevertheless, it didn't surprise him in the least when he turned back to the cart and found her dogging his steps as though reluctant to let him out of her sight.

Indeed, she followed him like a puppy, first to the front of the cart to unbuckle the reins and then to the pony's head to loosen the traces, and finally to the pen where she waited in silence while he rubbed down the weary animal before turning it loose. She trailed him as he made his way back to the cart, which stood in the front yard illuminated by the dim glow of the cottage lights.

"Miss me?" he asked conversationally.

"Certainly not!"

But Gemma was so close to him, that her nose bumped his back when he stopped abruptly.

"I think you did."

"I think you're mad." Her words fell like frigid icicles from her sweetly lying lips.

He couldn't help bursting into laughter.

"Stop laughing, MacEowan! It isn't funny!"

Still laughing, he began to rummage through the cart, which was loaded down with provisions. She kept close to him and when she bumped into him again, he turned to look down at her, his eyebrows arched.

"I thought you said you didn't miss me?"

"I didn't!" Gemma insisted, but she was standing so near that he could feel the warmth rising from her body. He pretended to busy himself with something inside the cart.

"It's just that . . ."

"What?" he prompted, but she didn't answer him.

"Gemma, what the devil's the matter with you?" he demanded. Whirling to face her, he bumped into her and sent her staggering. Catching her quickly, he pulled her toward him to keep her from falling.

"What is it?" he persisted huskily, drawing her closer so that his booted legs became tangled in the folds of her cloak.

"Nothing," Gemma mumbled, scarlet cheeked.

He refused to relent. He was enjoying himself too much. "Are you certain you didn't miss me?"

"N-no! I was just. . . . It was so *boring* here alone!"

"Then you must have missed me. Why else would you be bored unless you needed me here to provoke you?"

"That's utter gibberish!" she snapped, but she didn't sound angry.

"And I missed you," he added in a deliberately teasing voice so that she wouldn't suspect how deeply he spoke the truth.

Looking down into her tilted green eyes, whose memory had been haunting his every waking moment during the last two days, he was suddenly grateful for the presence of the pistol butt in her pocket, for it kept their bodies from meshing completely and letting her feel the intimate proof of just how badly he *had* missed her.

He struggled with the desire to fold her in his arms, to feel the warmth and the welcome of her kisses, then sweep her against him and carry her up to the loft for a night of unbridled loving. He'd been imagining the pleasure for hours on end as he wended his weary way homeward through the cold, and denying the worry that nibbled relentlessly at the edges of his mind that something had happened to her while he was gone.

Eachern had been so convinced that it had been a mistake leaving Gemma behind and that she had run away the moment Connor's back was turned, that Connor had come to believe as much himself. Never had he burned with such impatience to leave Glenarris, even though there had been so many pressing issues to settle—and not just gathering winter provisions and repairing the pony cart's damaged wheels.

Two full days had elapsed while Connor tended his long-neglected estate. He had worked long into the night dealing with accountings and ledgers, piles of bills and correspondence, myriad problems with his staff and tenants, and authorizing repairs and purchases and attending to hundreds of other maddening details. But by the end of the second day he had had enough. It was more than time to return home to Gemma.

"Wait until morning," Eachern had pleaded, for the sun had already slid below the hills and a chilly night wind had risen. "Ye'll get lost in the dark."

"I know the way," Connor had insisted.

" 'Twill be freezing i' the passes by now."

"I've got a coat."

"That nag of yours'll break its legs. Wait until light!"

"I don't intend to push him hard."

But of course Connor had, and he still couldn't quite credit the relief that had washed over him when the cart had cleared the last rise in the road, and across the dark moor he had seen the croft lights twinkling. So Gemma had kept her word and not tried to leave! Until that moment he hadn't really believed she would . . .

"MacEowan?"

He looked down at her as if starting from a dream, a delicious dream of seductive softness and warmth. "Aye?"

"You're hurting me."

Only then did he become aware that he was still holding her hard against him, his hands at her waist, the pistol crushed between them. Forcing a light laugh, he released her.

"I hope you brought me something to eat," she told

him in that nasty tone of voice that he had come to know so well.

"Aye," he retorted in the same tone, hiding his true feelings.

"Good things, MacEowan, not sheep stomachs or pig brains."

"For God's sake, lass, I know better than that."

I'm too tired to go on fighting tonight, he thought, aching. God, Gemma, can't you tell how much I missed you?

They stood facing each other across the width of the cart, Gemma with her chin tipped haughtily, Connor feeling tired and drained.

Just then a piteous whimper came from deep amid the sacks in the back of the cart.

"What was that?" Gemma asked, her head swinging toward the cart.

The tension eased from his body. "What was what?" he inquired, propping his arm against the wheel.

"Mmmm, mmmm, mmmm," came the pitiful sound again.

"It's an animal, isn't it?" she guessed. "Like a dog or . . . or . . ."

"Ah, yes," he said, straightening quickly to hide his grin. "I almost forgot. Eachern sent something for you."

"For me? What is it? MacEowan! Show me!"

He reached into the cart, feeling the same eagerness that had gripped him when he had presented her with the tin of chocolates the other night. The anticipation in her voice was impossible to resist, as was the expression of wonder on her face when he turned to lay the wiggling, whining bundle of black and white fur into her arms.

"A puppy! Oh, MacEowan, look. It's so tiny. What kind is it?"

"Some sort of terrier, I think," he replied, watching her, not the dog. "Eachern breeds them, but I can't for the life of me remember what he calls them."

They were hideously high-strung, yappy little things, and since Connor's tastes ran more to coursing breeds like the graceful deerhounds he kept kenneled at Glenarris, he had been dead set against Eachern giving this squirming whelp to Gemma. But seeing the rapt look that had crept over her face, he was suddenly glad he'd agreed to it.

She laid her cheek against the puppy's straining little body, and he felt an astonishing stab of envy at the way she crooned to it softly, in a tone she had never directed toward him. To cover his feelings he turned back to the cart, and although he was exhausted and had intended to unload the supplies in the morning, he began doing so now.

"You'll be glad to know I've brought plenty to eat," he told her over his shoulder. "Oats and cheese, cured ham and treacle, some brandy, eggs, and honey. I thought about bringing chickens, but I didn't think you'd appreciate having them roosting in our rafters."

He expected a lighthearted laugh in response to his teasing, but was rewarded with silence. Turning, he saw that Gemma hadn't heard him. She had started back toward the house, kissing and caressing that nasty little creature and cooing to it in a thoroughly disgusting manner.

He slumped against the wagon, defeated and knowing it. Women! For years now he had prided himself on understanding them, but that was before this wholly unpredictable brat had come into his life.

Chapter Seventeen

By the time Connor had finished unloading the last of the provisions and stacked them in a corner of the cottage to be unpacked in the morning, two things were immediately clear about Gemma's new puppy. One was the fact that it was not housebroken, which became apparent when wet circles and worse appeared in the middle of Gemma's fine Aubusson carpet.

The other equally disagreeable fact as far as Connor was concerned was the realization that the whiney little animal had taken an immediate and intense dislike to him. There was not one spot on his ankles that hadn't been mauled. Once or twice, when Gemma wasn't looking, he'd sent the savage creature tumbling backward with a violent shake of his leg. But the dog was a terrier, and so extremely stubborn, and a moment later it was back, yapping and snarling and growling at his boot heel.

Now as he stood looking down at the noisy cur, Gemma announced she was retiring and taking the dog to bed with her. She scooped the disgusting thing into her arms and it immediately reverted from a monster into an angel, contorting its body to lick her face and hands.

This was far more intolerable to him than the animal's other offenses and he protested vehemently.

"You're not welcome up there anyway," she informed him huffily, and without a trace of embarrassment added, "I'm having female troubles and I need my privacy."

Astonished, he said nothing as she ascended the ladder. He understood immediately what she meant, but could scarcely credit the calm way in which she had informed him of such an intensely personal matter. Was this the same woman who had nearly had the vapors when he'd undressed and washed himself for her benefit in the shepherd's hut so long ago? Or turned scarlet with shame when he so much as mentioned "underwear" or "lovemaking" or some equally forbidden thing?

Lovemaking . . .

His thoughts checked abruptly as he realized the implications of Gemma's statement. Bloody hell! How long did that mean he'd have to keep his hands off her? Three days? Four? Intolerable! He doubted he could wait even a few hours because he'd been thinking of little else since leaving for Glenarris, and anticipating nothing better during the long hours marking his return.

He had never thought that Gemma would be unwilling to accommodate him upon his return.

His heart softened at the memory of having loved her throughout that long, enchanted night before he'd left. He exulted, too, in the fact that Gemma had been so happy to see him upon his return. Oh, aye, she'd tried damned hard to hide it, but he was beginning to know the minx very well indeed. Her stammering and blushing and the way she'd stuck to him like glue while he unloaded the cart had told him that all those vehement denials falling from her lovely lips had been lies.

But now? Now, by God, he found himself tossed out on his ear in favor of a dog!

On the other hand, Gemma hadn't said anything about his not being welcome in her bed *after* her troubles were over, had she?

He hummed as he made a bed on the floor directly below the loft. Above him he could hear her moving around, and spent some time picturing her undressing in that narrow, cozy space. She was probably putting on one of those high-necked nightgowns designed to protect her modesty. But he already knew far too well what heart-stopping delights were hidden beneath that virginal attire.

Washed, undressed, and still lamentably aroused, he extinguished the last candle and crawled into bed. Gemma, too, had blown hers out, and now the cottage was plunged into a very black, very intimate darkness. Directly above him he could hear the clicking of the terrier's nails on the boards and then the unmistakable rustle of linens followed by a muffled giggle. His mouth thinned. He had no doubt that that four-legged monster was at this very moment cuddled up in the warm, curving spot that he himself yearned to occupy.

Flipping over onto his back, he closed his eyes and steeled himself for a sleepless night. But he had pushed himself far too relentlessly for the past two days, and in no time at all the ache for Gemma was replaced by the lassitude of weariness. His restless tossing ceased and after a while his breathing grew deep and even.

In the loft above, Gemma listened to Connor sleep, and was reassured. The fears that had gripped her during his absence had been reduced to absurdity the moment of his return. Once again the cottage was filled with cozy warmth, not emptiness. Turning onto her side, she pressed her cheek into the puppy's soft fur, glad for its company. Never mind that deep inside she would have preferred Connor's broad back to sleep against. At least he had returned to her unharmed, and she needed only to remind herself that he was there below her to drift easily into an untroubled sleep herself.

Connor was awakened by something warm and wet trickling down his bare heel, which rested on the floor outside the blankets. Prying open his heavy eyelids, he was groggily aware of a black and white blur squatting on the floor next to his bed. The warmth spread, becoming deeper and wetter, and with a howl he jumped up. Leaping around the growing puddle of pee, he snatched the puppy into his arms and tossed it outside. Cursing, he raced to pull his bedding to safety.

The sound of soft laughter brought him up short. Looking up, he found Gemma's curly head peeking down from the loft above.

"I'll give you a week to housebreak that thing," Connor growled, doing his best to sound dire. But it was difficult to appear threatening when Gemma looked so enchanting tousled with sleep and with her green eyes dancing.

"And if I don't?" she countered cheekily.

"We'll have a barbecue."

She shook her head in mock disgust. "Really! I know

you Scots keep a barbaric cuisine, but I never dreamed you'd stoop so low as to eat your own pets.''

"That, my dear girl, is not a pet. It's an abomination.''

Indeed, the abomination was already scratching at the door and whining piteously.

"Will you let him in?'' she asked sweetly.

"No. I have to mop up puppy urine and wash my feet.''

"Please?'' She raised her voice a little to be heard over the howling that had replaced the whine. "Pope is probably starving and I—''

"Who?''

"Pope.''

"Pope!'' He was incredulous. "What sort of daft name is that?''

"A very good one!''

"But your uncle told me you were Church of England!''

She burst into laughter. "We are! I was talking about the poet, not that fellow in the Vatican.''

"Alexander Pope?''

"Why, yes.''

Gemma regarded him suspiciously while he frowned. "How do you know Alexander Pope?'' they both asked in the same breath.

No young lady raised in a world as privileged as Gemma's could possibly have taken time from her piano lessons, her painting, embroidery, her rounds of parties and hunt balls and dinners to open a book of poems, let alone one of Pope's caliber, Connor thought. Pope's lengthy essays, and especially his pointed writings as a satirist, were not the stuff one would expect to interest a gently

220

bred girl. He also hoped she would not question his knowledge of poetry.

"Pope," he said again, not quite believing that Gemma had a grasp of more than the man's name. "Why Pope?"

Her eyes danced with amusement. "Isn't it obvious? He spent most of his life when he wasn't translating Greek ridiculing critics and other writers, and especially making fun of the king. I rather see *my* Pope shredding your ego in much the same way."

Which meant that she had known all along about Pope's nips last night at his ankles! Looking up into her smiling eyes, he burst into uproarious laughter. Oh, Lord, there was no woman like her.

Gemma, fully dressed, came sliding with childish enthusiasm down the ladder, her skirts hitched out of the way, which gave him a tempting view of *her* ankles.

Crossing to the door, she froze unexpectedly. "Good Lord," she said, startled, "where did you get that?"

He looked around, confused. "What?"

"That eiderdown."

"Hanging over the chair? I slept on it last night. Your abominable Pope almost ruined it just now."

Gemma fingered the plump bedding. "It's German, isn't it?"

Yes, it was, but he didn't intend to say so. German goosedown was expensive: twice the yearly income, and more, of a typical Scottish crofter. He'd retrieved several from Glenarris for use in the cottage without stopping to think that she might recognize them. "They may be German," he acknowledged vaguely. "I don't know." Then inspiration struck him. "I borrowed them from Eachern."

"Helios!" Gemma said breathlessly. "Did you see him?"

"Aye," he lied, for the colt was actually in Edinburgh, not at Glenarris. "Getting fat on oats and flirting with Eachern's mare. Eachern thought you might be lonely without him. That's why he sent the dog."

He watched her face soften and knew an uncharacteristic pang of jealousy. It was obvious that she thought more highly of his cousin than she did of him. They'd suit each other well enough, he thought nastily, both being young and not yet jaded, and equally pretty to look at.

Angered, he snatched up the water bucket and slammed outside.

Gemma stared after him, exasperated. Ooh! He was the most unpredictable person she'd ever met! What on earth had set him off this time?

Turning to the crates he had unloaded last night, she began unpacking the contents onto the shelves he had installed on that awful day when he'd been so angry with her. There were a number of sacks and tins obviously containing foodstuffs, but most of them baffled her completely. What were these, for instance? Some sort of bean, dried and hard as loch pebbles. And this pasty white stuff? She held it to her nose and sniffed. Ugh! Cooking fat? Lard? And these gray, crumbly things that months ago might have been cabbage leaves—what on earth were they?

The door opened and Connor came in. Crossing to the fire, he stirred the embers and set the water on to boil while Gemma surreptitiously removed the strange gray pellets from sight.

"Well," he said, looking expectantly at her, "what's for breakfast?"

She would rather die than admit she hadn't the vaguest idea what half these foodstuffs were, let alone how to cook them. But for the time being she could serve the perishables he had brought: the eggs, cheeses, cured meat, and oatbread. Hopefully, she could persuade him to go hunting for their supper, which should buy her a bit more time to acquaint herself with the mysteries of her kitchen.

Neither Connor nor Gemma seemed to find anything ironic about that first real breakfast they shared in their run-down old cottage. Surrounded by opulent carpets, tapestries, and works of art, they breakfasted off exquisite Royal Worcester china and with beautifully wrought silverware. To Gemma, who had eaten nothing save gamebirds and fish for three days, the crusty oatbread, cheese, cured meat, and butter and marmalade tasted heavenly indeed.

But by noon, Connor, who had been cutting peat on the moors all morning and building a winter shelter for the shaggy pony, was hungry again and wanting to be fed.

"What are we having to eat, lass?" he bellowed through the window in a tone that should have left her bristling but filled her instead with panic. What on earth was she supposed to do now?

She pawed frantically through the provisions. What did one normally serve at dinnertime? Visions of meals she had eaten back home rose tantalizingly before her: delicate soups, tender meats, vegetables picked fresh from the winter garden and prepared in a number of ambitious ways by Uncle Archibald's London-trained chef.

Soup would be nice, she thought hopefully. How did one make it? With stock, wasn't it? But she didn't have a soup bone, and no potatoes or carrots to help make it hearty. She didn't think Connor would be satisfied with a watery broth.

In the end, driven by desperation, she made porridge, if only because she did possess a vague idea as to how it was done. When the water in the hearth began to boil, she poured in the oats and stirred them vigorously with a long spoon. The concoction began to bubble and thicken, and she removed it quickly from the fire. After setting the table, she invited Connor inside with the pride of a Mayfair hostess summoning her guests to supper.

Connor washed up in the corner, as she tried to ladle the porridge into bowls. But the spoon wouldn't budge from the pot. It—it seemed to be stuck—!

"Well, well," Connor said heartily, scraping back his chair and sitting down. "Porridge. Backbone of the Scottish kitchen."

She tried her best to unobtrusively wrestle the spoon out of the cloying stuff, but the more the porridge cooled, the more it solidified. She began to panic, convinced it would soon become mortar. With a mighty heave she pulled the spoon free, but it came slowly and with an obscene sucking noise. Her wrist aching beneath the weight of the huge gray clot clinging to the spoon, she banged it on the side of Connor's bowl. The porridge plopped with a crash, and she and Connor looked to see if the bowl had shattered.

His amused blue eyes swept up to her face. " 'Twill certainly stick to the ribs," he observed.

"It—it was fine when I took it from the fire."

Connor rose slowly to his feet. "No harm done. We'll just add a wee spot of hot water."

And sure enough, she noted, with a bit of stirring, the porridge was rendered edible again.

They ate in silence, and Gemma wondered dismally how on earth she was going to prepare three meals a day for the rest of her life when she hadn't a clue how to cook.

Finally Connor finished the last few lumps in his bowl, and then patted his belly with every evidence of being well sated.

"Mmm. You did well, lass. I'm looking forward to supper."

She glanced at him sharply. Was he making fun of her? But Connor was a master of guile, and she couldn't read an untoward thing in his blandly smiling face. His mention of the next meal also served to divert her to a more pressing matter. What was she supposed to offer him for supper? She couldn't serve porridge again, but she had no idea how to prepare anything else. How could she? Never in her life had she spent more than a few moments in the Baird kitchen, and then only to steal a pinch of baker's chocolate or a piece of pastry from the dough board while dodging the Bairds' chef's irately brandished spoon.

Watching Gemma's shoulders sag, Connor felt his chest constrict with sympathy. He had only to look at the clumpy remains of the porridge in the pot to know what was troubling her. Poor, wee Gemma! Undefeated by highwaymen, an uncaring uncle, an opportunist of a husband and the harsh life of a Highland croft, she was laid low by that most historically female of all institutions—the cooking fire.

His cramping stomach reminded him of Mrs. Sutcliffe, the Glenarris cook, who had plied him with countless tempting dishes during his brief stay at the castle. And of Pierre Pous, the effeminate but immensely talented Frenchman Connor had brought back from Paris years ago and who had spoiled him with superb Continental cuisine ever since.

His hunger pangs warned that his own best interest lay in educating the girl in at least the rudimentary aspects of cooking, since he had no idea how long he would have to endure her meals before Eachern and the others allowed him to come home. While he was by no means an accomplished cook, he'd camped out often enough to understand the basic principles of throwing together a simple, edible meal. Since Mrs. Sutcliffe had drawn up the list of supplies he had brought back to the croft, he was certain that they contained the makings of the same hearty fare for which his Glenarris cook was revered. Surely he and Gemma could work through this very important aspect of their lives.

Their health, he thought wryly, might well depend on it.

Chapter Eighteen

And so began a strangely satisfying time in their troubled relationship. Forced together by necessity, and for once in agreement about what they hoped to accomplish, Connor and Gemma put aside their differences long enough to teach themselves—and each other—the rudiments of cooking.

For several days the peat fire was kept hot and the cramped cottage littered with the detritus of experimental menus. At first the results were largely inedible, and the dog spent most of the time cowering under the table as black smoke from some burnt offering, or objectionable fumes from yet another failed experiment, billowed into the air. But within a surprisingly short time those noxious odors became welcoming ones, and the once cowed puppy quickly returned to savaging Connor's ankles again.

They were surprised and pleased to discover a mutual

interest in cooking. Neither of them would have dreamed, back home in Edinburgh or in the Baird mansion in Derbyshire, that they would ever be forced to stoop to something as menial as meal preparation. But once the task was mastered it became an unexpectedly enjoyable one. There was no denying that they worked well together, and that they greatly enjoyed doing so.

Game was plentiful on the moor, and Connor was an excellent shot. Partridge, grouse, and waterfowl fell beneath his careful aim and were deliciously dispatched.

After having established a newfound truce with Gemma, Connor decided that venison should be added to their meals and as a result, he had been stalking a deer since dawn. There had been a hard frost the night before and the spoor was easy to follow. By the time the sun lifted clear of the mountain peaks, he was within range behind an outcropping of rocks and managed to squeeze off a shot.

When the deer fell, he laid aside his weapon and prepared to dress it. Only then did he realize that he had stupidly left his knife back at the cottage. Rather than leaving the deer where it was and going back for the knife, he slung the carcass over his shoulders and carried it down the mountainside.

He was hunkered down on the ground near the spring that bubbled from the earth just behind the cottage, elbow deep in blood and trailing organs, when Gemma found him.

"Come here, lass," he called cheerfully as he caught sight of her. "I'll teach you how to *gralloch*. That's the way a Highland Gael dresses a deer. You—"

But Gemma backed away, whitefaced, her eyes glued to the grass strewn with entrails and blood. Whirling, she started to run, then stumbled and went down on her knees and was sick.

It was the first time he had seen Gemma ill since that awful night on the moor near Bathgate. Although her worrisome cough had improved markedly, he had not forgotten the nightmare of her illness and the fear for her that had driven him like a man possessed to save her. He was beside her in an instant, desperate to offer comfort with his touch, but content to murmur soothing words because of the blood on his hands.

But he realized that his nearness brought no comfort when Gemma hunched over and retched again.

"Gemma, lass—"

"Go away," she told him feebly.

"Gemma—"

"Go away! M-murderer!"

He winced. He had not heard her speak that way for quite some time. Filled with helpless anger, he watched her totter back to the cottage where she was met by Pope, who pawed happily at her skirts. Scooping him up against her breast, she vanished inside.

Grimly he returned to his gory work. Damn the lass! Why did she have to choose something like this to be faint-hearted about? Properly cured and salted, the venison would last for weeks! Oh, aye, it had been a magnificent animal, tall and sporting a splendid rack, but its untimely death paled beside the necessity of having to eat to survive.

Worried that their tentative peace had been shattered, he nevertheless took great care to finish the job properly. He quartered the meat and scraped the hide and buried the offal well away from the croft so as not to attract marauding animals. Then he scrubbed himself with sand from the stream to remove every trace of blood, and washed his shirt and breeches before going back to the house.

Cautiously he peered inside, but Pope was under the table with his muzzle on his paws. Apparently the smell of blood had intimidated him as much as it had his mistress, for he made no move to launch himself at Connor's ankles.

Gemma was bending over the fire seasoning a pot of soup. She looked up as he came in but didn't say a word.

"Here," he said. Deftly he cut up some of the meat and added the cubes to the pot. Not long afterward a delicious aroma filled the air, and he had to smile when he saw Gemma's nose twitch.

"Nothing better on a chilly day than venison stew," he wheedled.

"You're right," she said.

Relieved that the storm had passed, he was careful to finish dressing and salting the meat later that afternoon, while Gemma and her beastly puppy were down by the loch. He would not distress her that way again.

Later that night, after Gemma had withdrawn to the loft, he worked by candlelight to prepare the deer hide for curing. He had it in mind to make a pair of mittens for Gemma, for the weather was growing increasingly cold and the delicate kid gloves she had brought with her from home would never keep her hands warm. He had a good laugh at himself as he sat down to work, for he supposed that this was how the ancient Picts had spent their long autumn nights: making deerskin clothing for themselves in the dim light of their fires.

Surprisingly, he had to admit that he had been enjoying himself of late. Strange, how much satisfaction a man could derive from making things with his hands, and providing food for his table by skill alone. Not that he would care to spend the rest of his life playing house like this, but now that he and Gemma had established a peaceful enough truce, there was a certain charm to their daily life together on this isolated moor. It was a time out of mind, an enchanting interlude from the hard realities of everyday strife, and he suddenly knew that he would always look back on these days with a sense of wonder and nostalgia.

Everything would be perfect if only Gemma would let him back into her bed again.

His cheek twitched. How long had it been since his return from Glenarris? Five days? Six? Long enough for Gemma's troubles to have ended, and for him to have grown increasingly randy what with working so closely with her in their makeshift kitchen, laughing over their failures, gloating over the meals that turned out edible, and discovering that there could be harmony, even pleasure, in old enemies doing things together.

Aye, he wanted her, and he thought that Gemma might want him, too, for he had not been ignorant of the way her eyes would rest on him sometimes when she thought he wasn't looking; or how the laughter would occasionally fade from her lips when their glances met and they would exchange a long, still look that wasn't funny at all.

With an effort he forced his tormented thoughts elsewhere. Too late. He found that he had grown too restless to sit still any longer. Laying his handiwork aside, he went to the door and stepped outside to gulp deeply of the frosty night air. The wind had risen, and it was sharp and cold, a northerly wind driving down from the wastes of the Arctic with storm clouds behind it. He knew this weather. There could well be snow by morning.

Shivering, he went down to the shed to check on the pony. Afterwards he filled both buckets—the pony's and the house's—with fresh water, for the spring pool might also be frozen by morning. Quietly, so as not to awaken Gemma, he stacked more peat by the hearth and closed the shutters. Crawling under the covers in his makeshift bed below the loft, he fell asleep quickly, but his dreams were of Gemma and gave him little respite.

"Connor!"

Slowly he pried open his eyes and was surprised to find harsh daylight dancing before them. In the midst of this blurry field huddled the lovely object of his dreams in that ridiculous wrapper she always wore, that virginal one with the high neck and long sleeves.

"What?" he croaked.

"Connor, it's snowing outside!"

"You woke me up for that?" Groaning, he turned over and covered his head with the blanket.

"But it's beautiful! There's plenty on the ground and more coming down. I've never seen the mountains look so pretty. Do come see."

He opened one eye to look at her. She was bending over him, beaming like a delighted child, her curly mop-top doing nothing to dispel the illusion. But he had only to lower his gaze to the rounded swell of her breasts against the virginal nightshirt to know that it was only that: an illusion.

Nothing childish about this woman, he decided, and he did the only thing a man could do when presented with such a tempting eyeful. Out shot his arm to circle her waist, and in the wink of an eye he had pulled the unsuspecting Gemma down beside him.

"Connor!"

At least she sounded more startled than mad, which he had to own was a vast improvement over the way she had reacted to his touch in the past. Encouraged, he threaded his hands through her short-cropped hair, loving the silky feel of it beneath his fingers. "What?" he asked lazily.

"Let me go!"

"No. It's your own fault, crawling into my bed all tousled and tempting while I'm lying in it."

"I did not crawl!"

But she had, and they both knew it. Lifting her easily with his strong hands, he brought her down on top of him so that only the eiderdown separated their bodies. Regrettably, the eiderdown was much too thick for him to enjoy more than a sensation of heaviness and warmth when he wanted so much more.

Sitting up, he took her by the waist and lifted her again. In one easy motion he threw the eiderdown aside, slipped her in beside him, and covered them again.

"There," he said, smiling into her eyes. "That's better, isn't it?"

It certainly was. He didn't protest as Gemma wrapped her icy toes around his feet. Still smiling, he brought her head down to his shoulder, and they lay for a time without speaking. It was the first truly intimate moment of their marriage; restful and sweet and entirely companionable.

Nevertheless, it was impossible for him to hold Gemma so close without wanting her, and he groaned in mingled need and dismay as his manhood rose hot and ready against her thigh. Shutting his eyes, he steeled himself for her escape from his bed.

But Gemma, with her infinite capacity for astonishing him, merely nestled closer and curled her body around his, fitting herself intimately against him.

Incredulous, he held himself still. His breathing was harsh, tormented, and his desire throbbed relentlessly between them. And then, with the lightness of a butterfly's wing, so light that at first he thought he must be dreaming, he felt the brush of her lips on his own. It was the first time she had ever turned to him without being asked or forced, and his heart thundered in response.

"Gemma—"

She opened her eyes and looked into his without lifting her head. "What?"

"Is it all right now?"

He could feel her smiling against his mouth. "Yes. It's been 'all right' for the last few days. Thank you for asking."

"Thank *you* for telling me!" he countered, teasing her because he felt ashamed all at once that she had actually felt the need to thank him for something as simple as thinking for once of her. Sadness welled within him as he thought of how often he had hurt her and treated her without a second thought.

Taking her into his arms, he rolled over, exchanging their positions so that she was now beneath him. But the tenderness remained in the touch of his lips on hers and in his hand that trailed softly to her breast.

God, how he had missed this—and her! He realized suddenly that it wasn't solely the urgency of sexual need that was making his heart pound in his chest, otherwise he would have sought relief with any number of very eligible ladies within a day's ride of Glenarris before coming back. No, it was Gemma with her disturbing kisses who made his senses drown, Gemma with her sweetly clinging body who left him aching inside.

Breaking off the kiss he reached for the hem of her nightgown. She lifted her arms obligingly, then wrapped them back around his neck the moment he tossed the offending article aside. He had been sleeping without clothes on, as he always did, and they both sighed as she settled her naked body against his.

Drawing back to look into each other's eyes, they smiled.

Down came Connor's mouth to claim Gemma's in a kiss that left no doubt as to his desire for her. His hot tongue clashed with hers and his big hands splayed across her buttocks, bringing her hard against his bulging manhood. She clung to him, wrapping her legs around his hips. Theirs was the give and take of a mutual passion born of the realization that both had come to this willingly, that this time neither force nor fear nor meek acquiescence had put in an unfair hand.

They kissed again and again, their arms linked around each other's necks and waists, their bodies melded, her thighs arching against his muscular ones. His hands stroked and revered and caressed, and beneath his passionate touch she swelled and bloomed.

"Touch me, too," he whispered against her mouth, and she reached down without hesitation to take his hot flesh into her hand.

Gemma, who had never permitted herself to be cowed, yet who had been so vulnerable, so innocent in everything, especially in bed, was now bold in every aspect of her life. With growing confidence she gave

Connor pleasure as he had pleasured her, touching him as he had taught her a lover should be touched. And when he was groaning with want she pulled him down with her into the softness of the bed, into the softness of her body.

Breath coming fast, Connor buried himself in the blooming wellspring of her love. Every impassioned stroke brought them closer to that wondrous peak until she held him tight to her breasts and cried out his name in a throaty sob. As she shuddered and rocked with the force of her climax, she felt Connor reach the same wondrous, bursting enchantment of fulfillment in which the universe tilted and turned, folded in on itself and went out.

Slowly, slowly, the room grew quiet. Ashes in the fireplace collapsed with a sigh. The puppy whined in its sleep. Outside the wind rattled coldly against the panes, but here, in the cozy croft, Connor lay lost in wonder, holding Gemma close to his heart. It's never been like this with anyone, he thought, dazed. Never.

He felt her roll away, and then she stood. In bare feet she climbed the ladder while he crossed his arms behind his head and closed his eyes to gloat.

"You all right, Gemma?" he did think to ask.

"Aye," she called back down.

"Kiss me when you come back?"

Her giggle warmed him. "Maybe."

He had no doubt that she'd comply. As a matter of fact, there she was now, descending the ladder while he lay, his eyes half-opened and a smile on his face, waiting for her worshipful touch.

The outer door opened and then shut on a rush of icy

air. What in hell was she doing? he wondered. Oh, aye, the dog. No doubt tossing it out for a piss while the two of them took a wee bit of time being—

"Yowww!"

Like a scalded cat he leapt from beneath the covers. "You witch!" he bellowed, slapping at the icy snow Gemma had dumped on his naked chest.

Her response was to burst into laughter.

"I'll kill you for this!" he howled, still dancing around the room.

"T-try it!" she taunted, laughing.

"What's so funny?" he demanded, his hands on hips as he glared at her.

"Y-you are! Men l-look so funny when they—they jump around n-naked!" She gestured unashamedly toward his bobbing genitals and doubled over in another fit of laughter.

Hard-pressed not to laugh himself, he swept her into his arms, where she shook convulsively against his chest. "That which you find so amusing only recently made you sob out my name," he reminded her.

"Y-yes." She giggled. "Isn't life a paradox?"

He had to laugh then, too, and hold her close while his heart rejoiced and the hard years of a lonely lifetime seemed to be washed from his soul. Yes, it certainly was.

Chapter Nineteen

The snow lasted barely two days, disappearing abruptly on the second evening beneath a sudden thaw. In the morning, Gemma watched as with great reluctance Connor put on his boots, then kissed her before going outside to cut peat. His departure was mourned by Gemma but welcomed by Pope, who danced around her skirts, barking for attention. But she was far too busy to give him more than a cursory pat. She had neglected more than the puppy in the last two days, and the heat rose in her cheeks as she remembered why.

Was it really she, Gemma Baird, who had behaved so wantonly? Crawling into Connor's bed and then refusing over the course of the next two days to let either of them get out of it? She had not known there could be so much bliss in being loved by a man again and again, and she suspected deep in her heart that Connor hadn't realized it either.

For two unbridled days and nights they had dropped all the hurts and anger that had always been like a wall between them. They had wisely made no mention of the past, nor of the future, and were rewarded with the blissful discovery of what the here and now could bring.

Connor had been gentle and kind, and more giving than she had ever known. He had taught her all of his formidable skills as a lover, and she had proved an apt and willing pupil. Which explained the heat that now spread across her face and her reluctance that morning to send him away from the cottage.

Nevertheless, she busied herself with cleaning up the remains of the few meals they had taken time to eat before Connor had swept her into his arms and back into bed. She shook out the eiderdown and brought it outside for airing. She swept the carpets and the floor and sorted the washing. The venison roast that had been tenderizing in a crock for the last few days was readied for the spit, and she reminded herself to take up the matter of purchasing a cow with Connor when he came in again. She had a longing for milk and butter, though she had no idea how to go about procuring either. Did Connor know how to milk a cow, and where would they go to buy a churn?

Provincial housewife, she chided herself, but she had to smile, for she had never dreamed that she would one day be fretting about menial things like churning butter, or that she could find such utter happiness in cooking and cleaning for Connor. Or that this new life of hers—so far removed from the stately halls of the Baird estate—could be so deeply satisfying.

On the other hand, she was no fool. She knew perfectly well that her new life suited her simply because she was viewing it through the golden haze of love.

Yes, she had to confess the impossible: she had fallen in love with Connor MacEowan. She knew it was love, because her heart had never ached like this or her limbs gone all weak and trembling simply because he was near. He made her feel the way no one in her life ever had before: cherished, wanted, as though she really mattered.

Tragically, there was one thing that prevented her happiness from being complete. She suspected that Connor did not love her in return. That was why she hadn't trusted herself just yet to voice what was in her heart. Above all else she feared being rebuffed. Oh, she believed firmly enough that Connor held her dear; no man who touched her as he did could be indifferent! And there were times when he would stop whatever he was doing and take her face in his hands and simply look at her, and she would shiver at what she saw in his eyes. That was when she would tell herself that surely, surely, she must matter to him.

But he had never said so, even though he must know how she ached to hear him say it. And how she ached to say as much to him. It was the only shadow that hovered over their otherwise unclouded bliss.

Gemma emerged from her troubled thoughts to discover that the pile of laundry she had been sorting had grown alarmingly large. She frowned as she stared down at it. There was no denying the obvious; she was going to have to do some washing—for the first time in her life.

The sun was warm on her back as she toted her basket to the stream that chuckled across the moor beyond the cottage. She would have preferred the wide, shallow spring pool behind the pony shed, but was afraid of contaminating the drinking water with the lye soap Connor had brought back. She gasped as she plunged her hands into the icy water, and thought longingly of the modern laundry room in the cellar at Uncle Archibald's, where the laundress and her daughters stoked the big kettles and boiled the linens amid the steam and the noise of the wringers and the smell of carbolic.

If Gemma had thought that keeping house was a dream, it was only because she had never done laundry before. In less than a minute she discovered that washing was drudgery.

She worked on her knees with her back aching and her hands reddened from the soap and the cold. She scrubbed and flailed and rinsed until she felt certain her arms would drop off and float away downstream. Which wouldn't be such a bad thing, considering that then she'd have an excuse to pass this torture over to Connor.

But the thought of cutting peat in his stead was no comfort. And she wasn't about to give up and have him laugh at her and call her lazy and spoiled, because she knew that that was what he thought of her—at least he had, before. So she kept on working, soaping and rinsing and spreading the dripping garments on the moor grass to dry.

Halfway through the table linens, Pope's excited barking brought her head around. Sitting back on her heels, she squinted in the bright sunlight, expecting to see Connor. To her astonishment she saw a pair of strangers trotting their shaggy ponies toward her.

She quickly stood, shaking out her damp skirts and running her hands through her tousled hair. She hadn't seen other people for so long that she felt awkward and slightly uneasy. She had no idea where Connor was. The pen beyond the croft, where he had been working earlier, was empty.

"Halloooo!" called the man in the lead as the ponies neared.

She did not return the greeting. Instead, she hid her chafed hands behind her back as the pair halted their mounts on the far side of the stream and looked her over with unconcealed interest. They were both around Connor's age, with tartan plaids wrapped in the Highland fashion around their shoulders. One of them had a tam on his dark head, the other wore no hat. Both of them sat their ponies astride despite the fact that their kilts were hiked well past their hairy white thighs.

She didn't know whether to laugh or blush. She had seen plenty of men in kilts on her journey through the Borders with Connor, but none of them had been riding horses. All at once she remembered Connor telling her that most Highlanders wore nothing at all beneath their kilts. Supposing that these two—?

"Excuse me," she said in a strangled voice. "I'll fetch my husband."

"Och, noo, lassie, wait!"

The Highland burr was so thickly pronounced that she halted in her tracks. Surely the locals didn't really talk like that, did they?

" 'Tis yew we werrre meanin' tae see," the man in the tam continued, rolling his r's with boundless enthusiasm. "Hearrrrd we had a bonnie wee brrride in Ferrrgus Dodson's auld crrroft!"

He dismounted as he spoke, and now he came sashaying toward her, his kilt swaying with every step. The other man, the shorter, blonder one, dismounted, too, but stayed near the ponies, grinning widely.

"Whot's yerrr name, lass?"

She eyed the taller one suspiciously as he halted before her, although she bravely held her ground. Somehow she doubted this scruffy pair intended to do her harm. Besides, if they had heard about her then they were probably neighbors, and she didn't want to insult them by revealing how uneasy she felt. But, oh, they were a disreputable pair, and the whiskey fumes rising from the one with the tam o'shanter was enough to make her eyes water! Where in blazes was Connor?

"I'm Gemma Bair—Gemma MacEowan," she told them politely.

"MacEowan! MacEowan, did ye hearrr thot, Angus?"

"Mmm," Angus grunted from beside the pony's head. He was digging around in his ear with a forefinger and didn't bother looking up.

"'Tis of a clan we be, lass!" Excitedly the big fellow flapped the trailing end of his plaid beneath her nose. "Green-blue-black! The MacEowan plaid, and prroud we arrre tae wearr it, isna thot richt, Angus?"

"Long live the clan," Angus intoned obediently.

"Where be yer mon, lass?" Tam O'Shanter inquired, fixing her with dark, devilish eyes. He must have been seriously drunk, for he seemed to be having a difficult time holding his laughter in check.

She bristled as it occurred to her that perhaps it was she who was being laughed at. How rude! Could she help it that they had caught her at her washing?

"Well, lass?" roared the one in the tam o'shanter, while the other looked on, picking his nose. "Where be yer mon?"

"I'm not certain. Perhaps I ought to—"

"Ah ha! Rrrun off, has he? Left ye tae do the washin' on yerr ain? Why, 'tis a maid he should brring ye, a maid tae do yer work an' keep yer wee hands bonnie. Though he'll no hae the cash tae be payin' a wench, will he, the penniless sot." He winked at her broadly.

"I assure you that we manage just fine on our own," she said with barely controlled fury. How dare this man insult Connor! Judging from that moth-eaten plaid and the swaybacked mount he rode, he was no better off himself.

"I'll see if my husband is back yet," she added stiffly. "He's been out cutting peat and—"

A roar of laughter cut off her words. She stared at the pair as though they'd lost their minds. What was so bloody funny? Didn't either of them ever cut peat? Surely they had to if they wished to keep those knobby legs warm during the winter!

Her shoulders squared, she turned her back on them and headed for the cottage. She had to quell the urge to break into a run when she realized that they were following close behind, clutching each other and chortling like madmen. Pope raced along at her heels, and Gemma wished that he were a mastiff so she could set him upon them with slavering jaws and savaging teeth. Neighbors or no, they weren't welcome here!

Turning past the stone wall near the pony's pen, she did break into a run. And she was about to burst through the cottage door when it flew open and Connor emerged on the threshold. He took one look at her face and then past her shoulder at the kilted, giggling pair who had halted on the far side of the gate.

"Go inside, Gemma." His voice was hard and dangerous.

Immediately the visitors set up a clamor of protest. "Och, Connor! Na need tae send the lass awa'!"

"We've only coom tae pay ourr rrrespects!"

Wide grins accompanied their pleas, though Gemma noticed that neither of the kilted jokers dared set foot beyond the gate.

A muscle twitched in Connor's lean cheek. She had the horrible feeling that he was about to explode. Her heart began beating rapidly, for she had never seen him so angry. What was wrong? Who were those two?

" 'Twas a long rrride frae Glenarris," Angus said, scratching at his privates. "Would ye be kind enow tae gie us a drram?"

It was too much for Connor. Bad enough that they were making fun of his heritage with their exaggerated accents and their insultingly brief kilts (and wearing the MacEowan tartan, no less!), but he would not have them set foot in the house he shared with Gemma, to let them gawk at her and ask rude questions and then laugh at her ignorant replies.

"Get out of here!" he said heatedly.

"Now, Connor," King Spencer pleaded, pushing the tam back on his head.

"Come away," Carter Sloane urged, taking King by the arm.

"Och, Connor, be reasonable," King entreated like a sorrowful pup. "We'll behave ourselves, won't we, Car—eh—Angus?"

"Aye," Carter agreed, though he didn't sound particularly eager anymore.

Wordlessly Connor took Gemma by the arm and

pulled her into the house. His pistols lay on the shelf near the door, and he inspected them carefully as he took them down. "Stay here."

Gemma's hands flew to her throat. "You're not going to shoot them, are you?"

"No. But I'd like to."

"Who are they?"

"Just a pair of drunks from the village. Harmless, though extremely crude. You'll stay here while I get rid of them."

It was not a question, but Gemma had no desire to disobey. Her nose pressed to the window, she watched as Connor stalked across the yard to where the grinning pair waited. His murderous rage had obviously not left him, but he seemed to be in control of it because he was speaking to them surprisingly civilly. Once or twice she even heard the tam o'shanter laugh and gesture toward the cottage. But each time Connor would shake his head, his lean profile forbidding.

After a few minutes more, Connor's rigid stance began to mellow. He tucked the pistols back into his belt. His forbidding scowl softened. Once or twice he even smiled. But she was relieved to see that he did not relent in any way toward the kilted pair.

Eventually, with obvious reluctance they turned to take their leave. As the tall one with the tam o'shanter waited for his companion to open the gate, Connor leaned forward and with his thumb and forefinger jerked up his kilt. For a nice, long moment she was treated to the flash of white male buttocks before Connor dropped the material and turned away, laughing.

The tam o'shanter never broke stride, but she saw the hot color rush to his cheeks. The blush deepened to crimson as the one named Angus also exploded with laughter. Then Angus turned and blew a kiss in Connor's direction before dragging his companion away.

Connor was still smiling when he returned to the cottage. She waited for him by the door. "Who were they? What did they want?"

"I told you. They're a pair of drunkards from Glenarris."

Glenarris! There it was again: that place Connor was always mentioning but never bothering to explain! "Is that where you went to buy provisions?" she probed, burning with curiosity.

"Where did those two find you?" he asked sharply, while he put away the pistols.

"Over by the burn. I was doing the wash."

"Did they tell you what they wanted?"

"Only that they'd learned I was here and wanted to meet me. Why didn't you want them to come in?"

Connor snorted. "Isn't it obvious? They were both dead drunk. And we'd both be better off if they never came again. I don't want their kind anywhere near you."

But she got the strange feeling that he had chased them away for an entirely different reason. Although she couldn't put her finger on her suspicions, she was hurt by the fact that he wasn't being honest with her. She was still so uncertain about her newfound love for him, and by the tenderness he had been showing her of late, that she was afraid to ask questions or make demands. She didn't think she could bear it if for some reason he reverted to his hateful old self.

Those two strange men . . . What was the truth behind their appearance today? Why had they made Connor so angry at first if they were, as he claimed, only a pair of harmless drunkards? And why did he still refuse to talk to her about Glenarris?

I must know, she thought desperately. She couldn't love a man as much as this and not know the first thing about him. In her happiness she had taken to pushing their unpleasant past away, but now the same old questions were coming back to haunt her once again. Loving him, she knew that if there was something in his past that he felt the need to keep from her, she had to find out what it was. To help him. And protect him. To love him as she wanted to, with all her heart and soul.

For the next few days Connor remained strangely irritable and preoccupied. He stayed away from the cottage for most of the daylight hours and out of her bed at night. Gemma found she had to be careful in what she said to him, because the least little remark served to incur his wrath. Even Pope stayed away, cowering under her chair whenever Connor was there and taking great pains not to relieve himself on Connor's bedding anymore.

One darkly overcast morning she came down from the loft to find Connor packing his leather satchel. She grew still at the sight, for she suspected what it meant.

After a moment he turned to her and said in an expressionless voice, "I'm going away for a time."

"Why?" she asked calmly, although it was hard to speak around the constriction in her throat.

"We need provisions. No telling when the blizzards will come, and we'll be snowed in until spring."

They had plenty of supplies left, she knew. But she knew that hard look on his face just as well. There would be no reasoning with him or trying to change his mind.

"May I come with you this time?"

"No."

She had expected as much, but it hurt anyway. With her back pressed against the ladder, she stood and watched him pack. He never even looked at her once. He might have been a thousand miles away.

When he was finished he merely slung the satchel over his shoulder and turned briefly toward her. There was none of the urgency, the barely concealed regret, in his leave-taking as there had been the last time. He merely reminded her curtly that his pistols were loaded, that she should keep the door bolted against any riffraff, and that he would be back as soon as possible, though he couldn't rightly tell her when.

At the very last he remembered to ask if there was anything she wanted him to bring back for her. She clenched her teeth. She hated being treated like an afterthought. Silently she shook her head.

"All right, then. Cheerio."

Once again she watched from the window as the cart rumbled off across the moors. Once again she prayed that Connor would turn around and wave. But he did not. He sat rigid and unmoving on the front seat of the cart, and eventually the trail took a sharp turn and he was lost from view.

Chapter Twenty

Connor was gone for eight days, endless days during which Gemma grew thin and haggard with anxiety. She slept badly and could scarcely think about eating. She tried hard to keep busy with menial tasks, for there were certainly enough requiring her attention: mending, cleaning, washing, stacking peat, toting water, polishing silverware, stringing up curtains over the tiny windows.

Now that she had Pope for company she no longer feared the dark nights, but the house, and her life, were empty without Connor. On more than one occasion she made up her mind to go after him, and once or twice had actually gone so far as to pack together the provisions she thought she might need along the way. But each time common sense intervened and she reluctantly put everything back. The weather had been bitterly cold of late and she had no idea where Connor had gone. Better to stay here and die of loneliness than to freeze to death in the mountains.

Eventually it occurred to her that she was trapped in the croft on this empty moor as effectively as she had been trapped in her life at Archibald Baird's. There, too, she had chafed to get away without any clear sense of where she wanted to go. But at least there her prison had been more far-ranging; she'd had Helios for companionship, and the warm countryside to ride in. Here there was only desolation, the harsh, forbidding landscape, and silence. But for the murmuring of the stream out back and the honking of migratory waterfowl she doubted that there would be any sounds at all.

She assuaged her loneliness by playing with Pope, games like tug of war with a pull she fashioned from discarded scraps of deerhide, or throwing sticks for him down on the loch shore. After one light snowfall she pelted him with snowballs, but that only depressed her because it reminded her of the morning she had dumped snow on Connor as he lay naked in bed, of the days when they had been lovers, companions, friends.

Many an idle hour was taken up with wondering how she and Connor had reverted to the cool hostility of their earlier relationship. She could not accept that a simple visit from those obnoxious Highlanders had been entirely responsible. There had to be more to it than that, but no amount of agonizing left her any wiser. When Connor returned she'd demand some answers!

If he returned. . . .

On the evening of the eighth day in the midst of an icy rainstorm that had made the last few hours of the trip a misery for himself and the pony, Connor approached the croft. He was exhausted, for he had pushed himself relentlessly, first to Glenarris, and then to Edinburgh, in pursuit of King and Carter.

Eachern had insisted on accompanying him to Edinburgh although Connor had told him his presence was unwelcomed. But Eachern had remained undaunted. He explained that he understood Connor's frame of mind, and although he couldn't blame Connor for being furious with Carter and King, he couldn't condone any bloodshed.

He had, he assured Connor, tried his best to talk them out of their madcap scheme to visit him at the old Dodson croft, but as usual they had turned a deaf ear.

But Eachern's concern had been well-founded, for in Edinburgh Connor and King had indeed come close to blows. Separated by Carter and Eachern, Connor and King had refused to back down, and it had taken a great deal of arguing on Eachern's part to keep them from calling each other out. None of them had ever dueled over a wager before, he had reminded them furiously. And wasn't it rather pointless to settle scores like callow youths?

Connor had reluctantly agreed. He would not settle the score with a duel however much he might want to, but he did demand an end to the wager.

King had immediately refused. Struggling to control his mounting rage, Connor had warned King in a deadly tone to keep away from the croft in the future. Wisely, King had agreed to that much. Connor's valet, Jamie, a disapproving witness to the entire unpleasant scene, had quickly shown King and Carter to the street while Eachern had poured Connor a stiff brandy.

The liquor had done much to soothe his raw nerves. It had been months since he had enjoyed such rare refinement. As the fragrant drink slid silkily down his throat, his tension had begun to ebb. His cousin, always quick to realize his changing moods, took advantage of the moment.

"Ye willna lose Glenarris for good if ye toss yer cards down now," Eachern had argued. "Ye've never lost anything to King or me or Carter ye've no been able to win back."

That was true, but Connor had refused to risk it. Furthermore, the winning of Gemma's affections had become a personal matter to him, a matter of pride and self-esteem. Now that King and Carter had seen her, he wasn't about to admit to them that a slip of a green-eyed lass had bested him!

He had brooded over this particular point for most of the long journey home, pushing himself and the pony throughout the daylight hours and long into the dark in order to hasten his return. Gemma had been softening toward him of late, and it was entirely possible that she might even be falling in love with him. He hadn't failed to notice the worshipful way she sometimes looked at him when she didn't think he was aware, and he had also felt the change in her kisses, so temptingly sweet.

With the clarity of hindsight, he realized now that he had made a mistake in letting King and Carter's depraved antics so infuriate him that he had treated Gemma with the manners of a bad-tempered boor before charging off in pursuit of them. He should have handled their appearance as a joke, shrugging it off with a laugh instead of allowing it to drive a wedge between Gemma and him. God knows their budding relationship was tenuous enough at the best of times.

Soaked to the skin and half frozen by the time he unhitched the pony, he stumbled wearily through the door of his croft. Daylight was waning into frigid night, and he wanted nothing more at the moment than to put his arms around Gemma and hold her close. How long had he been dreaming of letting her warmth and her softness ease the bitter cold from his body and his heart?

But her welcoming smile was not there to greet him. Instead, a thin, hollow-eyed creature met him at the door, and he forgot his misery.

"You're not ill again, are you?" he demanded anxiously.

Gemma's body stiffened. "N-no. Why would you say that?"

"Look at you, half worn to the bone! Haven't you been eating while I've been away?" he yelled.

"Look at *you*," she shot back. "Soaked to the skin! Don't you know better than to get out of the rain?"

A fine homecoming this is! he thought angrily.

They looked at each other, neither speaking.

I can't go on like this any longer, he thought wearily. I'm just too tired. He thought of Glenarris. There was too much at stake.

"Gemma, wait," he said softly.

She looked at him questioningly.

"Let's try this again."

"What do you mean?"

Wearily he went back out the door, trailing a puddle of water behind him. Then he reappeared, smiling. "Hello, lass. I'm home. Did you miss me?"

Laughing, Gemma stood on tiptoe with her arms outstretched and he pulled her to him. Within seconds she was as wet as he was, as he kissed her, starving for her touch. She burrowed closer into the circle of his embrace, warming him, loving him with her mouth and her hands.

"Oh, God, I've missed you," he murmured against her cheek, too tired to continue resisting the truth. "Do you know how good you feel?''

"No," she whispered. "Tell me."

Better than the brandy Eachern had poured for him, better than the ten-course dinner Monsieur Pous had prepared, better than the exquisite satin bedding he had sunk into on his first night home in Edinburgh. But he couldn't tell her that. And he didn't really have to answer. Gemma already knew.

"It's like coming home for the first time, isn't it?" she said softly.

Aye, it was, though it was dangerous to admit as much, even to himself. Because she was right. Walking into their croft and into her waiting arms was like nothing he had ever known. It was warmth and comfort, a sense of belonging that he had never realized was missing from his life until now.

He gathered her closer and turned his face into her hair, overwhelmed, and a little afraid. This was more than he had ever dreamed possible, more than he deserved from this woman who had suffered so unfairly at his hands. His face twisted with sudden agony, and his heart filled to bursting with all that he needed to say.

"Gemma—"

"Hush," she murmured against his mouth, for she was still standing on tiptoe with her arms locked about his neck. "You're soaking wet. And chilled to the bone. Come, warm yourself by the fire."

He allowed himself to be led, like a child, to the hearth where the peat fire burned. He was exhausted, drained of every ounce of strength. In his need to get home to her he had slept less than four hours a night, and he was close to collapse.

Gemma brought him a chair and knelt to pull off his

muddy boots. Easing the sodden coat from his shoulders, she paused a moment to rub and knead the stiffened muscles there. Connor groaned and his head fell forward.

When he was naked she rubbed him dry with a towel warmed before the fire. She remembered how wonderful that had felt when the girl at Mrs. Kennerly's had done the same for her after she'd been bathed in the sickroom. Connor had taken care of her then, and so she cared for him now. She knew that he was exhausted and that what he needed was not what she could give him with her body.

When she had dressed him once again in warm, clean clothes, she toweled and combed his hair. Connor sat with his eyes closed, and she pressed a gentle kiss to his lips. Then she went to the fire to fetch porridge and tea. While he ate she sat across from him, watching him anxiously.

When she saw the color slowly returning to his cheeks and some of the old twinkle to his eyes, she let out her breath in a long sigh, unaware until that moment that she had been holding it. She smiled, utterly relieved.

Connor, by contrast, looked at her and frowned. "Where's your supper?"

"Oh, I'm not—"

"You're skin and bones," he interrupted, rising to fetch a bowl for her. "I wouldn't be surprised if you told me you've eaten nothing for the last eight days." He grew still suddenly, his hand arrested over the kettle. "Not coughing again, are you?"

"No."

She did not fail to notice the way his big body relaxed.

Now Connor watched her while she ate, scowling throughout and half rising out of his chair when she laid aside her spoon before the last bite was finished.

Arching her brow at him, she scraped the bowl clean, unable to stop smiling for even a moment. She had never been so happy. Taking care of Connor, actually mothering him, had made her aware of a part of herself she hadn't known existed. It gave her something of the same, soaring pleasure as lying with him did, a sense of fulfillment that went beyond the physical, and left her heart bursting.

And he had let her care for him! Had welcomed her, in fact, not pushed her away with angry words or scorn. She could feel his unquestioning acceptance of her *right* to do these things like a drug in her blood, touching the deepest uncertainties in her soul and smoothing them away as though they had never existed.

She looked again at Connor's hard face and saw that it was relaxed with sleepy contentment. He looked so much younger, like the boy he must have been many years ago. In the shadows of the flickering fire the harsh planes of his cheeks and jaw were softened. His sensual mouth was touchingly vulnerable.

"Connor." She rose and took him by the arm. "You must sleep. You're half dead on your feet."

He stood, leaning into her, then turned and pulled her into his arms, tipping back her head and kissing her. But she stepped back and drew him to his bed, knowing he needed rest now more than he needed her.

"Where's the bloody dog?" he asked, his eyes slowly closing.

She chuckled. "I locked him in the shed. I thought you'd appreciate being spared his welcome."

He smiled. "Kind of you," he murmured, and drifted away.

* * *

Morning brought an end to the rain, although the wind was cold and the sky filled with shredded clouds. Gemma was up early stoking the fire and cooking breakfast, quietly so as not to awaken Connor, who lay without moving beneath the blankets. He must, she thought, have been utterly exhausted to sleep so deeply. Even the daylight brushing his face did not make him stir.

His was an unguarded face, she thought, studying it with an aching heart. It was as young and defenseless now as it had been the night before. She found she could not tear her gaze away. The careworn lines she had noticed there so often were gone, and she wished there was some way she could ensure that they remained away forever.

How could she make his life easier for him? For one thing, she must find a way to spare him the difficult journey to whatever town it was he went to for provisions. This last trip had nearly done him in, from the look of things, and it scared her to think of him risking his life in the wintry mountains and of her being alone again just so that they might have milk and flour. Perhaps if she wrote her uncle and asked for the rest of her money, she and Connor might be able to manage . . .

That thought brought her up short. Not too long ago she had been scheming to use her money to get away from Connor. And now? Now she was dreaming of using it to build a life for the two of them here in this remote Highland glen!

Why, Gemma, lass, she whispered aloud in Connor's own, lilting burr, *'tis a change of heart ye've had.*

Leaning over to peer lovingly into his sleeping face, she realized that it was true. She wouldn't mind spending the rest of her life right here in this croft, as long as Connor was there.

"Oh—!"

Without warning his hand shot out to clasp the front of her skirt and pull her down beside him. In the next moment he had encircled her waist and flipped her easily onto her back. Leaning over her, he propped an arm on either side of her head.

"How long have you been awake?" she demanded breathlessly.

"Long enough to know you've been mooning over me like a lovesick calf."

"I was not mooning! I never moon!"

Grinning like the wickedly handsome devil he was, he kissed her soundly. There was nothing weary or vulnerable about the kiss, the way there had been last night. This was the kiss of a man who deeply desired her.

Sighing, she slipped her arms around his neck and pressed herself eagerly against his warm body. She had hungered for this during the endless week of separation, and despite the dog howling in the shed outside and the breakfast scorching on the fire, she would not be denied.

Connor knew Gemma's body intimately by now, but still he took his time worshiping every lovely inch of it as he slowly undressed her. His hands caressed and stroked and touched, finding her as soft and yielding as he had envisioned during the dark hours of the long ride home. His heart throbbed in great, urgent beats as Gemma worshiped him in turn with her own seeking lips and hands. In a private lovers' language of murmurs and sighs they revered one another, returning always to draw sustenance from their seeking mouths, to kiss and pluck and link their dancing tongues together.

"Oh, Connor," Gemma breathed, lolling in his embrace.

Skimming his hands down to her buttocks, he lifted her against his throbbing manhood. They were both naked now, and the brush of skin on heated skin was electrifying.

Drawing back to look into each other's eyes, they were silent for a long moment, simply watching each other breathe. Then slowly, slowly, Connor shifted and slipped inside her.

His hips dipped down to burrow deeper, hers lifted to accommodate him. With arcane sweetness, they moved in the primal flow of love's ancient rhythm. Giving, receiving, flowering full so that every stroke lifted them higher toward the ultimate pleasure.

And it came quickly, an explosion of rapture too long denied, pouring like quicksilver into every nerve and fiber.

I love you, he thought, surging against her in triumphant release.

Afterwards they lay in sated exhaustion, their wilted limbs tangled together. Connor found joy in holding her close, her silky hair beneath his jaw, her hip resting against his belly. I love you, he thought again, but could not bring himself to say the words aloud, for he had never uttered them to anyone before and had no idea how to go about recalling them should they be met with scorn.

And so he lay there in an agony of uncertainty, longing to speak yet knowing he must not. He ached for her, knowing that therein lay the danger. The moment was ripe, and yet the bonds of the past would not release him.

At that moment the long neglected kettle collapsed into the flames.

"What now?" Gemma asked, dismayed, as he got up and fished out the blackened clump of tin with his gaff. It was the only kettle they had.

"No need to worry," he said with forced cheerfulness. "I brought plenty of cookware this time."

Gemma brightened. "You did? Where is it?"

He had to smile at her obvious delight. "Still in the wagon. Race you for it."

They hurried to be the first dressed and out the door.

"This isn't fair!" Gemma complained, struggling with the cumbersome hooks on her petticoats. "The least you could do is help me a little!"

But he knew better than to put his hands on that tempting body even for so innocent a reason as doing up the back of her gown. "Sorry," he said, pulling on his breeches, "it's your own fault for wearing those silly things to begin with."

"But I'm not the one who took them off," she shot back.

He grinned. Amazing, how quickly one could bring about a change of mood by indulging in a good squabble. "I'll see you outside."

"You don't play fair, MacEowan!"

He put his head back through the door. "I never do, remember?"

His smile faded as he stood outside surveying the walls of the cottage and the shed beyond it. Somehow his absence had served to make him aware of how truly shabby everything was. He saw now that an overwhelming amount of work needed to be done before the winter clamped down in its full savagery. The autumn had been uncommonly mild, but he had tasted enough of what was to come in the frigid passes of the Great North Road during the last three days. He would do well to take advantage of the short daylight hours left him before the blizzards came.

The pony nickered as he approached the shed, for he had been too weary to feed it the night before. To make up for his negligence he dumped extra grain into the bucket and then gave the animal's shaggy coat a vigorous brushing. Afterwards he unlocked the gate and released the whining Pope.

Barking, the little dog raced past him to the cart. Connor turned to see Gemma rummaging through the crates in the back. She barely paused to pet the animal before returning to the task. When he came up behind her, she whirled, her face alive with pleasure.

"You've brought so many wonderful things!"

Indeed he had. An embroidered footstool for her, a proper gentleman's shaving kit for him, extra blankets and a satin bolster, cookware and stemware, a crate of laying chickens, and several pounds of butter. Some of the supplies were new, bought in the stores in Edinburgh, and some of them had been filched from Connor's kitchen when the stern-faced Monsieur Pous had not been looking.

"How did you pay for all this?" she asked, climbing unladylike into the cart and clucking back at the hens, who had miraculously survived the cold night without shelter but were now irritable with hunger. "Did you use my money?"

"Aye," he admitted, and steeled himself for the explosion he knew was to come.

To his amazement she merely laughed. "Good for

you," she said gaily. "You've got sense after all."

No, he did not. Because if he did, he wouldn't let her dancing green eyes affect him so deeply. If he had any sense at all he would turn tail and run as fast as he could back to Edinburgh and the safety of his bachelor's home. Indeed, a man with sense would not take three quick strides to the cart and swing his wagered wife into his arms, nor close his eyes in pleasure as her slim arms locked around his neck and her parted lips sank to his . . .

It was Pope who interrupted the long kiss with a jealous attack on Connor's ankle. He tried unobtrusively to kick Pope away, but the dog was relentless, and after a moment Gemma started giggling.

"Best give up or he'll ruin your only pair of boots."

I've got dozens more at home, he longed to tell her. But since he could not, he had to feign suitable concern for the ones he was wearing and, very reluctantly, set her aside.

In companionable silence they unloaded the cart. It was almost like Christmas as Gemma exclaimed over every little item she unearthed. Connor watched, smiling, as she ran here and there hanging up her new pots and pans, spreading out the brocade shawl, setting the footstool just so near the fire. This happy creature cooing over a new teakettle couldn't be the same haughty shrew who had come close to murdering him over a casket of jewels, could it?

"This crate is heavy," she protested, interrupting his thoughts. "I can't wait to see what's in it. Will you lift it for me?"

He obliged, and after he pried open the lid, she plunged her hands into the straw packing. Delighted, she lifted out two of the bottles stored there. "Wine! Oh, Connor!"

"We can't survive all winter on water, can we?"

"Of course not. You clever man." She read the labels with approval, then dove in for the next two bottles. These were inspected as well, then happily set aside and the next pair withdrawn.

He saw the puzzled look that crept to her face as she examined them. He knelt down beside her, his hands propped on his knees. "What's wrong? I know you don't care for brandy, but I didn't think you'd mind if I bought some for myself."

"No, I don't," Gemma said vaguely. "But how—Did you select these yourself?"

"I did," he said, and then realized his mistake.

In the sudden silence his eyes met Gemma's. The brandy had come from his own cellar at Glenarris. It was an obscure label from a small family winery in the Grand Cru region of the French Champagne. Prohibitively expensive and older than Gemma, it was not the sort of liquor an ordinary crofting man with a taste for farmhouse ale would even know about, let alone care to consume. Indeed, it was the sort of drink intended for a palate refined over years, a taste that had to be developed slowly in order to be appreciated.

"I was in Inverness," he explained, breaking the silence. "Eachern was there, and he took me shopping. Those were his recommendations. He has a better understanding of wines than I do."

Gemma said nothing. Connor's words did not quite square with his behavior, for he had never before refused to look her in the eye when he talked to her. Yet his eyes were deliberately avoiding hers now, which made it painfully obvious to her that he was lying.

Why?

She pondered this as she got up and stowed away the rest of the provisions, soberly and quickly, the fun having gone out of it. In her mind she was carefully going over a number of things she had never paid any attention to before. Like Connor's indifference to her uncle's wealth and social standing when by rights it should have intimidated an ordinary man like him. And the way he had spoken to the Baird coachmen and the surly innkeeper in Kinkillie, as though he had been accustomed all his life to ordering others about. And she remembered now how Eachern MacEowan had deferred to Connor even though the younger man was obviously the better off of the two.

And what about Connor's ease in handling pistols, which were surely not the weapons of choice for a peasant? Or his knowledge of Alexander Pope and his remarkably learned vocabulary? And especially his taste for rare French brandy!

In a moment of startling clarity the pieces of the puzzle that made up this complex man suddenly fell into place. Her breath caught. Of course! She should have realized it long before, if anger and contempt hadn't blinded her to the obvious. Connor MacEowan was no crofter by birth. There was too much breeding in him, too much of the gentleman despite the fact that he worked so hard to hide it.

What had happened to him? What had reduced him to these harsh circumstances, and shamed him so that he could not confess his birthright to anyone? It would explain why she knew so little about him. He seemed to have no past beyond the mention of a place called Glenarris. And after all this time and the deep intimacy of certain aspects of their relationship, she still had no clue as to where—or what—Glenarris might be.

Her heart hammering, she wondered about the nature of the tragedy that must have befallen Connor and why he could not bring himself to discuss it with her. It could not have been any self-inflicted misfortune, for he was not the sort to fall victim to the lure of drink or gambling. And he was certainly far too shrewd to end up losing every guinea he owned on bad investments. And none of those circumstances, however tragic, would reduce a man of his caliber to wandering the English countryside in stinking attire and adopting such deliberately appalling manners.

It must, she decided soberly, have been a shattering experience, whatever it was. Enough to reduce a proud and highly educated gentleman like Connor to a half-demented pauper; to unhinge his mind to the extent that he had dared abduct against her will a young lady of his own class.

Her hands stilled and tears filled her eyes. Poor, poor Connor! If only she'd realized as much long before this. If only he had confided in her—although how could he? She'd never have believed him, and in her own hurt and anger would probably have kept on insulting and tormenting him exactly as she had done from the moment they'd been married.

Her cheeks burned, and she knew a shame that went beyond anything she had ever felt. She would have to make it up to him, and help him find his way back to whatever it was he had lost. But first she must convince him that he could trust her.

"I'll help you, Connor," she whispered, aching. "I'll help you, but you must let me do so, first!"

Chapter Twenty-one

Outside behind the cottage, Connor paused to wipe the sweat from his brow. It had taken him far longer to unload the cart than he had expected, but finally the chickens were housed in the pony shed and the last of the barrels of nails, tar, and thatch had been stacked beneath the eaves. If the rain held off a few days more, the shed would have the chance to dry out and he could begin building proper walls and a roof.

Then we'll have us a real croft, he thought, stretching his aching muscles and looking contentedly around him. Come spring he could start laying in a privy and enlarge the loft and the cooking area. With Gemma's help he could get a goodly amount of planting done as well. And if the winter wasn't too harsh, he might even get a root crop started before—

His pleasant thoughts skidded to a savage halt. Good bloody blazes! What on earth was he thinking? For one mad moment he'd actually forgotten who he was. Here he was, standing with his hands in his pockets, day-dreaming about the future like some common farmer! Planting crops, raising livestock, harvesting grain for a living? Thank you, no!

On the far side of the croft Pope set up a mad barking. Connor ignored him and kicked savagely at the barrels he had stacked with such care only moments before. What in God's name had possessed him to bring these stupid things along? What long-term plans had he been making, anyway? This was no life for him, or for Gemma, either.

"Shut that dog up!" he roared, for Pope was still barking, and the piercing yips were getting on his nerves.

The sooner he got back to Edinburgh for good, he thought furiously, the better. Autumn had been a pleasant interlude here with Gemma, but the winter would be harsh. Homesteading would quickly lose its appeal for him and his young wife once the two of them were trapped inside for weeks on end by howling blizzards and enormous banks of drifting snow.

His wife . . .

He was suddenly still.

What was to become of his wife when he went back to his old and very comfortable life in Edinburgh?

On the far side of the shed Pope kept up his infernal barking. Foul-tempered, Connor stalked around the shed toward the front of the croft. It would give him a great deal of satisfaction to boot that yammering beast right in the backside!

Rounding the corner, he drew up short. Three strange horses were standing in the small yard, their riders laughing uproariously at Pope, who was doing his best to leap up and savage their finely booted legs. The riders were dressed in the subdued green of formal hunting attire and had expensive guns slung over their saddles.

One glance told him that these were not local Scots. He guessed that they were Englishmen, whose kind traveled often to the Highlands at this time of year to bag grouse or deer or other wild game. The mild weather of the last few weeks must have attracted more than most and kept them afield far longer, which would explain why these three had ventured into so remote a glen as this one.

By now Pope had spotted Connor. Abandoning his attack on the huge horses, he ran barking toward him, his meaning clear. These strange men were a threat to Gemma, and the little terrier obviously expected him to do something about it.

Gemma, he now saw, was standing in the doorway watching. Her face was pale but she did not look frightened. Instead she looked angry. Spitting angry, in fact, and when one of the men caught sight of him and spoke to him, Connor understood why.

"Ah! This un be the lassie's husband, na doubt!" He spoke in the broad accents of a Yorkshireman. His manner was cocksure and thoroughly insulting. "We be doin' our best to convince the lass tedn't polite not to ask us in, but she won't budge."

Connor said nothing. Slowly he folded his arms across his chest and planted his legs apart. His expression indicated that he sided with his wife.

"It's been a tirin' morning," the second man added. His face was jowly and flushed an unhealthy purple.

The third man nodded. His contemptuous eyes regarded Connor as though he were little better than the dog cowering now at his feet. "We'd appreciate a spot by the fire and some whiskey." It was not a request.

"I haven't got any," Connor replied coldly.

"Well, well. Did ye hear that tone, lads? Fancies 'isself someone, don't 'e?" inquired the first man. "Not much reason," he added, looking the shabby croft up and down with unconcealed distaste. "But they do say Highlanders be a surly lot." As he spoke he aimed a stream of tobacco juice at Connor's boots.

The others laughed. Connor said nothing. Silence fell, broken only by the snorting and stamping of the horses.

"Well?" someone prodded eventually. "What about that whiskey?"

"Connor—" Gemma pleaded.

"Go inside, Gemma." He didn't even look at her.

"Right," agreed the hang-jowled one. "Get on up to bed and wait for we. Fancy a bit of a sniggle wi' the bitch, don't we, lads?"

The others guffawed.

"Na need to look so," the leader assured Connor. "Thou'lt be 'andsome compensated. Got a copper, Frank?"

A coin was produced from a waist pocket and tossed at Connor's feet.

"A' right, lads! Let's 'ave at the awd bitch!"

A moment later the three found themselves lying in a heap of tangled human limbs and stamping horses' hooves. Connor had unseated them with a lightning-fast attack, and now emerged from the cottage, armed. He drew back the hammers of the pistols with dual clicks. "I'll give you to the count of five to get out of here."

270

The fat one shook himself like a dog coming out of the water. "What the bloody—? 'Ow dare you!"

"One."

"Is it the copper? 'S truth, you can't tell me the wench be worth more'n that!"

"Two."

"C'mon, Frank," advised one of his companions. "The savage be touched in the 'ead, can't you tell?"

"Now't for it," the third man agreed, climbing stiffly into the saddle.

"Aye, 'tis best," the fat man, Frank, agreed sullenly, struggling to rise.

"Three."

Grunting, Frank swung himself onto his horse's back. His cap had come off when Connor knocked him to the ground and his hair was streaked with mud. The leader of the trio, who had not yet mounted, bent to retrieve it for him.

"Four," Connor warned, unrelenting.

Thinking better of it, the leader, too, got back in the saddle. A moment later all three of them were galloping out of the yard with Pope barking at their heels and the pony squealing after them from his walled enclosure.

"Five."

Slowly Connor lowered the pistols. Slipping back the hammers, he thrust them into his waistband. In a few short strides he reached Gemma, who stood frozen in the doorway.

"Did they hurt you?"

"No. They never even dismounted. Pope wouldn't let them."

Taking her arm, he jerked her toward the house. "Come on."

"Where are we going?"

Connor didn't answer. Mystified, Gemma watched as he began throwing things into his worn leather satchel.

"Connor! What are you doing?"

"Packing."

"I can see that, but why?"

"We're leaving. Get your cloak and gloves."

"But where—"

"Move, woman!"

Gemma did as she was told. By the time she descended from the loft, Connor had gone out to hitch up the pony. Coming up behind him, she said his name softly, but he did not acknowledge her.

"They didn't mean anything by it," she coaxed.

A muscle in Connor's jaw worked in and out. "Oh, didn't they? Offering to buy you for a bloody farthing? Thinking us so common that our rights don't matter?"

"They were uncouth, that's all."

Connor jerked savagely at the leather straps. "They would never have dared such a thing if they'd known who we were. It's only because they thought us lowly peasants, to be ordered about and paid off at whim."

"Well, aren't we?"

He swung on her then, his face black with fury. "No. No, Gemma, we're not. And it's time we settled that once and for all."

"What—what do you mean to do?" She looked at the pistols in his belt and then up into his hard face. "You'll never be able to catch them!"

"Is that what you think?"

"But if we're not going after them, then where—?"

"Glenarris. Get in the cart."

She hesitated, confused and apprehensive. "Can I take Pope?"

"If you must."

She scrambled onto the seat with the little dog in her arms. Taking up the reins, Connor climbed up beside her. She cast a swift glance at his face and then looked away without speaking.

Although the pony was still not recovered from its last, hard journey, it trotted off gamely enough. She turned to look over her shoulder as the cart swung onto the open moor. "My washing—"

"It will keep," Connor snapped.

She faced forward again and said nothing more.

They reached Glenarris late in the afternoon, after a ride in which not one word had been spoken between them for a number of hours. At first Gemma had tried to make conversation, but Connor had answered only in monosyllables, if at all. She sensed that his anger had by no means faded with the hours. Pondering this, she thought she understood why he was so angry. If he was indeed a former gentleman, as she now suspected, then of course he would be furious and bitter at finding himself treated like a callow beggar whose wife could be bought like a common strumpet. Why, Connor might even have once been better off than those boorish Englishmen, which would make their contempt doubly galling!

Although she ached for Connor, she did not know how to help him. The best she could do was respect his need for silence and leave him alone. Perhaps in time his temper would improve and he would tell her why they were going to Glenarris. She had been wondering for weeks what Glenarris was, but now she wasn't so certain she wanted to know.

Connor had brought along bread and cheese, and they shared it for lunch, washed down with a bottle of wine. All morning they had been traveling east across a wide moor with mountains ranking to the west and the south. The heather was no longer blooming, but Gemma thought the hillsides beautiful nonetheless, for the cold weather had painted them warm ocher, rust, and brown. There were more trees here than there were surrounding their croft, and the pines were of a green so deep as to appear almost black. Their resinous scent filled the cold air, and the discarded needles deadened the clopping of the pony's hooves.

Eventually the glen narrowed and the rolling hills sharpened into folds on either side of the unmarked trail. There were signs of human habitation now: tidy crofts with smoking chimneys, an occasional inn of white-washed stone, even a hunting lodge in the distance, its slate roof gleaming in the late afternoon sun.

Gemma noticed none of these, however, for not long after eating she had grown drowsy. The movement of the cart was like the rocking of a cradle, and after a while her eyelids drooped and her head fell forward.

"Go lie down in the back," Connor ordered after she had slumped against him for the third or fourth time.

She obeyed without arguing. Spreading her cloak on the straw she curled up with Pope beside her and fell asleep almost at once. It was a light sleep, alive with worry and incomprehensible dreams. Most of them centered around Connor, though there was something about this dream-Connor that she found disquieting. She felt compelled to escape him, but whenever she tried to run, she found herself moving with extreme difficulty, as though her feet were made of lead. Connor, who was not at all thusly hampered, caught her easily. Taking her by the shoulders, he began to shake and shake her. . . .

". . . Gemma, wake up. We're here."

She opened her eyes to find Connor leaning down from the seat and shaking her for real. Brushing the straw from her hair, she sat up and looked groggily around her. The cart had halted in the forecourt of a tiny inn with barren windowboxes and a forlorn garden.

A cobbled street led onward into the smallest village she had ever seen. No more than six houses stood facing each other on either side of the twisting alley. There was a market square with a fountain at the far end, and several stores: a butchery, a tavern, a bakery, and a dry-goods shop which boasted the services of a chemist on a faded limner's sign. Beyond the last house stood a tiny kirk with a sagging gate and tombstones leaning in the side yard.

There was no one about save a border collie that slunk away when Pope barked at it from the safety of her lap. But the village was by no means bleak, for the houses were tidy, and squares of welcoming light showed in some of the windows. Even the small crofts farther beyond the kirk were well tended and stocked with sheep and shaggy Highland cattle.

She took it all in, then turned to Connor. "Is this Glenarris?"

"Aye."

She waited, but he said nothing more. After a moment he set the cart in motion. She was startled when he turned away from the cobbled street rather than down it, but she didn't think he'd answer if she asked him where they were bound. She couldn't begin to imagine, unless it was to one of those outlying crofts there in the distance.

But these, too, were skirted as the pony trotted smartly along the trail, which wound in a wide berth around the village and the distant crofts before turning sharply to the west. Here the valley began to narrow as the hills— they were actually cliffs by now—rose sharply into folds and closed ranks over the glen.

As they neared the narrowing flume which made up the entrance of the glen, she gasped. An ancient castle with stone turrets and a keep clung to its promontory on the cliffs like a brooding bird of prey. Feudal arrow-slits showed along the massive walls, and as they came closer, she saw there were more along the parapets of the towers.

She sat quite still, unable to believe that this was their destination. The cart trail was climbing steeply now, and it seemed to be leading straight toward those towering walls. Stealing a glance at Connor's face, she saw that his expression was forbidding. He seemed a stranger to her now; no more the endearing lover of the last few days than the unkind monster who had first abducted her. She could not begin to fathom why he was bringing her here.

The pony was leaning hard into the traces, for the climb was becoming increasingly steep. She had no doubt that the fortress had been unapproachable in feudal times, when there probably hadn't even been a trail cut across the rocky face of the cliff. The castle loomed over them now, blotting out the late afternoon sky. The air was colder here, and very dark.

"Are we going up there?" she asked, craning her

neck and pointing high along the smooth stone wall.

"Aye."

"But how do we get in?"

Connor's smile held no humor. "There's a door around the far side. You'll see."

She half expected a drawbridge with an armored knight standing guard. Instead they followed the wall for more than a quarter mile before passing through a massive gate and entering a deserted stone courtyard. She blinked as she looked around her. There was surprising beauty in the arching doors and carved corbels, and a symmetry to the numerous stairs and towers, as if its ancient architects had saved their talents until the castle's defensive outer walls had been built. In fact, the approach along the cliff gave no hint that so much beauty existed behind those soaring walls.

"Fortification," Connor explained, echoing her thoughts. "Everything's built toward the back. For four hundred years this castle has never fallen to attack."

She didn't doubt it. But how would Connor know? And what was she to make of the arrogance that had crept into his tone? He sounded as if he were personally proud of the fact.

No one came out to meet them although the echo of the pony's hooves was loud in the stillness. Halting the cart near a massive iron tie, Connor looped the reins over the brake pole and stepped to the ground. She followed, searching the dark windows for a sign of life, any sign. Was the place deserted?

Connor didn't seem to think so. Barely waiting for her, he passed beneath a carved portal to rattle the hardware on the massive oak door. When it refused to yield, he rapped loudly with his whip.

No one answered. She could feel Connor's rising impatience.

Pope, who had been sitting quietly in the crook of her arm, now began to squirm. She set him down reluctantly and watched as he scurried off to sniff amid the roses in the bed.

"Pope!" she called in a loud whisper as he trotted off to explore the courtyard.

"He'll be fine," Connor said shortly, knocking again. "Leave him."

"There doesn't seem to be anyone here," she said with increasing hope as long moments passed and the door remained barred.

He turned to look at her. "Nervous?"

"Why shouldn't I be?" she countered stiffly. "You're acting so mysterious. What is this place? Who lives here?"

"I do."

She whipped around to stare at him, not sure that she'd heard right. Then all at once her expression softened. Her eyes filled with tears of understanding, and compassion. "Oh, Connor," she whispered, aching, "you should have told me. Were you the butler here? Or the sommelier?" she guessed, remembering his appreciation for fine wines.

"Good God! What on earth are you talking about, lass? I don't work here. I own this place. I'm the MacEowan laird!"

At that moment the iron bracings gave a deafening shriek, the sound magnified as it echoed up and beyond the high walls of the courtyard. The heavy door slowly swung back, but before the person on the other side could show himself, Connor had pushed his way in, dragging Gemma behind him.

"Who's there?" came a querulous voice from behind the door.

Connor moved obligingly into view. A grizzled old man wearing a moth-eaten plaid and house slippers squinted up at him. His mouth worked, but no sound came out.

"Who the devil are you?" Connor snapped.

"I might ast t'same of 'ee!" the old fellow shot back, finding his voice at last.

"You should know damned well who I am. Where's MacNeil?" he demanded. "Why didn't he open the door?"

"Who?"

"MacNeil, the steward."

"MacNeil of Perth?" the old fellow inquired, obviously bewildered.

"No, no, no! My steward, Keir MacNeil. Where is he?"

"Bain't no ane here wi't' name."

"Don't be ridiculous," he snapped. "He's been steward here for the past sixteen years."

The old man scowled. "*I* been steward. Na MacNeil."

Connor was more curious than angry. Who was this half deaf old fool? Why in hell was he pretending that he worked here? And where the devil was MacNeil? By God, there had better be some answers forthcoming soon! He had already suffered enough annoyance today dealing with those Yorkshiremen who'd offered to make a prostitute of Gemma.

"MacNeil!" he roared, his voice echoing to the rafters.

"Connor," Gemma implored, tugging at his coat sleeve.

He ignored her. Footsteps were tapping briskly through the darkness, and he looked up, scowling. "About time, MacNeil! What the devil's kept you? And who in blazes is this old duffer?"

But it was not Keir MacNeil with his ledgers and keys and distracted air. It was yet another stranger, a man who apparently did not know Connor either.

"May I inquire your purpose here?" he asked curtly, bearing down on them.

"I'm Connor MacEowan, laird of Glenarris and the MacEowan clan chief," he responded, more amused now than angry. He suddenly realized that a joke was being played here in the great hall, with himself as the victim. No doubt Eachern had rounded up all the Glenarris servants and replaced them with these two miscreants during Connor's absence.

"I'm very amused," he conceded generously. "Now tell me, where's my cousin?"

"Sir," the dark-haired fellow retorted in crisp Oxfordian English, "I must ask you to leave at once. The castle is at present unoccupied, and I am authorized to let no strangers in."

Connor had a good laugh at this. "A fine jest," he repeated. "You've made your point. But in the meantime my wife and I are cold and hungry. Tell Mrs. Sutcliffe we'd like supper within the hour."

He had been shrugging out of his coat as he spoke, but stopped as a soft gasp came from Gemma. Looking up, he saw that the man had drawn a pistol from his pocket and was pointing it directly at his chest. His laughter was replaced with cold impatience. "Enough of this. Let me pass."

"Sir, I cannot. I ask again that you leave quietly. I've no wish to summon the guard."

"The guard?" He gave a crack of disbelieving laughter. "Do you mean *my* men? Aye, bring them on if you will!"

"Connor—"

"Be quiet, Gemma!"

Apparently the old man in the shabby tartan had already thought to summon help, for at that moment a number of men emerged from various doorways amid the shadows. All of them carried weapons, and their icy expressions suggested that they were not above using them.

He did not recognize a single one of them, and by now he had completely lost patience with Eachern. Where the devil was the young blackguard keeping himself? No doubt somewhere close by, watching all of this with great enjoyment.

"I'm asking you again," he said coldly to the man with the pistol. "Where is my cousin?"

"Sir, I have already told you—"

With a growl, Connor knocked the man aside. In the next moment he found himself surrounded. His arms were seized, and before he could even express his astonishment he was being propelled through the door and out into the courtyard. Gemma, too, was escorted out in a similar fashion, though far more gently. Still, there was nothing gentle about the manner in which the great door was slammed and bolted in their faces.

"My God," he said after a moment.

Gemma looked at him. She pushed the hair from her

eyes and smoothed down her skirts. "I think we'd better go."

"Go? Don't be daft!"

"Connor, please. You're not well."

He turned slowly to look at her. "What the hell is that supposed to mean?"

Gemma bit her lip while tears sprang to her eyes. "Connor, please." Her voice quavered. "Please, let's go home."

"Damn it, woman, this is my home! And I'm bloody well going to put a stop to this lunacy right now!"

Taking her arm, he jerked her toward another doorway beneath a stairwell leading along the inner courtyard wall. Gemma stumbled unexpectedly and fell. He turned impatiently, but when she made no move to rise he went to his knees beside her.

"What is it, lass? Did you hurt yourself?"

She turned to look at him, and he saw with a queer blow to his heart that she had grown unnaturally pale. Gently he lifted her upright. "Gemma?"

She passed a trembling hand across her brow. "Can we go, p-please? I'm not feeling well."

His anger ebbed. Poor wee mite! Probably half starved and exhausted from the rough journey, and shaken by that unpleasant scene in the hall.

"Please, Connor?"

"All right, lass. Call your dog and we'll go."

As he helped her gently to her feet, he realized that he'd been wrong in bringing her here. This wasn't Gemma's fight, and he had had no right to drag her into it. Better to get her out of the way, make sure she was well fed and properly looked after, before he returned to deal with his double-dealing cousin.

Pope was already waiting in the cart, and Gemma scooped him into her arms. She said nothing as he untied the pony and turned the cart through the wide-standing gates. She kept her face buried in the terrier's soft fur as they clattered downhill, where the setting sun moved from behind the brooding stone walls to give them a welcoming measure of light.

He glanced often at Gemma's bowed head but did not speak. He knew there was no way of convincing her that he had been speaking the truth in the great hall at Glen-arris. Clearly she thought him mad, and the realization only made him want to murder Eachern all the more. The joke had been a clever one, but it had come at Gemma's expense, and he couldn't forgive his cousin for that.

After a time he realized that she was crying. She was hiding her tears in the little dog's fur but wasn't able to hold back the choking sobs that wrenched her thin frame.

He put his hand over hers. "Och, lass—"

"Don't worry about me," she said, giving him a watery smile. The sight of her wet cheeks fanned his temper to a heated burn. Eachern was going to regret those tears.

"I've not taken leave of my senses, Gemma," he said roughly. "I swear it. If you'll just—"

She moved to cover his mouth with her hand. "Hush," she told him softly. "We'll speak of it later."

And he obliged, if only because she looked so terribly pale and unwell, and because he knew that there was nothing he could say at the moment to convince her otherwise. He needed proof for that, and he would get it. But he would get it alone.

Chapter Twenty-two

The sun was no more than a faint orange glow on the westerly horizon by the time Connor brought Gemma to one of the tidy crofts beyond the village. They had passed it earlier that day. The prettiest of the crofts, with its painted shutters and windowboxes, it lay nestled in the folds of the hills far removed from the others, and that was precisely why he had brought Gemma here.

The croft belonged to Cullum Cowan, perhaps the most industrious and best educated of Glenarris's crofters. Cullum's wife, Mairi, was neat and motherly and could be trusted to look after Gemma properly. Furthermore, the Cowans had no children, which meant that there was no one at home but the two of them, and Connor knew that both could be trusted to keep their mouths shut.

Only Mairi was there when the cart rattled into the darkening yard, but she asked no questions and showed no surprise when he appeared on her doorstep with Gemma, claiming she was his wife.

"Coom in, coom in, I've the kettle t' boil," was all she said, and Connor knew at once that he had done the right thing.

Gemma's head throbbed from her earlier tears, and for some time now she had been suffering unpleasant bouts of dizziness. She had said nothing to Connor about them, reluctant to worry him further when he seemed so terribly agitated already. Now she sank gratefully into a chair, murmuring her thanks to the round-faced woman in the starched apron who offered her tea.

Near the door, Connor and the woman exchanged a whispered conversation. Gemma paid no attention. Her stomach had begun hurting again, and she wondered if perhaps she was getting ill from the cheese she had eaten earlier that day. But this was a different sort of pain, a sharp clenching that made her think of the illness that had nearly killed her on the journey north.

Oh, no, she thought, please, no.

Perhaps it was her flux? Wasn't that due again? But her mind was foggy and she was unable to think clearly as to the number of days that had passed since the last one.

The whispering ceased a short time later and the door closed on Connor's broad back. Outside, the pony whinnied, and the woman came back into the room, rubbing her hands together.

"Now, then, ma'am, 'tis a bit of broth ye'll be needin'. I'm told you're fair starved and—" She broke off as Gemma lifted her head. "Why, lass! What is it? Are ye no well?"

"It's nothing," she said in a difficult whisper. "A

stomach upset, nothing more. I shall soon be . . . I
think—''

Whatever it was that she meant to say was never uttered, for all at once the room spun crazily before her
eyes. She groaned, and the woman caught her as she
slumped forward in a faint.

Mairi led Gemma into the parlor when she recovered
from her fainting spell. But the young girl's health did
not improve after a few sips of tea, and Mairi was compelled to put her to bed, covering her with blankets as
chills overtook her and her fever began to climb.

Mairi saw no need to send for a doctor. No one in
Glenarris would dream of such a thing. The nearest one
was in Inverness, anyway, and a touch of influenza was
certainly no cause for alarm. But since this was the
laird's wife and since he had not seemed aware that his
wife was ill, she realized that she must do something.

The MacEowan had asked her to tell no one that he was
here, and especially not that he had brought his bride along
with him. But given that the wee thing had taken sick, she
thought it better for Cullum to send word to the castle. Hurrying to the front room, she peered outside to see if her husband was back. Normally he did not stay out long after
dark, but the yard and the village road were empty. She
prayed he would not be much longer.

But after a while, as time passed and she tended more
closely to the moaning girl in the bed, Mairi was glad that
Cullum had not returned. Though childless herself, she had
acted as midwife for a number of births in the village, and
she did not have to be told what was afflicting the Mac-
Eowan's young bride.

She watched as Gemma writhed in agony. Then the girl

clutched Mairi's hands and whispered, "This has happened to me b-before. When Connor . . . brought me here. He—he said it was probably the bad food we were given. This time I . . . I think it may have been the ch-cheese."

The cheese? Astonished, Mairi stared at Gemma, her eyes filled with pity. "Och, lass! Do ye no ken what it be?"

"It's the cheese, isn't it?"

" 'Tis no the food," she said sadly. " 'Tis the bairn. It's God's will that ye lose it."

Gemma regarded her with glazed, uncomprehending eyes. "The . . . the bairn?"

"Aye. The child. 'Tis a shame ye maun lose it, though 'tis thankful it's sae early yet. I daresay there will be others. Rest the noo. 'Twill be over soon."

"N-no!" All at once Gemma struggled to sit, but she bent over, bringing her knees up, and the sweat trickled down her temples. "Please," she panted, "there must be something you can do. Don't . . . don't let this happen!"

"I'm sorry, dearie," she said softly. " 'Tis beyond human help."

Gemma's face went white and she choked and closed her eyes. Tears seeped from beneath her lids, and Mairi wiped them away with a cool, wet cloth. Sighing, she took the girl's lax hands in hers. How well she could understand the wee lassie's agony! Hadn't she longed for children all her life, too? Though perhaps it was worse to expect a bairn and then lose it this way than to be barren altogether.

Mairi changed the soiled bedding and washed and gave Gemma fresh clothing. But the lass's fever was not abating, and Mairi was troubled. The miscarrying of a child was a natural thing for the most part, but the laird's wife did not show signs of regaining her strength. Instead she seemed weaker than ever, and feverish and confused.

"Don't—don't let him . . ."

"What, dearie?" Mairi asked, bending close.

"Connor. He mustn't . . . Don't let—don't let him know."

She was shocked. "But 'tis the faither's richt, lass!"

"N-no!" Gemma's bloodless lips barely moved. "He—he had no idea I was with . . . with child. I don't want him t-to know. Not—not now."

Mairi's heart ached. Obviously neither one of the young couple had known there was a baby on the way. Well, it was not Mairi Cowan's place to decide what was right or wrong for other people, especially not the laird and his young wife. Tiny thing she was, naught more than skin and bones. Small wonder she'd not been able to carry the bairn.

"P-please!" Gemma implored.

"There, there," she said, patting the hot little hand. She would respect the lady's wishes and keep her counsel. " 'Twill be our secret. Yours and mine."

Reassured, Gemma slowly closed her eyes. After a moment her pained features relaxed and Mairi realized that she had lost consciousness.

Oh, thank heaven, there was Cullum! He'd have to run to the castle and fetch the laird quick, no matter how tired he was. She intended to keep her promise to the lady about the child, but she would not neglect to summon the Mac-Eowan when it was clearly obvious that he should be here.

"Cullum!" she called in a loud whisper. "Cullum, where be ye? Ye maun coom at once!"

When Gemma awoke it was dark outside and rain was falling. She could hear the downpour hissing outside the window and feel the dampness in the chill air. Lying on her back in a huge bed with a canopy of dark brocade above her, she looked at it and tried to decide where she was. She had not slept in a four-poster bed since leaving Derbyshire. Was she home again at Uncle Archibald's?

Aye, that had to be it. She was awake now, and everything else had been a dream. A dream—or a nightmare—but now it was over. She had never actually met a wild-eyed rogue by the name of Connor MacEowan who had married her against her will and taken her to the misty Highlands of Scotland to keep house in a ramshackle cottage that was known as a croft. She had never seen a fortress called Glenarris or learned that her pauper husband was in truth its laird, which was another Scottish word she had dreamed about that meant "feudal lord" or some such thing. And she had never lain with that lord or learned to crave the pleasure of his touch, or especially been got with child by him and then lost it in the bed of a kindly woman whose name she didn't know.

A dream. Naught but a dream.

Then why did she feel so sapped of all strength and spirit? Why did she hurt this way?

She tried to sit up and felt a pain in her abdomen and the slow trickle of blood between her legs. Falling back, she laid her arm across her eyes.

Oh, God. Not a dream after all.

Which meant that this couldn't be her old bedroom at Uncle Archibald's either. Where, then, was she? Slowly she lowered her arm. The bleak daylight barely penetrated the room and she could make out little more than shadowy furniture and a huge stone fireplace in which the remains of a peat fire smoldered. So, she was still in Scotland. The rest of the world, she knew, burned trees. And since she was still in Scotland, then this had to be Connor's castle.

Connor's castle.

With difficulty she raised herself and climbed out of bed. This time there was no blood flow when she moved, and she managed to hobble to the window without falling. She felt absurdly weak and lightheaded. The window was set high in the wall, and she had to stand on a stool in order to peer out. The leaded panes were clouded with age and obscured by rain, but she could see other towers and plunging rooflines in the distance and, far below, the cobbled courtyard where Connor had first brought her in the cart.

Exhausted, she crawled back into bed. No one had told her the truth about Connor's ownership of this castle. No one had told her anything, in fact, because she had been too caught up in the physical agony of her miscarriage, and afterwards, too insensible to understand a thing. But snatches of conversation had come to her nonetheless as she had lain weak in the bedroom of the crofting woman whose name she still did not know.

"Go to the castle," the woman had said to someone, presumably her husband, as they whispered just beyond the bed in which Gemma lay. "Go at once and fetch the laird. Tell him his wife be ill."

"The MacEowan be married?" the man had asked in disbelief.

"Aye. But he asked that we keep the news 'tween un."

"Did he?" the man had said, sounding not at all surprised. "Always playin' games, s'truth! Tch, tch. I'm tired fit tae drop, lass. But I'll do as ye say."

And later:

"My wife will need absolute quiet, Mrs. Sutcliffe." That had been Connor's voice. Rough and authoritative, almost angry from the sound of it. "You'll see that she's left undisturbed while I'm away."

"Aye, of course, sir."

"And be absolutely certain that all her belongings are brought in from the old Dodson croft. I've already spoken to MacNeil about it, but I want you to know they're expected. They mean a great deal to my wife."

"I understand, sir. And we're deep sorry for t' scene in't hall when ye first came, sir. Mr. MacNeil says 'twas your cousin sent them strangers round while we——"

"I understand, Mrs. Sutcliffe. No need to explain. I've already gotten to the bottom of it. Now if you please . . ."

That was all Gemma could remember. The rest had been lost in a swirling haze of blackness and pain. But it was enough to convince her that Connor was in truth the master of Glenarris. And enough to raise many more questions than it answered. If Connor wasn't insane, as she had originally feared, then why on earth had he come to England posing as one of his crofters when he married her? Why *had* he married her when he obviously had no need for her money? Why had he lied to her repeatedly, and why hadn't he brought her here to the castle in the first place instead of that run-down croft?

Because something is wrong, she thought weakly. Horribly wrong.

She had to speak to someone, to find out what it was. But not Connor. She couldn't face him just yet.

What shall I do? she fretted. What's to become of me now?

But, weakened by the loss of blood, she could feel the pull of sleep replacing her agitated thoughts. Against her will her eyelids closed. Thoughts of Connor and of everything else ran together and faded as she found herself dragged into a heavy, dreamless rest.

*   *   *

When next Gemma awoke the rain was still falling and the sky had grown dark. A candle glowed at her bedside and someone had left a tray with a light meal and a glass of wine nearby. She wasn't hungry, only very thirsty, but she had no stomach for alcohol. Instead she drank the water in the wash pitcher, for it appeared to be clean, and then lay back, her supper untouched.

Once again she slept heavily, only this time she was disturbed by dreams and sensations of loss and pain. Toward morning she tossed restlessly and called out for Connor. Instantly there was movement beside the bed, but the hands that touched her were not the familiar ones that had tended her so patiently during her grave illness weeks before.

"Connor?" she murmured, longing for him.

"Hush, dearie," came a woman's voice, low and reassuring.

"Where—where is he?"

"Edinburgh."

"When will he be back?" she demanded like a fretful child.

"Mayhap today. Hush, dearie, sleep the noo."

Daylight had returned and someone had removed the bindings between her legs when Gemma awoke again. Stubbornly she willed herself to look, but there was no fresh blood. Moaning, she fell back against the pillows. The ordeal was over at last.

Marshaling her strength, she turned her head and saw that last night's supper tray had been replaced by another. This time she forced herself to eat the bread and fried eggs although she couldn't bring herself to touch the kippers. The tea was still hot, which meant that the meal had been carried in recently. What unseen servant had been charged with her care?

She had managed to eat a little and take stock of her surroundings when a bold knock came on the outer door. She sat up, her breath catching. Was it Connor?

The door opened a tiny crack and the blackest pair of eyes Gemma had ever seen were suddenly peering in at her.

"Who is it?" she asked hesitantly, her voice little better than a croak.

"Hah!" came an equally gruff response. The door swung wide and an old wrinkled woman with sharp eyes and an even sharper nose came shuffling in. She must have been tall once, but now was shrunken with age. She was wrapped mummylike in a plaid that was pinned at the shoulder with an enormous cairngorm brooch. The black, green, and blue pattern was the same one that had been worn by the drunken characters who had so enraged Connor when they had visited the croft so many days ago.

Gemma sat up. The MacEowan tartan, then. And that nose! There couldn't be another like it anywhere outside the family, which meant that this dusty old crone was in some way related to Connor.

"You're awake," the old woman exclaimed, leaning heavily on a gold-handled cane as she shuffled in. "And eaten, too. Hmmm. Seems ye'll live, after a'."

"Have you been caring for me?" she asked dubiously.

"Hee hee hee!" It was a rasping cackle. "Do I look like a ghillie, gel?"

"I-I'm sorry. What's a ghillie?"

"Ach, ah! I'd forgot you be a Sassenach! English, that

be. And a ghillie, m'gel, is a servant. I'll charge you I bain't one o' 'em!''

No, she obviously wasn't. There was too much of the haughty upper class in her bearing, however ancient she might be. And the diamonds winking on her gnarled hands could have pensioned off a score of servants for life, Gemma thought.

Unfortunately, she didn't seem inclined to enlighten Gemma any further as to her identity. She merely stomped to the end of the bed and stood there, staring. A musty scent of old lavender and mothballs clung to her faded plaid. She was so bowed and tiny that her fuzzy white head barely reached beyond the mattress, for the bed had been built upon an enormous frame which could only be scaled with the help of a set of stairs. Oak doors instead of curtains surrounded it, and they had been folded back.

''Not much t' look at, are ye?'' she clucked sorrowfully. ''My cats've dragged in better from t' gutter. Ha! Got spirit though, ain't ye?'' she added as Gemma scowled. ''Well, ye'd have to, I warrant, wedded to that nephew o' mine.''

''Your nephew?''

The black eyes, amazingly youthful in that wrinkled parchment face, snapped with spirit. ''In a manner o' speakin', aye. I'm Maude MacEowan. My brother James stood grandsire t' both Connor and Eachern. Arf!'' she added as Gemma frowned again. ''I see he hasna told ye much about the fam'ly, eh?''

''No,'' she said.

''Ha! He didna tell the fam'ly about his marryin', neither! Had to hear it frae Eachern's sister, who swears she took a poker to the lad afore he told her so himself.

Could've knocked me doon wi't feather! Our Connor? Wedded? That's why I thought I'd better coom an' look for m'self.''

She prodded Gemma with her cane. "Skin and bones, gel, skin and bones! Aye, they told me you been ill, but afore that Connor musta kept 'ee locked away in t' root cellar. Well, did he? I'd no put it past the bloody rogue.''

Fumbling around in her plaid, Maude MacEowan drew out a fat cigar and a box of penny matches. Gemma watched, horrified, as the old woman bit off the end of the cigar and spat it with deadly accuracy into the chamberpot. "You're tired, gel. I've talked too much. Always have, they tell me. Ha! Ha! Go to sleep the noo. I'll be back.''

"Wait, please!''

Joints creaked as the old woman turned, her movements painfully slow. "Hmm?''

"Is—I wonder—Could you tell me . . .''

"Connor? In Edinburgh. 'Tis why I came frae Inverness. Had t' make sure these shameless creatures were treatin' ye richt.''

But Maude MacEowan did not say who she meant. She merely tapped over to the door, tiny, bowed and muttering, taking the unlit cigar and the musty scent of the linen press with her. Outside in the hall she paused, and Gemma could hear the spurt of the match. A cloud of smelly smoke wafted inside, but that was all. The old woman did not return.

Gemma had barely time to recover her senses and rearrange her bedclothes before another knock sounded on the door. She looked up, wondering if Maude MacEowan had come back. But this time a robust woman with a red face and powerful arms came sweeping in, bringing the scent of freshly starched laundry with her.

"Auld besom!" she said without venom. "Told her ye wasn't to be bothered. When does she ever listen? Upset ye, did she, ma'am?"

"No," Gemma said truthfully. "Confused me, more like."

"Aye, that be like. Ach! And ye've eaten, I see! 'Tis the best way to bring back yer strength."

"Yes," she said dutifully. "Thank you. It was a delicious breakfast."

"Och, no need for thanks," the big-bosomed creature protested, looking pleased nonetheless. "I'm Ranna Sutcliffe. Cook and housekeeper here at Glenarris." She bobbed as much of a curtsy as her strapping frame would allow. "And how are ye today, ma'am?" she inquired, stacking the dishes onto the tray.

"Better, I think," she answered cautiously.

Mrs. Sutcliffe looked up, a kindly expression on her big-boned face. Their eyes met. "Are ye sure, ma'am? 'Tis I what be carin' for ye, ma'am. No ane else. There's been no ane let in't room exceptin' Miss MacEowan just now. Ye can tell me truthful."

Gemma felt as if a great weight had been lifted from her shoulders. Here, at last, was someone she could confide in. She smiled tentatively. Glenarris certainly had a strange cast of characters, but she had a feeling she was going to like this one.

"I—I haven't been . . . that is . . ." She felt her face grow hot, then plunged ahead. "The bleeding seems to have stopped."

"Ah, now! 'Tis as I've prayed."

Mrs. Sutcliffe seemed so genuinely pleased that

Gemma felt brave enough to frame a question of her own. "Who told you I was . . . How did you know what happened to me?"

Setting down the tray, the housekeeper crossed her arms beneath her imposing breasts. "Mairi Cowan an' I be first cousins, ma'am. She came along when the laird brought ye here to Glenarris. Told me what the trouble was an' how ye'd asked to keep it frae the laird. Now, I dinna hold wi' keepin' things frae 'Is Lordship, if ye'll pardon my sayin' so, ma'am, but this be a private matter an' I expect ye have yer reasons."

She looked as though she did not expect to hear them. She looked as though very little fazed her, either. Gemma could well imagine that Mrs. Sutcliffe never kept her opinions to herself. She wondered if it was Connor or Mrs. Sutcliffe who had the upper hand in running the household. She wondered, too, if Connor could beat Mrs. Sutcliffe at arm wrestling.

But no matter what Mrs. Sutcliffe might think about the matter, Gemma firmly believed that she had been right in keeping her condition from Connor. At first she had done so because she had thought him under enough strain already, what with the way he had deluded himself into believing Glenarris was his. Quite understandably, she hadn't wanted to burden him with more.

And now? Now she was no longer sure of anything at all. She had conceived Connor's baby, and lost it. Until she knew why Connor had married her and what he intended to do with her, she would hold that secret close to her heart.

"Meat," Mrs. Sutcliffe said unexpectedly.

Gemma looked up. "I beg your pardon?"

"I'm thinkin' supper, ma'am. Ye do need meat for

buildin' yer blood, ma'am, and yer strength. We'll put the color back in't cheeks afore the laird retairns from Edinburgh.''

With that Mrs. Sutcliffe swept out of the room with the breakfast tray in her big, capable hands, leaving Gemma overwhelmed and utterly exhausted. She would have liked nothing better than to sleep, but this time she found it impossible to escape from her traitorous thoughts by simply closing her eyes. They seemed to wander where they would, and always, always they came back to rest on Connor.

Her mouth twisted. She didn't want to think about him. Or about the child she had lost. Or why she should ache so because she had lost it.

I'm confused, she thought. And I hurt. Not only because of the child.

Sudden tears stung her eyes. She swallowed hard and turned her face into the pillow, too exhausted to think anymore. Not about Connor or the child or why Connor had lied to her all these many months.

But she wept nonetheless, for the baby she had lost before she had even known of its existence, and for Connor, whom she supposed she hadn't lost yet but expected to soon, since for the life of her she couldn't understand how she had gotten him in the first place.

Chapter Twenty-three

A cold, wet dawn was creeping over the sleeping city of Edinburgh as Connor, who had been up all night searching the Old Town for King and Carter, dismounted stiffly in the forecourt of his townhouse.

Rain hissed on the empty street and trickled down his face. He was met in the front hall by his valet, Jamie, who started to say something, then stopped as he saw the puddle forming at Connor's feet. Whipping off Connor's dripping cape, Jamie propelled him toward the parlor fire.

"Brandy," Connor commanded wearily.

The drink was already waiting. He downed it in a single swallow. After a moment his icy insides began to thaw. He turned to Jamie, who waited beside him, as patient as ever, for a chance to speak.

"I've been all over this damned town," Connor told him in a voice made raw by anger and fatigue. "You'd think those two were hiding from me deliberately.''

''I was just about to tell you—'' the valet began, when a mocking drawl from the parlor door interrupted him.

''There you are, old man. Took you long enough! We came straight from the club when we heard you were hunting us. What brings you to town?''

Connor turned. King and Carter. Both fashionably attired in dark suits with the requisite walking canes and silk hats. Both looking like wealthy, devil-may-care gentlemen who had stayed up all night doing nothing more strenuous than drinking and playing cards, as befitting their station in life.

He said slowly, ''Eachern told me it was your idea to replace my servants at Glenarris.''

''Nothing more than a precaution,'' King responded flippantly. ''You've been behaving so cursed odd since this wager began that we were afraid you'd be crying pax too soon. Apparently we were justified in our thinking, hmm?''

''Shall I fetch dry clothes, sir?'' Jamie asked.

Connor ignored him. ''You thought I'd give up,'' he repeated slowly. ''Was that before or after you'd goaded me beyond all bearing at Old Fergus's croft?''

Carter shifted uneasily. '' 'Twas but a jest, Con. You ken that.''

''And the servants who didn't know me,'' he persisted, ignoring him, too. ''That was most interesting, King. I'm convinced the idea was yours alone. It smacks of your unsavory touch.''

King made a half bow. ''It was.''

Casually, Connor strolled toward him. ''I want you to know that it was all in vain. You see, the bet's off. It was off the moment you showed up at the croft to harass Gemma.''

A flicker of surprise crossed King's aquiline features. "You can't be serious, Con."

"Oh, believe me, I am."

"Then Glenarris becomes mine, don't forget."

Connor shrugged. "So be it."

For a long moment no one said anything. Carter and Jamie looked appropriately thunderstruck, and King himself seemed rightfully taken aback. But before long a slow smile began to curve the corners of his mouth.

"My dear chap, surely you're not saying—"

"Aye, I am!" he interrupted tightly. "I want Gemma left out of this once and for all!"

"Then you're giving me Glenarris? Just like that?"

"I am. But, by God, you'd better leave my wife in peace hereafter!"

"Sir!" protested Jamie, who had stood by Connor's side since boyhood and had been privy to every wager he had ever made. "You canna mean that! You've had no sleep for days. Surely you should reconsider after you've had a proper rest and—"

Connor's mouth thinned. "I'm not going to reconsider."

"But, Con!" Carter exclaimed, disbelieving. "You can't just give in!"

"My wife has been ill," he said coldly, as if that were explanation enough.

Again there was silence. Embers popped in the hearth while the rain whispered against the glass outside. Connor's clothes continued to drip in a widening puddle at his feet.

Then King stirred. Tapping a finger to his lips, he said

thoughtfully, "I'm wondering why you're so concerned about the welfare of your . . . wife. The feelings of your victims have never mattered to you before, have they? You were charged with making her fall in love with you, Con. Could it be that *you've* done so instead?"

He took a menacing step toward King, whose head came up, but he held his ground.

The silence stretched ominously.

"Have you?" Carter shouted suddenly. "Come on, Con! Have you?"

" 'Tis no concern of yours," he said tightly.

"Methinks the gentleman doth evade the question," King observed mildly.

Peering into Connor's face, Carter let out a whoop. Laughing, he sprang forward to throw his arms around Jamie and gave the startled valet a hearty kiss on both cheeks. Then he began cavorting around Connor, prancing and waving his arms in the air.

"I knew it! I knew it!" he crowed. "You're in love wi' her, Con! You've got to be! Why else would you give up Glenarris just so we'd leave 'er alone? Did you hear, King? I told ye, didn't I? I told ye!"

"Would you mind telling me what this is all about?" Connor said through clenched teeth.

"But of course," King answered obligingly. "To tell you the truth, our intent was never—"

"You didn't lose the bet, Con," Carter interrupted, whooping. "King did. King! Ha! Ha! Ha! He said you'd never fall in love with anyone, heartless monster that you are, and I said you would. I said if we could only find one girl on this earth immune to your charms, she'd have you on your knees in no time at all trying to change her mind. That's why we chose Gemma Baird. Rumor had it she would never look twice at any man, even you. King said you'd never fall for her, but I bet him you'd go head over heels as soon as you discovered you couldn't have her. And you did! You did! Ha! Ha! Ha!''

"Then this whole pauper business," Connor said after a long moment, "was just a smoke screen. So I wouldn't suspect that the bet was really between you and King, and that it involved me, not Gemma."

"Aye!" Carter shouted, still laughing uproariously. "The tables were turned right clever, don't you think? Our own Con in love with that little goldy hair! Ha! Ha! Ha!''

Connor was consumed with rage, directed toward King, standing there with that look of smug amusement on his saturnine face. It was King who had been responsible for dragging Gemma into the bet in the first place. Innocent Gemma, who lay weak and deathly pale at Glenarris even now, having almost bled to death losing the child the two of them had created during the heart-stopping passion he had shared with her in the snug croft they had made their home.

Aye, he knew all about the child, for he knew Gemma as well as he knew his own heart and mind. She had not had to say a word to him about it, nor Mairi Cowan either. One look at the broken little thing he'd found lying abed at Cullum's croft had been enough for him. More than enough!

Now, in two swift strides, he crossed the room. Up swept his fist, moving in a blurring arc of well-honed muscle. Down went King, broken-nosed, spurting blood, instantly unconscious.

"I owed you that," Connor said without heat. "Jamie?''

"Aye, sir."

"I'll need a change of clothes. And so will you. We ride for Glenarris on the hour."

"Aye, sir."

"Carter."

The younger man gulped. "A-aye?"

"Get the fellow patched up, will you? He's bleeding all over my rug. And we'll have no more wagers in the future, understood?"

Carter nodded vigorously.

Connor stared dispassionately at the recumbent King. The unconscious man's nose was already swelling and turning blue, the bridge misaligned in the center of his once-handsome face. The bones were obviously smashed.

"Oh, and Carter?"

Already on his knees as he prepared to sling the unconscious King over his shoulder, Carter looked up. "Aye?"

"What did you gain from all of this?"

"Oh, my fair share." Carter's tone was decidedly smug.

"And that is?"

"His house."

"On Half Crescent Street?"

"No, no. The one down in Cornwall."

Connor started violently. "Good God! You don't mean Grambler Hall? But that's been in the Spencer family since, let me see—"

"Does it matter?" Carter asked, grinning. "They haven't owned it near as long as there's been Mac-Eowans at Glenarris."

"No," he agreed, smiling back. All at once the tension seemed to ebb from him, and he threw back his head and laughed, a deep-throated, lusty laughter which carried in it a note of triumph. "Well, well," he said when he could speak. "Grambler Hall. Quite a loss for the Spencers. Have you given any thought as to how King can win it back?"

"Oh, aye," Carter said, grinning, but did not elaborate.

Nor did Connor ask. For the first time in his life he seemed to have lost all taste for intrigue. At any rate, there was another, more pressing matter on his mind. Still grinning, he strode to the door, then turned as he remembered something. "Oh, by the way. Now that King has rendered his entire family homeless, I've a delightful little croft just west of Glenarris village I'd be willing to lend him for a time. Rent free, for old times' sake."

Carter hooted. "I'll be sure to tell him as soon as he comes round."

"Much obliged."

Upstairs in his bedroom, Connor quickly exchanged his soaking clothes for the clean ones Jamie had laid out. His earlier amusement had faded, replaced by a fierce urgency to get back to Glenarris and Gemma. He had no idea what he was going to tell her when he got there. He only knew that he had to find some way to make her understand that she—that both of them!—had borne the brunt of an ill-fated joke and that she must not take offense. He had never intended for her to be hurt.

For that matter, he had never intended for their relationship to progress so far that she conceived a child and placed her very life in jeopardy by losing it!

The thought was like ice water in his veins.

Nevertheless, he told himself fiercely, King and Carter had been sorely mistaken about his feelings for Gemma. Utter nonsense that he was in love with her! He had a fondness for the chit, and a powerful hankering for what they did together in bed, but that was as far as it went. His heart hadn't turned over when he'd seen her lying so pale and small and defenseless in Mairi Cowan's bed; his rage at King had nothing to do with anything beyond his discovering he had been betrayed; and he certainly wasn't burning with guilt now for what he'd done to Gemma, or for the truth with which he must hurt her when he returned. Ridiculous thought! Outrageous, in fact.

"Sir?" Jamie was standing in the doorway. "The horses are ready."

Wordlessly Connor shouldered him aside. In the forecourt he took the reins from the waiting groom and swung himself into the saddle. Barely giving Jamie time to mount his own horse, he brought his whip down viciously. The startled animal reared, then went clattering down the street as though the hounds of hell were behind it.

"Now, then," Maude MacEowan said, showing her toothless gums in a smile. "That be Brother James. Dead these thirty years, y'ken. A real Hieland laird, rarely set foot from Glenarris, and always wearin' the plaid, though 'twas against the law in those days. His son wasna like him. No like him at a'."

Gemma stood beside the old woman in the gloomy picture gallery on the upper floor of the castle's north wing. Her arms crossed, she gazed up at the portrait of the tall, kilted lord who looked so very much like Connor. ''His son? Do you mean Connor's father, or Eachern's?''

''Connor's, o' course. Eachern rare knew his own sire. Fever carried 'im off at twenty-six, when Eachern was still in schoolroom and his sister Janet a wee babe.''

Maude turned her gaze back on the imposing portrait with a snort of disgust. ''Now Alastair, Connor's father. No religion for him save money, and how to make the most of't. And make it he did. Hand o'er fist. First wi' France, buildin' up the cloth and wine trade after Waterloo. And then India. Tradin' wool and timber and dyes like them wealthy nabobs in Calcutta. Connor, of course, carried on after 'im.''

Maude strolled along the creaking floorboards, her cane thumping loudly. The scent of old-fashioned pomade hovered like a cloud around her. ''Neglected Glenarris, both of 'em,'' she added darkly. ''Though I daresay Connor's not so bad as Alastair. Still, there's plenty o' room for improvement. Thinks he's quite the humanitarian, ye ken. Hah! Lip service, that's a' it be! Just enou' tae keep his folk alive.''

Gemma walked silently beside the frail, feeble woman who barely reached her shoulder even though Gemma wasn't tall herself. But Gemma had already discovered that the old woman's intelligence and her ability to recall the past were phenomenal.

Thanks to Maude, she had already learned everything about Connor's childhood, which had been shortened and saddened by the early loss of his mother. As well, she had been presented with a complete history of every colorful ancestor whose portrait stared down at her from those soaring walls. She had listened, fascinated, to lengthy descriptions of clan wars and sieges and the struggles on behalf of the Stuart kings with which the MacEowans had indulged themselves over the centuries.

Maude knew, or remembered, every last detail. She had grown of age in this castle, had been chatelaine for many years for her own widowed father and later, after his wife's death, for her brother James. She had entertained George IV and his queen when they had toured the Highlands many years before Gemma's birth, and had presided over countless hunts and harvest balls and clan gatherings.

Indeed, for more years than Gemma could count, Maude had been called upon to balance the household accounts, manage servants, and oversee the rebuilding of the west wing after a disastrous fire. She had acted as midwife in delivering Eachern's sister Janet, and had wielded authority and weapons and peat cutters in her turn, and had—to Gemma's deep interest—changed Connor's nappies when he had been "naught but a bad-tempered babe."

In the brief hours since Gemma had felt well enough to leave her bed, she had learned a great many things from, and about, Maude. It was quite clear that most of the servants were terrified of the ancient harridan and that she thought nothing of poking her nose into every facet of their business. It was further obvious that, despite her staggering age of eighty-six years, Maude still had enough energy to take on an entire battalion of Coldstream Guards. More often than not she left Gemma panting whenever she whisked her off on a tour of the castle. Gemma wasn't afraid of her; she barely had time to keep up with her!

The castle itself was far and away more enormous than Gemma had ever imagined. Rooms opened onto rooms that opened onto other rooms or led along endless corridors to towers, raftered halls, and keeps. Only a portion of each level was in use, but Maude insisted that Gemma inspect every last, icy, unwelcoming inch. She was, after all, the wife of the present MacEowan laird, and mistress of Glenarris in her own right. She must learn the lay of her domain like the back of her hand before she could govern it properly.

To her surprise Gemma learned far more about domestic management than she ever had at the knee of the ogress Druscilla Baird. Indeed, running a bustling household like Uncle Archibald's was in fact far more intimidating than keeping track of the few servants who inhabited Glenarris's cavernous kitchens, the empty stillrooms and the wine cellar, and who looked after Connor's few needs whenever he was here.

Not that Gemma had any intention of ruling permanently over Glenarris, though she was sensible enough not to tell Maude as much. She had also realized, quite wisely, that she was not yet strong enough to leave the castle, especially not with winter settling fast upon the Highlands. She had already made the difficult decision to remain until spring, by which time her strength would hopefully return and she could risk the long journey south.

At any rate, she was not about to leave without Helios, who, as it turned out, was not down in the Glenarris stables as Connor had promised, but far away in Edinburgh. Even in this, he had lied.

Connor. In the space of a few hours she had learned more about her husband than during the entire stormy course of their marriage. Thanks to Maude, she knew that Connor had spent a lonely, neglected childhood and a miserable youth under the harsh boot of his domineering father. She knew that he had become profligate and dissolute upon the latter's death and that he had taken to indulging in dismayingly dangerous and oftentimes cruel wagers with his cousin and his disreputable friends.

Like the one involving herself. The moment Maude had mentioned the word *wager,* she had understood why Connor had married her. Everything he had ever said or done that had made no sense to her at the time had suddenly become startlingly obvious. She didn't doubt for a moment that Uncle Archibald had been privy to the truth all along. Small wonder he had been so quick to sell off his own niece to a fortune-hunting beggar!

Even so, a number of questions remained unanswered. Why, for instance, had Connor come to Derbyshire posing as a beggar rather than the Glenarris laird? Why had he brought her to that isolated croft near Arris loch rather than here to his castle? Had his objectionable masquerade as a lowly beggar been part of the wager?

She had no idea. But she intended to find out the moment he returned from Edinburgh. And afterwards, she would make certain that he never embarked upon another wager again.

"Drat!" Maude said suddenly.

Startled from her thoughts, Gemma looked around to find the old woman fumbling in the folds of her musty plaid. "Have you lost something?" she asked politely.

"Aye. My smokes. Left 'em in my room, I'll wager."

"Would you like me to fetch them for you?" she offered.

"Ye'll do no such thing, gel! Fetch 'em like a ghillie, indeed!" Maude snorted and then squinted searchingly at her. "Bah! I've kept 'ee out of bed too long. Ye're white as a sheet. Off wi' 'ee now!"

"But—"

"Gae on, lass! I'll see ye at supper."

"All right." Maude was right, she was extremely tired. "And thank you. I've enjoyed our afternoon together."

"Bah," Maude replied, and vanished into the gloom.

For a moment Gemma lingered beneath the frowning faces of Connor's family. Why was it that all of them looked so angry? she wondered. And why wasn't Connor's portrait here? She took another look to be sure as she made her way slowly back to her room. No Connor.

Perhaps he hadn't had the time or inclination to sit for a painting. None of the current MacEowan generation was hanging here, in fact. Not Connor or Eachern or that other cousin, Eachern's sister, Janet.

I ought to have *my* portrait done before I leave, she thought darkly. An honest likeness showing her as she was now: gaunt and hollow-eyed and shorn of hair. And instead of the name *Gemma Baird MacEowan*, they could simply inscribe the heavy gilt frame with the truth: *Ignorant Fool*.

"It's high time I left this place," she muttered aloud. But there were a number of things she wanted to do before then. She felt a strong need to repay Mairi Cowan for her kindness and care, and she really should take some time to help poor, overworked Mrs. Sutcliffe with the household.

Capable and strong as the housekeeper appeared, Gemma had already seen that she was sorely overworked and understaffed. Why, anyone with the least understanding of household management could see that

Connor left his servants struggling to keep up this enormous castle on a mere shoestring!

It enraged her that he could be so indifferent and uncaring. How supreme his arrogance to go through life abusing everyone without a second thought—his family, his crofters, his servants . . . and his wife.

I hate him, she thought passionately. And I'm going to make him pay for every selfish thing he's ever done!

Perhaps the tragic loss of her baby had also served to destroy all the budding love and trust she had ever felt for Connor. Her flowering heart had shriveled and died, and in its place burned the cool, steady courage that had sustained her through the lonely years of her childhood and the misery of those early days of her marriage.

Aye, she would have her revenge on Connor MacEowan and his heartless friends before she left. She would make them all cursed sorry that they had ever involved Gemma Baird in their foolish wager to begin with.

Tossing her head, she turned her back on the portraits of those illustrious MacEowans from whose loins had sprung the oh-so-arrogant clod she had married. To hell with him! To hell with all of them, in fact. She really should stay on at Glenarris until the entire MacEowan clan, not just Connor, was made to regret the fact that she had ever been one of them.

"Aye, why not?" she wondered aloud.

And with another toss of her head, she hurried back to her room to think and to plan.

Chapter Twenty-four

"Here you go, sir. Mind the strap."

Connor reached down from the saddle to take the flask Jamie offered. His master had been drinking heavily since they'd left their lodgings at dawn, and with Glenarris just over the ridge ahead, he showed no inclination of stopping.

In his opinion Connor looked awful. The shadow of a beard darkened his rugged jaw, and there were hollows beneath his eyes that had never been there before. Not until last night, when he had drawn Connor's bath in the private room they had engaged at the inn, had he really been able to take a long, hard look at him. What he had seen had disconcerted him enormously. Connor seemed to have dropped weight since the beginning of autumn and begun to show signs of aging. His manner was distracted and even more taciturn than Jamie remembered. Furthermore, while Connor had always been something of a drinker, Jamie had never known him to imbibe so recklessly.

It's this bloody awful wager, Jamie thought now, as he had so often since they'd left Edinburgh in such haste five days earlier. There was no doubt that this one had changed Lord Connor considerably, which was surprising considering that it was no more harrowing than any of the other wagers that had, over the years, grayed Jamie's own hair prematurely.

Usually Connor emerged unfazed and unruffled from all of his wagers, sometimes richer than before, sometimes not, but always self-satisfied and greatly amused.

But not this time.

What was it about this unknown English girl that had put such a harassed expression on Lord Connor's face? Turning in the saddle, he saw that Connor had drained the last of the brandy and thrust the empty flask into his coat pocket. His expression was harsh, and Jamie sighed, for he knew that look well. It was an unscrutable look which Connor had adopted since childhood so that no one could guess what he was thinking . . . or feeling.

A sudden suspicion struck him with the force of a physical blow. His mouth dropped open and he stared in disbelief at his master's harsh profile. Had Carter Sloane been telling the truth? Was Connor MacEowan in love with the girl he had married?

No, he thought, never in a million years! A strange sort of love it would have to be if it meant breaking King Spencer's nose and drinking oneself into a stupor on the Great North Road!

"Jamie!" Connor roared unexpectedly.

Looking up, he realized that he had allowed his mount to fall behind. I'm getting too old for this, he thought

314

glumly, flexing his frozen fingers.

It was late in the afternoon before they finally crossed the last, barren mountain ridge. The weather had remained tolerable for the most part, but now the wind picked up without warning, howling through their coats and stinging their eyes.

Jamie was greatly relieved when Glenarris village finally came into view on the moor far below. Smoke curled from every chimney, and the Arris River flashed silver in the watery sunlight. On a promontory across the glen stood the castle, as dark and brooding and secretive as its laird.

Connor drew rein to look at it, and Jamie followed suit.

"Well," Connor said after a moment. "There it is."

"Aye, sir."

"I suppose we'd better go."

"Aye, sir."

But Connor made no move to press the horses forward. Instead he sat there with the reins loose and an unreadable look on his face while the wind lashed at him.

Jamie watched him suspiciously. What was this? Cold feet? Since when had Lord Connor ever hesitated to barge into any place or situation?

I really must see this English girl, he thought. Everything seemed to hinge upon it. "Ready, sir?" he prompted.

"As ready as I'll ever be," Connor replied flatly.

At a brisk trot they descended into the glen and down the road to the village. They did not pause to warm themselves at the inn, nor chat with the few villagers who were out and about. Instead, Connor urged his mount through the square and past the kirk, then set off at a hard gallop over the moor. His pace did not slacken until he reached the steep trail flanking the castle walls. Here he slowed to a walk and waited for Jamie to catch up, then they passed in tandem through the wide standing gates.

Thankfully the howling wind did not penetrate the courtyard. The sudden cessation of its keening made the clatter of their horses' hooves on stone seem unnaturally loud. Rather than dismounting at the great front door, Connor trotted across the forecourt and into the stables, which ran the length of the outer wall opposite the gardens.

Connor slid stiffly from his saddle. Looping up the reins, he pulled off his gloves and took a scowling look around him. Without warning, he clapped a hand to his brow. "God's blood!"

Jamie whirled to see Connor glaring at a shabby black coach stored in an embrasure at the far end of the stable. It was an enormous, high-wheeled barouche left over from an ancient and more formal age, with rusted lanterns, pitted brass appointments, and a peeling coat of arms.

Jamie's heart missed a beat and he, too, cursed long and low beneath his breath.

"Maude MacEowan," Connor said in a voice of doom. He turned his head to address the shadows. "Stuart!"

A young groom came running to take the horses. "Aye, zur, welcome 'ee back, zur."

"How long has she been here?"

The youth drew up short and rolled his eyes. *Too*

long, his look said clearly. "She came na long after ye left for Edinburgh, zur."

"I should have known it." He drew a deep breath. He had no idea which of them he'd rather face at the moment: Gemma, who would be deeply wounded when he told her the truth about their marriage, or that harridan Maude MacEowan, who had no doubt been poisoning his wife with all manner of lies about his past from the moment she had set foot in the castle. Not that Gemma would need any encouragement to despise him once he had a chance to talk to her!

I need a drink, he thought despairingly. But the flask was empty.

Leaving Jamie to bring in the valises, he crossed the courtyard and, ducking his head, slipped through a small door behind the kitchen garden. There were more than a dozen ways to enter the castle, some known to the rest of the household, some not, and he had been using obscure little doorways like this one since childhood. He had no desire to encounter anyone until he'd seen Gemma.

Connor had expected to find the kitchens empty at this time of day, but to his amazement it was a veritable beehive of activity. Mrs. Sutcliffe and her scullery maids were stoking the enormous oven fires and running here and there between the oak tables and the pantry fetching slabs of meat, onions, breadstuffs, barrels of cooking oil, and flour for baking. All of them wore the harassed look that his servants always adopted whenever Maude was in residence.

He managed to slip through a side door without being seen. In the gloomy corridor, unfortunately, he was met by Keir MacNeil.

The elderly steward showed no surprise at discovering Connor suddenly in residence. The Glenarris servants were long accustomed to his unannounced comings and goings, and this time Connor could see that MacNeil looked more than a little relieved at his arrival.

The reason, of course, was Maude MacEowan, and MacNeil wasted no time in launching into a litany of complaints concerning the insult of being pressed into numerous duties that were no concern of his. Correspondence, inventory, cleaning and repairs—who the devil did the woman think he was? The housekeeper? The scullery maid?

Connor paid no attention. Outpacing the little steward with his long-legged stride, he ascended the staircase that soared up from the center of the great hall. Once on the landing, however, he paused. MacNeil was standing directly below still reeling off his endless complaints.

"All right, all right!" he called down to MacNeil. "I'll deal with it as soon as I can!"

"Thank you, sir!" his steward shouted back, but Connor was already striding down the corridor toward the bridal suite.

Though his steps didn't falter, his courage certainly did as he approached the magnificent set of carved double doors. More than a fortnight had passed since he had brought Gemma here from the Cowans' croft. He remembered carrying her down this same corridor, her weight frighteningly negligible in his arms. He clearly remembered laying her into the enormous box bed and staring for a long time down at her white, still face, seeing what illness and the hardship of the last few weeks and he himself had done to her. He had got her with child and she had nearly bled to death losing it, and all because he had used her without a second thought to satisfy a wager he had made with his friends.

Now his heart thundered as he knocked on the doors. Apprehension, anticipation, and dread warred within him.

"Gemma?"

No reply.

He knocked again.

Still no reply.

Slowly, his heart slamming painfully, he pushed open one of the doors.

The room was empty. The counterpane on the big Elizabethan box bed was neatly in place, the down bolster plump from disuse. The drapes had been drawn back from the arching windows, and in the weak daylight he saw that there were no candles on the tables, no water in the washbowl, no feminine articles left scattered about. No one was here; no one seemed to have set foot here for a number of days.

She'd left then. Gone home to Derbyshire. Maude must have told her the truth and driven her away. But how? How had the old witch known? Had Eachern told her? Had Maude simply guessed? Connor wouldn't put anything past her.

But it no longer mattered. Gemma was gone. She had packed her things and left in the dead of winter rather than stay behind to face him. And of course they'd let her go, Maude and the servants, because once Gemma set her mind to something even Maude couldn't have dissuaded her.

A red, raging tide rose before his eyes. His pulse pounded. Damn the stubborn wench to hell and back! Was she out of her mind? How could she even dream of running away in such a delicate state of health? Had she taken the cart? He hadn't thought to look for it in the stable, not after he'd caught sight of Maude's battered carriage. Had someone gone with her? Was she adequately dressed? God's Blood, he wanted answers!

He stalked back down the corridor. With every step his fury mounted until it was literally thrumming through his veins.

But at the top of the stairs he halted, alerted by the far-off slamming of a door. Light footsteps hurried across the thick carpeting toward him. His head came up. By God, he'd know her step anywhere.

And all at once there was Gemma emerging from the shadows. She was dressed in a gray woolen gown with a high, modest collar and unadorned sleeves. Though she was appallingly thin and hollow-eyed, there was a hint of color in her face, revealing its classic beauty. Her closely cropped hair had begun growing out and now it curled softly around her brow and ears and at her nape. She looked girlish and sweet in the demure gray gown, and thoroughly unapproachable.

As she caught sight of him she stopped abruptly, her heavy skirts swirling about her. "Oh," she said.

That was all. No words of welcome, no flush of pleasure on that lovely little face. Only a sullen exclamation and then stillness, like a sparrow crouching in the shadows of the hedgerow when a hawk circles overhead.

She knows, then, he thought dismally.

Something seemed to freeze inside him with the knowledge. His hands clenched slowly into fists. Sweat broke out on his brow. What could he say? What should he say? There was no way he could ever make this up to her!

"Hello, Gemma," he said at last.

"When did you return?" she countered politely.

"Only just. Your room was empty. I thought—"

"I moved to the one at the end of the hall. The bedroom with the blue flowered wallpaper. The other one was too big and gloomy."

The Blue Room. His mother's favorite. Isabelle MacEowan, too, had detested the darkness of the bridal suite with its heavy Jacobean furnishings and black oak paneling.

"I see you're up and about," he went on woodenly. "Is that wise?"

Gemma's slim shoulders lifted in a shrug. "I feel much better, thank you."

"But surely . . . considering what happened . . . two weeks of bedrest can't be enough, can it?"

She tossed her head. "For the influenza? Don't be silly! You know it would take more than that to kill me off."

The influenza. So she was not going to tell him about the baby. Should he tell her that he already knew? He cleared his throat. "Gemma—"

She interrupted coolly. "Where, by the way, is my colt? You told me he was here with your cousin. Your stableman says he's never laid eyes on him."

"I had him taken to Edinburgh. The stables there are far more modern, and my stableman is better experienced at handling studs."

"Ah," she said. "You have a house in Edinburgh, too? How very unusual for a pauper: a castle *and* a townhouse."

"Gemma—"

"Oh, my," she added hastily as the clock in the hall

below boomed three sonorous notes. "Is it that late already? Excuse me. I've much to do."

Baffled, aching, angry, he watched her run lightly past him down the stairs. Their interview had gone far worse than he had hoped. He couldn't even reach her anymore.

That wasn't as bad as I imagined, Gemma thought on her way downstairs. She had handled herself far better than she had feared. No tears, no shouting, no recriminations. Only a calm exchange of questions and answers. She was actually quite proud of herself.

The only thing that troubled her was the way her heart had lurched when she'd first seen Connor. How thin and haggard he'd grown. She had feared for one awful moment that he was ill. Well, now she knew that he wasn't, and he was back, and she hadn't succumbed to the vapors as she had worried she would.

All things considered, she'd been quite fortunate. She wasn't even angry at him anymore for marrying her just to win a bet. How on earth could she be? After the misery of those early days journeying north with him—hating him because she believed he'd married her for her fortune, and being forced to endure his cruelty—this cold, hard truth was far easier to live with.

Her only regret was that she had once wasted time feeling sorry for him. A gentleman down on his luck, she'd thought; once proud, now defeated and suffering from delusions. She had actually intended to use her fortune to set matters right for him, and coax him with the strength of her love back to a measure of sanity.

Bah!

"Gemma, wait, please."

She paused at the bottom of the stairs and looked up at Connor descending toward her. Well! It hadn't taken him long to recover his wits, had it?

They stood facing each other, Connor on the bottom step, she several feet away in the hall.

Neither of them spoke, both waiting to see what the other would say.

"Where are you off to?" he asked at last.

"The kitchen."

"The kitchen? What for?"

She arched an eyebrow. " 'Tis a wife's duty to see after the household, isn't it?"

"Yes, but—" Connor passed a hand across his eyes. "I don't understand. Does this mean . . . Then you're not leaving?"

Damn his bloody hide! Why did he have to look so tired and bewildered? It took all the enjoyment out of making him squirm.

Her chin rose. "Why should I leave? Have you looked outside recently? Winter's coming. I've no intention of traveling through the mountains at this time of year. Besides, this is my home now, isn't it?"

"Your—"

"Stop stammering, Connor, it doesn't become you. Yes, my home. You married me, didn't you? And whatever the circumstances, you're stuck with me for a little while yet."

Oh ho! So this was the game she had decided to play, was it? Stick the knife in him and twist till she had her revenge? Rather than run home immediately to her Uncle Archie with her tail between her legs, she was going to turn on him and gnaw him to pieces.

Not a pleasant prospect, in truth. Connor had already learned how savagely his wee bride could bite.

"Now, I really must be going," she added in that

haughty way of the old Gemma speaking down to her lowly beggar of a husband. "Excuse me."

He watched her sweep away, her head held high in that old, insufferable way of the spoiled little heiress. No doubt about it. Gemma had got her backbone back.

A dry cough brought his head around. There in the shadows, like some moldy specter, lurked his tiny, wrinkled great-aunt Maude, a veritable mummy in her faded MacEowan plaid. The last time he had seen her had been in early June at the Highland Games in Argyllshire. They had quarreled fiercely then, as they always did, over his neglect of Glenarris. He recalled having threatened to roast her tongue on a spit if she didn't quit lashing him with it. Maude had thumped him heartily on the backside with her cane for that one, and he had beat a hasty retreat. They hadn't spoken since.

Now they stood eyeing each other like bristling dogs ready to fall on the kill.

"Hello, Auntie. Still alive, I see."

"Hello, Nephew. Still putting yourself on the level with God, I see."

"If you're referring to Gemma—"

"I am!" Maude's black eyes glittered with anger. "Usin' her cruel, ye be, just like a' the other women in your disreputable past! Makin' daft packs wi' yer cousin an' that long-nosed Spencer boy for thrills, simple thrills, and not carin' wham ye be steppin' on, just so 'ee can hae yer fun! Well, mark my words, Connor, lad, wi' this ane ye've blundered! Regret it ye shall!"

"If you mean my marriage, I already do," he told her shortly.

Much to his fury, Maude merely looked pleased to hear it.

"And who on earth gave you leave to tell her about my betting?" he demanded, enraged. "Especially in her condition? You knew damned well she'd been ill, and the cause of it, too! Don't you dare try and tell me you had no idea what you were about, because I know you a damned sight better than that. You're naught but an addle-brained, interfering old hag who—"

"Lord, but there's heat in that great, cold furnace after all," Maude observed mockingly. "Well, ye've na richt to pass judgment on me, laddie! Na the way ye've used the bairn! And I wasna the one told her why ye'd married her. She's the one whot told me, for she did ken already."

"That I find hard to believe."

Maude shrugged and tucked her cane beneath her arm. He watched distastefully as she fumbled in her plaid for matches and lit one of her smelly cigars. He wished he could wring her scrawny neck here and now.

Maude glanced at him through a cloud of exhaled smoke and grinned a gummy grin. "I' my grandsire's time no ane questioned when the laird threw from the tower those who displeased him."

"Don't tempt me," he warned.

Maude cackled. Another cloud of bluish smoke settled around her head as she exhaled. She had been smoking for as long as he could remember. Even while still a handsome, much admired horsewoman she had actually smoked during the hunt, and sat with the men at their port and cigars long after the other ladies had discreetly retired.

Connor's mother had adored her, his father had loathed her. Most MacEowan men did, though the same couldn't be said for others of their sex, especially during

325

Maude's profligate youth, for she had been a fabled beauty in her day and her lovers reportedly legion.

Meddling old besom. He wasn't sure what he himself felt for her. As a child he had always delighted in her ability to turn his father's coldly ordered household upside down. She had always managed to reduce Janet and Eachern to tears at every family gathering, although Connor had found her more amusing than scary. Later, while growing into manhood, he had simply thought her daft and avoided her as much as possible.

On the other hand, he had often, and quite honestly, conceded that she was a far better man than he would ever be. She had always been a crack shot and good with a blade and, later, as she aged, became a force to be reckoned with wielding that gold-headed cane. She was bad-tempered, bad-mannered, crude, rude, and arrogant, but he had always had to admit (secretly, of course) that life was never dull with Aunt Maude around.

Unfortunately for him, the older Maude got, the more restless and bored and meddlesome she became. Somehow she always managed to catch wind of his presence at Glenarris, and it wouldn't take long before her musty old coach was seen rumbling up the hill from the Inverness road, bringing the scent of old lavender and the grave along with her and sending the servants into a panic.

At the moment though, he wasn't about to tolerate his great-aunt's presence. Not when he was dead certain that Gemma's coldness toward him was all the old woman's doing. ''What have you done to her?'' he demanded now.

Shrewd, unwinking eyes regarded him through a haze

of shifting smoke. "Done? Ye wound me, Connor. Not a thing."

"Hah. I smell something altogether objectionable here."

"Mayhap it be yer ain self," she shot back. "Reekin' o' the road ye be, an' whiskey an' the like. Do as I say and take a swillin' 'neath the pump, laddie. 'Tis high overdue."

He turned away from her quickly so that she would not see his grin. Old bitch! He'd have his hands full, with both Maude *and* Gemma obviously itching to do battle.

Where to begin? His hands on his hips, he considered briefly. With Gemma, of course. But first he'd actually heed the old harridan's advice and bathe and change his clothes.

Only then would he confront his rebellious wife and find out exactly how she intended to make him twist in the wind.

Chapter Twenty-five

When Gemma entered the kitchen, preparations for the evening meal were running smoothly. The smell of roasting meat hung in the air.

Her nose twitched. Even after nearly two weeks here at Glenarris, she still couldn't take Mrs. Sutcliffe's bountiful meals for granted. Not after the lean autumn she and Connor had endured foraging and hunting the area round their croft in order to feed themselves.

Her hands clasped behind her back, Gemma stood surveying the scene before her. When she had first felt well enough to get out of bed and take an interest in the Glenarris household, she had summoned Mrs. Sutcliffe and diffidently asked for the woman's help in learning the duties of a chatelaine. She had worried that the housekeeper would resent any intrusion into her domain, but apparently Gemma had underestimated her entirely. Mrs. Sutcliffe had professed herself delighted to do so.

The first thing she had asked of Gemma in turn was permission to hire a second scullery maid to help in the kitchen. How else, she had asked with a smile, was she expected to devote her own time to putting the meat back on Mistress Gemma's bones?

Relieved and grateful, Gemma had agreed. The new girl turned out to be a thin little thing from one of the crofts beyond the village, no older than twelve, but loyal and hardworking. Gemma had befriended her as best she could although Fiona Sinclair was painfully shy, and awed by her. After their first meeting, Gemma had taken Mrs. Sutcliffe aside and mentioned that it might be a good idea to put some meat on Fiona's bones as well.

"You'll find 'em all like that down i' the glen," Mrs. Sutcliffe had answered with a shrug. "All eyes an' baggy clothes because there bain't enow fat on their frames tae fill up the clothes they wear."

"But why?" she had asked, aghast.

Again a shrug from those broad, mannish shoulders. "Winters be hard here, ma'am."

But Gemma had noticed that after this exchange there was always an extra plate for Fiona, and even an occasional satchel of leftovers for the girl to take home with her at night.

As her own strength began to return and her conversations with Maude made her start to take an interest in Glenarris, she came to see that wee Fiona wasn't the only one who seemed badly undernourished. The grooms in the stable were unmistakably scrawny, as were the deerhounds Connor kept in his kennel. She had not had the strength to venture down into the village just yet, but she suspected that the situation there would be no different.

Eventually she began to realize that Maude had been right in claiming that Connor took little interest in managing his birthright. With increasing anger, she had set out to improve the situation, at least while the winter storms were expected to keep her trapped at Glenarris anyway. Connor may have treated her like an afterthought, but she was damned if she would permit him to go on being so indifferent to his own crofters!

Now, as she wandered through the cavernous kitchen deep below the magnificent staterooms of Glenarris, she took great satisfaction in seeing the huge kettles brimming with soup and root cellar vegetables, the heavy oxen turning on the spits, and Mrs. Sutcliffe kneading huge mounds of dough with her big, capable hands. There would be plenty of food for dinner even though Connor had shown up unexpectedly. More than enough to send out to the stables for the grooms to enjoy, and home with those servants who returned to their families in the village every night.

Gemma paused to exchange a few words with Fiona, who was using Mrs. Sutcliffe's freshly kneaded dough to shape bannocks at the worn oak table. Fiona had been told that the laird had returned and was in an obvious state of terror. Gemma had a lot of trouble coaxing her to smile, but finally succeeded after assuring the girl that, whatever she may have heard, MacEowan lairds did not eat children for breakfast.

Smiling, Gemma filched a pinch of yeasty dough before turning away. As she popped it into her mouth, her eyes fell on a man she had never seen before, standing in the shadows near the huge stone oven watching her. He was a pleasant-looking fellow, perhaps a little older than Archibald Baird, with graying hair and neat clothes.

As their eyes met, he straightened and came forward, bowing.

"Jamie Tendale, ma'am. Master Connor's valet."

Ah ha. Connor's valet. Interesting. Swallowing the lump of dough, she extended her hand. "How do you do, Mr. Tendale. I'm Gemma MacEowan. Did you accompany my husband from Edinburgh?"

"Aye, ma'am."

"Have you been with him long?"

"More than twenty years, ma'am."

"I congratulate you on your fortitude," she told him soberly.

Jamie burst into appreciative laughter. Then, appalled at himself, he immediately assumed his gravest manner. "I understand you're from England, ma'am."

"Yes, Derbyshire. I'm certain Master Connor told you the circumstances surrounding our marriage."

He couldn't prevent the heat from creeping into his cheeks. God's blood, the woman was direct! Small wonder she drove Lord Connor mad. He found he couldn't look away from the huge green eyes that met his without wavering, beautiful eyes they were, and solemn to the point of sadness.

"Yes, ma'am," he admitted honestly. "I'm sorry, ma'am."

He hadn't imagined it. They *were* sad, those tilted, leaf green eyes.

"Not as sorry as I am, Mr. Tendale."

"Mistress Gemma!"

She turned to Mrs. Sutcliffe who signalled to her with a flour-dusted hand, then turned back to him and smiled. It was a brief but dazzling smile that lit up her thin little face enough for him to catch a glimpse of its breathtaking beauty. In that one moment he understood clearly why King Spencer had chosen this young English lass for his wager with Lord Connor, and why his master had been acting like a bear with a thorn in his paw ever since he'd shown up in Edinburgh.

"Excuse me, please, Mr. Tendale," Gemma was saying ruefully. "It would seem I am needed. Mrs. Sutcliffe always frets whenever she cooks, though her meals are always without equal. But it was so nice to make your acquaintance. I'm glad you're here."

She certainly seemed to mean it. Apparently her animosity toward Connor did not extend to his personal servants.

Jamie watched her sweep away, small and lovely in her slim gray gown, and promptly fell in love.

Supper was served two hours later in the breakfast room, a far more cozy place in which to dine than the huge, drafty reception hall. The change of venue was Gemma's doing, and Connor wondered if she knew that his mother, too, had always insisted on taking meals here whenever the family ate alone.

Just as in his mother's day, the service was kept simple, with ironstone dishes and pewter utensils, while the family's needs were seen to by a single servant. In this case it was the ramrod-stiff Keir MacNeil, whose behavior baffled Connor because the man was all but acting as though he were lording over a state dinner at Holyrood Palace with the Queen and Prince Albert in attendance.

It didn't take him long to figure out that MacNeil was playing the obsequious chamberlain for Gemma's benefit. While he wouldn't go so far as to say the man was besotted, it was clear that the lovely Mrs. MacEowan had made quite an impression on the normally hide-bound fellow.

For some reason, MacNeil's fawning behavior irritated Connor. So did the way Gemma kept smiling at him. Before the first course was even cleared away, he had to fight the urge to lock Gemma in the root cellar and upend his steward in the privy.

Maude, quite naturally, only served to make matters worse. It was immediately clear to him that the ancient crone doted on Gemma and that the two of them had struck up a very amiable relationship. Never mind that his great-aunt had always professed to have absolutely no patience with members of her own sex. Throughout the meal she and Gemma argued over topics like old, bandy enemies and even laughed occasionally at some extremely off-color jokes. Connor's annoyance grew in equal measure with their obvious enjoyment of each other's company. He should have known that those two would take to each other!

Worse, neither woman seemed aware that he was even in the room with them. An occasional inquiry was directed his way for the sake of good manners, but if he chose to make some comment with regard to the topic they were discussing, they would both turn and stare at him curiously—as though he had sprouted horns, by God!—then turn right back to their gossiping.

Women! he thought furiously. What good are they, anyway?

Sawing savagely at his beef, he nonetheless found his eyes straying time and again to Gemma. She had changed for dinner, and was wearing a gown that she must have brought along with her from Derbyshire, for he had never seen it before. It was an informal tea gown of deep forest green, the skirts stiffened with crinolines, not the wide whalebone hoops of current fashion. The effect was breathtakingly feminine, for the wide skirts and tucked bodice accentuated her slim, lovely lines far better than the sensible working frocks she had worn at their croft.

As well, she had done something with her hair that was new, and which he found altogether disturbing. Now that her mop of yellow curls had started growing out, she had twisted them into a sort of knot that was pinned to her nape with a set of tortoiseshell combs. Returning good health, adequate sleep, and nourishing food had brought the sheen back into the golden tresses so that they glowed softly in the candlelight. Drawn back from her face, the new style highlighted the classic perfection of her cheekbones and the sensual beauty of her full-lipped mouth.

Watching her, he knew without a doubt that he wanted her. Wanted her so fiercely, that he ached with the need. How long had it been since he'd lain with Gemma, since they'd shared the soaring passion that had always marked their joinings? How long since she had held him in her arms and looked at him with desire and tenderness . . . and love?

He shot to his feet so swiftly that his chair went toppling over backwards. Both women broke off their conversation and stared at him.

"I've had enough," he growled, looking everywhere save at Gemma. "Excuse me." Without another word he strode out of the room.

* * *

In the huge, empty bridal suite, Jamie unpacked the last of his master's belongings. Candles had been lit in the sconces along the walls, and a fire burned brightly behind the grate. Orange light danced across the darkly paneled walls and on the huge Elizabethan box bed in which Mary, Queen of Scots, had once slept while a guest of the MacEowan laird.

The candles and the firelight did little to dispel the gloom, however, and an air of quiet neglect hung over the opulent furnishings. Jamie was startled when the silence was broken as the double doors crashed open and Connor stormed inside. His master's violent entrance wasn't surprising; Jamie was quite used to that. It was the timing that was startling, for the hour was early yet, and Lord Connor should have been downstairs at supper with his great-aunt and his bride.

"Good evening, sir."

Connor did not acknowledge his presence. Instead he crossed to the sitting room and poured himself a huge splash of malt whiskey, which he downed in a single swallow. Another followed. Jamie continued folding and putting away the fine lawn shirts while he followed Connor's angry movements with downcast eyes.

Holding a third whiskey, Connor began prowling the room like a restless bear. Anger seemed to rise like physical heat from his muscular body. At the window he paused to glare out into the darkness. The wind was howling down from the northern mountains, and a dusting of snow had already accumulated on the sill. After a long moment Connor turned away and resumed his pacing.

"Finished with supper, sir?" Jamie asked politely.

Connor's response was a low growl.

"I take it your great-aunt was present?" he added sympathetically, though he suspected that Maude MacEowan wasn't the one who had put Lord Connor in such a fine fettle this time.

"That woman has one bloody foot too few in the grave," Connor snapped.

"Aye, sir." He turned away to stow the shirts in the linen press.

"She's been spending altogether too much time with my wife. I should have known better than to leave 'em together!"

"Two peas in a pod, they are," he agreed affably.

Connor snorted. "Pair of wildcats, more like." Stalking into the sitting room, he refilled his empty glass.

"I don't know what to do with her!" Connor exclaimed, coming back into the bedchamber. "Should I send her away? Keep her here at Glenarris? Intolerable to think that I may have to spend the rest of my life with a miniature version of Maude MacEowan! I'd rather hang myself from the tower than put up with either one of 'em."

"Aye, sir," he answered sympathetically.

Lord Connor was obviously working himself into a fine rage. The whiskey glass nearly shattered as he slammed it down on the mantel.

Jamie thought it prudent to head off the pending explosion. "Sir—"

"What?" Connor barked without turning around.

"I have some—ahem—advice to offer."

Connor spun away from the fireplace. He looked as though he wanted to murder someone.

Playing for time, Jamie closed and locked the linen press and then prudently withdrew to the sitting room.

In the doorway he halted, a safe distance from his irate master. He cleared his throat.

"Well?" Connor snapped.

He took a deep breath and risked twenty-three years of faithful servitude by saying the words that lay nearest to his heart. "I think it's time you grew up, sir."

Connor stared at him. "What the hell does that mean?"

"Exactly what you think it does, sir."

"The devil take you!"

"Master Connor, sir," he plunged on bravely, hoping his demeanor did not even remotely reveal how wildly his heart was beating. But despite his terror, he forced himself to press on, the memory of Gemma Mac-Eowan's unhappy little face bolstering his courage. "In all the years I've known you, I've never said a single word about your . . . weakness for wagering."

"Aye, and I'm grateful," Connor snapped impatiently. "I know you disapprove."

"That isn't my point, sir," he said delicately.

Connor's brows drew together. "It's not?"

"No, sir. It's your—ahem—your character, sir. That part of you that seems to need constant stimulation, the thrill of pitting your wits against Masters Spencer and Sloane, though I daresay your cousin seems to have lost his taste for the stuff of late."

"His courage, not taste," Connor growled. "Eachern's a coward."

"Perhaps Master Eachern is finally growing up himself, sir," he pointed out.

Connor glared at him. "And I'm not, eh? Because I'm just as irresponsible and reckless as I was in my dissolute youth, eh? Stop stammering, man, it's what you mean to say, ain't it?''

Pained, he nodded nonetheless.

"And now you want me to *grow up*. Become responsible, a model landowner, accept the fact that I'm married and make the best of it."

"It does seem time, sir."

"Does it?" Connor turned back to the window. The handsome face reflected in the glass was ruthlessly cold. "I've more to worry about at present than transforming myself from callow youth into respectable middle age. My wife seems determined to make my life miserable."

Jamie mumbled something beneath his breath.

Connor whipped around. "I beg your pardon?"

Jamie squirmed. It was rare that he found himself on the receiving end of his master's rages. He thought again of Gemma's young, defenseless face. "I said that one can hardly blame her, sir."

It was probably the whiskey that saved him from being murdered. A sudden lassitude seemed to take hold of his master and he turned back to the window, his wide shoulders slumping, as he massaged the bridge of his nose.

"Go to bed, Jamie," he said curtly. "It's been a difficult day."

Did he mean the hard ride from Edinburgh or the silent battle with his wife which seemed to have begun the moment he'd walked through the door? Jamie wasn't sure, but the fact remained that Lord Connor had been pushing himself on precious little sleep of late, and enduring more than his fair share of torment at the hands of his friends, his great-aunt, and his spirited young bride.

He's brought all of it on himself, Jamie thought, but couldn't find it in his heart to be hard any longer. His devotion to Lord Connor was fierce and long-standing, his tolerance and ready forgiveness fueled by intimate relationship, for he was probably closer to Connor than anyone else was. He had always known what Eachern and Maude and everyone else in the family had missed: the extent of Connor's suffering when his mother had died and how cruelly his coldly autocratic father had assumed the responsibility of raising him.

He said quietly, "I'll ready your bath, sir."

Connor nodded wordlessly. There was an air of defeat about him that Jamie had never seen before. Understanding hit him like a blow between the eyes. His heart lurched. 'Od's blood! So that's it! He really *is* in love with the mite! Though it's more like abject misery than love, he thought sympathetically.

"I'd rather not stay here the night," Connor said suddenly, turning to survey the dark bridal suite, especially the huge bed with its privacy panels, which was clearly intended to be shared by two. 'Have my old room readied for me."

"But, sir! If you're married now, then the bridal suite—"

"Believe me," Connor said darkly, "I don't intend to stay that way for long."

Connor slammed out of the room while Jamie looked after him in silent dismay.

In the dark corridor, Connor ran into one of the maids coming up the back stairs. She was a scrawny wretch of a girl whom he had not seen before. She was carrying a tray in her thin hands and nearly dropped it when he loomed out of the shadows behind her.

"What's that?" he demanded, pointing to the tray.

"A p-posset for Mistress G-Gemma, m'lord," the girl squeaked.

"Where are you taking it?"

"The B-blue Room, m'lord. M-mistress Gemma's gone up to b-bed."

He scowled. "So soon?"

"She s-said she was t-tired, m'lord."

"Give it here."

The maid's jaw dropped. "M-my lord?"

He held out his hand. "Give it to me. I'll take it to her."

"The p-posset, m'lord?"

"Aye, the bloody p-posset!"

Ghostly pale, the girl obeyed, then scurried like a frightened mouse back into the shadows.

Forgetting her, he stalked down the corridor toward the Blue Room. Gemma's soft voice answered his knock. "Come in, Fiona."

He opened the door and stepped inside. A fire was burning in the grate and a single candle glowed on the dressing table. The heavy velvet drapes had been drawn, and a cozy warmth pervaded the room where tapestries hung and the furnishings were of golden oak and ash, far more inviting than the heavy Jacobean darkness of the bridal suite.

Gemma was sitting at the small dressing table unpinning her hair. As he entered she was just removing the tortoiseshell combs and shaking out her heavy curls.

The classic feminine gesture of her upraised arms and lovely, tilted head struck him an aching blow to the heart. How sweetly vulnerable a woman looked when letting her hair spill down her back; vulnerable, and unmistakably sensual.

"Have you brought the posset?" she asked without turning.

Her voice stirred him to life. Setting down the tray he crossed his arms and moved out of the shadows. "You really should hire a maid to do that for you."

Gemma whirled, gasping, then up came her chin, and down came the dark lashes over her stunning green eyes. He had to admire her for her quick recovery.

"I won't be here long enough to justify the use of one," she told him coldly.

His arms tightened over his chest. He was glad for the distance this seemed to give him from her. "Oh?"

Gemma turned back to her toilette. "Naturally I can't leave until the weather improves. Mr. MacNeil says that may not happen until spring."

"That's months from now," he pointed out. "You should reconsider getting some help."

Gemma's attention seemed focused on the pale reflection of her face in the looking glass. "And who will pay her wages? Me, or you?"

"I've plenty of money," he said tightly.

"I know that . . . now."

"Then hire yourself the bloody baggage!" He hadn't meant to get angry. He wanted nothing more than to sweep Gemma into his arms and bury his face in the hollow of her lovely white throat, to close his eyes and forget his weariness, his pride . . . and his loneliness.

Her chin rose even higher. "You'll have to send me a girl when you return to Edinburgh, then. I doubt any of your crofting women are qualified to be ladies' maids."

"What makes you think I'm going back to Edinburgh?"

She gazed at him. "Aren't you?"

He hadn't really intended to leave, but there was no mistaking the staggering disappointment in her stunned expression. It was obvious that he couldn't get away from Glenarris fast enough to suit her. All right, then, he'd oblige her! He'd be damned if he'd waste his time apologizing, wooing her into forgiving him, begging her to meet him halfway in recapturing the heart-stopping passion and, aye, the happiness, they'd known so fleetingly in Fergus Dodson's croft! As if he'd ever intended to do so anyway!

"You can let me know your requirements in the morning, before I leave," he said savagely.

Her eyes widened. "Tomorrow? But you only just arrived!"

"An unfortunate misjudgment on my part. You and Maude seem to be managing quite well without me."

"But . . . but surely you should spend a few days recuperating. You can't just up and lea—"

He interrupted her with a harsh laugh. "I would hardly call Glenarris a restful place nowadays, ma'am. I'm better off in Edinburgh, where peace and quiet is more assured. I'll be leaving very early in the morning, so there's no need to disturb your sleep on my behalf. Good night, ma'am."

Chapter Twenty-six

Rebuffed! Connor could scarcely contain himself as he stalked back to his own room. Slapped in the face more like, and by whom? That skinny, owl-eyed slip of a lass! Oh, he could see well enough now what it was going to take to win Gemma's precious forgiveness. Groveling, wailing, mayhap even the donning of a hair shirt and intense self-flagellation!

Well, he wasn't about to do it! He'd not go on his knees in front of that proud little witch and beg her pardon! Aye, he had used her thoughtlessly, been unkind and insufferable, but he'd done right by her in the end, hadn't he? After all, it had been for her sake alone that he had offered to call off the wager. Was it his fault that King had refused?

A tiny voice in the back of his mind pointed out that Gemma didn't know any of this, but he ignored it. He was too damned angry to listen to any nagging voices just now.

So Jamie thought him immature and irresponsible, did he? Well, what about Gemma? Wasn't it childish of her to treat him as though he were no better than the mud on her boots?

It's more than you deserve, whispered the tiny voice that was his conscience, but of course the remark only served to make him angrier.

I'm getting out of here before first light, he thought. I'll be damned if I stay under the same roof with that infernal woman another day! And to hell with the snow and the cold. I'll make it through those passes if it's the last thing I do.

Considering the conditions of the mountain roads at present, it probably would be.

Which would please Gemma mightily, his conscience pointed out.

Gripped by blinding anger, he refused to acknowledge it.

Dawn was already well established when a ruckus in the courtyard forced Connor to open his bleary eyes.

Stumbling to the window, his head aching from weariness and the previous night's drinking, he rubbed away the frost and looked out. The courtyard was filled with people, some on horseback, others in pony carts, still others on foot. The men were dressed in kilts despite the bitter cold, the women wrapped in shawls woven in the dramatic colors of the MacEowan clan.

"What in the bloody hell are they doing here?" he cursed aloud, although he already knew. His insufferable old great-aunt had summoned the clan, sending out word to

Inverness and Aberdeen and as far afield as Glasgow and Perth, letting the entire clan know that he had married. And now they were here, amassed in his courtyard, grim-faced, hungry, and cold, and probably too ill-tempered to accept Gemma with any sort of tolerance.

Dressing in furious haste, he knew he was right as he could hear them voicing their displeasure as they entered the hall. They were making enough noise to wake the devil, and when he reached the landing and looked down, he saw that they had trailed in a veritable river of muddy, melting snow.

"There he is!" shouted one of the Perth MacEowans, catching sight of him at the top of the stairs.

A chorus of complaints rose up to greet him, most of them aimed at his neglect of his crofters, which everyone considered the cause for the miserable night they had just spent as the snow undoubtedly had forced them to take lodgings in the small croft. The only ones who looked even remotely pleased to see him were his cousin Eachern and his half-deaf old uncle Leopold, whose German mother had been reviled by the clan her entire life for being a foreigner.

Connor surmised that it was exactly this suspicion of foreigners that had prompted his clan to answer Maude's summons after learning of his having taken a bride, an *English* bride.

And here they were, unannounced, unexpected, and thoroughly unwelcome. With extreme distaste, he looked down at the disorder in the great ancestral hall of Glenarris. Already the place was littered with garbage. One of Cousin Margaret MacEowan's pug-faced brats was blowing his nose in the fine Belgian tapestry hanging near the door. Ruan MacEowan, effeminate and simpering despite his rugged name, had brought along his yapping spaniels, which were relieving themselves on a suit of armor standing in an alcove. Where the devil was Pope when you needed him?

Good God and there was someone—he had no idea who—getting sick in the fireplace.

It was the last straw. Now not only was he stuck here at Glenarris for at least another day with his mutinous wife, but his entire objectionable family had sneaked into the castle to poke and prod and examine her!

Descending the staircase, he wished he'd done more to King Spencer than break his bloody nose.

"Gemma! Gemma, lass!"

Maude's excited voice was accompanied by the rapping of her cane on the door.

Yawning, Gemma slipped out of bed and slid back the bolt. As she opened the door, she could hear a faint tumult coming from the great hall, located far below in the opposite wing.

"What's going on?" she demanded, stepping back to let Maude enter.

The old woman looked positively triumphant as she swept in. "The clan be here!"

"Who?"

"The clan, gel! Connor's family!"

"I thought you said he didn't have a family. That his parents were dead and—"

"Och, aye, his parents be gone," Maude interrupted happily. "This be the rest of 'em. The clan, gel, the clan!"

What was a clan? Oh, of course. Anyone who was even remotely connected to Connor by blood or by marriage, or who bore the MacEowan name, or who claimed some other sort of fealty to the clan chief—in this case, Connor himself.

And Maude had said all of them were here? Here, in Glenarris, at this very moment?

She gulped. "How—how many are there?"

Maude looked smug. "Not a' be here, but enow tae matter."

"Just how many is that?"

"A score, mayhap more."

"A score? Do you mean twenty of them here in the castle? What on earth do they want? Why did they all decide—" She broke off and her brows drew together. "You summoned them here, didn't you, Maude? That's why you're looking so pleased with yourself, isn't it? Even though you knew Connor would be furious!"

"Heh! Heh!"

"But why? Why did you ask them to come?"

"Because it be time they met the MacEowan's wife, gel. Time Connor acknowledged he even *has* a wife! Shameful, the way 'e treats ye."

And this was supposed to make Connor look more kindly on his marriage to her? By summoning together his entire family, when Connor had never had a kind word to say about them? More likely than not, he would bitterly resent their invasion and hold her responsible!

And what on earth am I supposed to do? she wondered. Smile and curtsy and play the role of the blushing young bride when Eachern probably told every last one of them that Connor married me on a bet?

It was an intolerable thought. And a humiliating one. She just couldn't let Connor shame or belittle her again.

"Ye'll have tae feed 'em, gel," Maude was saying.

She looked up. "What?"

"Feed 'em. They'll be hungry after the long journey, not tae mention bein' stranded the nicht in Connor's

347

crofts with barely a crumb tae spare. Nothin' a Mac-Eowan likes more than 'is food.''

"Oh, I'm well aware of that," she agreed, more thoughtful than annoyed. Then, abruptly, her head came up and her shoulders went back. "Very well, Aunt Maude, I'll feed them. In fact, I'm going to serve those MacEowans a breakfast they won't soon forget."

Maude looked pleased. "I'll leave 'ee then."

"Breakfast in two hours," she called after the old woman as she stomped away.

For the next two hours, Glenarris Castle was the scene of considerable chaos. Because he rarely entertained when he was in residence, Connor's small staff was unprepared for such a huge influx of starving visitors. Long-unused guest rooms had to be opened and dusted, bed linens aired, fires laid on, and luggage unpacked. That poor new maid Fiona was kept toiling up and down the stairs with endless pails of hot water, while in the kitchen Mrs. Sutcliffe began preparing breakfast for thirty from her meager supply of rations.

He himself was not spared the inconvenience either. Every last member of his family insisted on an audience with him: Ruan MacEowan to ask for a loan, Angus MacEowan to discuss a thoroughly farfetched business proposition, the Inverness MacEowans to harass him about the sorry state of his crofts (never mind that most of their own crofts were in equally sorry states), and all of them to object to his marrying in secrecy, and to complain especially about his choice of an English bride.

"Now I remember why I never ask 'em over," he snarled to Jamie when he escaped to his rooms at last to shave and dress for breakfast.

"They're curious about meeting Mistress Gemma, sir."

"Curious? Livid, more like. Nobody travels from Inverness and beyond just to pay a courtesy call on a new wife. Where is she, anyway?"

Jamie shook his head. "In her rooms, I should think. Mrs. Sutcliffe said she won't make an appearance till breakfast."

"I'll bet she's hiding," he said darkly.

"Can you blame her, sir?" Jamie asked quietly.

He did not answer right away. He knew perfectly well that the next hour was going to be a hellish one for Gemma. He wished there was some way he could spare her the unpleasantness of being formally introduced to his objectionable kin, but there was really nothing he could do. Maude had planned the whole thing with too much cunning for him to get out of it now. Regrettably, Gemma was the one who was going to suffer.

"I've done wrong by her, haven't I?" he asked softly.

Before Jamie could answer, the chimes in the great hall boomed eight melodious tones. Further down the hall, he could hear the first of the guests begin exiting their rooms.

"Where's my coat?" he growled.

"I'll fetch it for you, sir."

Descending the stairs, Connor tried to remember the last time the great hall had been the scene of such a huge, impromptu feast. The long refectory table was formally set. Chairs had been brought in from every corner of the east wing, and the lovely Limoges china taken out of storage. The silverware had been polished and the stemware dusted. Keir MacNeil had donned a satin waistcoat for his role as majordomo, while the maids who would be serving the meal wore starched aprons and tidy mob caps. He had no idea where they'd found them.

There was an air of expectancy among his assembled guests. None of them had laid eyes on Gemma as yet, and it was obvious to him that she intended to make a grand entrance rather than greet his family at his side at the foot of the stairs as tradition demanded. He knew the MacEowans relished nothing more than a spectacle, as evidenced by their gathering at the foot of the stairs.

He wandered among them doing his best to be amiable. Though his family had always been an irritation to him, he went out of his way today to make them feel welcome, to mellow them so that they would receive Gemma kindly in turn. No matter how badly things stood between him and his wife, he wasn't about to stand by and watch her be fed to the proverbial wolves.

On the other hand, Gemma was quite capable of looking after herself.

Or was she?

He had a fleeting vision of her drawn, tired face as he had seen it last night, and with a heavy blow to his heart, he realized that she probably wasn't up to facing this boisterous bunch on her own. What was the matter with him? Why hadn't he gone to her rooms the moment he found out his family was here, and offered encouragement and the assurance that he would stand by her side?

His lips thinned. Nothing in his tumultuous life had ever frightened him before—not duels or fisticuffs, not murderous threats from irate husbands or cast-off lovers, nor the prospect of imprisonment, which had stared him in the face a time or two. So why then did a pair of big green eyes in a sad little face unnerve him so completely?

Because you're in love with her, you great, daft fool.

He was suddenly very still. The swell of laughter around him seemed to fade away beneath the pounding of his heart. Faces swam together and blurred into one sweet, lovely face whose eyes had once held his with brimming emotion and had touched his very soul.

How long had he been in love with Gemma and refused to admit as much to himself? How long?

Could it have happened during those passionate nights in their croft, when the hours had passed in a magical blur of kisses and touches, of whispers and laughter? Or long before that, when he had first seen her after she had become ill on the Bathgate road, in Mrs. Kennerly's bedroom with her hair lopped off short as a boy's and she had looked so fragile that he had simply wanted to hold her and protect her from the world?

Or had it happened before that, on the difficult journey north from England, when she had surprised him time and again with her quiet courage and her refusal to be cowed? Or on that very first day when she had appeared in the dining room of her uncle's house, regally beautiful, a stunning transformation from the battered harpy he had tended in the shepherd's hut?

It could have happened at any of those times.

Or all of them.

But it didn't matter.

The fact remained that he had broken King's nose for absolutely nothing.

He took a deep breath. His heart was throbbing in his chest. A hell of a time to make such a discovery, he thought. Why in the name of God hadn't he admitted the truth the moment King had accused him of being in love with Gemma, rather than reacting with denial and rage to such an unbelievable suggestion?

And what on earth was he going to do about it now? Any moment she was going to appear on that staircase, and he would be unable to prevent all the emotions he felt from showing on his face. By God, he didn't want her to see his heart in his eyes with a banquet hall full of interested witnesses looking on!

Get a hold of yourself, he warned.

As he turned away to pass a shaking hand before his eyes, he realized that the voices around him were dying away and that people were turning one by one toward the staircase. Silence fell with the force of a thunderclap.

A shock wave seemed to swell up from the very ground, and he, turning quickly toward the stairs, felt his world shatter.

"Oh, my God—"

Was that his own disbelieving voice he heard, or the stunned exclamations of everyone else in the room? He had no idea. All he knew for certain was that the ground had just dropped from beneath his feet.

There was Gemma, his wife, standing on the small landing halfway down the stairs. She was clad from head to foot in the MacEowan plaid, the dark weave of the fabric giving her skin a luminous quality and bringing out the deep forest green of her eyes. The folds of the plaid clung enticingly to her slim, lovely frame . . . but there all suggestion of beauty ended.

She looked as though she had just crawled from the gutter. In deliberate imitation of his own appearance the first time she had met him, her face and hands were smeared with dirt, her lovely curls greased and sticking out like a filthy scrub brush from her head. The Mac-Eowan plaid reeked of camphor and, worse, was anointed with horse dung.

Smiling graciously into the frozen faces gawking up at her, Gemma revealed a missing front tooth. As her eyes fell on him, she grinned and waved, then tugged impolitely at some unmentionable undergarment before traipsing down the stairs to join him.

His great-aunt saved the moment, clapping her hands to gain everyone's attention and herding them energetically toward the table to eat. No one dared look at Gemma as they took their places. No one uttered a single word of welcome or acknowledgment. Connor had never heard the great hall of Glenarris so silent. Imperiously, Maude signaled MacNeil to begin serving the meal.

Ashen-faced, MacNeil held out Gemma's chair while she seated herself with the aplomb of a queen. With all eyes upon her, she hunted through the folds of her plaid and removed her squirming dog, Pope. Setting him on the table next to her plate, she urged him to lap water from her fine crystal glass.

Connor was stunned.

This was a shattering breach of etiquette. While most of his family kept dogs and fed them from the table, they did not ever permit them to make contact with the service.

Around the table, he watched as his guests exchanged electrified glances.

Gemma smiled again and caressed the little dog's ears. "Welcome to Glenarris," she said gaily. "I'm sure Connor has told you who I am and how he came to take me for a wife. I'm sure all of you think him mad to have chosen me, and do you know what? I quite agree." And she laughed, revealing her awful, gap-toothed smile which Connor now could see had been achieved by Gemma's blackening out her front teeth. "On the other hand, a wager is a wager, and we all know that Connor is a gentleman of his word, eh?"

It was a nightmare meal for him. Gemma ate with her fingers, chewed with lip-smacking gusto, and made no attempt to quiet her gassy burps. At one point she spat a half-chewed piece of meat onto the floor for Pope, whereupon Great-aunt Charlotte of the Fiefmain sect of the MacEowans had to be escorted, swooning, from the room.

Conversation was strained. No one could utter a word without Gemma interrupting. Her comments were rude and insensitive, her language peppered with words that had even the earthiest of the MacEowan men shaking their heads.

The only one who seemed to be enjoying the spectacle was his great-aunt Maude.

Throughout the lengthy ordeal he sat without speaking, making eye contact with no one, his face and body so stony that he might have been a statue.

Not until the end of the meal, when half the guests had already stammered excuses and withdrawn to their rooms, did he scrape back his chair and come to his feet. All eyes save Gemma's turned toward him. He straightened his shoulders and looked calmly around the table.

"I trust you'll all excuse me until supper? I have work to do."

There was a chorus of relieved assent. It was the first time he had ever won their sympathy. He took a deep breath and allowed his eyes to fall on Gemma. "Good day, ma'am," he added tightly and, turning, left the room.

Chapter Twenty-seven

The long, still corridors of Glenarris had never seemed so empty to Connor. He walked swiftly through the gloom toward his bedchamber, his mind reeling.

So this was how Gemma had felt when he'd accompanied her home to Archibald Baird's and eaten like a barbarian in front of her. This was the humiliation he had put her through, this intolerable, burning shame that made his stomach lurch and his pulses pound.

Only now did he understand her aversion to him as she had watched him belch, spit, and smack his way through that elegant meal. Only now could he understand her helplessness and pain. For the first time in his life, he had been forced to trade places with a victim of his bets. The effect was devastating, made all the worse by the fact that it was Gemma who had suffered so cruelly at his hands.

Jamie was waiting for him in the sitting room of his

private suite. The heavy drapes had been drawn back from the narrow windows. Cold sunshine beat against the glass.

Agitated, he peered across the snow-covered mountains, assessing the weather. Jamie stood silent in the shadows. His valet, too, had witnessed the stunning vengeance wrought by Gemma downstairs.

"Pack my things," Connor said, finally breaking the silence hanging so heavily between them.

"Sir?"

"We're leaving for Edinburgh on the hour."

"For Edinburgh?"

"Aye. Don't stand there gawking, man! Pack my things!"

"But—but the mountain passes will be under five feet of snow! Surely, sir, you don't expect—"

"I do. Stop looking so stunned. I told you last night we were going to leave."

"Aye, but that was before—I thought—"

"Will you stop that blasted stammering!"

"Excuse me, sir, but I don't exactly relish the thought of dying out there," Jamie responded, wounded.

"Don't worry. We'll plan our route differently this time." Connor's voice had lowered to a soft monotone. He shrugged out of the elegant coat he had donned to officially introduce Gemma to his family. "We'll only use those trails that assure us an inn or a farmhouse for shelter each night. It may take considerably longer, but I intend to get through."

"Of course, sir," Jamie answered dutifully, then cleared his throat. "May I ask, sir, the reason for this unexpected departure? I thought that with your family here—"

"No, you may not."

"I know that Mistress Gemma humiliated—"

He turned to look at Jamie, a long, hard, silent look.

His valet's gaze faltered and slid away. Poker-faced, he laid a valise on the bed and unbuckled the leather straps.

"On second thought," Connor said suddenly, "perhaps you'd be better off staying here. Who's down in the stables this time of year?"

Jamie thought a moment. "That fellow Sutherland and the two McKenzie lads."

"How old are they?"

"I'm not certain, sir. I can ask Keir MacNeil."

"Then do so. And send for the oldest. Let him know he's to accompany me to Edinburgh."

"And I, sir?"

"You'll stay here and get rid of my family. As soon as the weather breaks I want them gone. And for God's sake, keep them away from my wife!"

"Of course, sir."

When his bags were packed and the horses saddled, Connor went to the Blue Room to bid farewell to Gemma. Against all better judgment, he sought her out one last time, and found her in the sitting room just finishing her bath. She was being attended by little Fiona, who took one look at him and scuttled away without waiting to be dismissed.

Sitting near the fire drying her freshly washed hair, she now stood up and turned to face him, drawing her satin wrapper tightly about her.

He cursed inwardly as he looked at her. Why couldn't she still be dressed in her dung-smeared plaid? He had thought that telling her goodbye would be easy. How wrong he'd been—as usual! She looked enchanting in her clinging emerald wrapper with her hair drying softly around her lovely face.

He wished he could distance himself completely from this achingly beautiful woman. He wished that he wasn't so acutely aware at the moment of being in love with her. He wished, more than anything, that they could turn back the clock and find themselves once again in their cozy croft, and that he was still ignorant of the magnitude of what he had done to her.

It was this knowledge that was driving him away. Not, as Jamie had thought, because he could not bear the humiliation of what Gemma had done to him in the great hall with all his family present. Connor had never cared a whit what his family thought. In fact, a perverse part of him had actually taken pleasure in the shock Gemma had dealt them. Served them right for having invaded Glenarris in the first place!

No, he was leaving Glenarris simply and solely because of her. Simply and solely because today he had had his first taste of the pain he had put her through, and had known at once that there was no way he could ever make it up to her. The wounds he had inflicted went too deep for reconciliation.

While she may have begun loving him a little (or so he could only hope) during that blissful autumn in the croft, he knew that she could never forgive him for this ultimate betrayal. There was no sense in staying. He must set her free and hope that one day she would come to hate him a little less.

Oh, God, but it was difficult to hold fast to his convictions as he faced her across the room with the sunlight torching her lovely body from behind. Her golden hair made a soft aureole around her head, and her eyes, so wide and deeply green, seemed to reach out and invade his very soul.

He said abruptly, "I'm leaving."

He couldn't meet her eyes, but looked instead at the floor between them.

"Oh? Where are you going?"

She sounded cool and detached, like the old Gemma, the one who had always despised him.

"To Edinburgh."

Gemma gasped softly. "You can't possibly mean that! You'll never make it through the passes! The snow—"

"Believe me, I intend to," Connor interrupted. His expression was cold as he finally lifted his head to look at her. "Now more than ever."

He can't get away from me fast enough, she thought numbly. She'd succeeded, then. She'd driven him away.

"Well," she said aloud, her tone carefully unconcerned, "if you really must . . ."

"Aye, I must," he assured her.

Neither of them said a word as they avoided looking at each other. Then their glances collided, slid away, only to return.

I must have been mad to humiliate him so, she thought. At the time, her decision to dress up like a guttersnipe had seemed a stroke of genius, a way to pay Connor back for all the hurts she had suffered at his indifferent hands. Only it hadn't been. Her triumph had turned to ashes in her mouth the moment she had seen his expression as she swaggered down the grand staircase with her tooth painted with boot blacking and her clothes reeking of the stable.

She had known in that one moment that there could be no pleasure in causing him pain, in shaming him before his collected family, in trampling his pride, which had once angered her so that she had often dreamed of killing him. None of that mattered anymore. Nothing mattered but the fact that she had shamed him so deeply. So great was his humiliation that he was risking his life in the snowbound mountains to get away from her. Any love that he might have felt for her during those bittersweet days in their croft was gone now, snuffed out for all time. She suspected that she'd not be able to rekindle it. Once again her gaze swept up to cling with his.

Connor, I'm sorry, she ached to say, but pride and fear and the lonely years of childhood kept her silent.

An awful moment passed. Down below, the sound of voices came faintly from the great hall. A woman was arguing with Keir MacNeil about the woeful lack of servants in the castle.

Connor grimaced and looked at her. "I'm leaving my valet behind. He may appear harmless, but I assure you he'll clear them out soon enough. Take your troubles to him while I'm gone, ma'am. I promise he can be trusted."

"Then you're really leaving." It wasn't a question; it was more a despairing acceptance of the truth.

Connor turned away and fussed with his cuffs. "Aye. You'll be quite comfortable here until spring. As I said, if you need anything, go to Jamie."

She didn't answer as Connor crossed to the door. On the threshold he turned to look at her. She stood, her hands at her throat, her lips trembling.

"Under the circumstances," he added coldly, "I think

it's probably a blessing that you lost our baby.''

Connor turned away quickly, and she recoiled as though he had struck her. The bedroom door squealed loudly as he closed it.

All that remained for Connor now was to descend the back stairs to the service pantry where Jamie awaited him with his coat and gloves, and then out into the sharp, cold air and beckon Bertie McKenzie to bring his horse. Seconds later he and Bertie were trotting across the courtyard and through the wide standing gates, their pack pony following behind.

Fortunately, the weather proved merciful. Southerly winds and the less severe conditions along the coast provided the land with more rainfall than snow. Although the rain reduced the roads to quagmires of slipping ooze, it served to keep the thermometer well above freezing so that he and Bertie got through to Edinburgh with surprisingly moderate discomfort.

And there Connor remained for the next two months. He busied himself with his long-neglected household, his shipping firm, and his warehouses, although the latter provided less and less work as the winter progressed and his fleet was forced to sit idle in the frozen harbor.

He, too, found himself with more and more time on his hands, a situation that quickly proved intolerable. Before leaving Glenarris, he had instructed Jamie to send detailed news concerning his wife and his family, but during the slow-moving weeks following his departure, not a single letter had made it through. Thus he had no idea if Jamie had succeeded in ousting the MacEowans from the castle or if Gemma had managed to play still more objectionable tricks upon them. Quick-tempered, sleepless, and drinking more than he should, Connor was reduced to prowling his townhouse like a caged and dangerous tiger.

Martinmas came and went, as did Advent Sunday. The Christmas season drew near, and finally, at long last, a letter arrived from the north. He had no idea how many hands it had fallen into during the long journey south, or how it had managed to arrive at all. He didn't care. All that mattered was that here was news at last, and that the letter's seal was still unbroken when it arrived on his doorstep.

While the half-frozen messenger was permitted to warm himself before the kitchen fire, Connor took the letter into the study and shut the door behind him. Wintry darkness had fallen, and he had to light the candles to dispel the gloom before he could unfold and read the tattered pages.

Jamie's handwriting was scraggly, and the ink had run where snow or rain or unwashed hands had touched the brittle vellum. Nevertheless, he had no difficulty in deciphering the news that all was relatively peaceful at Glenarris. No reference was made to his family, so he assumed that the clan had long since decamped and that the actual news of their going had more than likely been recounted in a previous letter that had gone astray.

Mistress Gemma was well, Jamie had written. She had spent the last few days in bed with a touch of the flu but had recovered sufficiently to begin laying plans for a rather ambitious St. Stephen's Day feast that would involve all of the servants in the castle. Falling back on ancient Glenarris tradition, she had decided to invite every last one of Connor's crofters.

"Good God!" he burst out. Had Gemma lost her

mind? Dismayed, he read on.

Jamie's personal feelings on the matter, and that of the collective household, were not mentioned. The valet was far too proper to offer opinions in a letter to Connor, but he thought he detected a note of desperation in Jamie's simple comment that "it would seem everyone invited has firm plans to attend. Mistress Gemma seems determined to spare no expense in ensuring a lavish spectacle for all."

Which was all it took for his long-simmering temper to explode. Not since his mother's time had a feast been held for Glenarris tenants on St. Stephen's Day, which fell, if he remembered correctly, on the 28th of December every year.

Long-forgotten memories of poorly dressed and unwashed children crowding the great hall arose in his mind. He could see the children's parents, grannies, and uncles and aunts jostling and begging for food while craning their necks for a glimpse of the laird's lovely wife, who always made her grand entrance on the staircase before descending to distribute gifts and sweets to the horde.

A grand entrance.

He was suddenly still, his anger replaced by a dreadful certainty. How well he could remember the last grand entrance Gemma had made on that same staircase! In a soiled MacEowan plaid with a missing front tooth and dirt-smeared cheeks, she had given him every bit as good as she'd gotten, and provided the fodder of family gossip for years to come.

There was no doubt in his mind that she intended to do exactly the same with his crofters. Since no one among them save Mairi and Cullum Cowan had ever seen her, Connor could well imagine how eagerly the curious would flock to Glenarris for a chance to look at the laird's English bride.

And Gemma would be ready for them, by God! He didn't doubt for a moment that she'd once again insult his family tartan by smearing it with horse dung, and show the collective tenants just what a beauty their laird had married by blackening out her tooth and rubbing dirt in her hair. The thought of being humiliated in front of his tenants was far more galling than bearing the same shame in front of his family. Good God! He couldn't bear the thought of being emotionally castrated in front of the men, women, and children who for centuries had worked MacEowan land and owed their fealty to MacEowan lairds.

It was all the excuse he needed to emerge from his lengthy lethargy. All the anger and frustration he had tried to subdue with drink and hard work ever since his return to Edinburgh came howling to the fore. He'd not let Gemma get away with this, by God! He'd just as soon shackle her to the dungeon walls for the rest of her life!

"Thomas!" he roared, nearly unhinging the door as he strode outside to call loudly for his acting valet. "Thomas! Get that scrawny arse of yours in here!"

An old man came scuttling from the kitchen like a frightened rat. "M-my lord?" he squeaked.

"Pack my things!" he shouted. "And send for Bertie McKenzie. We're leaving for Glenarris at first light."

Chapter Twenty-eight

Gemma awoke to the sound of water dripping from the eaves outside. Standing on tiptoe at the window, she saw that the massive icicles which had festooned the roof line for weeks on end were thawing. Down below, the brook flowing beneath the castle walls was frothing with winter runoff.

Clapping her hands excitedly, she hurried to dress. For days now she had been waiting for such a thaw, even though she was embarrassed to admit that she had been doing so only because its advent had been predicted by Fiona's great-grandmother, Rula Minka. Minka's Romany name and her rumored ability to see into the future were gifts from her gypsy heritage, and Fiona had insisted that her predictions always came true.

Fiona had also told Gemma that most of the Glenarris crofters were afraid of the ancient crone, and even Fiona spoke of her in an awe-filled voice. Gemma, on the other hand, had taken an instant liking to the strange old woman after hiking with Fiona up to the remote mountain hut where Minka lived with a shaggy sheepdog named Grigori. Pope and Grigori had become fast friends, and Gemma and Minka had laughed watching them tumble in the snow.

It was during that visit and over tea that their conversation had turned to the weather, and Minka had told Gemma to expect a brief thaw before Christmas. "The snow will melt," she had predicted, "and the water in t'rivers will rise. The roads will be passable, but only for a spell. Ye've chosen the time of yer party well."

"How did you know I was planning a party?" She had asked, surprised.

"Grandmama can see into the future," Fiona had piped up, brewing another kettle of tea over the peat fire.

Gemma hadn't been able to keep the skepticism from showing on her face, and Minka had smiled when she saw it. "I dinna read tea leaves like a gypsy, child. I dinna have a crystal ball. I dinna look at the lines o' yer palm and tell ye o' yer happiness or sorrow."

"Then what do you do?" Gemma had asked, returning the old woman's smile.

"Come here, child."

Gemma had settled herself on the small stool at Minka's feet. Outside, the wind had howled, but in the tiny cottage it had been cozy and warm. Pope and Grigori had been napping near the fire while Fiona hummed as she filled the teacups. A sense of peace had settled over them all.

Minka, as wrinkled and shrunken as Maude Mac-Eowan, had leaned forward and taken Gemma's face in her hands. Her gnarled, arthritic fingers had surprising strength. Looking solemnly into Gemma's eyes, Minka had said softly, "Oft times the future be written i' our hearts. Oft times it be there for a' to see, though few ken how to look."

"Can 'ee see summat in Mistress Gemma's heart, Grandmama?" Fiona had asked eagerly, crossing to the old gypsy's side.

"Sorrow," Minka had said immediately. "And emptiness."

Gemma had felt her cheeks grow hot. She had willed herself not to squirm out of Minka's grasp.

"There be an ancient tale told and retold by my people," Minka had gone on, her dark, clear eyes still holding fast to Gemma's. "A fairy tale perhaps ye, too, have heard, child. 'Tis of a lovely princess who promises all she holds dear to an ugly green frog."

Fiona had giggled. "A *frog*, Grandmama?"

Minka had ignored her. "The evil enchantment isna broken until the princess kisses the frog."

"And he in turn becomes a handsome prince, and they live happily ever after," Gemma had put in impatiently. "Yes, I've heard the tale." How bitter the knowledge that it hadn't come true for her. She had kissed her frog and found out that he was indeed a handsome prince, but still as ugly on the inside as he had once appeared on the outside.

So much for looking into the future! Minka had done nothing more than guessed at Gemma's past.

"There still be time," Minka had insisted, but Gemma had heard quite enough. She hadn't wanted to burst into tears in front of Fiona merely because Fiona's grandmother had recounted some silly fairy tale.

"About this thaw—" she had said, detaching herself

gently from the old woman's grasp. "You say enough of the snow will melt to free up the roads?"

Minka had shut her eyes and let her hands fall into her lap. Without looking up, she had nodded.

That had been welcome news, and Gemma had preferred to think about it rather than brood over the ridiculous exchange between herself and the old gypsy woman. She had been hoping for such a break in the weather for weeks, because everyone at Glenarris had been trapped indoors by howling winds and heavy snowfall since Connor's departure. Why, even the short hike up to Rula Minka's hut had taken more than two hours of wading through hip-deep drifts.

"Do ye ken why Mistress Gemma wants the snow tae melt, Grandmama?" Fiona had asked eagerly.

Minka had opened her eyes and smiled at her great-granddaughter. "Why don't ye tell me, bairn?"

"So the footmen can cut a fir tree from Lord Connor's forest! Mistress Gemma says we're tae have a real Christmas tree for St. Stephen's Day!"

Gemma's announcement that the great hall at Glenarris would be graced with a Christmas tree had been met with considerable skepticism—except by Fiona, who worshiped her and believed she was capable of anything. Everyone else had scoffed, for no one at Glenarris had ever heard of such a thing.

Gemma had tried hard to explain the custom, which had been introduced into England only recently by Queen Victoria's German husband, Prince Albert, but everyone had looked at her as though she were mad. Not just the servants and the crofters, but even Connor's family, most of whom had been trapped at Glenarris by the weather.

As she left her room, she thought about the Mac-Eowans. By and large, they were a decent sort, and it hadn't taken Gemma long to make peace with them. Even Great-aunt Charlotte, that temperamental termagant who would have been family matriarch but for Maude's stubborn refusal to die, had eventually professed her approval of Gemma.

Gemma's suggestion that the entire family remain at Glenarris for the Christmas holiday had been met with great enthusiasm. Years had passed, they had told her, since those at Glenarris had last marked such festivities, and her disclosure that the tenant farmers would be taking part had made the older MacEowans grow misty-eyed and nostalgic.

They had also forgiven Gemma her shocking behavior on the morning of their arrival. She knew that Maude had made certain they were all told of the scandalous circumstances surrounding her and Connor's marriage, and afterward sympathies had landed square at her doorstep, and not at Connor's any longer. Never mind that Connor was the MacEowan laird and she an English-woman brought into the family without their knowledge. Stand by her they would, they had told her, which was why a number of them agreed to remain on at Glenarris until the holiday season.

Now as she entered the morning room for breakfast, she was surprised at how grateful she felt for their company. Though many of them did end up braving the snow and the cold to return to their homes, a handful had remained, among them ancient Uncle Leopold, the last surviving son of the thirteen born to Dorothea MacEowan, Connor's German great-grandmother. Doddering and half deaf as he might be, Uncle Leopold had taught Gemma to play chess and dance the Highland Fling, and her empty days had been brightened watching the old codger butt heads with Maude, which seemed to happen whenever the two of them were together in the same room.

Now, thanks to the break in the weather predicted by Rula Minka, the next few days would be extremely hectic.

While Glenarris footmen scoured the glen for a suitable yule log and the much ballyhooed Christmas tree, Gemma and Fiona enlisted the help of the crofting children in gathering evergreens and holly to decorate the great hall and make ornaments for the tree.

Gemma's enthusiasm couldn't help but rub off on the household, and soon there was a noticeable air of festivity around the place.

But Maude, Jamie, and kindly Mrs. Sutcliffe fretted that she was pushing herself too hard. They declared she was much too thin, and often coaxed her to eat. Most nights she tumbled into bed exhausted, which she knew worried Maude and the housekeeper, but for which Gemma was grateful. The nights had been so hard to bear, considering that she had spent most of them awake, aching for Connor. At least now all the holiday preparations made her so tired, she fell instantly asleep.

As fulfilling as Gemma's life might seem, she had never felt more empty or alone. It seemed to her as if all the color had been washed out of her life with Connor's leaving. She could still eat and breathe and talk and work, but inside her she felt nothing but a numbing void. Is this what being in love was all about? If so, she hated it. Why, open any book of poems and one could read any number of rapturous descriptions about the ecstasy of love, when in truth it was like a millstone around the heart, a cold, dark thing that left a person feeling more dead than alive.

I suppose I should go back to Uncle Archibald's when spring comes, she thought often. Then maybe I won't feel so awful anymore.

But the future didn't bear thinking about. She couldn't tolerate the thought of spending the rest of her life in the colorless void that was her existence without Connor. Better to throw herself from the highest castle wall than to go on facing such emptiness--which explained in part why she had thrown herself into the Christmas preparations with something very like desperation.

Inevitably, finally, the big day arrived. Everything was ready. The last candles had been dipped, the last ornaments fastened to the tree, the floors and furnishings given their final polishing, and the finishing touches put on the feast. The pair of oxen that had been turning on the great spits for days were hoisted down and readied for carving. The Christmas puddings were stacked away in the creamery, the barrels of ale and wine rolled up from the cellar, and every last piece of silverware was polished and laid out on the enormous banquet table.

The laundry room, which had been filled with steam for days as long-disused linens and formal shirts and breeches and ladies' dresses were washed and ironed and hung at the ready, was empty at last. Uncle Leopold had enthusiastically applied boot blacking to everyone's shoes, while Gemma had distributed the contents of her jewel box and lady's trunks to the delighted women of the serving staff. A final inspection was made in which the entire household took part, and now there was nothing to do but await the hour when the first guests would arrive.

Gemma had been up since dawn helping belowstairs and in the guest rooms. Despite her fatigue, she was happier than she could remember. Surely this grand feast was going to be wonderful!

But as evening fell and she withdrew to her rooms to bathe and change her clothes, she suddenly was dismayingly close to tears. Surely it wasn't because she wished that Connor was here! Nearly two months had passed since he'd left for Edinburgh, and not one word had been heard from him. She knew that Jamie wrote him regularly, but Connor had never bothered responding to a single one of his letters. She could only assume that he simply didn't care enough to answer them: not for Glenarris, and certainly not for her.

She had written him herself, more than once, without Jamie's knowledge. She had described her plans for the Christmas season and asked, diffidently, if he would make an effort to appear, if only because he was the official head of the household and laird of the MacEowan clan.

Not one of her carefully penned missives had received an answer.

"Well, I don't care!" she said now, sinking into the bathtub that Fiona had kept hot for her. Every muscle in her body ached from the hard work of the last few days, and the scented water felt wonderful to soak in.

Gemma looked down at herself and saw how thin she had grown, and wondered painfully if Connor had been taking his ease with another woman since his return to Edinburgh. She could not imagine a man as lusty as he was going long without a woman, and since she was unavailable, then surely he must be seeking diversion elsewhere.

Scowling, she leaped from the tub. She was not going to let thoughts of Connor ruin her Christmas! In fact, she wasn't going to let thoughts of him bother her at all anymore! It was time to put the past behind her and stop mooning over that pig-headed, blackhearted clod.

Darkness fell swiftly. Down below in the chapel on the far side of the castle bailey, a single bell pealed. To Gemma, it was a joyous sound, heralding the commencement of the holy Feast of St. Stephen. Along the gates and the soaring castle walls the grooms were setting out torches to light the way for the arriving guests. As the first stars began to pulse in the cold night sky, the stable doors were thrown open, drenching the courtyard with warming light while Keir MacNeil swept the last of the snow drifts from the front portal.

Looking down on the busy scene from high in the east wall of the castle, she felt her heart grow light. She had never had any pretensions about her place in the family, or dared call herself mistress of Glenarris in anything but name. But viewing the busy courtyard and listening to the bell extolling the winter solstice, she felt a strange sense of peace wash over her. For tonight, at least, she belonged to a place and a family. For tonight, at least, she would welcome visitors to her own home, and would be accepted by them as hostess in her own right. Connor might have rejected her, but tonight she would be part of his family and his clan. She intended to enjoy that sense of belonging to the fullest. Tomorrow there would be nothing left her but the memory.

A knock sounded on the door and Fiona's expectant

face appeared. "They be comin', ma'am! Master Jamie's seen 'em on the hill. 'E says the whole glen be travelin' together."

A shiver of excitement fled down Gemma's spine. It was just as Mrs. Sutherland had described for her. In Connor's mother's day, she had said, the great gates of the castle had always been thrown open like welcoming arms to receive the entire procession of visitors all at once. They would be greeted at the door by the Glenarris staff, headed by the steward and the housekeeper, and the curate from the village. A prayer of welcome would be said, and in the great hall there would be drinks for everyone: mulled cider and ale, and lemonade for the children. The Glenarris pipers would play traditional tunes while everyone waited with mounting impatience for the laird and his lady to make their entrance on the grand staircase.

Well, Glenarris didn't have a piper anymore, but the stablemaster, Mr. Diamid Jeffries, had promised to dust off his violin and play a few tunes. Nor would Gemma descend the staircase with the MacEowan laird to receive her guests, because Connor would not be there.

Once again she told herself it didn't matter. She only hoped that the crofters would find the transformed ancient castle as magnificent as it had been when Connor's mother had welcomed them into it. Every nook and cranny was decorated with candles, evergreens, and ropes of braided gilt. Boughs of ivy and blood-red holly were entwined along the mantels and balustrades, and bright ribbons and bows festooned the ironwork and the furnishings. Gemma had outfitted the servants in satin finery for tonight's festivities and had even tied a red ribbon around Pope's neck.

Oh, and the Christmas tree! She had selected a fir that stood more than thrice the average man's height, and a pair of powerful draft horses had transported it to the castle. It had been winched upright with the help of every manservant, and the thick trunk was held in place by enormous spikes and draped with deep crimson velvet to hide the carpenter's handiwork.

The fragrant bows that donned the tree were illuminated by candles in tin holders forged by the Glenarris blacksmith, and under Gemma's guidance, the crofting children and women of the household had labored well into the evening hours painting, cutting, whittling, and sewing decorations. Even Aunt Maude had helped to string the cranberries and dried oranges into garlands that were twined with gold roping.

At first, Gemma had lamented that none of the lovely German mouth-blown glass ornaments were available in Scotland, but when she had seen the inspired creations of glitter, sequins, and colored tissue paper the excited maids had fashioned, she was thoroughly enchanted.

To top the tree, she had made an angel of fine tulle and Mechlin lace—which she had cut from the bodice of one of her nightgowns, which no one but Mrs. Sutcliffe knew. And at the tree's base, the floor was piled high with baskets brimming with goodies which would be distributed later to each family. She had also managed to coax Jamie into playing Father Christmas.

Fiona's excited prancing around her caught Gemma's attention and she swept off her shawl and took a last look at herself in the dressing table mirror. How different she appeared now from the last time she had readied herself for a reception in the great hall! Then she had been trembling with terror and telling herself that she *must* go through with her plan if she wanted revenge on Connor once and for all. Her courage had almost failed her when she had glanced into this same mirror and had seen the black-toothed hag staring back at her. But she had stiffened her spine and done what she felt she must, although revenge, she had quickly discovered, was nothing but a cruel deception, a two-edged sword which had cut her just as badly as it had Connor.

Now, with Fiona urging her to hurry, she thrust the awful memories away. She had dressed with more care tonight than at any time since her debut. Gone was the moth-eaten plaid with its rubbings of manure. In its place she had donned a satin damask tea dress the color of Highland heather. The bodice and sleeves were trimmed with ribands of the MacEowan tartan, which she had stitched on, the bold colors a perfect contrast to the subtle lavender gray. Her full skirts were draped over wide whalebone hoops, a fashion rarely seen in Scotland beyond the glittering reception halls of Holyrood Palace.

Her hair was arranged in a loose knot gathered at her nape with pearl-studded netting, which was also fastened with a fluttering riband. Around her throat and on her fingers she wore her mother's emeralds, which Jamie had returned to her shortly after Connor's departure. She knew Jamie had not understood the reason for her tears when she accepted the treasured casket, but she suspected that Connor had known she would shed them and had therefore—quite cowardly, in her opinion—charged his valet with their return to her.

Little Fiona reverently fingered the shimmering satin of the magnificent gown, and when Gemma mischievously lifted her skirts and showed the girl the whalebone contraption that held them aloft, Fiona's eyes nearly popped from her head.

"Oooh, ma'am!" was all she could manage.

At that moment there was a shout from the courtyard. Racing to the window, Fiona pressed her nose to the glass. Gemma subdued the urge to do the same. It would be unladylike to spy on her guests.

"Well? Are they here?" she demanded.

"Aye!" Fiona's voice was muffled against the glass. "It be a' of 'em, ma'am! A great crowd! I see Mither, and Faither, an' Uncle Jock . . . Oooh! Taddy Feillich be here as well! Look! He's walkin' wi' a stick, an' Mairi Cowan, what doctored 'im, said he'd no be off that broken leg 'til spring! Do look, ma'am!"

But she didn't want to. She was filled with a sudden rush of stagefright. She had met most of the Glenarris crofters already, and although they had welcomed her politely into their homes, she supposed that coming to the castle itself was an intimidating experience for them.

Actually, it made her feel better to know that they were just as nervous as she was. And it helped, too, to remember that they were honest, simple folk who had treated her kindly from the first and never behaved as though they held her responsible for Connor's neglect.

Because neglect them he had! She had been appalled to discover the condition in which some of the Glenarris families lived. Why, old Fergus Dodson's croft had seemed a veritable palace compared to the smoky, windowless huts into which she had been invited. She had sipped tea from dented iron mugs and been offered scones from slabs of wood because plates were simply not at hand. She had been asked to admire babies whose swaddlings weren't clean, and played with children with open sores and bare, filthy feet.

Upon her return to the castle after the first of those visits, she had vented her anger toward Connor to Maude, loudly lamenting the fact that she could do nothing to help those poor families. His great-aunt had agreed that Connor did little to improve his crofters' lives, but since the practice was common throughout the Highlands, she had treated Gemma's impassioned vows to make improvements with an indulgent pat on the hand.

As though I were a temperamental little lap dog! Gemma had thought.

Nevertheless, she had kept her word. While the astonished MacEowans looked on, she had organized a massive cleanup of the castle. Every room and closet and storage alcove was emptied of its excesses, and long-disused beds, blankets, furnishings, and especially precious clothing and lamps were doled out to the poor of the glen. Huge bolts of muslin, wool, cambric, and linsey-woolsey were brought out of the attics and divided among the women of each household to sew into the shirts, trews, and jackets their kinfolk so desperately needed.

Gemma had not been rewarded with an outrush of gratitude for any of it. The Glenarris crofters accepted the gifts with a healthy measure of distrust. They had suffered generations of hardship and were unused to, and quite suspicious of, any show of kindness from their clan leaders, Maude had explained to her. And it would take some time for Gemma to win them over.

Nevertheless, Mrs. Sutcliffe and Fiona had told her that the crofters' general opinion of her was favorable, and those who still remembered Connor's mother, Isabelle, spoke approvingly of Gemma's actions, even wistfully of the return to those genteel old days. Others scoffed that she was wasting her time since she would never be able to bring about a similarly positive change in their indifferent laird. News that Lord Connor had departed for Edinburgh without her had spread among the crofters. She was shocked to learn that they were not surprised by his behavior and that they thought him restless, unhappy, and spoiled by too much wealth to appreciate a gift as fine as she.

Again, Fiona's prodding broke into Gemma's reverie and she hurriedly left her room.

Jamie was the first to spot Gemma standing on the landing, peering down at the crowd staring openmouthed at the beautiful Christmas tree. Mr. Jeffries, who had been fiddling a passably good rendition of "Good King Wenceslas," was at the bottom of the stairs. Looking up at Gemma, he quickly broke into a rousing version of "Scotland the Brave."

As the beloved anthem skirled softly into the air, all conversation ceased and everyone turned toward the staircase, where Gemma stood bathed in the golden glow of the candles. Jamie heard the sighs around him as she slowly descended the staircase, her wide skirts grazing the railings, rustling softly, magically. Emeralds sparked on her slim fingers and at her creamy throat, and the seed pearl netting made her golden tresses appear dusted with starlight.

A little girl squirmed in her mother's arms and took her finger from her mouth long enough to lisp loudly, "Be that a angel, Mummy?"

Jamie smiled and thought it was a moment that could not have made more of an impact on the people gathered in the hall had Gemma and her staff rehearsed it for weeks.

Applause started spontaneously at the bottom of the stairs, then spread like quicksilver throughout the hall. Jamie couldn't imagine a man in the room who wasn't smitten by the sight of Gemma. Nor could he imagine that there was a woman who didn't sigh with envy.

In the midst of the noise and the drama, the great front doors burst open and a blast of arctic air swept inside. The applause died away as Jamie and the other guests whirled, shivering and scolding, at the cold and the untimely intrusion of so late an arrival.

Two half-frozen men staggered in, and Jamie glanced up at Gemma who stood on the staircase, looking over the heads of those gathered below. Her hands flew to her throat and she gasped. Jamie quickly turned back to the intruders and saw that the taller of the two had pushed back the hood of his cloak to reveal the thin, unshaven face of his lord and master, Connor Mac-Eowan.

Chapter Twenty-nine

Silence had fallen over the hall. For a long moment no one stirred. All eyes were on Connor, who advanced unsteadily into the room. His every movement was painful, as though he were on the verge of collapse. The crowd parted silently to let him through.

At the foot of the grand staircase he halted. Slowly he raised his head to look up at Gemma. Across the distance their eyes met.

He wavered from hunger and fatigue, but Gemma stood as still as an alabaster statue.

At long last he spoke. His voice was hoarse, but loud enough to carry. "Good evening, ma'am. It seems you've started the festivities without me."

"We didn't know when to expect you, sir," she answered. Her voice, too, sounded clear and calm in the utter stillness.

"Forgive me," he added, this time turning to take in

the entire assembly so that they, too, would know they were included in the apology. "Bertie and I were detained by the weather."

Holding fast to the railing, Connor began to ascend the staircase. Gemma held her ground, though she seemed to have forgotten how to breathe. Her heart was slamming wildly against her ribs. Would he knock her down when he reached her side? Spit in her face? Or would he drop unconscious to the floor before he took another step? Good Lord, he was naught but a walking specter, more dead than alive! His clothes were in tatters and his eyes were red. What had kept him from perishing on his way here from Edinburgh? Over his shoulder, in the hall below, she could see them pouring whiskey down the swooning Bertie McKenzie's throat.

It seemed to take forever for Connor to reach her side. Her spreading skirts prevented him from standing on the same step, so he mounted to the one above, where he stood towering over her, an icy giant with those unnerving hollow eyes.

"If I recall," he said, addressing the hushed crowd below, "it has always been tradition for MacEowan lairds to make a speech at the commencement of the yuletide festivities. As you can see, I've not had time to shave and change my clothes, let alone prepare a proper welcome."

A few reluctant grins appeared on the upturned faces below.

"Bertie and I haven't had a bite to eat for three days," he went on. "I hope you'll understand if I dispense with the customary words of greeting and get straight to the feasting. Mr. MacNeil, will you do the honors, please?"

A cheer arose and a mad trample toward the banquet

table began. For a time Gemma stood watching the confusion below, pretending to ignore the man towering at her shoulder.

"Bite that lip any harder and it may fall off, ma'am," he said.

She stiffened, but didn't dare turn around.

"Shall we go down and join our guests?" he asked, offering his hand.

She was afraid to touch him, although she knew she must. Taking a deep breath, she put her hand in his. As Connor's icy fingers closed around hers, she felt shaken by an unexpected rush of longing, and gladness because he was here and he was safe. But she had learned to school her face well since her marriage, and tensed her jaw as they went down the stairs together.

Many heads turned to watch their descent.

Although he was by now thoroughly lightheaded from hunger and exhaustion, Connor took his time leading Gemma toward the banquet table. Servants and crofters alike came up to bow and curtsy and offer their good wishes. He was astonished that Gemma seemed to know most of his crofters by name. Why, he couldn't recollect half the faces around him!

Surprising, too, were the number of MacEowans in attendance. There were Eachern and Janet, and Cousins Sophie and Margaret. Stuffing his face at the table was that social vermin, Ruan MacEowan. And how in hell had horse-faced little Winnifred and her whining husband Rupert made it back from Glasgow? Was it possible that they'd never left Glenarris to begin with? How many others had remained here despite the explicit orders he had left with Jamie for their immediate expulsion?

Maude was probably still in residence, too, he thought grumpily. The old bat would never vacate the premises until she was bodily removed, and sure enough, there she sat near the fireplace in an armchair the footmen had carried in for her, puffing away on one of those disgusting cigars and flirting outrageously with several brawny, grinning farmers.

Over in an alcove under the minstrel's gallery stood ancient Uncle Leopold holding a shouting match with some white-haired crone who appeared just as deaf as he was. Connor couldn't believe his eyes.

"How in the world did he get back here?"

Gemma followed his gaze. "Uncle Leopold? Why, he never left. As a matter of fact, he's moved back to Glenarris for good."

"What?"

He had stopped so suddenly that Gemma, whose hand had been resting on his sleeve as tradition demanded, was spun around to face him. Her skirts belled against his legs and she nearly bumped his chin with the top of her head.

"I invited him to stay," she spoke into his chest. "There was no question of his returning to Glasgow once the snow came, and he sounded so lonely when he described his home there."

"So you invited him to move in with us. Just like that."

"The castle is enormous," she said coolly. "I didn't think—"

"No, you never do," he interrupted. "Wee, impetuous Gemma. Won't you ever grow up?"

She lifted her eyes to his. "I *have* grown up," she

told him with quiet dignity. "Now I think it's time that you did, too."

Oh ho, that did it! He had never been so glad to feel himself growing angry. It had never felt so good to let the blood pump hotly through his frozen veins and to have his fighting instincts rise up from their lengthy dormancy.

Why in bloody hell did everyone keep insisting that *he* was the one who needed to change? Why was *he* the one they called irresponsible, spoiled, and out of touch with reality?

But just as quickly, the fight went out of him. He was simply too weary to argue with Gemma now. And, to tell the truth, a part of him deep inside realized that what she said, that what Jamie and Eachern had said as well, was partially true.

All right, largely true. He couldn't stand here and look around and fail to see what Gemma had accomplished in his absence. Exhausted and half starved as he was, he couldn't fail to see how this magnificent feast and the glowing faces around him contrasted sharply with his usual neglect of his clan's tradition, his own crofters, his family, and his wife.

Especially his wife.

"Gemma—" he began, but was too tired to go on. His eyes closed and he wavered on his feet. Instantly he felt her slim hand on his arm. Opening his eyes, he found her lovely little face smiling up at him.

"You must come and eat now, my lord," she said lightly. "If you wait, there'll be nothing left."

Gemma knew that he was at the end of his strength. She knew, too, how much his pride would suffer if his family and his clan saw any evidence of his weakness.

Doing her best to prop him up without looking as though she were, she led Connor to the table and fed him mouthfuls of nourishing shepherd's pie while the delighted guests looked on. Jamie appeared at Connor's elbow with a bracing dram of whiskey.

Connor drained the glass with one hand while keeping the other around her waist. While he drank, Jamie and Gemma exchanged a glance of mutual understanding.

"Perhaps you'd like another, sir," Jamie suggested as Connor handed him the empty glass.

"Aye."

As the valet hurried off, Connor glanced down at her. "Thank you," he said softly.

Her eyes swept up to his. They exchanged a long look, but before either could speak, they were interrupted by Jamie holding another drink.

After Connor had drained the glass and made short work of the salmon rolls and venison strips she insisted on feeding him, he strolled with her around the great hall, exchanging pleasantries with his guests and his family as etiquette demanded.

He seemed completely recovered—unlike Bertie MacKenzie, who had been carried off on a makeshift stretcher by several burly footmen. Gone was his frozen look which had unnerved her and their guests when Connor had first stumbled in. He appeared relaxed and never once moved away from her side.

Only she knew that Connor clung to her for lack of strength to stand on his own, but she would not have abandoned him even if she could. Her heart was singing with the joyous realization that he needed her. For tonight, at least, they had put their differences behind them and, for the sake of the crofters, the family, and this festive occasion, had established an outward truce.

As the bounteous food began disappearing and the ale barrels emptied, the crowd grew boisterous. Stablemaster Jeffries, who had been scraping away heroically on his single violin, was now joined by a number of crofters whose inhibitions had faded with the consumption of Connor's fine ale. MacNeil brought in a pair of fiddles, as well as a moldy set of bagpipes which, once cleaned and warmed up, produced a surprisingly pleasant sound. The little band was joined by Connor's uncle Leopold, who had served as drum major in the 7th Highland foot and kept time surprisingly well, despite his deafness, by banging Aunt Maude's walking stick on an overturned kettle. Servants, crofters, and family alike were quickly drawn into a spirited dance.

Connor had neither the strength nor the inclination to join them. Instead he stood against the wall with Gemma at his side, watching the jubilant crowd twirl and leap and laugh uproariously. Not since his mother's time had the great hall rung with such merriment. He was startled to realize how much he had missed it.

Once again he found his gaze straying to Gemma. Only now did he understand how tirelessly she had struggled to put together a feast of such epic proportions. Proof of her spectacular success lay in the fact that his moody family and deeply suspicious crofters were all out there on the dance floor making complete fools of themselves.

A hand clapped him on the shoulder. "Splendid party, old man," came a familiar voice in his ear.

He turned, grinning. "About time you came to pay your respects, you miserable sot."

"I thought it best tae wait till yer mood mellowed.

Whiskey'll do that, eh, Gemma? Ye look enchanting, m' dear. Fair enough tae eat.''

To Connor's amazement, Gemma didn't bristle like an offended cat as she would have if *he* had dared to say as much! Instead she giggled like a brainless school-girl and permitted Eachern to press what was, in Connor's opinion, a far too intimate kiss on her cheek.

Scowling, Connor moved to step between them, but Gemma had already turned away from Eachern and slipped her hand back beneath Connor's arm. He wasn't sure she was aware of what she did, for she and Eachern were still chatting amiably, but the intimate gesture warmed him far more than the whiskey had.

He forced himself to concentrate on what Gemma and Eachern were saying. They were talking about the Christmas tree, and Gemma was describing the difficult task of winching it upright and decorating the top branches with a ladder. The ease with which they spoke together made him suspect that Eachern hadn't been a stranger at Glenarris during his absence. Black jealousy gripped him, for he had always suspected that Gemma fancied his easygoing cousin far better than she did him.

Bloody idiot! he told himself harshly. After the way you treated her, she'd fancy the lowliest shepherd above your sorry carcass.

Ashamed, jealous, aching with something he couldn't name, he tried to free himself from Gemma's grasp. To his surprise, she held fast, tugging him deliberately back to her side. Frowning, he looked down at her and caught a glimpse of something that was very nearly desperation in her eyes before she smiled brightly and made another offhand remark about the tree.

He was suddenly very still. Was it possible that

Gemma needed him as much as he needed her? Was his presence here in some way necessary to maintaining the uncaring facade she showed the world tonight?

He looked at her closely and for the first time saw the false brightness in her eyes, the strained manner in which she spoke and moved, and the tiny frown line etched between her brows. Obviously the task of fooling the guests into believing they were happily married was taking its toll on her, too.

In that moment the evening lost its sparkle for him. He found that he had to restrain himself from roaring out that the party was over and then physically pushing every last person out the door. He wanted to scoop Gemma into his arms and carry her to bed, insist that she rest, for she looked so careworn and fragile, like a piece of glass that might shatter at any moment.

Was he responsible for that? It didn't bear thinking about.

Eachern said, "May I partner yer wife for a dance, Con?"

"No, you may not."

"Of course you may," Gemma said at exactly the same moment.

Connor glared at her.

She smiled back. Apparently she was quite determined to go on playing the game. Still smiling, she took Eachern's hand.

"Wait a minute," Eachern protested, holding back. "I just thought o' summat."

"What?" Connor and Gemma said together.

"Where's the mistletoe?"

Connor frowned. "The what?"

"The mistletoe." Eachern was turning this way and

389

that, looking at the evergreens that festooned the candle-lit hall. "It's tradition tae share a kiss when ye be standin' beneath it. Did ye no hang any inside, Gemma? Shame on ye for yer cowardice!"

"Why, Eachern," Gemma countered, wagging a finger at him, "don't you know mistletoe is pagan? No British church sanctions its use at this time of year."

Eachern looked glum. "But now I've no excuse for stealin' a kiss!"

She smiled mischievously. "Do you need an excuse?"

Oh, but this was too much for Connor. Wordlessly he took Gemma by the hand and dragged her away.

He got no more than a few steps across the floor when his path was blocked by Cullum Cowan and several other burly crofters. "Mistletoe?" Cullum cried gaily. "Did I hear summat 'bout mistletoe?"

"Aye," Eachern told him gloomily. "Connor's English bride kens naught aboot it."

"Well, we happen tae have a sprig right here," Cullum declared triumphantly. "Time for a lesson, eh, lads?"

And Cullum was boosted, grinning, onto the shoulders of his laughing companions so that he towered high above Gemma and Connor. While a number of couples broke away from the dance floor and crowded around to watch, Cullum held the tattered sprig of mistletoe over Connor's head.

"Only one kiss," Connor was instructed, "and ye'll have tae remove a berry as payment when ye're through. 'Tis tradition, ye ken!"

Connor was livid, Gemma scarlet with embarrassment. Everyone else looked expectant and bright-eyed from too much good ale. There was a great deal of laughter and jostling and catcalls.

Connor wondered if it would be seemly to take the mistletoe and cram it down Cullum's throat.

The heckling grew louder. More and more people were leaving the dance floor, attracted by the noise. Uncle Leopold saw what was going on and played a drumroll on his kettle. The moment was in danger of becoming absurd.

Connor turned helplessly to Gemma. She looked back at him, feeling equally helpless. She had no doubt that her face was redder than the holly berries. Two spots of color were burning high in Connor's cheeks as well.

Awkwardly, like untried lovers, they came together in an acceptance of the inevitable. Connor's arms went reluctantly about her waist. Her hands linked hesitantly around his neck. He drew her to him clumsily, the heavy hoops of her skirts getting in the way. Her cheeks burning, she stood on tiptoe and raised her face to his.

Their lips met hesitantly, almost shyly. Connor's beard scratched her skin. She trembled like a leaf in his embrace. She had forgotten his overwhelming masculinity, his sensual skill at taking her mouth with his own and using it to draw the very breath from her body. She had expected an impersonal peck. It was so much more than that.

Her trembling faded and the rigidity went out of her. Her body became pliant in his powerful embrace, and her resistance melted into softness.

Dimly, through the pounding of her heart, she heard the approving roar of the crowd. At the same time she felt Connor begin to shake with silent laughter. Instantly

she pushed hard against his chest, indignant and breathless.

Raucous hoots and off-color remarks greeted her
hasty escape. Embarrassed, she refused to look at anyone, especially Connor.

Aunt Maude pushed her way to the front of the crowd.
" 'Tis high time we a' went hame," she announced.

Groans and cries of dismay greeted her.

The old woman held up her hands. Tiny as she was,
she commanded instant silence. "Leave the newlyweds
tae their own reunion, will ye? 'Tis lang past midnight
an' we'd do best tae find our own beds."

"I'd like to share mine with her!" someone hollered,
pointing at Gemma.

Everyone laughed. Even Connor gave a wide smile,
but Gemma bowed her head.

Then, slowly, good-naturedly, the assembly broke up.
Connor ordered the Glenarris wagons brought out for
those who had arrived on foot. Even Maude graciously
provided the services of her ancient coachman and
musty barouche for the elderly and infirm.

Before they left, Gemma made certain that every family was presented with a gift basket. One by one, the
children came forward to curtsy and to receive their
Christmas treats. Some of them were gripped by shyness
and had to be coaxed forward by their older brothers
and sisters. Others, who knew Gemma better, did not
hesitate to give her a hearty embrace. She returned all
their hugs with fond ones of her own, uncaring of the
smeary prints the children left behind on her magnificent
skirts.

Watching from the shadows, Connor felt something
touch him whenever a child's thin, clinging arms

wrapped around Gemma's slender neck. The baskets were a surprise to him as well. Each and every one of them was stuffed with essentials considered priceless in this remote Highland glen: sewing needles, tincture bottles, skeins of knitting wool, bandage gauze, and tins of food and preserves. There were frivolous things as well: stick candies and chocolates, shiny ha'pennies, and even a whittled toy or a whistle.

Where on earth had she come by such things in the dead of winter? How on earth did she understand so completely what these impoverished people desired?

You're a mystery to me, Gemma MacEowan, he thought, certainly not for the first time. He had a sudden vision of the infinite delight there would be in uncovering all the secrets about her.

But not for him. He knew that he could no sooner make peace with this self-assured stranger than with the old Gemma who had clashed wills with him so ferociously in the past. It galled him to realize how ill at ease he felt around this woman. He had come back to Glenarris expecting Gemma to humiliate him in front of his entire clan. Instead he had found a soothing scene of cozy domestic order, of peace and goodwill and permanence that made him feel like a stranger in his own home.

Frowning, he looked up to see that the last of the baskets had been distributed. The good people of Glenarris were making their way into the frigid air amid much laughter and cheerful good nights. In no time at all the beaming MacNeil had ushered them out and closed the great front doors. The heavy bolts echoed as they were slid into place, and then, abruptly, Gemma and he were left alone to face each other across the length of the great front hall.

Chapter Thirty

The candles sputtered softly in the background while Mrs. Sutcliffe wordlessly directed the staff to begin clearing away the remains of the feast. Uncle Leopold and Aunt Maude were on their way upstairs, and a pair of yawning footmen were extinguishing the embers in the great hearth.

Connor looked at Gemma. Without acknowledging him, she went to stand in front of the Christmas tree, absorbed in watching the candles burn out one by one.

She turned to face Connor before he was even close enough to touch her. For a moment they stood looking at each other without speaking. Then he gave her a faint smile.

"What an incredible evening. You must be exhausted."

"I am."

"May I show you upstairs?"

She cast a quick look at his outstretched hand. Once again she was afraid to touch him, but once again she knew she had no choice. How warm and strong his fingers were, and how her own trembled when she placed them in his big palm.

As they walked toward the stairs, Connor lazily turned her hand around so that he could lace her fingers through his. She cast him a startled glance. The gesture was so intimate, so familiar. Was he even aware that he had done it?

Neither of them spoke until they reached the upper landing.

"Are you still in the Blue Room?" he asked.

She nodded wordlessly. She didn't trust herself to speak. A thousand questions were tumbling through her mind. Did he intend to accompany her inside when they got to her bedroom door? If so, would he confront her tonight or wait until morning? Was he furious with her for organizing that spectacle downstairs? She had used MacEowan money to finance the whole affair, after all, since she hadn't had access to her own funds.

More importantly, what would he have to say about her future? Had he made a decision about their marriage during the months he'd been in Edinburgh? Did he plan to annul their vows now or wait until spring, when she was ready to leave Glenarris for warmer climes?

Absurdly, or perhaps it was the wine influencing her now, the one thing she wanted to know above all else was what he had thought of the kiss they'd exchanged beneath the sprig of mistletoe. Had he realized, as she had, that none of the passion and sexual attraction between them had diminished despite how far apart they may have grown? Had he felt the same stirring of unfulfilled longing that had flowed sweetly through her veins when his mouth closed over hers?

He must have! Why else would he be holding her hand so intimately now? Why else would he be escorting her to her bedroom, which could not in any way be misconstrued as a simple mark of courtesy? She could not remember a time when they had ever been courteous to one another.

Though why should she care? Just because you ached for a man didn't mean you had to give in and make love with him, did it? There were far more compelling reasons to avoid him right now than there were reasons to welcome him back to her bed!

The wisest thing under the circumstances, she decided, would be to send him away *before* they reached the door to her bedroom. That way neither of them would be tempted to recapture the stirring urgency of their earlier kiss. That way there would be no chance of misunderstandings or embarrassments. She would be spared the agony of trying to guess whether he intended to accompany her inside or wait to be invited.

Not that she wanted him to come in.

Oh, blast it all, yes she did! She could no sooner deny the pull between them than she could the need to breathe. The worst part about it was that she didn't know how to go about inviting him inside without compromising her pride.

Send him away now, she thought in panic, before it becomes an issue.

But she had always been impetuous and unwise, and had probably drunk far more tonight than she should have. She might not love Connor anymore (as if she ever had!) but a wild, wicked part of her yearned to do battle with him tonight and, aye, to feel his kisses and his touch.

It seemed like an eternity to her before they reached her bedroom door. Connor turned her to face him, and with an odd little smile, lifted her hand and brought it to his lips.

"Good night, ma'am."

She stared after him, her jaw dropping, as he walked away down the corridor. That was it? A simple peck on her knuckles and a polite good night? After all the agonizing she had done on the way up here? How dare he! She wasn't going to let him get away with it!

"Connor!"

He turned and waited while Gemma hurried after him. Her gown rustled sharply in the stillness.

"What is it?" he asked, his smile wary.

Lifting her lovely little face, she asked bluntly, "Why did you come back?"

He groaned inwardly. He should have remembered that Gemma never, ever made things easy for him. At any other time he would have relished squaring off against her, but at the moment he was just too tired.

"I'd prefer talking about it in the morning, Gemma."

"Well, I don't," she informed him crisply. "You'll only be well rested then, and too good at making excuses. I'd rather confront the truth here and now."

"I was afraid of that," he muttered beneath his breath.

"I heard that," she said, glaring. She was obviously spoiling for a fight, and he knew better than to deny her.

He gestured wearily toward the door. "Could we talk in privacy, at least?"

Her bedroom was dark. As Gemma went around closing the drapes and priming the lamps, he settled himself tiredly on the edge of her bed.

"I wasn't sure what you were going to do to me when you came up those stairs tonight," she confessed, her back to him as she trimmed the lantern wicks. "I thought perhaps you'd kill me in front of everyone."

"Not advisable. Too many witnesses," he murmured.

Gemma couldn't help chuckling. She wasn't the least bit tired anymore. She felt charged with excitement, like a soldier ready to leap into battle. She supposed that she was a little drunk, too, because she felt wonderfully lightheaded and very, very brave, something she had never been in Connor's presence before. Was the wine responsible for that, or was it the fact that the more time she spent with him, the more she came to realize that their relationship had changed?

She thought about this as she bent to coax the hearth fire back to life and pour fresh water into the ewer on her dressing table. She knew perfectly well that she was no longer the ignorant girl Connor had spirited away from Derbyshire so long ago. How could she be? For the past six weeks she had singlehandedly managed an enormous feudal castle. She had tamed Connor's hostile family and made peace with his crofters. She had planned and presided over an enormously successful feast to which nearly a hundred people had been invited.

No one who had accomplished such things could remain an innocent any longer! Was it possible that her newfound self-esteem had finally served to elevate her to equal footing with the sophisticated, worldly man she had married?

Poking again at the embers, she sneaked a look at Connor over her shoulder. He was sprawled on her bed in a rather ungentlemanly fashion, his limbs akimbo, his eyes red-rimmed, his jaw covered with unbecoming stubble. The journey from Edinburgh had taken its toll on his clothing as well, and his expensive boots were nearly worn through at the soles. Not much of the urbane sophisticate in evidence tonight, that was certain!

"Do you regret marrying me?" she asked suddenly.

His bleary gaze found hers. "I've aged thirty years since the day."

"Well, whose fault is that?" she countered archly. "I mean, you should have realized from the outset that I wasn't going to be docile about the whole thing, especially not after finding out I was the victim of your childish betting!"

She turned away from the fire as she spoke and now she hitched up her skirts and, unbuckling the whalebone hoop, let it click softly to the floor. Stepping around it, she went to the ewer to wash, her heavy skirts trailing like a train behind her. "I didn't really plan to bring this up, but now that I have, it seems as good a time as any to talk about what you intend to do with me. You see, I'm not really certain I want to return to England come spring. There's so much to do first, here at Glenarris and down in the crofts, and I'm starting to think that you won't care enough to do it."

"Hmm," came the response from the bed.

"I'm serious, Connor! The children in the glen need to go to school. They need to be taught to read and write. So do a lot of their parents. And a doctor! How difficult would it be to bring a doctor to the glen several times a year to treat them? Uncle Leopold says your mother always made sure they had decent clothes and shoes on their feet, but after she died nothing was ever done for them. Maude says you're mostly to blame. She says you spend all of your time chasing after women and behaving scandalously with your cousin and those friends of yours, and now that I've met them I'm not at all surprised.

"I think, too," she added in a rush, bending over the ewer to rinse the soap from her face and hands, "that you and I would both be better off if you went back to Edinburgh as soon as the weather clears. You don't seem to care about Glenarris, so why bother to stay? I can handle everything here by myself, with MacNeil and Mrs. Sutcliffe to help. I've been doing it all along, you know. And . . . and since I don't think you really care much for me, either, or Uncle Leopold, or Great-aunt Maude, wouldn't it be easier for everyone if you just left us alone?"

She waited with bated breath for an answer.

"Connor?"

No reply.

Drying herself with a towel, she whirled to face the bed. And had to laugh, rather ruefully, to herself. He was asleep. One arm was thrown across her pillow, the other cradled beneath his head. His harsh, handsome face was relaxed and vulnerable in the flickering candlelight, and her heart couldn't help turning over as she looked at him. The amusement faded from her smile and was replaced with a bittersweet longing.

Crossing to the bed, she gently drew off his boots and covered him with the goosedown tick. Connor never stirred. Straightening, she stood for a moment looking down at him. Then, taking liberties she would never have dared had he been awake, she reached down and took his face in her hands. With her palms curved along his unshaven jaw, she caressed his relaxed, unsmiling mouth with the tips of her thumbs. Her heartbeat accelerating, she bent over him and planted a kiss on his brow.

''I love you,'' she whispered.

It was an admission that she had long dreamed of making to someone, anyone, just once in her life. Never mind that it wasn't true, that it was really the wine speaking tonight and not her. Because she had never uttered those words to another soul, she could scarcely credit the way they made her heart clench and the tears sting her eyes.

Three simple words. How powerful they could be—if and when they spoke the truth.

Almost reluctantly, she reached over and extinguished the bedside light. With her long skirts trailing behind her, she went through to the sitting room and stretched out on the narrow daybed where Fiona sometimes slept. Closing her eyes, she willed herself to sleep, but it seemed a long time before her breathing quieted and her strained expression relaxed at last.

Connor's sleep became increasingly disturbed. Images of the hardships he had endured while crossing the mountains plagued him, as did the memory of his hunger and the biting cold. No man in his right mind would have attempted such a journey, and yet he had done so.

Another dream seemed to come from far away and touch some hidden part deep within his soul. A woman's hands, cool and welcoming against the roughness of his face, caressing him tenderly. A woman's lips upon his brow, the lovely scent of her surrounding him as she whispered three words that he had heard often enough in his wild, dissolute life, yet which he realized all at

once had never been uttered with such resounding truth:
I love you.

"Gemma," he whispered, but it was all part of the
dream, and after a moment the hands went away and he
was alone.

Connor awoke with a pounding headache and in a foul
frame of mind. Somehow he couldn't help having the
feeling that he had bungled something terribly important
last night.

Staggering out of bed, he splashed his face with the
icy water in the ewer. Shaking himself dry, he looked
around and realized with a start that he wasn't in his
bedroom. Incredibly, he was in his mother's old suite—
the one with the heavy blue drapes and the blue velvet
coverlet and the Turkish rug woven in deep blue green,
which some brilliant ancestor had fittingly dubbed the
Blue Room.

Only it wasn't his mother's anymore. It belonged to
Gemma.

He sat down heavily on the bed and put his head in
his hands. How in the hell had he ended up here? Oh,
Lord, he remembered now, and the moment he did, the
nagging feeling that had been with him since waking up
suddenly found a name. Lunacy. Insanity. The stupidest
thing he had ever done!

He didn't know whether to laugh or weep. He only
knew that he'd never mishandled a situation so badly
before. Here, on this very same bed, he had sat and
watched his tipsy wife actually undressing in front of
him last night! And what had he done? Lost his nerve
like some Frenchie milquetoast, then passed out like a

common drunkard, and so completely missed his chance to make love with her!

God alone knew how much groveling he'd have to do to get an opportunity like that again!

Groaning, he fell back against the pillows and covered his eyes with his hands. Dimly he began to recall other, equally tormenting things about the previous night: the feel of Gemma's hands on his face, her willowy slimness as she removed her hoops and stood with upraised arms before him, and her endless chatter, which he had been too tired to make any sense of. All except for one thing: Her insistence that he cared nothing for Glenarris, and how much better off everyone would be if he returned to Edinburgh and left them all the hell alone.

Gladly! he thought with sudden fierceness. By God, he'd had enough of this entire rotten crew, and his bloody wife in particular! She was right—he'd be far better off in Edinburgh where she couldn't nag and harp and drive him utterly mad. But before he obliged her he wanted to make sure she understood clearly whose castle and clan this really was, and who still held the upper hand in their tiresome relationship.

Back in his own bedchamber he found a bath drawn for him and his clothes neatly laid out on the unused bed. Obviously, Jamie had not forgotten his duties although everyone else in the castle seemed to be dancing to Gemma's tune.

To his annoyance, he found it hard to maintain his temper while indulging in the luxury of a hot bath. And it was even more difficult to continue holding a grudge against Gemma when he made his way downstairs some twenty minutes later and saw how splendidly the Christmas tree and the other yule decorations served to warm the gloomy hall in the daylight. Womanly touches were evident in the brightly polished windowpanes, the tastefully hung draperies, and the homey linens draped over the numerous wooden tables. The furnishings in the small anterooms he passed had all been regrouped in a tasteful fashion and fresh paint applied to the moldings and trim. There were new faces among the staff as well, young girls with freshly starched mob caps and aprons who greeted him with curtsies and shy good mornings.

By God, he thought, Gemma's a better laird than I am!

A murmur of voices led him to the morning room. Pausing in the doorway, he found Gemma presiding over an enormous breakfast with Janet and Eachern, and those ancient quacks, Uncle Leopold and Aunt Maude. Gemma had just concluded a ribald jest about last night's party that was greeted with a chorus of raucous laughter. Even Janet, Eachern's normally sour-faced sister, had joined in, which made Connor shake his head in disbelief. He couldn't remember the last time he'd seen the old spinster smile, or known Glenarris to be so full of life. Was there no end to the changes wrought in this gloomy place by his astonishing young wife?

"Ha, looka there!" Uncle Leopold shouted. " 'Tis Connor hisself, back frae the dead."

All heads turned, but it was Gemma whom Connor sought. His heart skipped a beat. Was it possible that there was a trace of anxiety in her expression as she set down her teacup and lifted her gaze to his? Maybe he imagined it, but he could have sworn that she was searching his face intently for some lingering trace of the hardship he had suffered on his journey from Edinburgh. Not finding any, she relaxed visibly.

Only wishful thinking? Perhaps so, but he felt warmed through and through. His mother had been the only person in his memory who had ever fretted about him, and for just this once he allowed himself the luxury of believing that Gemma actually cared, that it mattered to her that he was warm and dry and the difficult journey from Edinburgh had left no permanent mark upon him.

He wished he could speak to her privately, but that was impossible. Eachern was already on his feet, coming around the table to slap him on the back. Maude and Janet were insisting that he come in and have something to eat. Reluctantly, he broke eye contact with Gemma and took a seat between the two.

"Good morning, Uncle," he said loudly to the old man across from him.

"Eh? What's that?" Uncle Leopold asked.

"I said 'good morning'!" he repeated loudly.

"No need tae shout!" Uncle Leopold protested. "Here, Gemma," he added, turning to her, "feed the lad! 'Twill help calm his temper."

"I very much doubt it," Maude and Janet said in unison.

Connor joined in the group's laughter, and the atmosphere lightened appreciably.

"There were a lot more of you MacEowans in attendance last night," he remarked, his eyes sweeping over the faces of his family. "Are you the only ones still here?"

"What's that?" Uncle Leopold demanded. "Who shot a deer?"

Smiling, Gemma patted the old man's hand. "Not a deer, Uncle! Connor wants to know how many of last night's guests are still here!"

"Sorry! Can't hear too well, ye ken!" Uncle Leopold shouted back.

He was a wizened gnome of a man who had been an accomplished practical joker in his day. Connor had forgotten that in his youth he'd been very fond of him. In the last few years he had come to look upon the old man as little more than an annoyance. Maude, too. But here, in the cozy surroundings of the oak-paneled morning room, they seemed to have lost their bite. Why, even Janet was looking a lot less hidebound than usual as she smiled at him and offered to pass the bramble jelly.

No doubt about it, he thought in astonishment. Gemma had somehow managed to mellow them. Or was it him? Had she somehow succeeded in making him more tolerant toward these people with whom he had never had a bit of patience?

The thought brought a rueful smile to his lips. He stole a glance at Gemma while buttering his scone. It pleased him to find her watching him, and she blushed as their glances met, aware that she'd been caught.

"Do you know," he told her innocently, "I slept like a log last night."

Her blush deepened. "Did you?"

"Aye. My only regret is that I dozed off too soon. So many interesting things were going on."

He knew she understood very well what he meant, as the blush on her cheeks deepened to scarlet and she looked hastily away.

She had done something different with her hair, he noticed. Plaited it in some newfangled way that made her appear delectably young and innocent. Her cream-colored morning frock was trimmed with gray and green and made her look so freshly virginal that he wished he could sweep her into his arms and have his way with her right there on the breakfast table.

Curse her! How could she turn so calmly back to her tea when she knew how much he ached for her? The worst thing about it was that matters between them were now more complicated than ever. This self-assured woman sitting across from him in her lovely cream gown and grown-up hairstyle didn't need him anymore. She had made that quite obvious when she had asked him oh so calmly to get out of his own house last night. Even though he could still make her blush like a holly berry, he doubted that he could bend her will by wooing her as he had done so easily and delightfully in Fergus Dodson's croft.

The memory cut him deeply. The knowledge that he had only himself to blame brought a rush of defensive temper. Did he really want to set matters right with this arrogant new Gemma, ask her to stay, to spend the rest of her life at his side, and be his wife in every way?

Aye, goddamn it, he did!

He should have realized as much from the moment he had first met the impetuous, sharp-tongued beauty sitting across from him and from the thousands of ways she had shown him that he couldn't live without her.

The irony of it all was that Gemma didn't seem interested anymore. She had moved so far beyond him that he doubted he'd ever be able to catch up. He had held her heart in his hands and been too stupid to treasure it, had trifled with her deep loyalty and her boundless affections and paid the price by losing both.

Gemma didn't want him anymore; she wanted Glenarris.

She wasn't interested in rehabilitating him; she

wanted to improve the lives of his crofters.

How on earth was he going to convince her that he was worth keeping, too?

I still have Helios, he thought. Perhaps Gemma and I can strike some sort of bargain—

But it wasn't a simple bargain he wanted from her. Not by a long shot.

"What's the matter, Con? Have ye swallowed a worm?"

"Oh, leave him alone, Eachern," Janet chided. "He's never worth much i' the mornin', ye ken."

"Or afternoon or evenin' either," Eachern snorted.

He fixed his cousin with a baleful eye. "You have a very high opinion of me, I see."

"Nothing ye don't deserve," Eachern shot back.

Connor laid aside his fork and knife.

"Och, Con, I didna mean aught by it," Eachern said hastily.

"No bloodshed at the breakfast table, please," Aunt Maude commanded around a mouthful of oat cake.

"I've had enough of this," Connor growled. Coming to his feet, he directed his gaze to Gemma. To his surprise, he saw that she had bowed her head, and when he looked at her closely he could have sworn that her lower lip was trembling.

God's blood! Was the lass near tears? Surely it didn't matter to her one way or the other if he was as surly as a bear and went around picking fights with his cousin!

Or did it?

Gemma, he thought, aching. What will it take to convince you I'm not the man I was?

Scowling, he looked at the others seated at the table. Eachern and Janet were looking aggrieved and Uncle

Leopold appropriately vacant. Only Maude was bold enough to make eye contact with him.

"My apologies, Eachern," he said at last. The words had a hard time coming out. He wasn't used to apologizing. "I'm not myself this morning."

"No, that ye bain't," Eachern agreed in wonder.

"Gemma," Connor added before his courage failed him. "I'm sorry. I apologize to you as well."

Gemma's head came up and her startled eyes met his.

"For what?" Maude demanded, bristling. "What did ye do tae the gel?"

He didn't answer. He was looking at Gemma as a drowning man in heavy seas might look to the lights of a fast-approaching ship. For both of them there could be no mistaking the significance of the moment. In her acceptance or rejection hung the balance of his very existence.

Gemma was wholly unprepared for the moment. Quickly she hid her shaking hands in her lap. Her heart seemed to have risen to her throat and formed a hard, burning lump there that made it impossible to breathe.

"Gemma," Connor said urgently, as though they were the only people in the room.

Oh, how often he had looked at her like that during those enchanted days in the croft! As though the very light within him would die if she so much as turned away! But he had been living an utter lie back then. How was she to know he wasn't deceiving her now?

"Oh, gae on, lass!" Aunt Maude said impatiently. "Tell the bloody heathen he's pardoned so we can get on wi' our meal!"

Good old tart-tongued Maude. As refreshing as an icy wind in the face, or a blow to the side of the head!

Gemma's hands stopped their trembling. "I'll give it some thought," she told him coolly.

"Aye, I'm sure you will," he agreed, sinking back into his chair.

Chapter Thirty-one

Gemma swept down the long hall of the third floor in the castle's west wing, her arms full of linens. Most of her guests had departed Glenarris yesterday morning, the day after the St. Stephen's Day feast, but some had elected to stay on through New Year's. Though she had at first welcomed them, she found herself wishing now that they would all go home. She was short-tempered and jumpy as a cat and couldn't bear listening to another word of advice from well-meaning family members concerning her relationship with Connor.

What relationship? she wondered angrily. They'd been avoiding each other like cowardly enemies for two whole days, and those few times when necessity forced them together, they treated each other with icy aloofness. They might just as well have been total strangers than husband and wife!

Her expression was mulish as she opened the door to

411

the bedroom vacated just that morning by Connor's cousin Winnifred and her husband Rupert. To her relief, she saw that they had left the room in decent order, not at all like those Kirckaldie MacEowans who had drunk too much at the banquet and stayed up all night playing rugby in their suite! Oh, Mrs. Sutcliffe had been beside herself when she saw the broken glassware, the overturned furniture, the torn wallpaper and mutilated paintings.

Connor had been far more philosophical. "That's what happens when you allow Kirckaldie MacEowans to inbreed," was all he'd said, shrugging.

Gemma had been hard-pressed to control her laughter. A look of amusement had passed between her and Connor behind the irate housekeeper's back. How well they understood each other! What a shame they couldn't be reconciled.

It will never happen, she thought now, setting down her linens in an armchair and ferociously stripping the bed. Connor still seemed perfectly willing to return to Edinburgh the moment the weather broke, and never objected whenever she reminded him that she was going home to Derbyshire come spring.

She had originally planned to remain at Glenarris longer; until the summer crops had been planted and her ambitious plans for a school and a medical clinic had been put into practice. But two days of living beneath the same roof with Connor had shown her it would be wiser to leave as soon as possible. She couldn't go on pretending any longer that nothing was amiss in her life when she was utterly miserable and her heart ached more and more with every passing hour. It was simply too exhausting to continue feigning indifference.

412

Bunching up the used linens, she tossed them aside. Laying the new ones across the mattress, she found she had to hitch up her skirts and scramble onto the bed to tuck them in. Unladylike behavior to be sure, but there was nothing she could do about it. At least no one could see her!

A chuckle from the doorway brought her head around. Connor stood on the threshold with his hands in his pockets, watching her.

She sank back onto her heels in the middle of the enormous bed. "How long have you been standing there?"

"Long enough."

She scowled at him. "Well, the least you could do is give me a hand."

"Certainly." He strolled inside and halted in front of her. "What do you want me to do?"

She gestured. "Take that end there and fold it under. No, not like that! 'Twill only come up the moment someone lies on it. Haven't you ever made a bed before?"

"Honestly? No."

"Time you were shown, then."

Scrambling off the bed, she nudged him aside and showed him the proper way to smooth and tuck the freshly laundered linen. He nodded and leaned forward as though to get a better view of what she was doing as she bent and tucked and bent and tucked.

Straightening unexpectedly, she whirled and caught him staring. His face immediately assumed a bored expression.

"Now the bolsters," she instructed. "Can you handle them, do you think?"

413

"I suppose so, though I didn't really come here to play housemaid."

"Then why are you here, pray tell?"

"Because one of the scullery girls swears she heard a strange noise up here last night."

She frowned. "A strange noise? What do you mean?"

He shrugged. "Some bumping and thumping, that sort of thing. She insisted all the family was downstairs and this entire wing should have been deserted. I thought it best to scotch any rumors of spooks and goblins before the talk takes hold among the staff."

She laughed. "Ghosts at Glenarris? How intriguing."

"Not if you're superstitious. Then it's downright scary."

She snorted. "I'm sure there's a very simple explanation for strange noises in this wing."

His brows arched. "Oh?"

"Your Drumcorrie cousins are staying in the rooms at the end of the hall."

"So?"

"Oh, really, Connor! Isn't it obvious? They're a randy pair and I doubt they sleep much at night. Why do you suppose they're always late for dinner? And where do you suppose they slip off to whenever they disappear for an hour or so? Into any empty bedroom they can find, the more remote, the better. You know how newlyweds are."

"Do I?" he asked quietly.

She gasped as though he had struck her. Heat flooded her cheeks.

"Ah, young love," he said mockingly. "I agree they do seem unable to keep their hands off each other. Delightful to know they've been sneaking around my dom-

414

icile trying out this bed and that for a fast tumble.''

''Connor, don't—''

''Don't what?'' he demanded as she broke off and turned away.

She shook her head, refusing to look at him.

''Don't bring up the subject of 'young love'?'' he persisted angrily. ''Don't mention that at one time we couldn't keep our hands off each other either?''

''N-no! That's not it at all!''

''Then what? Why this sudden virginal embarrassment? I've seen the way you look at them whenever they bill and coo and practically undress each other at the breakfast table! You envy them, Gemma, don't you?''

''D-don't be ridiculous!''

''Ridiculous? How strange. It seems to me you always look wistful when my cousin Roddy puts his hand down Caroline's dress.''

Her mouth trembled. ''Now you're being crass! And I'm not wistful! I'm—I'm . . .'' But the proper words failed her. How on earth could she think up an appropriate lie when everything he said was so infuriatingly true? Stamping her foot, she spun away from him.

Connor watched in silence as she tossed the bolsters onto the bed and jerked the covers over them. Instead of being angry, he felt elated. In a fine fettle like this Gemma was in over her head, he knew. And why should she be feeling out of her depth unless she agreed with everything he'd just said?

A shaft of hope speared through him. And longing. Because he, too, ached for the same things she did.

Gathering together every ounce of his courage, he took a deep breath and moved toward her. Quietly, almost diffidently, he paused behind her as she stood with her back to him. She stiffened as he put his hands on her shoulders, but did not move away.

"Gemma—"

"Connor, please." Her voice shook. "Go away."

He stepped nearer, his breath brushing over her nape. "Do you really want me to?"

"N-yes! I-I've work to do, and I don't w-want you in that way anymore."

His hands continued to knead her shoulders. "What way?" he asked softly.

Gemma made an impatient movement without turning around. "You know."

Oh, aye, he did. And while her words told him one thing, her body was telling him quite another. He could feel the way she trembled and her breathing hitched, and he knew that he had only to slide his hands from her shoulders to her pert, tempting breasts, to find her nipples straining against the fabric of her gown.

The thought made his heartbeat quicken.

This was the closest he had been to his wife for far too many weeks. His fingers ceased their kneading and moved to encircle her slender neck. Beneath his thumbs he could feel the pounding of her pulse in her throat.

"Gemma—"

With his voice and the pressure of his hands Connor turned Gemma around to face him. She stood with her head bowed and her hands at her sides, as though hoping that by ignoring him he would simply disappear.

But he didn't. Instead his hands slipped upward to cup her face and gently tilt it back. Her eyes were closed— not in anticipation of his kiss, but because she wanted desperately to shut him out. It was the only thing she could do to resist him. Her body had betrayed her by refusing to move away no matter how hard she might wish to.

"Kiss me, Gemma," he whispered huskily. "Kiss me the way you used to."

"I can't," she whispered back, tremulous, near tears.

"Why? Have you forgotten how? Here, let me remind you."

Slowly, hypnotically, he lowered his mouth to hers. At the same time, he brought one hand down to the small of her back, and in one fluid motion fitted her against him. He half lifted her off the floor and his mouth sought and found hers.

Groaning, he cradled the back of her head with one hand while his other arm tightened around her waist, pressing her even harder against his swollen manhood.

She moaned low in her throat. How long had she hungered for this man? Too long to deny him what he asked for, she knew. They were husband and wife. Surely there could be no harm in letting him love her just this once? After all, if she no longer ached for him physically then surely she could fight him all the more easily?

Why not? Why not?

Betrayed by passion, yearning for release, she opened herself to him for the last, lovely time. Greedily she clung to him, her arms moving upward to wrap around his neck, her skirts crushed between them as she pressed herself against him.

"Gemma, oh God," he groaned.

"Just this once," she whispered against his mouth.

"Just this once," he agreed. "I swear it."

He lifted her into his arms. With her skirts hiked above her waist, she straddled his hips as their mouths sought and tasted and worshiped in turn. His hand found her breast, and she gasped and let her head fall back.

Immediately he swung her onto the newly made bed. Still standing, he bent over her. His fingers worked the fastenings on her bodice and then his dark head bent to her swollen nipples. Laving them with his swirling, dipping tongue, he stroked his hands downward. In mounting urgency, he removed her frock and tossed it aside.

Without waiting for him to remove her undergarments, she pulled him down on top of her. Only that thin layer of silk, and his clothing, separating them.

As he leaned over her, he slipped the last of her garments from her and rained urgent kisses upon her naked flesh. At the same time, he shamelessly invaded her secret core with his wonderful, experienced hand. His practiced touch made her dewy while she writhed and moaned. Her entire being was inflamed with lustful, burning desire.

"Connor, please—" she breathed.

Neither could wait for him to get his clothes off. Instead, he merely unhitched his breeches and let them fall to his ankles. Her legs fell open beneath his urgent command. With a groan, he settled his weight atop her and in a moment of breathless triumph, slipped inside.

"Ohh!"

Her eyes widened. She had forgotten how perfect, how magnificent, was the moment of their joining. Her hips swirled up to meet him while he thrust deeply, then reared back and kissed her before filling her again.

The rhythm was timeless perfection. Like hand to silken glove they fit, swept along on a mounting tide of pleasure. Heat flowed and damp skin slid sweetly against damp skin. Their arms clung and caressed, their lips entwined, and their breath intermingled.

With every thrust he heightened her rising passion. She moaned and rose toward him, her hands gripping the bunched muscles of his arms, her heels hooked around his calves. She could feel the tension building within him and she arched her throat so he could press his lips against her wildly beating pulse. Their limbs entangled, their breathing tortured, they moved in unison toward fulfillment.

It came like the roar of a tidal wave. Spasmed, they clung together while Connor cried out her name, while she, sobbing, clung to him.

Oh, Connor, she groaned inwardly as the flaming passion bore her aloft, love me, love me, please . . .

At long last the room was still. The bed had ceased its tortured rocking. On the silken sheets they lay entwined, their bodies still shaking with the violence of their lovemaking.

Flushed with triumph, Connor lifted his head from Gemma's shoulder and smoothed the damp hair from her brow. She opened her eyes and smiled at him, a dazzling smile that pierced his heart.

"You," he said softly, taking her face in his hands and peering into her beautiful green eyes.

"What?" she whispered when he said nothing more, only caressed the hollow of her cheeks with his thumbs.

"Just that. You. There's never been one like you, Gemma MacEowan."

Her lips curved. "I know."

"Shameless baggage."

They lay still, smiling into each other's eyes, afraid to risk more at the moment than simple teasing. For a long while there was silence while their breathing quieted and their bodies rested.

Then from downstairs came the distant slamming of a door. Muted voices sounded in the corridor.

Although the voices faded immediately, they served to remind Connor and Gemma that the castle was occupied and that the bedroom in which they lay was not a private one. They had even neglected to shut the door.

"They'll be looking for me soon," she said.

Sighing deeply, he eased himself away from her.

Slowly Gemma sat up, brushing her hair from her eyes. She felt stiff and bruised, but gloriously sated. And uncertain and not a little shy as she watched Connor swing off the bed and cross the floor naked to shut the door. She sat with her arms around her updrawn knees, secretly admiring his body while he dressed.

When he straightened to adjust his cuffs, their eyes met and grinning, he moved to the bed and bent to kiss her. She obligingly lifted her mouth to his.

"Mmm," he said.

Shamelessly, she reached up and locked her arms around his neck. Taking her by the hips, he lifted her against him. In one swift motion he came upright with her legs straddling his hips, their kiss unbroken.

"Connor!" she breathed, scandalized.

He drew back just enough to smile into her flushed face. "What?"

"I haven't any clothes on!"

His dark eyes gleamed. "Believe me, ma'am, I'm well aware of it."

"But—but what if someone comes in?"

"That didn't matter a moment ago."

"Well, yes, but this is different!"

"Oh?"

"I'm naked and you're not!" She reared back to glare at him. "Stop laughing! It isn't decent, Connor! Put me down this instant."

To her surprise—and disappointment—he did. And stood laughing down at her, his hands propped on his hips, a devilishly handsome giant who seemed to know her every thought and mood.

"Can I make love to you again?"

Her cheeks grew hot. "No! I—I've work to do."

"Hah. A lame excuse."

"No, really, Connor, I do."

Still grinning, he planted his legs apart and folded his arms across his wide chest. "Such as?"

Slipping off the bed, she scrambled around him and scooped up her discarded undergarments. As she did so, she reeled off a list of chores, most of them real, some of them not. Anything to keep his mind from following where his eyes were going, because she could feel the heat of his gaze upon her as she laced up her corset and pulled on her stockings.

"—And Mrs. Sutcliffe says the laundry's piling up and we're out of lye, and of course there's dinner to worry about, and Mr. Buchanan's coming at three-thirty—"

"Who?"

"Mr. Buchanan, from the village."

"You mean the curate? What in hell does he want?"

She stepped into her gown and hitched up the wide skirts. Shrugging into the sleeves, she said, "He's coming to talk to me about a school."

"A school?"

She turned slowly, alerted by some change in his voice which told her this wasn't welcome news to him. "Yes, a school."

"For the village children, you mean. With a teacher and desks and supplies, that sort of thing."

"Yes," she said warily.

"And who's supposed to fund all that? Me?"

She bit her lip. "I was rather hoping you would."

"So now I'm to play handmaiden to your Lady Bountiful."

"Only if you want to."

"And where were you going to get a teacher?"

She closed her eyes for a long moment, then opened them again. In silence she crossed to the mirror hanging on the opposite wall and began to brush her fingers through her hair. When she spoke, her voice was weary. "Never mind, Connor. I hadn't really intended to involve you anyway."

"Gemma, I only want to make sure that any investment—"

She swung around to face him. "Investment? Is that how you see it? You can't put a value on those children, Connor! It's your duty as their laird to see they're adequately housed and clothed and taught to read and write!"

"Is it?"

"You always resort to sarcasm whenever I want to talk about something important," she said scathingly. "Why is that? Are you afraid of confrontation?

He said nothing, setting his jaw at that stubborn angle which let Gemma know how futile their situation remained.

"Nothing has changed between us, has it, Connor?" she asked sadly.

"Why should it?" he demanded. "Every time I turn around, there you are telling me how much you despise me, how selfish I am, how I'm never going to grow up and assume responsibility for Glenarris. Well, what about you, Gemma?"

"Me?" she asked, startled. "What do you mean?"

He gestured angrily around him. "Jamie's told me what you've done for my family and my crofters, and believe me, I'm grateful. I saw for myself the night before last how grateful the crofters feel toward you, too. But what's the point in all of this? What's the point in talking about a school and a doctor and giving them hope when you're only going to run out on them in the end? It's easy to play the kindhearted lady of the castle when it means no more than packing cute little baskets and putting up a Christmas tree! But what about a real commitment? There's work involved in starting a school and a clinic and all those other ambitious reforms Jamie says you have in mind. What good is starting all that and then running away before you've finished? Better not start at all than make promises you don't intend to keep. Go back to Derbyshire, Gemma. Go home now, before you do any more damage!"

He uttered those last words in a tone that left her reeling. Slowly, slowly, she turned away from the mirror. Her heart was pounding so hard that she thought it might burst from her body.

There it was. The truth at last. He was sending her away. He had had his last fling with her, had won his bet and kept Glenarris, and she wasn't needed anymore.

In the doorway, she turned and said quietly, not looking at him, ''I was going to offer to teach them, you know.''

Then she was gone, leaving a deafening silence in her wake.

Chapter Thirty-two

The chill between Gemma and Connor at dinner was obvious. Gemma appeared at the table puffy-faced and silent and Connor had schooled his face in an expression of cool disdain. He knew his family sensed the tension. Even Maude saw the need to keep her mouth shut. Chomping on the end of her unlit cigar, she vented her displeasure on the innocent servants instead.

Connor noted that the courses were carried in and removed in due time by footmen who gave the impression that they were walking on eggs. Conversations were strained. Far too much wine was consumed. A sigh of relief seemed to come from everyone when MacNeil brought in the brandy, signaling that the meal was over at last.

"Just a moment," Gemma said as the ladies prepared to rise.

Everyone froze and looked at her, and Connor lowered his head.

"I want everyone to know that I'm leaving Glenarris," she said, her voice steady.

"When?" Uncle Leopold barked.

"In the morning."

"And where be ye gang, gel?" Maude demanded.

His head bowed, Connor held the stem of his brandy glass without lifting it to his lips, awaiting Gemma's answer.

"To Inverness," she said calmly. "I've made arrangements with Janet. I'll be staying with her until the weather clears and I can go home to Derbyshire."

His eyes slanted toward Janet. Blushing furiously, she made a small, helpless gesture with her hands. He lowered his eyes again but heard the rustling of satin and the scraping of a chair.

"Excuse me," was all Gemma said, and he heard her exit the room.

He felt his family's eyes on him, but no one said a word.

His grip tightened around the stem of his glass. In the utter silence, the sound of it shattering beneath his hand was like an explosion.

When Eachern found him a short time later, Connor was pacing his study. He refused to acknowledge his cousin until Eachern closed the door none too gently and all but shouted his name.

"What?" Connor barked, turning.

"Will ye stop behavin' like a barbarian? Go an' talk wi' the lass."

"Talk with her? I'd prefer strangling her!"

"Well, go ahead, then! At least 'twill improve yer

damnable temper. But before ye throttle the life out o' her, will ye at least tell her ye be i' love wi' her? Mayhap 'tis a' she wishes tae hear.''

"Hah!" he said nastily.

Eachern scowled. "What could it hurt? Ye've tried all else, haven't ye? Don't tell me ye're scared!"

"Scared? Of course not! Don't be stupid. It's just that I'm—I'm—she—oh, go to hell, Eachern!"

"Connor," Eachern said seriously, "I dinna think 'ee can hide behind yer anger na longer. Ye'll lose her if ye do.''

"So what? I'll be a damned sight better off, and you know it!"

"For God's sake!" his cousin shouted. "Ye'll no be happy without her. Surely ye ken that, man!"

He didn't say anything to that. He just stood there, his pacing arrested, his hands hanging at his sides.

"Go!" Eachern said urgently.

"For heaven's sake!" he exploded. "Gemma will never listen. She doesn't give a damn."

"How do ye ken? How do ye ken unless ye ask? Go, Connor! Dinna wait another moment! Go!"

Agonizing silence. Then he said slowly, "Do you really think I should?"

"Great bloody balls!" Eachern screamed. "Get out o' here!"

Connor moved like a zombie toward the door. There he hesitated, staring down at the floor. Then he looked up, a faint smile playing on his lips.

"You know, Eachern, you're not as dim as I thought."

"Neither are you," his cousin shot back.

They exchanged grudging smiles.

Out in the corridor, his heart pounding, Connor waylaid one of the parlormaids. Gemma, he was told, had gone down to the laundry with Eachern's sister.

Taking a deep breath, he crossed to the cellar steps and descended deep into the bowels of the castle. Since pre-medieval times, while Druids and Picts practiced their sorcery and bloody religious sacrifices in the remote corners of Scotland, the cellars of Glenarris had been known to exist. In those early days they had not been proper cellars, but a series of caves and dark, twisting tunnels carved into the very walls of the cliff. Some had been used for storage, others as dungeons, and the layout of the many chambers and antechambers had been known only to the MacEowan lairds themselves. In times of siege they had sheltered the families and livestock of the clan, and in times of peace stored the bounty of plentiful harvests.

In his grandfather's day, when the last of the Stuart kings had been defeated by the English and peace seemed assured for the foreseeable future, many of the dungeons and unused tunnels had been sealed off. Root cellars and wine cellars were established, and a surprisingly modern laundry put into place. Located directly beneath the cavernous kitchens, the huge kettles of boiling water and the roaring fires that fed them served to heat the stone floors above, a pleasant benefit for the kitchen staff on bitterly cold winter mornings.

Connor couldn't remember the last time he had descended so far below the earth. As a boy he had haunted these dark corridors with his cousins and friends, but as a young man he had abandoned such horseplay, and had rarely interested himself in the workings of the castle laundry once he became the MacEowan laird.

Now he wondered if perhaps he shouldn't modernize this long-neglected part of the castle. Not since his grandfather's day had anyone thought to improve so much as the lighting or the ventilation. The worn stone steps were slick with moisture that dripped from the icy walls, and the lamps lighting the way emitted clouds of black, smelly smoke.

Not a particularly pleasant place in which to work, and for the first time in his life he felt a twinge of sympathy for the washerwomen from the village who toiled here several days a week under Mrs. Sutcliffe's stern guidance. Aunt Maude had been right, and so had Gemma. He had ignored his responsibilities far too long.

Gemma. . . .

Already he could hear the sound of her voice rising from the bottom of the stairs. The glow of lamplight illuminated the entrance to the washrooms, and when he paused in the doorway, he saw Gemma and his cousin talking animatedly with the pair of washerwomen. Gemma was apparently describing for them the raising of the Christmas tree, which the pair had seen for the first time at the banquet two nights ago. She had her back to the door and so did not see him come in, but Janet and the washerwomen did.

Gemma turned around, and he had to admire the way she maintained her composure in front of the curious women. Crossing to him, smiling for their benefit, she took his arm.

''Hello, Connor. Mrs. Kintyre tells me you've not been down here for ages. Do come see our wonderful new machine. It agitates the laundry so that the ladies don't have to, and then wrings the water out for them. Mr. MacNeil arranged for this one to be put in a few months ago. It took weeks for the parts to arrive, and days and days until they put it together, but here it is.''

''By all means, show me,'' he said, sounding equally affable. He was not about to provide his servants with fodder for gossip any more than Gemma was. Feigning deep interest, he allowed her to show him the huge vats and the mechanical arms of the wringer, and the rollers of the mangle. Gemma could not know what it cost him to stand beside her and keep all that he was feeling from showing on his face.

Just talk to her, Eachern had said. Just tell her the simple truth: that he was sorry for hurting her, using her, that loving her had made him realize the full error of his ways.

And love her he did; so badly that it scared him, so much that he had only to stand here beside her and let her nearness wash over him to know that peace and belonging, and an end to all loneliness, lay within his grasp.

''Gemma—'' he said suddenly, interrupting her but not caring.

She fell silent immediately and lifted her eyes to his. Only then did he notice how wide and strained they were, and how anxious she seemed. His heart constricted. Oh, Gemma! What it must cost you to play such a role. And how I must have hurt you to drive you into hiding behind it each and every time we're together!

On the other hand, could it mean that she loved him still—if she had ever loved him at all?

The possibility so staggered him that he found himself unable to utter a single word. And so he merely stood there looking at her while she stared back at him.

At last she took a deep breath. He could see the effort

it caused her just to gather her courage to speak.

He said quickly, quietly, ''No, Gemma. It's all right. It's my turn now. You've done so much more than you ever should have—and far more than I ever deserved.''

''I don't understand, Connor. What—what do you mean?'' Her voice was a tremulous whisper.

''Come,'' he said softly. ''We can't talk here.''

But as he reached out to take her hand, a shrill scream came from one of the washerwomen. He whirled, while at the same time thrusting Gemma protectively behind him.

''Oh, my God,'' he said softly, looking at the doorway.

''What is it?'' Gemma demanded, trying to peer over his arm that was holding her back.

Then she gasped, and Connor knew that she had seen the man who stood in the shadows of the arching doorway, a tall, dark-headed man with a hideously deformed face and black gaps where his teeth should have been.

He was holding a pair of German dueling pistols with ivory grips, and Connor recognized them long before he realized who it was that held them. He whistled softly and went still, his hand tightening in warning around Gemma's arm.

''Aye, Con, it's me!'' King called to him. ''Or what's left of me, I should say.''

Slowly he strolled into the cavernous room, paying no attention to Janet or the cowering washerwomen. With the light full on his mangled face he didn't look quite so awful, because the shadows no longer distorted his features. But there certainly wasn't much left of the devilishly handsome rogue he had been.

Nor could there be any mistaking the malevolence radiating from him as he halted a few feet in front of Connor pointing the pistols at his heart and looking at him slowly up and down. "You did quite a number on me, old friend."

He shook his head. "I never hit you hard enough to knock out your teeth."

"No, not at first. They took a while to abscess and fall out. The nose is ruined, though, don't ye think?"

"Looks aren't everything."

King's narrowed eyes glared toward Gemma. "Looks aren't everything," he repeated slowly. "I guess you'd know that better than me, Con. After all, you ended up the winner despite the ugly beggar you were. Glenarris, the Baird fortune, the girl, they're all yours now."

"What are you doing here, King?" he asked coldly.

"Why, I've come to ask for your help, of course."

"Oh?" Connor felt Gemma's trembling fingers grip his arms from behind. Instantly his hand came up to cover them and squeeze reassuringly.

"What sort of help could you possibly need?" he asked calmly. "And how the devil did you get here? When did you arrive?"

"The night before last, toward the end of the festivities. A charming St. Stephen's Day, I might add. What a pity I wasn't invited." King's cold eyes again went to Gemma.

"Do you know I've been cooling my heels in Inverness for weeks now, living off the largess of my disgusting relations while listening to all the gossip coming from Glenarris? Seems your bride has made quite an impression on folks hereabouts, Con. I understand she won the respect of your entire clan by humiliating you thoroughly at breakfast one morning. There, there, no need to scowl so," King added, grinning. "You'll have to admit 'twas brilliantly executed. Better than some of our own pranks, eh, Con?"

"King—"

"I'm told she charmed 'em all in the end," King went on, waving one of his pistols dismissively. "Even that batty great-aunt of yours." He looked over at Gemma and touched the pistol to his forehead. "I salute you, Mrs. MacEowan."

Gemma said nothing, but Connor could feel her shaking against him. He willed her to remain calm, aware that King had become unhinged; that he was irrational and dangerous, and that he kept looking at Gemma with an expression that made all of Connor's primitive instincts rise to the fore.

"Anyway," King went on, "I heard so many glowing reports about young Mrs. MacEowan that when I found out about the St. Stephen's Day feast I decided to take a look for myself. I slipped in through the terrace door the other night when everyone else was leaving. I spent the night in one of the unused bedrooms in the west wing. Nobody even knew I was there, except for one of your maids who heard me thumping around."

"You didn't have to sneak in," Connor told him. "You could have announced yourself and been welcomed."

"Really? Looking the way I do? Do you know I make babies cry and women scream when I walk down the street?"

"It couldn't be as bad as—" he began, but King interrupted him with a snarl.

"Isn't it? That's easy for you to say with your stunning looks still intact and your beautiful wife standing adoringly at your side. I always envied you your looks, Con, even more so now that I've lost my own. And as for your lovely wife . . .'' King broke off and thoughtfully scratched the side of his head with the barrel of one pistol.

Connor said quickly, to distract King from Gemma, ''You said you came here to ask for my help. Whatever you need—''

''I need money,'' King said icily, ''to compensate for the loss of Grambler Hall. Do y' know my family's out on the street, Con, and none too happy about it?''

''That wager was between you and Carter Sloane,'' he reminded King. ''Why don't you go to him?''

''Because he doesn't have the one thing I really want at the moment, Con. More than money, actually. Your lovely bride. If you'll recall, I'm the one who spotted her first, but I'm willing to take her now, soiled though she be. I appreciate your taming her down a bit, though.''

He lunged toward King, but Gemma kept him back with a desperate grip.

''How touching,'' King sneered. ''So quick to protect him from harm, Gemma? Could it be that you've fallen in love with him after all?''

''King—'' he warned.

''You're right,'' Gemma interrupted clearly. Stepping away from him she faced King with her chin high, placing herself directly in the line of fire. ''You're absolutely right, Mr. Spencer. I do love him. And I'm asking that you please, please, leave him alone.''

Connor turned to her. ''Is it true, Gemma?'' he asked hoarsely.

Her beautiful green eyes clung to his. ''Yes.'' Her

answer was a tremulous whisper.

"Oh, God." His mouth twisted. "How could you, after everything—"

"None of it matters," she said fiercely. "It never did."

In that one moment everything between them was stripped to its barest essence. They stood facing each other, a man and a woman who had found in each other the very reason for life itself.

"Gemma . . . Oh, God." Connor passed his shaking hand across his eyes. "I had to leave that morning when my family came and you joined them for breakfast dressed in rags. You made me realize that there was no sense in saying I was sorry, not after how deeply I'd hurt you."

"I thought I'd driven you away forever," she protested, her voice thick with unshed tears. "And when you came back during the party, when you came up those stairs more dead than alive, I thought—I thought you were going to kill me."

He uttered a soft, broken laugh. "I came back because I thought you were going to humiliate me all over again. I didn't think I'd be able to bear it. But kill you, Gemma? No," he said, aching, "not when the very thought of you was the only thing that kept me alive on the way here."

Her eyes were wide. "It—it was?"

His heart wrenched with pain. Words simply did not exist to describe to her what she meant to him. Lover and wife, companion and soulmate, mother and nurturer, the very reason for his existence. Without Gemma there was no purpose, no light, no need to go on living.

But without having to utter a single word, Connor saw

that everything that was in his heart, everything that he thought and felt and wanted and needed, was reflected in Gemma's eyes.

"Connor—" she whispered.

"Gemma—" he replied, and held out his arms.

"How very touching," King sneered, and the moment shattered like fragile glass.

With deliberate slowness, as though flaunting his total lack of fear, Connor reached for Gemma and put her safely behind him once again. "You say you need money, King." His voice was calm and slightly mocking, the tone he had always used with King. "I can give it to you. All you want. And my townhouse in Edinburgh. Your parents should find it adequate, perhaps even preferable to that drafty hall out in the Cornish wilds."

"Oh?" King's voice was frigid. "I understood from Carter that you were willing to give me that run-down old croft of yours, not your lovely townhouse."

He went cold inside. So there it was. An offhand remark made in the heat of the moment after he'd shattered King's nose, coming back now to haunt him. He could well imagine with what smug pleasure Carter had repeated that ill-advised remark to the defeated King.

In that one moment he saw clearly that there would be no negotiating with his old friend tonight. He realized that King had crept into the castle with one thought in mind: to humiliate him before destroying him. And he obviously intended to do so by using Gemma.

"Actually," King was saying with a lopsided grin that twisted his deformed face hideously, "I could use that croft of yours after all. Perhaps that's where I'll take your lovely bride when I leave here and have my way with her in the same honeymoon cottage where the two of you fell in love. How utterly fitting that would be.''

''You're not leaving Glenarris with her, King,'' he said quietly.

King's demonic eyes gleamed. ''Over your dead body, I suppose? Don't worry, old chum. That's easily arranged.''

His remark brought a gasp from Gemma and loud wails from the washerwomen, who were cowering with Janet behind the bleaching vat. Obviously having forgotten them, King now turned his head and looked at them.

That was what Connor had been waiting for. Shoving Gemma out of the line of fire, he lunged toward King. He knew he didn't have much of a chance because King was a dead shot, with lightning-fast reflexes. But he knew, too, that this was the only chance he would get.

Unfortunately, King had already turned back to him, and the moment he saw Connor he fired both pistols point-blank.

The explosion was deafening. Powder flashed and the shots roared, and Connor staggered backward and briefly broke stride. Gemma screamed, but he threw himself at King and sent him sprawling to the floor.

Connor knew that King had made a mistake in discharging both of his pistols at the same time. But his old friend's reactions were still fast, and now he used the empty pistols as clubs, smashing their butts into Connor's jaw and ribs.

Blood was spurting out of him from somewhere, but he was blinded by too much savagery to feel any pain, and King was too busy defending himself to take stock of how badly Connor was wounded.

Weakening, Connor felt his viselike grip around King's throat while they wrestled on the floor begin to slip. At that moment, throwing all of his weight into a brutal hook, King hit him in the same place on his jaw where the pistol butt had landed earlier. Grunting, he lost his hold—long enough for King to roll him over and emerge on top.

Then King turned quickly, but didn't have time to deflect the blow that Gemma aimed at his skull with the heavy stirring stick she had snatched from the laundry vat. The impact sent King hurling backward. At the same time there was a thunder of footsteps in the doorway of the laundry and Connor saw the blue flash and heard the loud report of a gun. King jerked a second time, but the shot had been unnecessary. Slowly he toppled to the floor where Connor lay sprawled in a pool of blood.

Epilogue

In the loft of Fergus Dodson's croft, Connor lowered Gemma on the bedding and silenced her laughter with a deep, pleasuring kiss.

The loft window was open and the warm spring air caressed their naked bodies. His hand caressed her breast, and sighing, she wrapped her arms around his neck and kissed him back, her breath mingling with his in wonderful gusts.

They knew each other so intimately, but still every kiss, every touch, every coming together was a thing of wonder. For weeks after the shooting, she had feared that Connor would be lost to her forever, and she had not gotten over that fear as yet. There was certainly enough to remind her of that awful night in the Glenarris laundry. Worst was the scar that ran from Connor's shoulder down to his chest—left behind by the plowing path of a bullet—that would remain with him for the rest of his life.

The torn muscles had taken a long time to mend, but the months of convalescence had held a certain magic that neither of them had anticipated. It had been a time of discovery and awakening for both of them, of quiet conversations with her at his bedside, holding his hand while he stroked her hair. It had been a time of winter fires and weeks of seclusion when the snow piled high on the windowsills and there was absolutely no reason for them to venture outside even if they had wanted to, which they had not.

Eachern had generously taken care of all the legal matters involving Reginald Spencer's death, while Jamie had attended the inquest at the magistrate's court in Inverness in Connor's place, seeing that Connor was bedridden and it had been Jamie's own shot that had felled King that day. Eachern's sister had joined forces with Aunt Maude in taking over Gemma's role of looking after the crofters during what turned out to be a fierce winter, while Mrs. Sutcliffe ran the castle with her usual unruffled efficiency.

Their generous efforts had freed Gemma to care solely for Connor, who had lost enough blood to kill a lesser man, and had succumbed to a high fever when his wounds festered. She had tended him with the same unswerving devotion he had shown her in the long days of her own illness at Mrs. Kennerly's inn.

Small wonder that the memory of those frightening weeks remained with her still, and perhaps with Connor, too, given the urgency with which he made love to her every time they were together. But nowadays there was gentleness, too, in their union and in their lives. Connor had become tender and compassionate and as her own high spirits and laughter slowly returned with the coming of spring and the knowledge that he would live, he in turn grew increasingly mellow, a far more contented version of his former restless self. Perhaps the old beldame Minka had been right in predicting that Gemma's love would turn an ugly frog into a handsome prince, because the transformation had ended up going far deeper than simple appearances.

And now they had departed for their long-postponed honeymoon. They had told no one where they were going, only exchanged smiling looks whenever anyone guessed some faraway and exotic location. Only Jamie was privy to their secret, and he had vowed not to reveal it even under threat of death.

The ancient croft had survived the harsh winter with surprisingly little damage. A few hours of solid work was all it had taken to render it cozy once again.

"I'd rather be here with you than anywhere else on earth," Connor confessed now to Gemma, lifting his mouth from hers to smile deeply into her eyes.

She stretched like a contented cat beneath him and threaded her fingers through his thick black hair. "I wish we could spend the whole summer here."

"Well, then, why don't we?"

"Don't tempt me," she warned, but it was already too late. Closing his eyes, he lowered his face to her naked breasts. She continued to ruffle his hair while his lips found her nipples and began to lave them gently.

Her eyes slipped shut as well. Her hands moved to the back of his head, holding him while he suckled and ignited the fires of passion deep within her.

Rising up when she moaned, he folded her around

him, into that intimate fit where Connor ceased and she began.

His breath was uneven now, and hers seemed to have caught in her throat. It was always this way between them, a stormy readying and then the hushed moment before the wonder of coming together.

I love you, Connor's smoldering gaze told her.

I love you, hers answered.

Their joining was a breathless soaring, a coming together of sheer opposites, of Connor's mighty maleness slipping easily, wondrously into her dewy womanhood. And in that moment of wonder they stilled, as they always did, to gaze into each other's expectant faces. The look they exchanged needed no words. They had come too far together not to know what the other was feeling.

Then, with a breathless sigh, she caught him to her. Wrapping her legs about him, she brought him deep inside her while he took her mouth with his. Their lips parted and their tongues met in a mating kiss that was a joyous celebration. Motion flowed between them, at once familiar, at once gloriously new. And at the end he turned his face into her throat and poured all that was his to give into her while she clung to him, shuddering and calling out his name.

There was silence in the loft for a long time afterward. Then came the murmur of Connor's voice, as warm and drowsy as summer rain as he lay above her, still entwined with her in passion.

"I think the bread's burning."

She tightened her arms around his back and hooked her heels over his hips so he would realize that she wasn't about to let him go. She nuzzled his neck before whispering back, "It can fry to a crisp, Connor Mac-

Eowan. What do you care?''

Grinning, Connor propped himself up on one elbow and looked down at her. "You're right. I don't care." He traced his finger along the tip of her nose. "But we're going to have to get up sooner or later. I've a fence to mend and trappings to clean, and peat to cut because the nights are still deuced cold—"

"Is all of that really so urgent?" she protested, smiling at him.

She arched her body against his as she spoke, stroking him shamelessly, tenderly, and was rewarded with an answering spark in his mellow gaze. Taking her face between his big hands, he leaned over her.

"Don't you ever get enough, Mrs. MacEowan?"

"No," she whispered back.

"I was afraid of that."

"It's your own fault, really. If you'd never started any of this back on that journey from Derbyshire—"

"Aye, you're right," he acknowledged, smiling. "It's my fault for destroying your innocence. Ah, well. One thing about me is that I always own up to my responsibilities. And one of those is making sure I always finish what I've started."

"Have you started something?" she asked innocently, even though she could feel him throbbing inside her once again.

"Hmm. Perhaps I have. Or is that Pope wiggling between us?"

She giggled and then shifted subtly to accommodate the insistent demands of her husband's body. Connor, his eyes darkened with renewed passion, laughed triumphantly and lowered his mouth to hers.

And the loft was silent once again.

DANCE of the FLAME

ELAINE BARBIERI

**Elaine Barbieri's romances are
"powerful...fascinating...storytelling at its best!"**
—*Romantic Times*

Exiled to a barren wasteland, Sera will do anything to regain the kingdom that is her birthright. But the hard-eyed warrior she saves from death is the last companion she wants for the long journey to her homeland.

To the world he is known as Death's Shadow—as much a beast of battle as the mighty warhorse he rides. But to the flame-haired healer, his forceful arms offer a warm haven, and he swears his throbbing strength will bring her nothing but pleasure.

Sera and Tolin hold in their hands the fate of two feuding houses with an ancient history of bloodshed and betrayal. But no matter what the age-old prophecy foretells, the sparks between them will not be denied, even if their fiery union consumes them both.

_3793-9 $5.99 US/$6.99 CAN

An Angel's Touch

Time Heals
SUSAN COLLIER

Tired of her nagging relatives, Maeve Fredrickson asks for the impossible: to be a thousand miles and a hundred years away from them. Then a heavenly being grants her wish, and she awakes in frontier Montana.

Saved from the wilderness by a handsome widower, Maeve loses her heart to her rescuer—and her temper over the antics of his three less-than-angelic children. As her angel prods her to fight for Seth, Maeve can only pray for the strength to claim a love made in paradise.

_52030-3 $4.99 US/$5.99 CAN

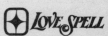